If My Father Loved Me

ROSIE THOMAS

If My Father
Loved Me

THE OVERLOOK PRESS
New York, NY

This hardcover edition first published in the United States in 2017 by
The Overlook Press, Peter Mayer Publishers, Inc.

141 Wooster Street
New York, NY 10012
www.overlookpress.com

For bulk and special orders, please contact sales@overlookny.com,
or write us at the above address.

Cataloging-in-Publication Data is available from the Library of Congress

Manufactured in the United States of America

2 4 6 8 10 9 7 5 3 1

ISBN 978-1-4683-0261-5

For DCM
With love always

If My Father Loved Me

ONE

'My father was a perfumer and a con artist,' I said. 'You would like him. All women do.'

I was telling Mel this, my dear friend Mel, on what was then still an ordinary night.

We had arranged to meet in a new restaurant and I had got off the tube one stop early and walked for ten minutes to reach it. It was that tender time between winter and very early summer that is too fragile and understated, in the city, to count as a proper spring. The plane trees in the great squares were shyly licked with pale green and there would be cherry blossom in suburban gardens. I noticed that the sky was pale grey, almost opalescent, and shafts of light like cathedral pillars struck down between the concrete buildings.

When I arrived Mel was already at the table, waiting for me. She was wearing her leather jacket and her hair frizzed out in black spirals all round her face. Her trademark red lipstick was still fresh, not yet blotted with eating and drinking. She stood up when she saw me and we hugged, laughing with the pleasure of seeing one another and to acknowledge the small festivity of a new restaurant, the familiar sprawl of London outside the windows, the stealthy approach of summer and also the fact that life was kind to us both.

As we sat down Mel said, 'Let's get a bottle of wine and order some food, then we can talk.'

Mel and I have been saying this, or a near version of it, all through the five years that have gone by since we met. The talk is always the most important ingredient, although food and wine are right up there too. It was our interest in cooking that brought us together, on a week's master class hosted by a celebrity chef at some chichi and terrible hotel in the Midlands. The first time I saw Mel she was wearing her black curls bundled up under a white cook's cap in a way that was all about business and nothing about looking fetching, and I liked her immediately. She was quietly laying out her knives while our fellow students were crowded up at the front trying to catch the chef's attention. (And that was just the *men*, Mel said.)

She looked confident and successful. It turned out that she knew how to cook and wasn't afraid of the bad-tempered prima donna who was supposedly there to inspire us. I wasn't the only one who warmed to her, but it was to my room that she brought a bottle of wine on the second evening and it was to me she chose to open her heart. I learned that Mel Archer was trying to come to terms with the knowledge that she was never going to have a child of her own, let alone replicate her fecund mother's perfect family. It was causing her pain, like a bereavement.

In my turn I told her that I was newly divorced. I was hard up and quite depressed and I had a daughter who was trying single-handedly to recreate the cliché of the teen rebel queen, as well as a six-year-old son who was going through an awkward phase. The one that had lasted since he was four days old.

We were both going through a difficult time in our lives.

'We should swap problems,' Mel said.

She made me laugh, and we opened another bottle and the talk went on and on. At the week's end we came back to London with some overblown new recipes, a shared sense of relief that we would never have to work in a commercial kitchen under our master chef's direction and a friendship that we both knew would endure.

Over the years I have told her everything, and nothing.

'What are you going to eat?' Mel asked, when we had studied the menu.

'The pasta, I think.'

I always choose what I want to eat very quickly. While I waited for Mel I looked down the line of tables. They were placed close together and I could eavesdrop on two or three overlapping conversations. There were the first-daters craning eagerly forward over their plates and the married couple who had run out of things to say. On our other side were a noisy quartet of old friends and three young women of whom one was leaning forward through a veil of cigarette smoke to say to the others, 'Just wait and see, he'll be regretting it within, like, six weeks.' The red nail polish she was wearing looked the same shade as Mel's lipstick.

I felt a little quiver of affection for her and the other diners, for the arrangements that we had all made in order to be here and the problems with parking, and the balancing acts about how much to drink and whether or not a pudding would be permissible. I loved the city and felt happy to be here in the middle of it with Mel for company. At that moment, I wouldn't have changed a single thing about my life.

'What do you think of this menu? Scallops and mushrooms is always a good combination,' she finally decided. 'I'm going to have that.'

A young waiter took our order and Mel chose a bottle of Fleurie from the list. A different waiter came and poured the wine, taking care with a wrapped napkin not to spill a drop on the bleached wood of the table top. A new recruit, not yet confident.

We clinked our glasses before we drank.

'How's Jack?' Mel asked. She shook a Marlboro out of the pack and lit it, then leaned back in her chair to look at me. Jack is my son.

'Not bad,' I said cautiously. 'And Adrian?'

'So-so.'

3

Adrian was Mel's current boyfriend, if that's a word you can still use when you aren't young any more. At least, not young in the sense that my daughter Lola is young, although on the other hand at twenty she is so precisely of the modern world, so experienced and knowing, that I sometimes think she could be my mother instead of the other way round.

Mel and I have both turned fifty and we are therefore invisible except in the technical sense to, say, the young waiter who took our order. He was nice-looking, brown-skinned, with black hair slicked straight back from his face. I could see him stepping around the female trio and exchanging eye contact as he slipped them their starters. He said something that was evidently cheeky and they all laughed.

I don't remember anyone mentioning the fact to me when I was as young as Lola, but you don't feel yourself growing older. You reach an age – which probably varies according to your history and personal circumstances, but in my case was twenty-seven – and there you are, fully formed. As time passes you note your failures and allow yourself to appreciate what you have done well, but there remains the inner individual who isn't aware of alteration either mental or physical. Inside my skin, a millimetre or so beneath the eroding surface, I remain twenty-seven years old. It's a shock, when riding the escalator in Selfridges or somewhere, to confront an unexpected mirror and be obliged to check the discrepancy.

We've talked about this, of course, Mel and I. Being invisible to waiters and white-van drivers and brickies doesn't bother us. What is alarming is the possibility that when we do start to feel our age, it might all happen at once. What if we go from being twenty-seven to being sixty-seven in a day, suddenly getting infirm knees and crochet shawls and a fondness for *Book at Bedtime*, crumbling away into old ladies as the light falls on us like Rider Haggard's *She*?

'That will be scarier than *Alien*,' Mel said.

Joking about our worries is something we have always been able to do together. What else should we do?

I lifted my glass of wine again. 'Here's to now,' I said.

Being old hasn't happened yet, that's what the toast means, in spite of the escalator mirror's warning and in spite of our awareness that it will, that it must.

'To now,' Mel echoed happily.

The waiter came with our food. He put Mel's dish of scallops down in front of her and she immediately picked up her fork to take a mouthful. I had chosen mezzalune di melanzane, half-moons of ravioli stuffed with aubergine. We sampled our own portions and then traded forkfuls. Mel chewed attentively and pronounced my ravioli to be drab, and I agreed with her.

'Go on,' I said.

We had started talking about Adrian and I was watching her face as she relayed her concerns. I also wanted to enjoy the restaurant's brightness and the sweet damp night outside, and the animated faces of the three women and the way the waiter's long white apron tucked round his waist just so, by listening for a while longer instead of talking.

And there is another presence, too. A shadow at the back of the room, a black silhouette beyond the restaurant plate glass, already waiting.

I can smell him, even, although I haven't put the awareness anywhere close to words. It's still only premonition, a cloudy scent stirring in the chambers of my head, but he is *there*.

I don't know it yet but it's not an ordinary night.

Mel sighed. 'You know, Adrian always makes me feel that he would like me to pat his cheek and say *well done*, or on the other hand *don't worry*. He needs approval all the time. It's tiring.'

'Maybe the reassurance he really needs is that you're not going to leave him.'

'I can't give him that assurance, unfortunately.'

We have been here before. We exchanged smiles.

5

'Fucked up by my happy family history,' Mel shrugged, only half joking.

Mel has never married. She is the middle child of five siblings, petted by two older brothers and idolised by two younger ones. Her father was a fashionable gynaecologist with a practice in Harley Street, and her parents had a house in the country as well as a Georgian gem in London. The Archers took their children skiing in Switzerland every winter and to Italy for summer holidays, although all this was many years before I knew Mel. Her widowed mother now lives in some style in South Kensington and her brothers do the kinds of thing that the sons of such families usually do. Mel insists that her childhood was so idyllic and her father such a wonderful and benign influence that she has never found a man or an adult milieu to match them.

All this I know about her.

'What was your childhood like?' she asked me, when we first met and we were finding out about each other.

'Nothing like yours.'

And this was nothing less than the truth.

Mel's dark eyebrows lifted.

'It was ordinary,' I lied. 'There isn't much to tell,' I said, 'except that my mum died very suddenly when I was ten. I lived quietly with my dad and then eventually I grew up.'

'That's very sad,' Mel said warmly.

'Yes,' I agreed. I didn't volunteer any more, because I don't like to talk about my childhood. The past is gone and I am glad of it.

'What are you going to do?' I ask now, eating my ravioli.

'About Adrian? End it, or wait for it to end, I suppose.'

'You don't love him.'

'No. But I like him and I enjoy his company, quite a lot of the time.'

'Isn't that enough?'

She looked at me, tilting her head a little so that the ends of her curls frayed out against the background of the restaurant's shiny turquoise wall. If I reached out my fingertips to touch, I thought, I would feel a tiny crackle of electricity.

Mel said, 'You're the one who's been married and who lived with another man as well. *Is* it enough?'

I gave the question proper consideration. When Lola was eleven and Jack was three, and I was married to Tony, I fell deeply in love with a man called Stanley. It wasn't that I didn't care for my husband, because I did. Almost from the day I met him he made me feel that I was at anchor in some sheltered harbour while the storms raged out at sea, and for years I believed that was what I wanted. Tony was and is a good man who cared for the three of us. But sometimes I did long for the danger of towering waves and the wild wind filling my sails.

Stanley was gale force, all right. He was eight years younger than me. He was a not very successful actor who made ends meet by doing carpentry and he came to do some work in our kitchen. He was handsome and funny, utterly unreliable and unpredictable, and he stirred a longing in me that I have never known before or since. I couldn't take my eyes off him, or my hands either. He would turn up and tell me that I was beautiful and intoxicating, and that I was all he had ever wanted. Happiness and wonder at seeming to mean so much to someone like Stanley made me suspend my natural disbelief.

Then he would disappear and in his absence the world went completely dark. I did try to convince myself that I was a wife and mother, and what I felt was mere lust, but I knew it wasn't. When he came back again, when I was actually with Stanley, it was as if nothing else mattered. Not my children, my husband, my old friends, or our well-rubbed and fingermarked everyday world. What I wanted, *all* I wanted, was this. This passion and delight was the marrow at last where everything else grated like dry bones.

After two months of agonising I left Tony for Stanley and

took the children with me. I truly believed that there was nothing else I could do.

Lola accepted the fait accompli with which I presented her, more or less, and although she never warmed to Stanley, she and I still managed to stay friends. Lola has always had an enviable degree of self-reliance. But Jack was already an insecure child, given to bad dreams and absence of appetite, and the upheaval tipped him severely off balance. At twelve, he still hasn't recovered his equilibrium.

Tony and I sold our house, and I bought a much smaller one with my half of the money and Stanley came to live in it with us. For a few months I was shockingly happy, even in the face of my children's discomfort and Tony's misery. But then, slowly and inevitably, things began to go wrong. Stanley did less carpentry and spent more time in the pub. Then he went off with a travelling production of *The Rocky Horror Show* and met Dinah, who was playing Janet.

I was afraid that I would die without him, but I also thought that to be abandoned was no more than I deserved.

It's not a very original story and I'm not proud of this portion of my life. I'm sorry for what I did and regret that I can't put it right, not for Jack and Lola, or Tony either. Remembering the hurt I caused by abandoning my family makes me recoil and wish I could slam shut the doors of recollection. I can't, of course, and I think about the damage every day.

But even so, and with the benefit of experience, what I really think – now that Mel has asked me – is that you can compromise in love as in all other things. If you have to, that is. But it's much better not. If you give up your independence to share your life with someone, it should be a state of existence that improves on being single.

Sometimes, not all the time of course, but sometimes, when you're sitting down to breakfast opposite each other or getting into a car together or just lying quietly in each other's arms, you should catch your breath and think, being with this person here and now is what lends reason to and makes logic of everything else in the world.

I thought this, for just long enough, about being with Stanley.

If you don't have these times that snag your breath and make you smile with happiness, and if all you are doing instead is rubbing along, wrapping up the packages of irritation and disappointment and sliding them out of sight, then you would be better off alone.

'Is it enough to share your life with someone you like well enough, but don't love?' I repeated.

Mel nodded.

'No, it's not enough,' I said.

'Of course it isn't,' she agreed.

Mel and I knew that we were fortunate, because we'd often discussed it. We had evenings like this one. We could do our work, eat out, book holidays, see friends, choose films, argue about politics, cook meals, laugh and talk a lot. Once in a while drink too much. True love in addition would have been magnificent, but I knew that I didn't want to sacrifice any of the above just to settle for a compromise, for a merely pale and ersatz version of love.

I also thought that maybe Mel herself thought a little differently from me. With Adrian and his predecessors she had devoted more time to the pursuit of passion than I ever did. But then, Mel didn't have children to consume her energy, draining it with their needs and the exhausting negotiations of parent–child love.

Mel's own cheerful explanation for her persistence would have been that she was still looking for a man to replace her daddy. Whereas I had run so far and so fast from mine that by now I had shaken off all male bonds altogether. Except for Jack, of course.

Mel's thoughts must have been travelling along a path parallel to mine. And, as often happened, they moved faster. 'Tell me about *your* father. I don't think you ever have, not properly. What was he like? Do you look like him?'

'Not really. Our eyes and hands are the same shape.'

Her questions made me shiver.

I had been thinking about him as I walked through the opalescent evening. I could feel his shadow here in the restaurant. There was no reason for this tonight of all nights, other than premonition, but he was already in my mind.

'Go on.'

I told her, reluctantly, that my father was a perfumer, and a con artist.

Mel fixed all her formidable attention on me. Her black eyes held mine and I knew that if I chose to say more she would listen intently. If I should happen to need advice or a reliable insight, those would be forthcoming too. But all my instincts told me – as they always tell me – to hold my tongue and to keep my history to myself. 'You would like him, all women do. He was a perfumer's "nose",' I added.

Stay there, stay away, I wanted to warn him. The shadow was lengthening as he came closer.

'Go on,' Mel repeated. She was ready to be fascinated.

With only the one obvious exception, myself, women did find Ted Thompson utterly magnetic. He was a good-looking man, for one thing, with the looks of a Forties movie star. He loved being told that he resembled Spencer Tracy.

'Do you hear that, Sadie?' he would say and laugh. 'Your old man? What do you think?'

'I can't see it,' I'd mutter. 'You just look like my dad.' That was what I wanted him to be, just my dad.

The real basis for his success with women, though, was his interest in them. He had a stagy trick of cupping his target's upturned face in his hands and then breathing in the warmth

10

of it as if the skin's scent were the most direct route to knowing its owner. He would close his eyes for a moment, frowning in concentration, then murmur, 'I could create such a perfume for you. The top notes sweet and floral to reflect your beauty but with the firmest base, cedarwood with earth and metal tones, for your great strength.'

Or some such nonsense, anyway.

'His job was to mix essences, the building blocks of scent, to create perfume. He told me it was like painting a picture, making the broad brushstrokes that give the first impression and then filling in the details, the light and shade, to create the fragrance that lingers in the memory.'

As I talked I was thinking about the words from my childhood, ambergris and musk and vetiver. Not the scents or essences themselves because I didn't inherit Ted's nose and could barely have distinguished one from another, but the pure sounds of the words with their velvety textures. I recalled them the way other children might remember television programmes or ice-cream flavours, and I was back to being ten years old again. I could hear the click of heels on the unloved parquet of our hallway and the scrape of unpruned garden branches in the wind, working like fingernails at the glass of the front room's bay window.

'Why did I never know that? It sounds highly exotic.'

'Yes.'

It was exotic, in its way, Ted's world. But you couldn't describe my growing up on the edge of it as anything of the kind.

'What about the other thing? The con artist bit?'

'That's a manner of speaking. Perfume is nothing more than a promise in a bottle, Ted used to say. It exists to create an illusion.'

My discomfort was growing. I didn't want to talk to Mel about my father. We had reached an unspoken truce long ago, the old illusionist and me, and chatting about him and his life's work, even to Mel, was outside the terms of the agreement.

11

'I thought smell was the truest of the senses.'

'Smell may be. But perfume, on the other hand, is meant to disguise and flatter, and lead the senses astray.'

'I have just realised something. You never wear it, do you?'

'No,' I said.

Mel always moved in a cloud of scent. She changed her allegiances but the emphasis was constant. Ted wore cologne. He had created one for himself and he used it liberally. I never thought it suited him. It was too salty and citrusy, too fresh and clean and outdoor, and when I was a child the discrepancy between the man I knew and the way he smelled was always troubling. The scent rose in my head now, like the first warning of a migraine.

'Why?'

'I prefer the smell of skin,' I smiled. I remembered the way Lola and Jack used to smell when they were babies.

'What's the real reason?'

'There's no other reason,' I said.

I put down my knife and fork, placing them very precisely together between uneaten half-moons of ravioli.

Mel stared at me for a moment, then she lightly held up her hand. If I didn't want to talk about my father she wasn't going to force me to and I appreciated her tact. But in the little silence that followed I understood that the closed topic made an uncomfortable feeling between us. Mel was hurt by my reticence. For the first time, she had noticed that I wasn't entirely open with her. This meant that she was wondering what else I held back and how well she did know me, and therefore whether our friendship was really as close as she had let herself believe.

I wanted to reach out and take her hand, and tell her not to mind.

I wanted to assure her that I hid nothing except my history, and this no longer mattered to me. But I didn't do it and the moment passed. The brown-skinned waiter came and took our plates away, asking me if everything had been all right.

'Fine,' I murmured. 'Just a bit too much.'

Mel sat back in her chair and lit another cigarette. The three young women had ordered puddings and were enjoying a chocolate high. The quartet of old friends had already left, hurrying back to relieve their babysitters. The noise in the restaurant was slowly diminishing.

'How's your mum, by the way?' I asked.

She looked at me as if she were going to protest that this blatant change of topic was beneath me, but then she shrugged. 'She's being quite difficult.'

This was not new. Mel's glamorous mother had become elegantly and minutely demanding in her old age. We talked about her for a while, until the atmosphere between us warmed again. We exchanged some news of Caz and Graham, my oldest friends whom Mel had met many times and with whom she was now friendly in her own right. She asked about Penny, my business partner, and Penny's lover Evelyn, and Evelyn's baby, Cassie. I gave her the small pieces of information eagerly, trying to make amends.

Then we studied the pudding menu together. Mel spotted it first and her face puckered with delight before she started laughing. She pointed the item out to me.

Pecan, almond and walnut pie (contains nuts).

Mel and I collected menu misspellings and absurdities. Lola maintained that this was very sad and middle-aged, but it was a source of innocent amusement to us and we didn't care. The addition of this latest one helped us to forget the doubts I had raised by putting a wall round my past.

'I'm going to put my nut allergy right behind me and have that,' I said.

'Split it with me?'

'Done.'

While we ate our nuts we talked about the Government's ridiculous plans for the tube, and about our respective jobs, and a film about South America that Mel had been to with Adrian, which I wanted to see. The restored rhythms of the evening were familiar and precious to me, and I regretted that I had caused any disturbance in them. Maybe some time I could talk to Mel about Ted and the way I grew up, and maybe even should do so. But not now, I thought. Not yet.

It was eleven o'clock before we found ourselves out in the street again. A cool wind blew in our faces, striking a chill after the warmth of the restaurant.

Mel turned the collar of her leather jacket up around her ears. 'Call me later in the week?'

'I will,' I promised. I felt full of love for her, and stepped close and quickly hugged her. 'You're a good friend.'

I saw the white flash of her smile. And I could smell the warm, musky residue of her perfume. I couldn't identify it by name, but I thought it was one she often wore.

'Trust me,' Mel said. 'I do.'

She touched my shoulder, then turned and walked fast up the street. Mel always walked quickly. She filled up her life, all the corners of it.

I retraced my steps more slowly to the tube station. I liked travelling on the Underground late at night and watching the miniature dramas of drunks and giggling girls and hollow-eyed Goths and couples on the way to bed together. I never felt threatened. I even liked the smell of Special Brew and Kentucky Fried Chicken, and the homely detritus of trampled pages of the *Evening Standard* and spilled chips. That night there was a ripe-smelling old dosser asleep in one corner, and a posse of inebriated Australian girls who tried to start up an in-compartment game of volleyball using a red balloon. Two gay men with multiple piercings looked on coldly, but the tramp never even stirred.

The walk at the other end through the streets to my house was much quieter. The street lamps shone on parked cars and skips and front gardens. Once, on this route, I saw a dog fox at the end of a cul-de-sac. He stood silently with his noise pointed towards me and his ears delicately pricked. I was surprised by how big he was. After inspecting me he turned and vanished effortlessly into the darkness. Tonight, however, there were only cats and a couple of au pair girls hurrying back from an evening at the bar on the corner of the main road.

I was thinking about Mel as I walked, reviewing the little breach that I had caused and telling myself that it didn't matter, it was nothing, our friendship was strong enough to weather it. If Mel had a fault it was her possessiveness, her need to feel that she was at the centre of her friends' lives. Of course she would hate any suggestion that she was shut out.

The houses in my street had steps leading up to the front doors. As I walked under the clenched-fist branches of pollarded lime trees, I had glimpses of basement kitchens barred by area railings. I saw alcove bookshelves, the backs of computers and the occasional submarine blue glimmer of a television, but most of the downstairs windows were already dark. I reached my steps and walked up, my house keys in my hand. The lights in our house were all on. Lola must still be up.

I turned the Yale key and the door swung open. In front of me lay the familiar jumble of discarded trainers and shopping bags, and the council's plastic boxes for recycling bottles and newspapers. Lola's old bicycle was propped up against the wall even though she hardly used it nowadays, and one of the three bulbs in the overhead light fitting was still out. I had been meaning for days to bring up the stepladder from the basement and replace it.

Jack was sitting on the bottom stair. His face was a motionless white triangle under a stiff jut of hair. His arms were wrapped round his knees and his chin rested between them. His eyes fixed on mine.

15

'Jack? What are you doing? Where's Lola?'

My voice sounded sharp. The main feeling I had at the sight of him, out of bed at almost midnight, was irritation. He should be asleep. He should be recharging, ready for another school day. He should be many things that he was not.

'Lola's in her room.'

'So should you be.'

I put down my bag and eased past the bicycle handlebars.

'Why?'

It should be obvious even to a twelve-year-old boy that midnight is not a suitable time to be sitting around on the draughty stairs in a house in which the central heating has gone off for the night. But it was – or used to be – Jack's way to question the obvious with earnest attention, as if even the simplest issue were a matter for philosophical debate. Most recently, though, he has more or less stopped talking altogether.

I sighed. 'Please, Jack. It's late. Just go to bed.'

He stood up then, pulling his pyjama sleeves down to cover his fists. He looked small and vulnerable. He said, 'There's some bad news. Grandad has had a heart attack.'

I turned, slowly, feeling the air's resistance. 'What?' I managed to say.

'Mum, is that you?'

Upstairs a door clicked and Lola materialised at the head of the stairs. She ran down to me.

'What?' I repeated to her, but my mind was already flying ahead.

That was it. Of course, it was why he had been in my thoughts tonight. I had smelled his cologne, glimpsed his shadow out of the corner of my eye even in the slick light of a trendy new restaurant.

Was he *dead*, then?

Lola put her arm round me. Jack stood to one side with his head bent, curling the toes of one foot against the dusty mat that ran down the hallway.

16

I looked from one to the other. 'Tell me, quickly.'

'The Bedford Queen's Hospital rang at about nine o'clock. He was brought in by ambulance and a neighbour of his came with him. He had had a heart attack about an hour earlier. They've got him in a cardiac care ward. The Sister I spoke to says he is stable at the moment.' There were tears in Lola's eyes. 'Poor Grandad.'

'We tried to call you,' Jack said accusingly.

But I'd forgotten to take my mobile phone out with me. It was on my bedside table, still attached to the charger. I put to one side my instant regrets for this piece of negligence. 'Is there a number for me to call?' I asked Lola.

'On the pad in the kitchen.'

I led the way down the stairs to the basement with my children padding behind me.

The light down there was too bright. There were newspapers and empty cups and a layer of crumbs on the table.

'My father. Mr Ted Thompson,' I said down the phone to a nurse on Nelson ward in the Bedford Queen's Hospital. She relayed the information that Lola had already given me. 'Should I come in now?' I asked. I didn't look at them, but I knew that Jack and Lola were watching my face. We hadn't seen their grandfather since Christmas. We observed the conventions, meeting up for birthdays and Christmases, prize-givings and anniversaries, and we exchanged regular phone calls, but not much more. That was how it was. Ted had always preferred to live on his own terms.

'I'll check with Sister,' the nurse said. A minute later she came back and told me that he was comfortable now, sleeping. It would be better to come in the morning, Sister thought.

'I'll be there first thing,' I said, as though this was important to establish, and hung up. Lola put a mug of tea on the counter beside me.

'Thank you,' I said.

Jack lifted his head. 'Is he going to die?'

He was over eighty. Of course he was going to die. If not immediately, then soon. This was reality, but I hadn't reckoned with it because I wasn't ready. There was too much unsaid and undone.

'I don't know.'

I put down my tea and held out my arms. Lola slid against me and rested her head on my shoulder. I stroked her hair. Jack stood a yard away, his arm out of one pyjama sleeve. He was twisting the fabric into a rope.

'Come and have a cuddle,' I said to him. He moved an inch closer but his head, his shoulders, his hips all arched away from me.

After a minute I pushed a pile of ironing off the sofa in the window recess. Lola and I sat down to finish our tea and Jack perched on a high stool. He rested his fingertips on the counter top and rocked on to the front legs of the stool, then on to the back legs. The clunk, clunk noise on the wooden floorboards made me want to shout at him, but I kept quiet.

In the end Lola groaned, 'Jack, sit still.'

'It's quite difficult to keep your balance, actually,' he said.

Lola sniffed. 'What if he's going to die? I don't want him to die, I love him.'

'So do I,' Jack added, not to be outdone.

It was true. My children had an uncomplicated, affectionate relationship with Ted. They teased him, gently, for being set in his ways. He remembered their birthdays and sent them occasional unsolicited cheques. In a corner of myself I envied the simplicity of their regard for each other.

I stroked Lola's hair. 'Let's all go to bed,' I suggested. 'Grandad's asleep. If anything changes they're going to ring us. We'll see him tomorrow.'

I followed Jack up the stairs into his bedroom. I sat on the end of the bed and he lay on his back with his arms folded behind his head.

'Are you all right?' I asked.

'Can we tell Dad what's happened?'

'Of course. In the morning.'

Tony wouldn't appreciate a call about his ex-father-in-law in the middle of a week night.

Jack turned on his side, presenting his back to me.

'I'm going to sleep now.'

'That's good.' I leaned over and kissed his ear, but he gave no response.

The air in Lola's room was thick with smoke and joss.

'Lo. Have you been smoking in here?' Obviously.

'We've been sitting worrying, waiting for you to get back.'

'I know. I'm sorry.' Did all mothers have to apologise so often? Was this the main transaction in every family, once your children stopped being little? Or was it just the case in *my* family?

'Goodnight, Mum.'

'Goodnight, darling. I love you.'

In my own bedroom I turned on the bedside light and drew the curtains. Then I lay down on my bed, still fully dressed. I stared at the ceiling. Now that I tried to picture my father's face, I couldn't conjure up his features. All I could see was his shadow.

'Don't die,' I ordered the dark shape. 'Not until I've had a chance to talk to you.'

I felt cold, even though the room was warm. I knew that I was afraid of his going, but it was at a distance, as if I couldn't reach inside my own heart and get at the fear and the love that went with it. I was reduced to making a numb, dry-eyed acknowledgement, a nod in the direction of real feelings, as though my emotions belonged to someone else.

TWO

They had put him in a small room off the main ward. There he was, lying on his back, his head propped on pillows. I saw that his profile had become a sharper, bonier version of the one I knew, as if layers of fat and muscle had been scraped away from his skull. His nose looked bigger and his skin was pale and shiny, stretched tight over the bones.

I hesitated at the door but he opened his eyes and turned his head to look straight at me. 'Hello, Sade. Sorry about this. Damned nuisance.'

I smiled at him. 'Hello, Dad.'

All night and as I drove out of London I had been dreading this moment. I had been afraid of how he would look and of what we would say to each other with the spectre of death in the room. Now that I was actually here I saw that he was hooked up to wires and tubes ran into his arms. He looked ill, but still not so different from his usual self, and my fear was not in speaking of painful matters, but that he might go away before we had a chance to talk at all.

There was a red plastic chair in the cramped space beside his bed. I sat down and took one of his hands, lacing my fingers with his. We had so rarely touched each other. Somewhere deep inside my head I could feel the pressure of tears, but I knew I wasn't going to cry. 'How do you feel?'

He ran his tongue over his lips. 'Rough as a bear's back.'

'What happened?'

'Chest pain. I rang Jean Andrews and she came right over.'

I knew Mrs Andrews. She was Ted's neighbour. It would have been Mrs Andrews who came here with him in the ambulance. He was wearing his own pyjamas, and his glasses and a paperback book were lying on his bedside locker, so she must have packed his bag for him, too. She was probably the last of the line of Ted's girlfriends, or 'aunties' as I was taught to call them when I was little, although I don't believe Jean really performed any services for my father beyond looking out for him and bringing him the newspaper.

'Why didn't you call me?'

He moistened his lips again. There was a covered jug and a plastic beaker on the locker, so I poured some water and held the beaker for him while he drank a mouthful. Afterwards I took his hand once more.

'Thanks. I thought I'd see the quack first, let him take a shufti. Might all have been a false alarm.'

The vocabulary made my neck stiffen, just a little, as it always did.

Ted had served in the RAF during the war. He was not a pilot but an aircraftsman, working on the maintenance of Spitfires that flew in the Battle of Britain, although he didn't like to be too specific about his exact rank and responsibility. When on the back foot he still reached for words like prang and crate and willco, as if this threadbare old slang could lend him some extra strength or status.

He lived increasingly in the past, like many old people, although the difference with Ted was that the geography of that other country was largely imaginary. But the boundaries between truth and illusion didn't really matter all that much, I thought. Not any longer.

My fingers tightened on his. 'I'm here now,' I said.

'How's my cutie? And Jack?'

When she was a little girl Ted always called Lola his cutie. He was delighted to have a granddaughter, although he protested that it made him feel old. 'She's going to be a heartbreaker,' he used to say. 'Just look at those bright eyes.'

I should have made sure he saw more of his grandchildren on ordinary days, not just the set-piece ones armoured with conventions and pressured by expectations. I should have tried to forget my own growing up and let the next generation make amends for our failures.

'Lola's just fine. She's going to come in and see you later, or maybe tomorrow. And Jack's okay, although he doesn't like school that much.'

'Neither did I when I was his age. I used to sit next to a boy called Peter Dobson. He would shake his pen deliberately to make blots all over my work, and he and his chums used to lie in wait for me after school and pull my books out and run off with my comics.'

'I don't think things have changed for the better.'

I realised that there were pins and needles in my arm and my wrist ached with the tension of lightly holding his hand. I shifted my position and he asked, 'Are you comfortable?'

'Yes. Are you?'

He sighed, restlessly shifting his thin legs under the covers. 'Not very.'

A nurse came in. He was young, dressed in a white jacket and trousers. He glanced at the whiteboard over the bed and I followed his eyes. A note in bright blue magic marker, scrawled over the previous occupant's smeared-out details, declared that this was Edwin Thompson, 'Ted'. 'Hello, Teddy-boy,' the nurse said, examining the bags that leaked fluids into my father's arm. 'My name's Mike. How are you feeling? Not so good?'

'I feel as you would expect, having had a heart attack last night,' Ted answered. I smiled. Ted didn't take to being patronised, even in his hospital bed.

'And who is this young lady?'

'I'm his daughter.'

'Well, now then, I need to do your dad's obs and then the doctors are coming round. Could I ask you to pop up and wait in the visitors' room? You can come back as soon as rounds are over.'

'I'd like to talk to his doctor.'

'Of course. Not a problem.'

I walked up the ward, past bedridden old men, to sit and wait in a small side room.

A long hour later, the same nurse put his head round the door. 'Doctor will see you now, in Sister's office.'

As I passed I saw Ted lying on his back in the same position. His eyes were closed and I thought he must have fallen asleep.

The consultant cardiologist was a woman, younger than me. I shouldn't have been surprised, but Ted had talked about the quack and finding out what he had to say. That was Ted all over: proper jobs, like this one, were done by men.

The doctor held out her hand, with a professionally sympathetic smile. 'Susan Bennett,' she said and we shook hands.

I sat down in the chair she indicated.

I remembered the shadow that had slid into the restaurant last night and found myself repeating over and over in my head, *don't, please don't say it, just let him get better . . .*

Susan Bennett explained that it had been a serious attack, bigger than they had at first suspected. A large proportion of the heart muscle had been affected.

I listened carefully, intending to work out later what was really being said, but I understood quickly there was no need to try to read between the words. Dr Bennett gave me the unvarnished truth. There was no likelihood of long-term recovery, she said, given the damage that had already occurred. The question was when rather than if the end would come, and how to manage the intervening time.

'I see,' I murmured. The voice in my head had stopped. All I could hear was a roaring silence.

I realised that Dr Bennett was asking me a question. She wanted to know, if there were to be another huge heart attack, how I felt about an attempt to resuscitate my father. Did I want them to try, or should they let him go in peace?

'I . . . I would like to think about it. And perhaps to talk to him about it. What usually happens in these cases?'

What am I *supposed* to say, I wondered? No, please just stand aside, don't bother to help him? Or, I absolutely insist that your technicians come running to his bedside with their brutal paddles and try to shock him back into the world?

'Every case is different,' she said gently. 'I'm sorry to have to give you bad news.'

'Does he know?'

'We haven't told him what I have just told you, if that is what you are asking.'

'He's over eighty,' I said, as if his age somehow made the news slightly less bad. What I actually meant was to deplore the total of years that he and I had allowed to pass, until we had unwittingly reached this last minute where his doctor was telling me that Ted was going to die soon.

She nodded anyway. 'If there is anyone else, any other members of the family, it might be a good idea if they came in to see him soon.'

'How long is it likely to be?'

'I don't know,' Susan Bennett said. I liked her for not pretending omniscience. 'We'll do what we can to keep him comfortable.'

I walked slowly back to his bedside. I noticed the shiny floors with a faint skim of dust, and the chipped cream paint of the bed ends. Ted's eyes flickered open as soon as I sat down in the red chair. He wasn't asleep – he had been waiting for me.

'Did you hear what that nurse called me? *Teddy-boy*,' he muttered in disgust.

24

'I know.' We both smiled. I leaned over his hand as I took hold of it again, studying the map of raised sinews and brown blotches. Please don't die, I wanted to beg him. As if it were his choice.

'What did the doctor say?'

'That you have had a heart attack. They're monitoring you and waiting to see what will happen over the next few days.'

'Yes?'

'She sounded optimistic.'

But my tongue felt as though it was sticking to the roof of my mouth. *Coward, coward, coward.* I shouldn't be lying to him, but my father and I were not used to talking to each other about matters like love, or guilt, or disappointment. Was I supposed to start now, going straight to dealing with impending death? And how was I going to say it? You are going to die. And so I want to tell you that I love you, even though I haven't said so in forty years, and that love is in spite of everything, not because of it?

I bit my lower lip until distracting pain flooded round my mouth.

Ted only nodded, lying wearily against his pillows. He was looking away from me, out of the window at the grey angle of building and the narrow slice of cloudy sky that was the only view from his bed.

If he asks anything else, I resolved, I will tell him the truth. If he wants to know whether he is dying, he will ask me. Then we can hold each other. I will put my arms round him and help him and look after him, whatever is coming.

I waited, trying to work out the words that I would use and listening with half an ear to the sound of trolleys moving on the ward. A nurse walked past the door with a pile of linen in her arms and I watched her black-stockinged ankles receding.

The silence stretched between us. I rubbed the skin on the back of Ted's hand with the ball of my thumb, noticing how

25

loose and papery it felt. He didn't say anything, but the muscles of his chin and throat worked a little, as if he wished that he could. As the minutes passed I began to long for talk, even if it didn't mean much, or anything at all, just so long as there was some exchange between us.

The last few times we had seen each other, Ted reminisced about the war and about the make-do years that followed it when he was first married to my mother. He talked a lot about the glory days of the Fifties too, when he was discovering that he could follow his nose into a career that allowed him to meet rich women and powerful men. He spoke of the old days with a longing for his lost kingdoms, although oddly enough he never romanticised his gift itself. (He was always matter-of-fact about the mystery of creating perfumes. 'It's chemistry, memory and money,' he used to say. 'And mostly money.')

I thought now that maybe I could reach out to him by talking about the past, even though it was such a quagmire. I tried harder, flipping through the scenes in my mind's eye, searching for some neutral time that I could offer up. 'Do you remember that day when you took me in to the Phebus labs? I must have been six or seven, I should think.'

'Old Man Phebus,' Ted said quietly.

I can't remember why Ted took me to work with him on that particular morning. Maybe my mother was ill, or had to go somewhere where she couldn't take me. Outside school hours she and I were usually at home, occupied with our quiet routines that were put aside as soon as Ted came in. We were happy enough on our own together, Faye and I, yet even when I was very young I understood that hers was a make-do contentment. It was only when Ted was there that I saw her smile properly. For people in shops, occasional encounters with neighbours, even for me, there was a tucked-in version bleached by melancholy. Because I didn't know anything different I thought that was how it was for all families. Fathers went out and eventually came back, redolent of the outside world, and mothers and children waited like patient shells to close themselves round this life-giving kernel.

That day Ted and I travelled to work by bus, and I sat close up against my father in the blue, smoky fug on the top deck. It was exciting to ride so high above the streets, and to be able to look straight in through smeary windows and see cramped offices and the rumpled secrets of half-curtained bedsits. Phebus Fragrances occupied a small warehouse building off Kingsland Road, in Dalston, on the fringe of the East End. It seemed very far from our house in a north London suburb. There was a bomb-site to one side of the warehouse, and summer had turned the piled rubble lush with the blue-purple wands of buddleia and the red-purple of willowherb. It must have been the school holidays because there were children out playing on the open space. I held my father's hand as we walked from the bus stop and felt sorry for them because they weren't going to work as I was.

Anthony Phebus was Ted's earliest mentor in the perfume business. Ted always called him the Old Man. Ted had started working for him not long after I was born, as a bookkeeper and general office administrator, although of course he didn't actually have any bookkeeping skills or relevant office experience. In the years after the war he did a variety of jobs, from van-driving to working as a garage hand, but when I was born he decided that it was time to move up in the world. He applied for the job with Mr Phebus and impressed the old man so much with his apparent expertise with figures that he was offered the position on the spot. I knew this part of the story well, because Ted liked to tell it with a wink.

'I learned on the job.' He smiled. 'Always the best way. You don't know what you're going to be able to do until you have to do it, and when you have to it's surprising what you *can* do.'

In any case, Ted Thompson didn't stay long with the ledgers and file cabinets in the outer office. Anthony Phebus's business was as a commercial fragrance supplier. If a perfume house wanted to design a new scent, or if a manufacturer of face powder or shampoo needed a fragrance to set off a new product, they commissioned Mr Phebus to develop one for them. In his laboratory, with a tiny staff and minimal investment, the old man would mix and sniff and frown and adjust and finally come up with a formula that he would sell to the manufacturer. Sometimes he made up the perfume oil itself, juggling with money and loans to buy in enough raw materials just as he played with the balance of ingredients in his latest creation. Cosmetics manufacturers knew that he would give them what they wanted. Quite soon after joining the company Ted was helping him to do it. Phebus Fragrances was a long way down the scale from Chanel or Guerlain, but the old man did enough business to survive.

When we arrived Mr Phebus was at his desk in an untidy cubbyhole of an office, but he stood up straight away and came round to shake my hand. I was frightened of his eyebrows. They were white and jutted straight out from his forehead like a pair of bristly hearth brushes.

'And so, Miss Sadie, you work hard and make my fortune for me today?'

I looked up at Ted for confirmation and he gave me a wink, followed by his wide smile.

The 'lab,' as Mr Phebus and Ted always referred to it, was a windowless room lined from floor to ceiling with ex-WD metal shelves. On the shelves, drawn up in precise rows, were hundreds and hundreds of brown glass screw-top bottles. Each bottle was labelled or numbered in the old man's neat, foreign-looking script. In the centre of the room was a plain wood table with another clutch of bottles ranged on it in a semicircle, a line of notepads and pens, a pair of scales and some jars of what looked to me like flat white pencils. There was a sink with a dripping tap and some bright overhead lights.

'This is where we make our magic, eh?' Mr Phebus laughed. 'Where your good father learns to make dreams for beautiful women.'

I didn't like the reference to beautiful women or their dreams, not in relation to my father. The only women he should have anything to do with were Mum and me. I kept my mouth shut in a firm line and waited.

'Sit down here, miss,' Mr Phebus said and I slid into a seat. As well as having alarming eyebrows, I thought he talked in a funny way, as though 's's and 'th's were 'z's. When I was older I learned that the old man had been an analytic chemist in Warsaw, but he had come to London with his wife before the war. He started work with a cosmetics house and he turned himself from a chemist into a perfumer by sheer hard work.

'Your father, Mr Ted here, he has what we call a nose,' Mr Phebus grandly announced.

I remember looking at my father's face and realising it was a handsome one compared with Mr Phebus's, and feeling proud of my father's youth and good looks. But his nose seemed relatively unremarkable. 'So have I,' I retorted, pressing the end of mine and squashing it.

'We shall see,' the old man said. I thought he was not very observant if he couldn't see it already.

The three of us sat down at the plain wood table and Ted gave me my own jar of the flat white pencils. Now I could see that they were in fact strips of thick blotting paper, the same size as the spills my mother used for lighting the gas. Mr Phebus was humming and setting a line of the little glass bottles between us. He unscrewed the top of one with a flourish and told me to take my blotter. I glanced at Ted and he pointed to the white paper strip. Mr Phebus already had one and as I watched he slid the tip of it gently into the liquid in the bottle.

'Now you,' he said. I copied him exactly as he lifted the blotter to his nose and breathed in. His eyebrows twitched and I looked again at Ted, wanting to laugh. My father pressed his forefinger against one nostril and winked again. I sniffed hard at my dipper, as Mr Phebus had done. A dense, sweet cloud instantly filled my nose and rushed up through the secret insides of my face until it seemed to squeeze its fingers round my brain. I coughed and closed my eyes, and as I let my hand fall the scent's power receded, although I could still feel the pressure of it above my cheeks and the stinging shock in the tender membranes of my nose.

'What is that?' I whispered.

Mr Phebus said, 'That is lavender. It will be one of the top notes of the scent we are working on today.'

'Lavender's blue, dilly dilly.' I had heard the song on *Listen with Mother* and I was pleased to make this unexpected connection. But Mr Phebus held up his hand and frowned. We were working. The lab was no place for rhymes or any kind of inattention. He unscrewed another bottle and we went through the same process, dipping and smelling. This one was nasty as well as strong. The stink was sharp, like cats or the brown-tiled lavatories at my school, and I screwed up my face in disgust.

'Cassia,' Mr Phebus said. 'Very important. You must remember that not all perfume essences smell sweet and pretty. We often use these sensual animal stinks like musk and civet for our base notes, to anchor the structure. Men and women are animals too, you know, and we all respond in the same way.'

I frowned at him, battling my incomprehension.

The door opened and a woman with her hair swept up on the top of her head looked in at us. 'Phone call for Mr Thompson,' she said.

I shivered on my wooden seat with pleasure at the importance of this. We didn't have a telephone at home. Ted sprang up and went out, not remembering to look round at me. Mr Phebus went on unscrewing bottles and motioning to me to dip and sniff. Some of the smells were like flowers pressed and squeezed to make them powerful instead of sweet and gentle, others were surprising, reminding me of orange peel, or Christmas, or the sea at Whitstable where we had spent a summer holiday. By the time my father came back there were ten used white dippers on the table in front of me. I was beginning to feel bored and slightly queasy.

'Now, miss,' Mr Phebus said, pulling at the thistly tuft of one eyebrow. 'Pay no attention to your father. Can you remember which one was lavender?'

Ten dippers with their tips discoloured or turned translucent by the oils now lay on the table in front of me. I stared at what was left of the evidence and then reluctantly I picked up several in turn and sniffed at them again. My head felt muzzy and too full of potent fumes. The dippers smelled less strongly now; their separate characters and the names Mr Phebus had given them had become hopelessly confused. I took a wild guess. 'That one?'

'No, that one is jasmine.'

Ted laughed and sat down again on the wooden chair beside mine. He tilted it back on two legs with his arms folded, in the exact way my mother told me not to do at home. My eyes were stinging. I felt that I had let him down.

'Don't worry, you can learn the difference if you try hard enough,' Mr Phebus said. 'I managed it. I spent many years of hard work, memorising thousands of notes, which is what we call the different basic scents and that is only the very beginning of what a perfumer must know. He must have other skills too, and most of all he must have imagination that lifts him from being a mere technician into an artist of fragrance.

'I am an artist, in my small way, but only of the fourth or maybe third degree. But your father here' – he paused for effect,

31

with his eyebrows pointing at me – 'he is, at once, a natural. He smells a note only once and he remembers it. And he knows, because the artistry is in his heart and in his mind, he knows what he will add and what he will withhold to coax from these bottles, these not romantic little jars, the dreams of women.'

Women and their dreams, again. I was torn between pride in my father and a new discomfort that rubbed at the margins of my understanding. I didn't like the feeling of insecurity that came with it.

'Of course, he still has very much to learn. *Many* years of practice.'

Ted laughed out loud delightedly. 'Better get on with it, then.' He was always enthusiastic in those days. He rubbed his hands and smacked his lips, full of raw appetite for life. I didn't recognise his hunger then for what it was, but I already knew that my mother entirely lacked what Ted possessed. I loved her, of course, and I took for granted her devotion to me, but she wasn't thrilling in the way my father was. She was always there and I never noticed her constancy until she wasn't any longer. One morning she was at home and that same afternoon she was never coming back. That's how sudden her death was from the brain haemorrhage. Afterwards, when I thought about her, I would remember her quietness and restraint. She used to brush my hair and tie ribbons in it, looking down or away instead of into our joint reflections in the mirror of her kidney-shaped dressing table. She wore plain jerseys and calf-length colourless skirts that hid her pretty legs. It was as if even before she left us altogether she occupied only the corners of her own life. Whereas Ted joyfully overflowed out of his, and ran in a hot current through hers and mine as well.

Mr Phebus said, 'Let's have Black Opal three and four, then.'

Ted brought some bottles from the shelves and they drew their notepads and jars of blotters towards them. The two of them began nosing and muttering together, and I half listened while unfamiliar words washed over my head. They talked about heart and base notes and aldehydes and sparkle and synthesis, and the names of natural essences and the chemical polysyllables of synthetics rolled off their tongues. I didn't remember tongue-twisting phenylethylene or galaxolide, but the mysterious-sounding beauty of naturals – vetiver and musk and mimosa – did stay with me.

They were still with me now as I sat by my father's bed and held his dry hand. Only the names, not the scents. I failed Mr Phebus's first test and I knew I was not an artist like Ted.

I was talking too much, I realised. It would be tiring for him. 'Do you remember?'

'How old were you?' he asked, restlessly moving his legs and frowning with the effort of recollection.

'Six, or seven.'

'Back in '56, then.'

I was pleased that he knew the year of my birth. I wouldn't have placed a bet on it. 'Yes.'

'We were working on contract for Coty.' His hand moved a little in my grasp, as if he were trying to reach for something, and then fell back again. 'I don't remember the day. It must have been boring for you.'

We're so polite to each other, I thought. We are like a rough sea swirling under a thin skin of ice.

While the old man and my father continued with their sniffing and scribbling I began to fidget and rock on my chair. I made a wigwam of dippers and then, with a hasty movement to stop it collapsing, I knocked over a bottle. The bottle rolled across the table and stopped in front of Ted.

He raised his head, his forehead corrugated with irritation and his eyes cold. It was a look I had seen often enough. 'Why don't you go out and sit by Miss Mathers?'

33

Miss Mathers was the woman with piled-up hair. I had seen them laughing together and heard Ted call her Babs, but I understood that she was Miss Mathers to me. I stood up obediently.

Miss Mathers gave me some pencils and some sheets of paper to draw on, then went back to her typing. She rolled letterheads and pale-pink and green flimsies sandwiched with carbon paper into her black-and-gold typewriter and busily stabbed the keys. Once or twice she answered the telephone in a sing-song voice: 'Phebus *Fray*grances.'

At twelve thirty Ted and I went out. After the dimness inside the warehouse the sunshine was so bright it made me blink. We strolled down Kingsland Road to a pub and I sat on a bench in the sun while Ted went inside. My excitement flooded back with the novelty of all this and I swung my legs so my white socks flashed. Ted brought out lemonade and a cheese sandwich for me, and a pint of beer and a ham-and-pickle sandwich for him. He took a long swallow of the beer and rubbed the froth from his clipped moustache. Then he slid a packet of Players from his pocket and lit one. He blew out the smoke in a long plume and sighed with pleasure. 'Not a word to a soul,' he said to me, pressing his lips with the side of his index finger. 'No good for the old *nose*, booze and fags, are they?'

I was awed to be part of this conspiracy. The old man and Miss Mathers would have had to torture me before I would have breathed a word about my father's lunchtime habits.

The afternoon of that day was the same, except that the hours seemed longer than the morning's. My father and the old man were shut up in the lab together and Miss Mathers largely ignored me. I drew some desultory pictures on my sheets of paper and looked at shiny brochures with pictures of women and tins of talcum powder in them. Yet as Ted and I finally rode home in the bus, along Holloway Road and up to the Archway, I felt utterly triumphant. The new words I had learned still rang in my head: mimosa, musk, amber. Mr Phebus had given me a folded ten-shilling note when Ted took me into his office to say goodbye. But the best of it was the new footing I felt that I was on with Ted himself.

Before now, he had gone out in the mornings and come back again at night with the newspaper, a kiss for my mother and a joke for me. He brought different sounds and smells and a new atmosphere into the house with him, but I had no picture in my mind of where he had been. Quite often he was away at night too, or for days at a stretch, on business for Mr Phebus.

But after today, I felt that I was a part of his other world. There had been beer on his breath as we walked back to the warehouse after the pub, and he had put pennies into a chewing gum machine on a wall. We were both chewing one of the little white pillows as we walked diagonally across the bomb-site to the warehouse door. I had heard him joking with Miss Mathers, although I didn't like the soft teasing sound that crept into his voice when he spoke to her. At Miss Mathers's suggestion, I had carried their pot of tea into the lab at four o'clock. Ted and Mr Phebus were both in their shirtsleeves with scratched notes and discarded dippers spread everywhere, and I understood that they were too preoccupied to glance at me. I accepted my lack of importance with proper humility.

The impression of that day stayed with me for years. It defined my notion of work, as the utterly exotic somehow hemmed in by the tedious progress of hours. At the end of it, as Ted and I marched up the garden path to the house where my mother was waiting for us, I kept my thrilling new awareness locked inside me.

My father was an artist of the first degree. He was a nose.

The house that night seemed colourless and smaller and overfamiliar and my mother even quieter than usual. 'What did you do?' she asked, as she brushed my hair. The sheets on my bed were smoothed down and I knew without looking that my hot-water bottle with the rabbit cover was in its proper place.

'Drew some pictures,' I answered evasively. I didn't want to share the experience, even with her.

'That's nice.'

I didn't ask about her day's absence. Maybe she had been to see the doctor about her headaches. Sometimes they made her eyes red and swollen so she had to lie down on the double bed, a small shape hunched up on the green candlewick cover with her back turned to the door.

'It wasn't boring,' I told Ted now. 'I loved it.'

'He was a good perfumer, the old man, a craftsman. I learned everything I needed to know from him. No business sense, though. None at all.'

I had to lean closer to catch his words. His voice seemed to be fading to an echo of itself and his eyes were gradually falling shut. I thought he might be drifting into sleep and I had to stop myself from grasping his hand and shaking it hard to keep him with me. I watched the shallow rise and fall of his chest under his pyjama jacket.

Then his eyes snapped open again and he struggled to sit upright. 'It stinks in here,' he complained. His nostrils flared and deep lines pulled the corners of his mouth downwards. I sniffed the air and caught a whiff of vomit and a faint fecal undertone. If even I could smell it, the ward must indeed stink to Ted's sensitive nose.

I sandwiched his hand between my two. 'We need something stronger to block it out. I've got an idea. Shall I go out and buy some perfume to spray round?' I could hear the cheeriness in my voice cracking and shivering like the sea ice, with grief welling up from beneath. 'What would you like? Joy? Vent Vert? Or one of your own? How about Black Opal or Iridescent?'

'I've smelled enough perfume for one lifetime,' Ted said irritably.

I bent my head and waited. And then, when I finally stole a glance at his face, I saw that this time he really had fallen asleep.

I went down to the hospital visitors' car park, where I could use my mobile phone, and called Lola to relay the news.

'Oh God, Mum, I'm sorry. Poor Grandad. I'd better ring in and cancel my shift,' she said at once. Lola worked in a bar during university holidays. At least she's at home, I told myself, not up in Manchester as she was all term-time. We agreed that she would collect Jack from school in her car and they would come straight up to the hospital.

'Drive carefully,' I warned her.

'Of course I will.'

Next, I telephoned Penny at the Works, as we call the book bindery and small print shop we jointly own. Penny and I have been business partners for twelve years. I have always loved the physical weight and dimensions of fine books, the texture of paper, and the variety and intricate grace of typefaces, and Penny possesses the rare combination of design flair and business acuity. We work well together and although there are no great riches in what we do, we make an adequate living out of our leather bindings and hand-set printing.

'Don't worry,' Penny told me. 'Don't even think about anything here, I'll handle it. And I'm here if you need me, okay?'

Next I spoke to Caz. Caz has been my friend since we lived in adjacent rooms in a decrepit student house thirty years ago. We were married in the same year, and she and Graham had their two boys in quick succession, not long after Tony and I had Lola. We have shared the quotidian details of our lives ever since, to the extent that if I think of myself as having an extended family, Caz and Graham and their children are it.

'What can I do?' Caz said, as soon as I told her the news. If there is ever a favour to be done for someone else, an empty slot in a rota or a spare pair of hands required, Caz is always the first to volunteer.

'Will you have Jack, if I have to stay over at the hospital? If Lola can't hold the fort, that is?'

Jack didn't currently get on all that well with Dan and Matthew, Caz's boys, but in this emergency he would have to make the best of it.

'Of course,' she assured me. 'Anything else? What about some shopping? Or listen, I've got a chicken, I can roast it and bring it over . . .'

Caz and I both use food as shorthand for love. With Mel and me it's more a matter of romance and theatre.

Caz was saying, 'It's very sudden. He wasn't ill before, was he?'

'Yes,' I agreed. 'It is very sudden.' I don't think that even Caz, whom I have known for all these years, has ever really noticed how little I actually talk about my father or about the past.

'I'll be thinking of you, darling,' she said in her warm voice. 'Call me as soon as there's any news.'

Finally I dialled Mel's office direct line. After I had told her what had happened she said, 'That's quite strange, isn't it? The way we were talking about him last night?'

'Yes.'

'Do you want me to come up and keep you company?' It was a generous offer. Mel worked for a big headhunting company and I could guess at the rapid mental diary reshuffling she must be doing, although there wasn't the faintest hint of it in her tone.

'No. But thank you.'

'Sadie?'

'Yes?'

'You can't change or even affect what's going to happen, you know. You just have to accept this, for him and for yourself.'

Mel understood me well and my need to control what went on around me. She knew that it was disturbing for me to feel powerless, as I did most of the time where Jack was concerned, although she didn't know what had made me this way.

'I know,' I murmured.

After she had rung off I sat down on the low wall of the car park. The morning was grey under a monochrome sky, with none of the luminous quality of the evening before. Cars rolled through the entrance and circled past me, looking for slots. A young man in a Peugeot skidded into an empty place and leaped out, clicking the remote locking as he sprinted towards the hospital doors. His wife must be in labour, I thought. I watched an old couple extricate themselves with difficulty from their Honda. The wife took a pair of sticks from behind the passenger seat and gave them to her husband, waiting with exaggerated patience while he shuffled himself into the 'go' position. They set off on the journey towards the doors together, without having exchanged a word. A big Asian family filed past, followed by a white girl who looked younger than Lola pushing a baby in a buggy. All these people had their different reasons for coming here, to this place of crisis, and all of them brought with them the weight of their anxiety or the bubble of hope. Ted was dying, but so were other people behind the stained concrete façade, and at the same time others were struggling with pain or dreaming of recovery, and babies were fighting their way out into the light. Being part of this random community made me feel less isolated and the walls that contained my feelings seemed to grow thinner, as if they might rupture and I might be able to give way to grief.

A florist's van drew up and the driver began unloading cellophane-wrapped bunches of flowers finished with puffs of gaudy ribbon. The last item to appear was a wicker basket with a huge hoop handle and a ruff of paper enclosing a mass of pink and white carnations. The sight made me smile and remember the day Lola was born. She was handed to me wrapped in a blanket, and I looked down into her fathomless black eyes and felt a stirring of love I had never known before.

Ted was living at that time with an auntie called Elaine. It was Elaine who sent flowers and a card ('It's a Beautiful Baby Girl!') signed in both their names, with a line that read, 'Your Dad's up to his eyes, nothing new!'

When the driver came back from delivering the flowers he leaned against the back doors of the van and lit a cigarette. He saw me watching him and called out, 'Just taking five, eh?'

'Why not?' I called back meaninglessly.

But suddenly the sky seemed to lighten and the diesel-heavy air of the car park softened and sighed in my ears. I could feel the gritty surface of the wall under my fingertips and hear the swish of traffic out on the dual carriageway. The stitching on the leather strap of my handbag was coming undone and I stared down at the tiny frayed ends of thread and the puckered edges of the stitch punctures. Real time and place blurred and swam almost out of my reach. It was one of those rare moments of extreme physical and mental awareness, when even the smallest incident seems to contain infinite richness and a profound meaning that only narrowly evades capture. I was wide awake, but I felt the altered dimensions of a dream world beckoning me. I swung my feet up on to the wall and rested my head on my bent knees. Behind my eyelids, in this quietness, I could talk to Ted and he to me. The dialogue had always been running back and forth between us, in this other place, the old skeins of angry words and bitter words tangled with the words of love and faith, which were the ones I wanted to hear and speak now.

We failed each other, I said, I you and you me, but it was not a failure on such a scale that we are apart now, today of all days.

I was still sitting there, caught up in my inner conversation, when the driver climbed back into his seat. He tooted his horn at me as he rolled away and at once I jerked back into ordinary awareness. I should be sitting at my father's bedside instead of hovering out here with my mind freewheeling in space. I hurried across the car park and in through the revolving doors, past the coffee shop and gift stall, and took the lift up to the ward. In the airless, medical-scented atmosphere I already felt as if I had been at the hospital for days.

Ted was still asleep. His mouth had fallen open and his breath clicked faintly in his throat. I took my seat once more beside him but didn't try to hold his hand in case I disturbed him.

The hours passed slowly. The nurse who looked in from time to time explained that he was connected up to monitors that were watched over at the nurses' station. He was stable, he said, at present.

At the distant end of the afternoon Lola appeared. In this stuffy room my daughter looked supernaturally beautiful and healthy, with her bright eyes and polished skin, as if all the threats of mortality had been airbrushed out of her face. I clung briefly to her, breathing in her sweet and perfectly familiar smell. Jack sidled in in her wake. He edged round the bed and, after a quick glance at Ted, leaned his forehead against the window and stared out. I hugged him too and he submitted briefly, although I could still feel the tense curve of his body arching away from me.

'Have you had something to eat?' I asked him.

'Yeah. Lo fixed me a sandwich. I ate it in the car.'

The red chair was the only one. Lola went out to the main ward and borrowed another. She handed me a bag of apples and took a framed photograph out of her nylon rucksack. It was of herself and Jack and me, taken on last year's summer holiday in Devon, the one that usually stood on the dresser in our kitchen. For once we were all smiling, looking straight into the camera, and now I noticed that each of us had a variation of Ted's strong features overprinted on our own. She placed

41

the picture on Ted's locker, angled so that he could see it when he woke up. 'I thought he might like it,' she said, 'if he wakes up when we aren't here.'

The love implicit in the simple gesture touched me and I felt sorry that I hadn't thought of it myself. 'A very good idea.'

'We're all he's got,' she said matter-of-factly and this was the truth. There was no wife, not even an auntie, now, if you didn't count Jean Andrews. I didn't know who Ted's friends were, if there were any remaining.

'How is he?'

Out of the corner of my eye I saw Jack's head half turn at Lola's question. He wanted to hear but didn't want me to see him listening.

'Holding his own,' I said. I was afraid that even though he seemed to sleep, he might hear what we were saying. I would tell them Dr Bennett's verdict later, out of Ted's earshot.

Lola nodded. 'Go and get a cup of tea, Mum and eat some fruit. I'll be here.'

'Do you want to come with me, Jack?'

'No,' he said.

I carried a polystyrene cup of tea out into the car park and sat in my place on the wall, sipping the tea and eating an apple. The traffic was heavier now, with after-work visitors arriving and a short line of cars waiting for a free slot built up at the entrance. I tried to recapture some of the comfort of my earlier unspoken dialogue with Ted, or even the sense that with the dying and the newborn and the passers-through we were part of a generous community, but there was nothing. I felt lonely and sad for him, and disappointed in myself.

But there's still time, I thought. I can still reach him.

'He woke up,' Lola said when I reached the ward again.

'Yes?'

'We chatted for a bit, Jack, didn't we?'

'Yeah. He asked Lo about uni and me about school. He was

okay. Then he just sort of shut his eyes and went to sleep again. He didn't see the photo, though.'

This was a long speech for Jack. Hope began sliding through my veins. Outside on the main ward there were relatives gathered round the beds of the old men, two nurses were pushing a trolley loaded with pill bottles and checking lists of medication, and a woman in a green overall was offering tea and biscuits. It wasn't over. In a week, maybe, Ted would be sitting up too and choosing a biscuit from the Tupperware drum. In another week or two I could be driving him home. I would bring him back to my house and slowly, slowly, we would learn a new language for each other. I could tell him that he had made me suffer when I was too young to deserve such treatment and he could explain to me what had made him do it. We would listen to each other and make sense of the unintelligible, and then slowly stitch up the weave of forgiveness.

Anything was possible. Everything was possible.

The three of us settled round his bed. On one side Lola stroked his hand and talked to him about her house-share friends at university, young people he had never heard of let alone met. She talked easily and I knew that Ted would like the sound of her voice with its regular gurgles of laughter. Jack flitted around the room. He leaned on the windowsill for long minutes and watched the birds coming to roost among the huge metal cylinders on the hospital roof, then turned away to pick with his thumbnail at a leprous patch of paint on the bed end. I sat still and watched the rise and fall of Ted's chest. It already felt like routine to be sitting here. Was it only yesterday at this time that I had been walking through the shimmering evening to meet Mel?

Time passed slowly. The ward quietened as the visitors drifted away. I was half expecting it, but no one came to tell us it was time to leave. A new nurse, just arrived on night duty, came in to introduce herself and to change one of the packs of fluid that drained into Ted's arm.

'How is he?' I asked softly, thinking of the monitors at the nursing station.

'There's no change.'

That meant there was no deterioration. I smiled my leaping gratitude at her.

At nine o'clock I told Lola and Jack that they should go home. It was over an hour's drive and Jack had school in the morning.

'Aren't you coming?' Jack asked.

'I'll stay here a little longer. Lola will see you into bed.' I glanced at her over his head and she nodded. 'Or if you'd rather, you can go to Caz and Graham's.'

'No,' Jack said at once.

Lola bent over and kissed her grandfather's forehead, then touched her fingertips to his lips. 'See you later, Grandad,' she whispered.

Jack touched the small steeple of bedclothes over his feet and snatched his hand back. 'Bye,' he mumbled. He followed his sister to the door and then hovered, torn between the impulse to rush back to Ted's side and the need to keep his own distance from me and his sister. Sometimes Jack was so transparent I thought I could read his hurt and put everything right for him so easily; at others I was afraid I hardly knew him. 'Bye,' he said again. Lola was leading and he followed her.

'Drive carefully,' I warned automatically. 'I love you both.'

'Yes, Mum.'

I sat down yet again. An hour dragged by and Ted rolled his head on the pillows and feebly shifted his legs. The Night Sister suddenly appeared with the first nurse. They moved rapidly around him, checking his fluids, and the tubes and wires that led into him, and calling him by his name.

'What's happened? What's wrong?' My voice was sharp and loud.

'There are some new signs. The doctor's coming.'

I was squeezed out of my place at his side. Ted's eyes were wide open now and I could see how much it hurt him to breathe.

'Dad? Dad, I'm here . . . I . . .'

I couldn't finish what I was saying because the doctor arrived and I was edged further away to make room for him. I stood obediently outside the room with my arms wrapped round my chest. The old men were mostly asleep although pools of light lapped one or two of the beds. I waited until the doctor came out again. He was wearing a dark-blue shirt under his white coat and a name tag that read Dr Raj Srinivasar. I saw all this in a split second. He indicated that we should step a little distance away.

'Doctor?'

'I'm sorry. The undamaged portion of your father's heart muscle has been working very hard since the attack and we have been helping him as far as possible with drugs to stimulate the heart's natural rhythm. But I am afraid even this is gradually failing him now. I think Dr Bennett explained?'

I bent my head. 'Yes.'

It had been human but utterly vain to hope, of course. I wanted the doctor to go away and take the nurses with him, and leave the two of us together. Dr Srinivasar knew this, because when I had composed my face and turned back to Ted he was lying quietly, alone again, under a dim light. I closed the door of the little room and took my place in the chair once more. I thought there were fewer wires clipped to him now and the levels of liquid in the bags hanging over his head didn't change.

He was awake and he didn't look as if he was in pain. Keeping him comfortable, Dr Bennett called it. Ted licked his lips and his neck muscles worked as if to squeeze words out of his ruined heart. 'You've been a good girl,' he whispered.

Automatically, defensively, keeping my long-learned distance I muttered, 'Not really.'

I wasn't ready for Ted's praise and in my unpreparedness I couldn't have assured him in return that he had been a good father.

I would have snatched my answer back if only I could, but Ted surprised me. He let his head fall further back against the pillows and laughed. It was a small coughing echo of his old laugh, but still there was no mistaking it. He said one more thing after that, on a long breath. I thought it was 'my girl'.

As the minutes ebbed and I waited I knew that now it was too late for us to make our spoken allowances to each other. He lay with his eyes closed and the rise and fall of his chest grew shallower until I could no longer see it. I pressed my face against his cheek. Tears began to run out of my eyes and into the sheet. I put my arm under his shoulder as if I were going to lift him up and held him close against me. If I could have lifted him properly and carried him across the divide before laying him down again to rest, I would have done it. As I wept I told him, the angry words and the bitter words threading with the words of love, that I loved him and I hated the childhood he had given me, and I would always love him. He didn't answer and I didn't expect him to. I knew that he was dead.

I sat with him for a little while; then there seemed no point in staying when Ted himself had gone. I took the framed photograph off the locker and tucked it under his arm where he could hold it close to his heart. Then I kissed him on the forehead and touched his lips with my fingers, as Lola had done. I closed the door of the room very quietly.

Dr Srinivasar and the Night Sister were waiting for me.

'I'm sorry,' the doctor said. He shook my hand, very formally.

'Thank you,' I said.

The Sister put her arm round my shoulders and led me into the empty visitors' room.

'Would you like to sit in peace for a while? Let me bring you a cup of tea?'

I shook my head. 'No, thank you, Sister.'

'There is a chapel in the hospital.'

I shook my head again. Ted had never been very godly and I took after him.

There was only one place I wanted to be and that was at home. We established that I would come back to complete the formalities relating to the death and I thanked her for everything that had been done for my father. I went out once more to the car park, now deserted under a heavy dark sky, climbed into my car and drove back dry-eyed to London.

Lola was waiting up for me. I told her that Ted Thompson was dead, then we sat down and cried for him together.

THREE

The room was light and bare, with tall, plain windows. Rows of wooden seats faced a pair of non-committal flower arrangements on either side of a secular-looking lectern. The atmosphere was subdued, naturally enough, but also utilitarian. The light-wood coffin under a purple drape was utilitarian too, which was inappropriate for Ted, whose life had been many things but never that. And at the same time as I was thinking about the crematorium chapel and the flowers, and the coffin I had selected with the undertakers' discreet guidance, I was also reflecting that Ted wouldn't have cared what arrangements were made for his funeral. Or would have affected not to.

'I haven't got to sit through it, have I?' I could hear him snort in the half-irritable, half-jovial way that he adopted in his later years. 'Just do the necessary and make sure all and sundry get a drink at the end of it.'

I also wondered how abnormal it was to be standing at a funeral and thinking like this. But then our life together, Ted's and mine, hadn't been usual. Mel's family had been normal, or Caz's, or Graham's. Not ours.

Mel was sitting a few seats behind me. She had never met Ted, but she insisted that she wanted to come, out of respect and to keep me company. Caz and Graham were with her. They had met him a handful of times, at my wedding and the children's birthday parties, and the occasional Christmas celebration in the intervening years.

'I liked your dad. Of course I'm coming to his funeral,' Caz declared.

Ted had liked her, too. I remember him flirting with her at my wedding reception. He had probably cornered her in some alcove, before cupping her round face between his two hands and breathing in the scent of her skin as if she were some exotic flower. 'I could create such a perfume for you,' he would have murmured in her ear. This routine worked like a charm with a surprisingly wide range of women. Not with Caz, of course, although it would have been a matter of pride for him to have a go. But with plenty of others. More than I could or would want to remember.

Lola and I sat on either side of Jack in the front row of seats. Lola was wearing black trousers and a tight red jersey that made her glow like a damask rose in the colourless desert of the chapel.

Rosa damascena, from which the essential perfume oil attar of roses is distilled. In Bulgaria, principally. I was surprised by how much I remembered about Ted's craft.

Lola blotted her tears with a folded Kleenex and glanced down at the two black feathered wings of mascara printed on the tissue. Jack sat upright and stared straight ahead of him, dressed in a tidied-up version of his school uniform.

When I broke the news to him, on the morning after Ted's death, he said, 'I see.' And after a moment's thought, 'It's very final, isn't it?'

'Yes. Although he's still here in a way, because we remember him and because we'll go on talking about him as long as we are alive.'

Jack gave me one of his withering looks, as if he saw right through this threadbare platitude, but he didn't pass any comment.

Apart from the six of us, the other mourners were Ted's two first cousins on his mother's side, who had come down from Manchester. There was no other family left. Then there was a handful of Ted's neighbours, led by the large and forthright Jean Andrews, and the landlord and a couple of regulars from the pub Ted used to go to. I had never met any of these people before, but they filed up to me at the chapel door, and shook my hand and told me how sorry they were. A great character, your dad, they said. Thank you, I murmured. And yes, he was.

There was also an old woman wearing a ratty fox fur over a shapeless bag of a coat and a crumpled black felt hat with a bunch of silk-and-wire lilies of the valley pinned to one side. *Muguet*, Ted called the flower. It was one of his favourites. The yield of natural oil from the blooms was minimal, and so the fragrance was usually artificially created.

The woman in the black hat had nodded coolly to me as she walked in, but she didn't introduce herself or offer condolences. I assumed she was one of those eccentrics who like to see a decent send-off, regardless of whether or not they actually knew the dear departed.

There were perhaps twenty-five people in all. Muted piped organ music whispered around us.

On being given the nod by the crematorium officiator, who wasn't exactly a vicar and who certainly wasn't lively enough to qualify as master of ceremonies, one of the cousins hobbled to the lectern. He read that passage from Canon Henry Scott Holland about not having gone away, but being in the next room, still with you. I thought it was a fine and comforting piece of writing, but unfortunately untrue. Ted *was* completely gone. The shadow of himself that he had lately become had followed the younger man, with his Spencer Tracy looks, his laugh and his silk ties and his perfumes, off and away out of our reach.

Lola's shoulders shook and she pressed the Kleenex to her

face. I reached around Jack to rest my hand in the smooth dip between her shoulder blades.

After the reading there was a hymn, 'All Things Bright and Beautiful', which I had chosen for no more significant reason than that Ted sometimes hummed it while he was shaving. He would turn his face from side to side, catching the best of his reflection in the mirror above the bathroom sink as he whisked on the soap lather with an old bristle brush. Then with his lips twisted aside he would razor a long, crisp channel through the white foam, all the way from his cheekbone to his jaw. The humming was counterpointed in my memory by the dripping and clanking of pipes in our chilly bathroom.

Or maybe I never actually *saw* any of this ritual, only imagined that I had. And maybe I also imagined the conspiratorial half-wink he gave himself as the words of the hymn played on in his head, *all things wise and wonderful*, as if he were saying to himself, that's you, my boy.

After the hymn the officiator gave a short address. Lola and the cousins and I had provided as much background as we could about Ted and his life, and it was a good attempt at a tribute, given that he had never met him. Practice helped, I supposed, since the man was probably doing this several times a day. He spoke of Ted's popularity, his love of life and its opportunities, and his gifts as a perfumer. We were just shuffling to our feet again, to the first notes of the organ voluntary that the cousins had suggested to accompany the coffin's slow slide between the curtains, when Jack scrambled past me. I thought for a second that he might be going to be sick, which had been one of his specialities as a younger child, but he pushed me back when I went to follow him. He marched up to the lectern and took his place behind it, and the recorded music was abruptly switched off. Lola and I glanced nervously at each other. He had given no indication that he wanted to make his own tribute and I regretted that I hadn't thought of asking him.

Jack cleared his throat. 'My grandad,' he began. We waited in silence. 'My grandad told me when I was just a little kid that pigeons are vermin.'

After another beat of silence I heard from the back of the room a snuffle that might have been suppressed laughter. I stared hard at Jack, seeing his stiff hair and the way his baby's face would settle into the aggrieved lines of pre-adolescence. He didn't blink.

'At our other house before . . . before Mum and me and Lola moved, they used to sit on all the upstairs windowsills and on the gutters, and Grandad didn't like all the . . . all the . . . mess they left. He pointed at it when I was going to bed one night and said it was smelly and they were dirty. And I looked at their feet, the ones that were standing on the windowsill, and they were all, like, scabby. Their plumage was dirty as well.'

This all came out in a breathless rush. *Plumage* was a very Jack word. Lola was signalling to him, little patting movements with her hands that meant slow down, speak slower, but he didn't see her. His gaze was fixed on the back of the room.

'I said, are all birds dirty, then? And he said, I remember it really well, he said no, birds are beautiful, they've got the gift of the air, all the freedom of the sky and it's just the poor pigeons who live in London and eat rubbish and everything and sit on top of *our* dirt that makes them dirty. So they're vermin in the same way as rats, because rats are really clean creatures, in fact. He told me that as well. Anyway . . .'

Jack paused and now he did look at his audience, letting his eyes slide over us. He had got into his stride. We all sat without moving.

'Anyway, after that I got interested in birds. I liked the idea of the freedom of the sky. I wanted to think about them not being all vermin with diseased feet from living on our mess. So

I started watching them and learning about them, and he was right, they are beautiful. Seabirds especially because the sea belongs to them as well as the sky, if you think about it. So it's because of him. That I like birds. I owe it to him.' He nodded sideways to the coffin under the purple drape. 'That's what I wanted to say, actually. Grandad knew about things. He didn't always let you know that he knew, but he still knew. He was interesting, like that.'

The rush of confidence subsided as quickly as it had come. Jack's voice trailed away and his gaze returned to the floor. We sat in silence for a few long seconds, waiting to see if he wanted to add anything else. At last the officiator cleared his throat and stepped forward, and at the same moment Jack's head jerked up and he swung round to face the coffin. 'I love you, Grandad,' he blurted out. There were tears on his eyelashes. Then he turned round and marched back to his place between Lola and me. I tried to put my arm round his shoulders but he shook it off.

The piped music started up again. The curtains at the back of the chapel slowly parted and with a faint mechanical creaking the coffin slid forward. I kept my eyes fixed on it, feeling the faint tremors of Lola's weeping.

Then I began to think about my mother.

I could remember her calling me in from the garden – *Sadie? Sa-aa-die!* – where I was playing some complicated and solitary only-child's game.

I was ten when she died. I have so few memories of her and yet this tiny moment was suddenly crisp and rounded out with the sound of a radio playing in a neighbour's garden, and the suburban scents of dusty shrub borders and cooking. It was exactly as if I were standing there beside the rosebushes again, torn between playing and responding to her call.

Yes? I answered now, silently and pointlessly, but there was no more. It was strange that Ted himself, who had been so vividly alive and such a forceful presence all my life, should seem absent from these proceedings, while my shadowy mother, dead for more than forty years, was close at hand.

I wish I had been able to go to my mother's funeral. I think Ted sent me to a neighbour's, although I can't remember the precise circumstances. He excluded me, anyway and later he swept my mother out of our lives and made it as if she had never existed.

Ted's coffin had travelled the full distance. The curtains swished shut behind it and we all stood silently while the organ voluntary wheezed to an end.

Afterwards we walked out into the bright daylight. There was some more handshaking and subdued conversation. The family and neighbours already knew that there was to be a gathering back at Ted's house, and there was a slow movement towards the handful of parked cars. Polished shoes crunched on the gravel path and two or three people patted Jack on the shoulder as they passed.

The old woman in the black hat was waiting with the sun showing up the dust on her defiant fox fur. She came towards me with her head tilted expectantly. She had purply-red lipstick, gamely applied to pursed lips, and powdered cheeks. 'You'll be his daughter,' she said. 'I am Audrey.'

This meant nothing to me. I had never seen her before. She wasn't one of the aunties. It occurred to me that it was her snuffle of laughter I had heard when Jack launched himself into his pigeon speech. 'Thank you for coming,' I murmured. 'Would you like to join us for a drink, back at . . .'

But Audrey had already turned her attention to Jack. 'And you're his grandson. I liked what you said about him. You were quite right, Ted knew about things and it was one of the games he liked to play, not letting you know what he knew and then surprising you when you least expected it. Birds, or whatever it might be.'

Jack nodded, looking at her and sizing up the unwinking fox eyes and sharp fox faces that hung down over her bosom. I turned away because I had to speak to the undertakers, and when I had finished doing that and was ready to shepherd the last of Ted's neighbours back to his house, Audrey was nowhere to be seen.

'She went,' Jack said and shrugged, when I asked him.

Ted had lived for the last seven years of his life in a red-brick terraced house in a side street within two miles of both the hospital and the crematorium. He liked to joke in his deliberately bluff, I-dare-you-to-be-bothered way about their convenient proximity. On my infrequent visits there I felt that, like all Ted's places, it was too full of wedges of memory, bits of furniture or ornaments or even kitchen implements, that propped open doors of recollection and so let images back into the daylight that I would have preferred to remain in darkness.

After the crematorium, the neighbours and pub friends and Ted's small family reassembled at this lumberhouse of inanimate memory triggers. Everyone came back, except the mysterious Audrey. Mrs Andrews had been in to air the rooms and do some dusting, and as a result the place looked tidier and emptier than it had done when Ted was alive. Caz and I had made an early-morning lightning swoop on Marks & Spencer's and bought in enough finger-food to fill several trays. She worked her way round the guests with these while Graham and I followed with gin, Scotch or wine. We made it our job to fill and refill glasses as soon as they were half empty. The atmosphere lightened as people ate and drank, and then grew positively jolly. Jean Andrews's cheeks turned pink and she told the Manchester cousins stories about growing up in Oldham. They tried to find acquaintances in common, without much success from what I could overhear as I passed by with my bottles.

The noise level rose. The pub landlord told a couple of

jokes, on the grounds that they had been favourites of Ted's, and everyone laughed.

Jack sat on the stairs and read a book while people trod past him on the way to the bathroom. He glowered when anyone tried to speak to him or congratulate him on his impromptu speech, particularly me. Lola's tears had dried up. She moved between the groups, with the attention of one or two of the younger pub men fixed on her. She caught my eye once and winked. Caz and Graham still circulated with drink and food, and Mel just circulated. In the narrow room with Ted's shiny brown furniture and faded curtains she seemed bigger than the rest of us, and Technicolored alongside our dark clothes and muted pastel faces.

After a while I glanced at my watch. It was well past the lunch hour and I wanted to look in at work before the end of the day because there was some urgent finishing to do. I raised my eyebrows at Graham, who is used to standing in for a husband at times like this.

When I called Tony to tell him that Ted was gone, he had said how sorry he was, then asked immediately when the funeral was to be.

'Sadie, that's the one day I can't come. I've got to go to Germany for a big client meeting.'

I knew he would have come, if he possibly could. Tony is like that. He does the right thing. 'Don't worry. Graham and Caz will be there. We'll organise it together.'

'I know they'll support you. But I'm truly sorry I can't be there as well. Ted was my father-in-law for fifteen years.'

'It can't be helped,' I said. I too would have liked Tony to be here today, for my own sake as well as Lola's and Jack's. But there was no point in regretting his absence now, or at any other time.

'How are you?'

'I'm all right,' I told him.

'And the kids?'

'They're here.'

'I'll talk to them. I'm thinking of you, Sadie.'

'I know. Thanks,' I said and passed the receiver to Lola.

When we were first divorced, Jack and Lola both spent plenty of time with their father. We had agreed on unlimited access and it worked well. But in the last five years, since Tony met his new partner and particularly since the birth of their twin girls, the weekend visits have become less regular. This is no one's intention, it's just that Tony has less time to spare for children who can already feed and dress themselves. Lola is fairly sanguine about it, but Jack minds.

Graham glanced around the room, judging the atmosphere. 'A few words, maybe?' he suggested to me in a whisper.

I cleared my throat and stepped into the middle of the room while he rattled a spoon against a plate.

I had no idea what I was going to say. I don't remember what I did say, except that it can't have been very inspiring. Everyone listened politely, anyway. I thanked them again for coming, and lifted my glass that had one and a half mouthfuls of red wine at the bottom of it. Luckily everyone else's glasses were well charged.

'To Ted.'

The echo began as a muted, respectful chorus. But the next thing I saw was the faces all around me breaking into smiles and there was a sudden little wave of clapping, and some stamping and cheering. *Ted, Ted, Ted.* Jack's white face poked round the hallway door.

'My father,' I added to the chorus, but under my breath. It wasn't my unmemorable words that had provoked this, of course. It was Ted himself and I was being made aware of his popularity for perhaps the last time.

I looked around the room again, searching for a synthesis between my knowledge of him and what all these other cheerful, rational friends and neighbours felt. There was his dented old armchair but even as I stared at it I couldn't shift the cold wedge that separated my memories of Ted from everyone else's.

I shook my head and looked for the faces of my children and my old friends. They jumped out of the gloom at me, full of warmth and life. Mel's red lipstick. Caz's hennaed bob, Graham's bald patch and habitual anxious frown. And Jack and Lola, my flesh and Ted's too.

This is what matters now, not *then*, I rationalised. History's gone.

I found myself with my fingers wrapped round my now empty glass, fondly beaming back at all of them. And my smile must have been particularly noticeable because there was another surge of clapping and cheering. How Ted would have *loved* all this.

It was another moment before everyone noticed that they were involved in an outbreak of spontaneous celebration, but when they did the applause gently faded into shuffling and coughing. This was a funeral, after all. Still smiling, Jean Andrews began dabbing her eyes.

My short speech and the clapping were taken as the signal for everyone to make a move. Caz and Mel swept plates and glasses into the kitchen as Lola and I stood by the front door, thanking everyone all over again for coming.

'If only he could have been here.' Jean Andrews sighed as she squeezed into her coat. Half an hour later Caz's and Graham's Volvo followed Mel's Audi down the road. Lola and Jack and I were left standing on Ted's doorstep. The children looked at me, waiting for a lead. I closed the door firmly, double-locked it and dropped the keys into my pocket. Memories were neatly boxed up inside it with Ted's clothes in the wardrobe and the old tea caddy with the pictures of the Houses of Parliament rubbed away where his thumb always touched the same spot.

'Let's go home,' I said.

In the traffic on the M1 Lola told me, 'I think that went really well.'

'Yes, it did.'

I flicked a glance in the rear-view mirror. Jack was sitting sideways with his feet up on the back seat and his head tilted against the passenger window. There was no telling what he thought.

It was after five o'clock when I finally reached work, but that didn't matter. Penny and I are self-employed and we put in the hours to suit ourselves. Her house is the end one of a pretty Georgian terrace, but it's East- rather than West-End Georgian. The houses themselves were once fine but have become dilapidated and even recent gentrification hasn't improved the immediate surroundings, which are grimy, traffic-clogged and unsafe after dark. Not that that worries Penny.

I walked down a small cobbled alleyway past the side of her house, under a sign that reads 'Gill & Thompson Fine & Trade Bookbinders'. The old brick outbuilding, backing on to a murky stretch of the Regent's Canal opposite some gasometers, was one of the main reasons why Penny bought the house when we first set up in business together. It had originally been a coal depot, where the long barges down from the Midlands unloaded their cargo, but together we cleaned it up and – roughly – converted it into a book bindery.

That was what I did, and do. I am a bookbinder, in the way that Ted was a perfumer. But without the mystery, of course.

I opened the door into the shop part of the bindery. Across the counter that divides it from the workshop I saw Penny. She was standing over a stitched book, rounding out the spine ready for backing. She was using the little old Victorian hammer I found at a bindery sale and bought for her, and she rolled and banged away at the stitching to make exactly the right swell that would form the spine of the bound book. She was so immersed in the job that it took several seconds for her to register the sound of the door opening and closing. But then she looked up over her half-moon glasses and saw me. 'Hi,' she said.

I walked round the counter end and took my apron off its hook, winding it round my middle and tying the strings without looking or thinking about it, the actions being so familiar.

'I'm glad that's over.'

My job was lying at the end of my bench. The dark-blue cloth-covered book boards for Ronaldshay's three-volume *Life of Lord Curzon* that we were restoring for a regular customer of ours. The finishing, the gold lettering on the spine, still remained to be done, ready for the bound books to be collected tomorrow.

'Are you okay?'

I picked up the first boards and stroked the cloth with my thumb. It was a good job, clean but nothing flashy. 'Yes.'

I opened the as yet unbound book and automatically checked the title page. Then I put the board in the holder and adjusted the screws to position it correctly.

Penny was still standing with her hammer resting on the bench. 'You needn't have come in tonight, you know. Not straight from your father's funeral. I could have done *Curzon*.'

'I know.' I smiled at her. Penny's a good finisher. 'But I wanted to.'

It was the truth. The concentration on a defined job, technically demanding but finite in scope, was just what I needed. And the bindery, with its ordered clutter and smells of glue and skins, is a soothing place. I always find it easy to be there.

Penny nodded and went back to her tap-tapping with the hammer. I switched on the heating element in the Pragnant machine and reached for a drawer of type. I decided that I would do the title in two pulls, and then put the author's name and the volume number together in the third panel. Using tweezers, I picked the type from the drawer, dropped the letters and spacers for *The Life of* one by one into the slot of the type holder and checked them. The characters have to be placed upside down and although I can read as quickly that way as the right way up, it is still too easy to make mistakes.

The work absorbed me. Penny and I settled into the easy silence that we often enjoy when we are on our own in the bindery. It's different when Andy and Leo, our part-timers, are there. They like to play music and talk about the jobs in hand. It's still comfortable, but different. Less symbiotic.

I measured the available space on the book's spine with my dividers, then checked it by eye. However carefully and accurately the lettering is placed, if the result looks wrong to the eye then it is wrong. I put the board back on the stand and slipped the foil out of the way. I pressed the handle forward gently to make a blind pull, just an impression of the letters lightly tapped into the cloth that I could rub away if they were misplaced. When I examined the result I saw they were indeed in the wrong position. About a millimetre too high.

I sighed and clicked my tongue, and Penny heard me.

She glanced over her specs at me. 'Let me do it.'

'Pen, I want to do it myself.'

I rolled the bar down by what I calculated to be the right amount and did another blind pull. This time it was exactly right.

Even though this was a routine machine-blocking job that I had done many hundreds of times before, I still had to summon up some courage to make the gold pull. If I got it badly wrong there was no chance of a repair. The boards would have to be made and covered all over again, and with the margins Penny and I operate on, and the backlog of work waiting to be done, we can't afford the time. I took a steadying breath and pressed the operating lever forward. The type kissed the blue cloth and I pressed harder, going in with a smooth bold movement, and the gold tape frazzled as the letters burned out of it. I eased the handle back and bent forward to see the result.

There it was, *The Life of* in strong, gold, block capitals on the dark-blue cloth. I'd gone in a little too heavy, perhaps, and laid on a touch too much foil, but I could fix that. I stood back in a glow of satisfaction.

However many times I do it, finishing always gives me the most pleasure of all the stages of binding a book. I love the shape and balance of the letters, and the grace and infinite invention that are possible within the conventions of traditional tooling and decoration.

'Good,' I said.

Penny finished her rounding and backing job with a final burst of tapping. She took off her glasses and ran her hand through her short hair with the result that it stood up on the top of her head like a grebe's crest. I knew about grebes from one of Jack's bird posters. 'How did it go?'

What do you say about a funeral? 'It was . . . well, processed.'

'I know what you mean. Coffins on a conveyor belt. Mourners by numbers.'

'A bit like that. Sort of next please! Jack made a speech, though.'

'*Did* he?' Penny was surprised, not surprisingly.

'About pigeons. It was Ted who set off his interest in birds by telling him about the way pigeons live in London. He made a whole address out of it at the ceremony.'

'I think that's very appropriate.'

She was right. I was proud of Jack.

'And then, at the drinks afterwards, everyone clapped and sort of cheered and tapped their feet when I made a toast to Ted.'

'Ah.'

I took up the second cover and squinted at the panel where I would place the blocking. This second volume was thicker than the first and I would have to make an adjustment to positioning. I pinched at the spaces on the spine with my dividers, not wanting to expose my feelings to Penny.

She put her book in the press. It was a good edition of Keats's *Letters* that we had restored and were going to rebind in full calf. Tomorrow she would paste a backing on the spine and cut the endpapers. I planned to hand-finish the leather binding with gold and blind tooling, the full works. It was a tasty job, as one of our old tutors at college would have said. If only we had a few more like it, as well as our regular bread-and-butter work of binding Ph.D. theses, law reports, photographers' catalogue boxes and presentation Bibles.

'I'm going to head inside,' Penny said. 'Evelyn's going out and she wants me to give Cassie her tea and put her to bed.'

'See you tomorrow,' I said.

I made the pulls for the second and third volumes, using just the right pressure this time, then discarded the type and set up *Lord Curzon*. I loved the quiet in the bindery on evenings like this. Behind me, the tall window that looked out over the canal darkened and the pale struts of the gasometer supports briefly glowed like the skeleton of a spaceship.

If I was thinking about anything as I worked it was Penny. We had met as art students at Camberwell and had learned the principles of bookbinding together. We hadn't a clue how to do the job, even when the course was finished, but we both went on to work in other binderies. I found a job as a very junior assistant to Arthur Bromyard, one of the great artist-bookbinders, while Penny went into a busy and aggressive trade bindery where most of the other workers were men. She was bullied there and responded by becoming even more superficially prickly and defensive than she had been at Camberwell. We stayed friends, just about, but she was scathing about what she regarded as my sheltered and arty-farty existence under Mr Bromyard's gentle tutelage, and I thought she was wasting her talents banging out dozens of legal buckram-bound law reports day after day and standing up to the taunts of brutal men who didn't understand her manners or motives.

I blocked in the rest of the title and the author's name and the volume number on each of the three books, then laid out the results on the bench to examine them. The first pull had indeed been a bit too heavy. I took my little ivory-handled penknife out of my drawer and scraped very gently at the gold to loosen the excess. The penknife had once belonged to the Old Man, Anthony Phebus, who had given it to Ted. Years later Ted had handed it on to me, asking offhandedly if I could find a use for it, and I had discovered that it was good for just this purpose. I blew the dust away and rubbed my blocking lightly with a duster. Perfect, even though I had to pass the verdict myself. Within the constraints of time and resources, of course.

I found a paste tray and a roller, and briskly applied PVA glue to the boards. Once the books were glued into their finished covers I could go home. The sky against the window was completely black now.

Half an hour later I was placing the bound volumes in the old wooden press, neatly interleaving them with paper so the moisture in the glue didn't cause any cockling, when the door opened again. I began turning the screw to tighten the pressure and looked to see who it was. I could hear running feet, but I couldn't see anyone.

A second later Cassie burst round the corner of Andy's bench. 'Sadie! Sadie!' she shouted.

Cassie was nearly three, the daughter of Penny's partner Evelyn and a musician from Grenada. It was a year since the lovely but distracted Evelyn had left Jerry and brought herself and Cassie to live at Penny's.

I had never seen Penny happier than she was with Evelyn. In fact, I didn't think I had even seen Penny happy at all before, although there had been a series of women, even in her miserable days at the blokey bindery.

'*What* are you doing here?' I demanded.

'Seeing you,' Cassie yelled triumphantly.

I swung her off the floor and she sat astride my hip. She was wearing a zip-up fleece over Tellytubby pyjamas and smelled of warmth and soap. 'Why?'

'Because you are silly.'

I reached for my duster and dropped it over my head and face. 'How about now?'

This was greeted with hoots of laughter. She twitched the duster off my face and rubbed her boneless button nose against mine.

I cleared a space on my bench and gently sat her down. I didn't really like seeing Cassie in the bindery. There were too many instruments of harm in here, too many long-bladed knives and mallets and jars of glue and size. The sight of her anywhere near the big old hand-operated guillotine with its grinning, curved metal blade made sweat break out down my spine and in the hollows of my hands. I blew a raspberry against the back of her plump, pale-brown neck and told her to sit still.

I never worried about my own two when they were small the way I feared for Cassie. It was only when I got older and Lola and Jack didn't need and certainly didn't welcome my physical protection that I started to.

But Evelyn didn't worry about Cassie either. She let her play on the bindery floor, where she chewed strips of discarded goatskin and banged her head on the iron legs of the guillotine. 'Let her play, Sadie,' she would say with a shrug.

Penny came in with a tea towel over her shoulder.

'Pen . . .' I began.

65

She held up her hands. 'I know, I know. But she wanted to come and see you on her own. You're here and I was watching her all the way.'

Penny was incapable of refusing Cassie anything. She loved the child with an absorbed, half-unbelieving passion. I loved her too; the familiar weight of a baby in my arms, the softness and tenacity and scent of her. I missed my own children's infant selves – Lola was already overtaking me in the adult pecking order and Jack was angular and rejecting – and Cassie filled some of the space they had left empty. So she moved between the three of us women, bathed in the constant light of our adoration.

'I'm just finishing,' I capitulated. 'Do you want to stay here with me, Cass, and then I'll carry you up to bed?'

'No bed.'

'Yes bed.'

'No.'

'Yesyesyesyesyesyesyesyesyessss.'

'We'll see,' she suddenly bargained and I could hear her mother's sweet cajoling voice. Evelyn seemed other-worldly, but she always got exactly what she wanted.

After I had checked that *Curzon* was properly positioned and all the machines and lights were switched off, I hoisted Cassie into my arms again, locked up and followed Penny up the path to the back door of the house.

The ground-floor rooms interconnected and together they functioned as kitchen, living area and bindery office. There were books everywhere, and newspapers, heaped up on battered but good-looking furniture. Penny's rooms had always looked the same, in whichever of her houses, but since Evelyn's arrival there had been some changes. She had feng shui'd the place as soon as she moved in, shifting the position of the table, lining up chairs and introducing frondy plants and scented candles. It was funny to see her *Hello!* magazines alongside Penny's *London Review of Books*.

Penny was sitting at the computer making up invoices. This was usually my job.

'I'll do those tomorrow.'

I put Cassie down and she immediately ran away and hid.

'Sade, will you tell me why you're rejecting all offers of help and sympathy?'

I played for time. 'Am I?'

I felt fraudulent, that was why. I had hardly cried yet for Ted and I couldn't map even the outlines of what his loss meant to me. What could I look for from my friends, when I couldn't locate my own grief? All I felt was numb, and exhausted to realise that my relationship with my father wasn't going to end with the mere fact of his death. It was going to go on and on, for ever, the old disabling argument between love and bitterness.

Penny sighed. 'Never mind,' she said gently.

'Shall I put her into bed?' I asked.

'Yeah. Tell her I'll come up in a minute.'

I found Cassie behind the sofa, her usual hiding place. She let me carry her upstairs to her bedroom, on the second floor next to Penny's and Evelyn's. It was at the back of the house, and looked out over the bindery and the gaunt ribs of the gasometers. I drew the curtains, dark-blue ones with gold stars, and turned on the man-in-the-moon nightlight.

'Time to go to sleep now.'

'Lie down too.'

I slid under the duvet with her. She put her thumb in her mouth and began winding one of her curls round her forefinger. Lying there with my arms round her and her breath on my face, I felt some of the sadness melt away.

Downstairs again Penny was standing looking out of the window at the little backyard. Evelyn had put some tubs out there and there had been a spring display of daffodils.

'She wants you to say goodnight. She's nearly asleep.'

'Do you want to stay and have a glass of wine?'

My own children would be waiting for me at home. 'Thanks. Not tonight.'

'See you tomorrow, then.'

I touched Penny's shoulder. She was much shorter than me. She had always been squarely built and now, in her contentment, she was putting on weight.

I walked home along the canal towpath. The gates that gave access to it were locked at dusk, but the railings were easy to climb. Muggers and junkies hung out down there, especially in the thick darkness under the bridges, but tonight I wanted the silence and solitude of the path instead of threading the longer way through the busy streets. Lights were reflected as broken tenements of yellow and silver in the flat water, and dripping water echoed my footsteps. The city traffic sounded muffled; the rustle of rats clawing the litter in the rough grass on the land side was much louder. I walked briskly and saw no one.

Lola was on the phone. She mouthed 'hello' at me as I came in. When she hung up she said, 'Mum, that was Ollie. I said I'd go and meet him and Sam for a drink, is that okay with you?'

She had stayed in with Jack, waiting for me to come back. Having her at home in university holidays had great benefits for me, although I tried not to take advantage of this too often. And I was glad that she felt like going out with her friends tonight. She had cried enough for Ted. I smiled at her. 'Of course it is. Where is he?'

'He said he was going to bed.'

'Did he talk to you?'

'What do you think?'

'I think he didn't talk to you.'

'Precisely.'

Lola and I have always discussed almost everything. Once she had forgiven me for leaving her father and got over the extremes of adolescent rebelliousness that followed it, that is. I feared sometimes that because I didn't have a husband I admitted too many of my anxieties to her, but her response always was that she would rather know what affected me because whatever it was actually affected all three of us. Lola is always level-headed. In her case at least the cycle of family wrongness has been broken. And even her concern about Jack's oddness wasn't as deep as mine. 'Sure, he's kind of a weird kid. But not as weird as some, believe me. He'll grow out of the bird thing, and the not talking. Probably when he gets a girlfriend.'

'I'd just like him to have some friends, let alone a girl.'

'Mum, he's okay.'

She picked up her denim jacket now, with its badges and graffiti, and stitched-on bits of ribbon and braid. She was eager to get on her way. 'Are *you* all right?' she asked.

'Yes. Yes, I am.' So I didn't share everything with her.

Lola whirled out of the house. I went upstairs, knocked softly on Jack's door and, when there was no answer, turned the knob. Sometimes he bolted it but tonight it opened. The light was out and I could hear his breathing, although something told me he wasn't asleep. 'Jack?'

There was no answer.

Cassie's room had been sweet with the innocence and trustingness of babyhood, but in here all I could pick up was the darkness of rejection.

'Goodnight,' I whispered.

FOUR

He walked off up the road, very slowly, his bag slouched across his back and the soles of his trainers barely lifting off the pavement. At the corner he paused and looked right and left, but he never glanced over his shoulder to see if I was still standing in the doorway of the house. I watched until he turned left, in the direction of school, and plodded out of my sight. Only then did I go back inside and begin to put together my things for work.

I was shaking with the tension of the morning. It was the third day of the summer term and every morning so far Jack had refused to get out of bed. Then, when I finally hauled him out from under the covers, he refused to get dressed. He didn't speak, let alone argue; once movement became unavoidable he just did everything very, very slowly.

'Jack, you have to go to school. Everybody does. It's a fact of life.'

He shrugged and turned away. While I stood over him, he had got as far as putting on his school shirt and it hung loose over his pyjama bottoms. I could see faint blue veins under the white skin of his chest and his vulnerability made me want to hold him, but I knew if I tried to touch him he would pull away.

'Jack, we have to talk about this.'

'*Talk*,' he muttered finally, as if the mere suggestion exasperated him.

'Yes, talk.' I struggled to be patient and moderate. You could ache for him, for what he was going through, and at the same time irritation made you long to slap him. Hard.

'Mum.'

'Yes?' I said eagerly.

'Go away if you want me to get dressed.'

'I'll make you some toast. Would you like an egg?'

'No.'

'Downstairs in five minutes, please.'

Five minutes turned into fifteen. He ate his toast very slowly while I sat waiting.

'You're going to be late.'

'Oh *no*.'

'For God's sake,' I snapped, 'what's the matter with you? What's wrong with school? If you won't talk to me or anyone else how can we help you? What's wrong?'

Jack fumbled with a knife, then dropped it with a clatter. He looked around the kitchen as if surveying his life, and then said out of a pinched mouth, 'Everything.'

The bleakness of this was unbearable.

I remembered how it felt to be his age, at the mercy of the world and powerless to change anything. I tried to touch his hand but he pulled away as if my fingertips might burn him.

I took a breath. 'Jack, listen. It just *seems* like everything, you know. It isn't so bad. There are lots of things you enjoy and look forward to.' Although if he had pressed me to name them, I couldn't have got much beyond seagulls. 'And you've got us, Lola and me, and your dad as well. If we try and work out what's most wrong, I can help you.' This sounded feeble, even to my own ears.

There was a small silence. Then he said flatly, 'You?'

71

I understood that *everything* mostly meant his life in this house, with me and without his father.

It wasn't that he didn't see Tony: the three and a half weeks since Ted's death had spanned the school Easter holidays and the two of them had been away together for three days' fishing in Devon. Lola could have gone too, but she had preferred to stay in London. Once or twice a month Jack went over to Twickenham to spend a night with Tony and his second family, and there were weekday evenings too when he and Lola went out for pizza or a film with him. But that wasn't the same as having a father who lived in the same house and didn't have to portion out his time with such meticulous care.

Everything wasn't school and friends or the lack of them, although I wanted to believe that it was. The trouble was home, and home was mostly me. In the last few weeks and months Jack had gradually stopped communicating, had withdrawn himself from our already dislocated family, but he had never let me hear the roots of his unhappiness as clearly as in that one word, *you?*

I wished just as much as he did that he had a live-in father. I wished he didn't have to live with just two women, or that he and Lola were closer in age, or that he had been born one of those children who found it easy to make friends. And I wished that I had been able to break the cycle that began with Ted and me, and rolled on with me and Jack, in the way I had apparently been able to break it for Lola.

The silence extended itself. The need to cry burned behind my eyes, the pressure of years of denied weeping swelling inside my skull, but I didn't cry and my inability to do so only increased my sense of impotence. Unwitting Jack, my unlucky child, was the focus of this mighty powerlessness. I couldn't make the world right for him, I couldn't even make the dealings between us right. Sympathy for him was squeezing my heart so I could barely speak.

'I'm sorry,' I managed to say.

He pushed back his chair and stood up. 'Going to school,' was his only response.

I went with him to the door and watched him until he was out of sight. I longed to run after him, to go with him and shield him through the day, to turn his *everything* into nothing that mattered and let us both start again, but I couldn't. It was hard to accept that after all the promises I had made to myself when they were small, about always being close to my children and never letting them down, there was still a breach between Jack and me. Ted was dead and gone but somehow his damned legacy was right here in our house with us.

I was angry as well as impotent. I slammed my hand down on the kitchen table, so hard that the pain jarred through my wrist bones, but nothing changed and my head still hurt with not crying.

I snatched up my bag and went to work. It was too late now to walk, even along the canal. I had to drive, in a 9 a.m. press of buses and oversized trucks, and when I arrived I made a mess of cutting some endpapers out of some special old hand-marbled paper that Penny and I had been saving. I had to throw the ruins away and use a poor substitute. Penny kept her head down over her work and although I could sense Andy and Leo glancing at each other, I didn't look their way.

When I got home again Lola had already gone out to her bar job. In two days' time she would be going back to university and she was trying to earn as much money as she could. Jack was sitting in front of the television, still wearing his outdoor jacket and his school tie. He looked grubby and utterly exhausted.

'How was your day?' I asked. I was going to make shepherd's pie for supper, his favourite.

'All right.'

'What lessons did you have?'

73

'The usual ones.'

He didn't take his eyes off the screen but I didn't think he was really watching it. There was wariness in the hunch of his shoulders and his fingers curled tightly over the arms of his chair.

'What did you do in the lunch break?'

'Nothing.'

I threw three potatoes in the sink and began peeling. 'So, it was a pretty uneventful day, then?' He twisted his shoulders in a shrug. But when I started browning the meat and vegetables, and he assumed my attention was elsewhere, he let his head drop back against the cushions. Then, when I glanced at him again, he had fallen asleep.

We ate dinner together – at least, Jack sat at the table with me, but he had a bird book open beside his plate. I was, temporarily, too tired of the battle to make any protest. He ate ravenously, though, as if he hadn't seen food since breakfast time.

But the next morning, to my surprise, he put up less resistance to getting up and getting dressed. When the time came to leave, he shouldered his bag and silently trudged away. Maybe he was beginning to accept the inevitable, I thought. Maybe the tide had turned.

That day Colin came into the bindery. He lived with his mother, somewhere on an estate that lay to the east of Penny's house, and he was a regular visitor. He pushed the door open, marched in and laid a heavy carrier bag on the counter. Penny was working on a big case for a photographer's portfolio and Leo was trimming boards at the guillotine. Andy was on day release and in any case it was my turn to deal with Colin. We took it roughly in turns, without actually having drawn up a rota.

'Morning!' he shouted. He had an oversized head that looked too heavy for his shoulders and his voice always seemed too loud for the space he was in.

'Hello, Colin. How are you today?'

'All the better for getting this finished.' He began hauling a mass of papers out of his bag. Penny and Leo were suddenly completely absorbed in their jobs.

My heart sank. Colin had been writing a book ever since he first came in to see us, and would regularly turn up with fragments of it that he wanted us to discuss. It was going to be a cookery book. He had chosen us, he announced, to be his publishers. Penny and I had often tried to explain to him the difference between binding an interesting collection of personal recipes and publishing a cookery book, but he took no notice. The sample material, in any case, usually consisted of recipes torn from women's magazines and annotated with drawings and exclamatory scribbles in a variety of coloured inks, so we hadn't worried too much about the day of reckoning. Now, apparently, it had finally arrived.

'I have to have the books ready soon, of course. Mum'll want to give one to all her friends, won't she?'

A tide of magazine clippings, jottings on lined paper, sketches and headings like 'A Good BIG Dinner' blocked out in red felt-tip capitals spilled over the counter. They were accompanied by a nasty smell. Some of the papers were very greasy and I spotted a flaccid curl of bacon rind sticking to the reverse of one of them. I stopped myself from taking a brisk step backwards.

'Colin, we're not book publishers. I told you that, didn't I?'

He gazed around him with an ever fresh air of surprise and bewilderment. 'Yes, you are. I know you are. Look at all your books.'

'We just put covers on them. We restore old books, we bind people's academic theses, we take care of books that have already been published.'

'Exactly.' Colin nodded triumphantly. One of the most exhausting aspects of dealing with him was the way he agreed with your disagreement and just went on repeating his demands. 'So you can put covers on mine. I'll pay you, you know. I'm not asking for something for nothing, not like all these refugees coming over here and expecting to get given money and big houses. It's not like that, you know.'

'I know, Colin. But we aren't publishers. Putting a cover on ...on your *manuscript* here, that won't get it into the bookshops like Smith's in the High Street where people could buy it. That's a completely different process. You have to ... well, you have to have the text edited and all these recipes would have to be tested. Then artists and marketing people would have to look at designs for it, and thousands of copies would have to be printed by a big commercial printers, and then salesmen would have to sell it to booksellers ...' I felt weary myself at the mere thought of all this effort.

'Exactly.'

'But we don't do any of these things, Colin.' I reached out for his plastic bag and very gently began putting the rancid pages into it. From past experience I knew and feared what was likely to come next.

He watched me for a second or two, then he grabbed the bag from me and began hauling the contents out again. 'It's my book.'

'I know, but I can't publish it for you because I'm not a publisher.'

'My book's important, I'm telling you. It's taken me a long time, these things take time to do properly.' His voice was rising. We tussled briefly with the bag, me putting in and him taking out. The bacon rind dropped in a limp ringlet on the counter. 'I'm not stupid, don't make that mistake. I'm as good as anyone else and I was born here, not like these blacks and the rest of them.'

Leo's mother and father came from Trinidad. He went on lining up trimmed law reports as if no one had spoken. True to form, Colin was now shouting. And equally predictably, the phone rang.

Penny went to answer it. 'Gill and Thompson, Bookbinders. Good morning. Oh, yes. Hello, Quintin.'

Colin was thumping the counter and shouting that we weren't bookbinders at all, didn't deserve the name, not when we wouldn't do a simple job of work for an ordinary person, who had been born here, not like some of them.

Quintin Farrelly was our most lucrative, knowledgeable and exacting customer. He was the owner of the Keats *Letters*. Penny blocked her free ear with one finger and struggled to hear what he was saying. 'Yes, yes. Of course we can. Sorry, there's just a bit of a noise in here.'

'I'll tell you what, Colin,' I said. 'There's something we could do for you, if you'd like it.'

He stopped shouting, which was what I had hoped for. 'What?'

'Well. Let's have a look at what Penny's doing, shall we?'

I took him by the arm and showed him the photographer's portfolio. It was A2 size, in dark navy-blue cloth with a lining of pale-green linen paper. The man's name, Neil Maitland, was blind tooled on the lid. Colin examined the job with an aggrieved expression.

'What do you think of it?'

Penny gave me a grateful thumbs-up. She wedged the handset under her ear and reached for the order book and work diary. 'Yes, Quintin, I'm sure we can do that for you.'

'It's nice,' Colin admitted, rubbing the green interior with a heavy thumb.

'We could make you a beautiful case like this, and you can put your recipes and pictures in it, and then your mum can show it to all her friends.'

'Can I choose the colour?'

'Of course.'

'And it would have to have my name on the lid, not this Neil's.'

'Of course.'

'Any colour?'

'Any colour you like, Colin.' Including sky blue pink.

He expressed a preference for red. He left his bag of papers with us, stressing that it was to be kept in the safe whenever we were not actually working on it, and promised that he would call in again tomorrow to see how the job was progressing. Penny hung up, after asking after Quintin's wife and the Farrelly children.

'Christ on a bike,' Leo muttered as the three of us raised our eyebrows at each other. 'Anyone want a coffee?'

Jack was sitting in his armchair again when I got home from work, apparently absorbed in *Neighbours*. He looked dirtier, if that were possible, and even more exhausted than he had done yesterday. An empty plate blobbed with jam and dusted with toast crumbs rested on the floor beside him. It was Lola's last night at home. She was ironing, also with her eyes fixed on the television. The forgiving winter gloom that usually hid the worst of our semi-basement kitchen had given way to a watery brightness that announced summer and showed up all the layers of dust as well as the peeling wallpaper. The place needed a spring-clean. The whole house needed a spring-clean and a new stair carpet wouldn't have done any damage either. I let my bag drop to the floor.

'Good day, Mum?' Lola asked.

'Er, not bad, thanks. What about you?'

She nodded. 'Yeah.'

'Jack?'

Just the way that he shrugged his shoulders made me want to yell at him. I took a deep breath and began rummaging in the freezer. It was going to have to be defrost du jour tonight, because I didn't have the energy to start a meal from scratch.

As soon as *Neighbours* was over Jack removed himself upstairs. I sat on the sofa and watched the remainder of Channel 4's News, and when Lola finished her ironing (leaving a pile of Jack's and mine untouched) she brought over two glasses of red wine and joined me. She kicked off her shoes and curled up so her head lay against my shoulder and I stroked her shiny hair.

'I'll miss you,' I said, as I always did when she was about to go off. I did rely on her, more than I should have done, for companionship but also for the lovely warmth of her life that I enjoyed at second hand – the parties and nights out clubbing that she'd describe in tactfully edited detail the next day, the long phone conversations, the friends who dropped in and lounged around the kitchen, and the certainty that anything was possible that seemed to govern them all.

'I know, Mum. I'll miss you too. But I'll be back for the weekend in a couple of weeks.'

'So you will. Is there any more of that red? How does he seem to you, the last couple of days?'

'He' was always Jack in Lola's and my conversations.

'Very quiet.'

'But he's been making less fuss about school the last couple of days. I think maybe the worst's over.'

Lola said, 'I hope so.'

Jack ate most of the dinner, finishing Lola's portion even after he had devoured his own second helping, then wiping his plate clean with chunks of bread torn off the loaf.

Lola tried to tease him about his appetite. 'Hey, bruv. Is school food getting even worse?'

'I was hungry, okay? What's wrong with that?'

'I never said there was anything wrong. Sorry I asked.'

After dinner Jack retreated again and Lola went out to

meet some friends. She had left the ironing board folded but hadn't put it away. I did the obligatory brief two-step with it as if it were a reluctant dancing partner and finally managed to set it horizontally on its metal strut. I took the first of Jack's school shirts out of the basket and began pressing a sleeve. The steamy smell of clean laundry instantly filled my head. The olfactory nerve is the largest of the twelve cranial nerves; smell is the swiftest as well as the most powerful of the senses. My eyes stung, then filled up with tears and as I bent my head they dripped on to Jack's shirt, making translucent islands of damp in the white polycotton. I finished the shirt and began another but I was crying so hard I couldn't see properly. I hadn't been able to cry for weeks on end and now I was sobbing over the scent of clean laundry just because it reminded me of the way home should smell, of cleanliness and care and therefore security.

'The ironing? Don't do the bloody ironing,' Mel said when I called her.

I sniffed, wiping my eyes with the back of my hand. I didn't properly understand the tears, that was the worst part of it. If I had been thinking of Ted, it would have been different. But in the last month whenever he had come into my head it was with a numbness that cut me off even from the relief of missing and loving him. I thought with dry precision instead about our life apart.

'Are you there? Sadie?'

'Yeah, I'm here. Sorry. I really don't know what this is all about.' I could hear Mel at the other end lighting up a Marlboro and exhaling.

'Your dad died. You're grieving for him.'

I was going to say, I almost *did* say, 'It's not like that.'

Mel had told me how bereft she felt when her adored father died and that wasn't how it was with me.

'Do you want me to come round?' she asked.

'No. Yes, I do, but it's late.'

'Then let's have dinner tomorrow.'

'Lola's going back to Manchester in the morning. I can't leave Jack.' I didn't want to leave Jack, in any case. He needed me, even if he didn't want me.

'I'll come to you. I'll cook something for the three of us. Don't be late home, dear.'

Jack didn't answer when I knocked on his door. I called goodnight and told him to sleep well.

Lola saw Jack and me off in the morning and said goodbye. She would drive herself north later in the day.

Colin came in twice to the bindery, and on the second visit he was aggrieved to discover that we hadn't even started work on his box.

'There are twelve other jobs ahead of yours in the line,' Penny told him, it being her turn.

'Why isn't mine as important as theirs?'

'It's not a matter of importance, it's just that you can't jump the queue. We're busy here, in case you hadn't noticed.' She was brusque, but Colin tended not to notice subtleties like that.

'Well. I've had some more thoughts about how I want it.'

'Don't you want to hear our estimate first of what it's going to cost?'

I was trying to signal to her to go easy, but Colin was grandly insisting that cost didn't matter to him. His money was as good as anyone else's. The phone rang and as I was nearest I picked it up. A voice I half recalled asked for Mrs Bailey.

'Speaking.' At the same time I was frowning because although Jack and Lola went under Tony's name, after the divorce I had deliberately reverted to my own. To Ted's, that is. I had been happy to accept Tony's when we married, but once I had rejected him I didn't deserve the shelter of his name, did I? I went back to being just Sadie Thompson again.

'This is Paul Rainbird, at the school.'

I remembered now that I had spoken to him when I called to say that Jack would be away on the day of the funeral. He was Jack's head of year.

'Is something wrong?' Penny and Colin dwindled, their voices obliterated by the rush of blood in my ears.

'No, nothing at all. I wanted to ask how Jack is.'

'Why?'

'We haven't seen him for three days. Is he ill?'

'He's been at school all week,' I said stupidly.

'No, I'm afraid he hasn't.'

The lack of protest in the mornings, the dirtiness and exhaustion and his appetite in the evenings fell belatedly into place. Wherever he had been going for the last three days, it hadn't been to school. Dismay at my own obtuseness and sharp anxiety for Jack overtook the usual nagging concern. 'I'd better come in and see you.'

Mr Rainbird said he would be at school until six that evening. I looked at my watch. Ten to four. Colin was reluctantly shuffling out of the door.

I untied my apron and hung it up, turned off the heating element in the Pragnant and closed the open drawers of type. 'Jack's been bunking off,' I told Penny. 'I've got to go in and see his teacher.'

The school wasn't far from our house, so it didn't take me long to drive there. As I parked the car there were streams of children coming out of the gates. I pushed my way in against the current, assaulted by the noise and the display of attitude. Children came in so many shapes, sizes and colours. Some of them stared, most didn't bother. There were so many different statements being made within the elastic confines of school uniform, so much yelling and kicking and threatening and ganging up. Survival was the prize of the fittest – and you could see which kids were the natural survivors. They were the cool ones and the disciples of the cool ones, and the others who hung around on the fringes and took their cues from them. The rest straggled on in ones and twos, keeping out of the way, trying not to attract too much attention.

Lola had been the coolest of cool. She had achieved this by breaking every school rule and defying me daily about her clothes and her hair, and her attitudes and the hours and the company she kept. But even so, even when she was at her most grungy and rebellious, on some deeper level we had still been allies. When we weren't fighting, she told me secrets. Not hers, that would have been too incriminating, but her friends'.

'Isn't fourteen a bit young?'

'Mum, you mustn't breathe a *word*.'

I took this as her way of alerting me to what she was doing or about to do herself, and no doubt her friends' mothers did likewise. Lola and I were both women and for all our differences we had the comfort of being the same.

In my mind's eye now I saw Jack, and he was smaller and paler than all these children, and *different*. Different even from the wary singles. He was churned around by the alarming tide as it swept him along. I clenched my fists into tight balls in the pockets of my coat, wanting to defend him.

I found my way to the Year Seven office at the end of a green corridor lined with metal lockers.

'Sit down, Mrs Bailey,' the teacher said, having stood up to shake my hand. There was just about room in the cubicle for a second chair.

'Thompson,' I murmured. 'I'm divorced from Jack's father.'

Briefly my eyes met the teacher's. Mr Rainbird was wearing a blue shirt and slightly shiny black trousers, and his colourless hair was almost long enough to touch his collar. He looked tired. If, without knowing him, I had been forced to guess his occupation I would have said English teacher in a large comprehensive school. We faced each other across the desk piled with exercise books and mark sheets and he nodded, registering my statement, before we both looked away again.

'Is Jack being bullied?' I asked.

'Has he said so?'

'He hasn't said anything. I know he's not happy at school, not the way my daughter Lola was, but I didn't know it was as bad as this.'

'I remember Lola.' Mr Rainbird nodded appreciatively. 'Although I never taught her. How's she getting on?'

'Fine.'

There was some shouting and crashing outside the door, and several sets of feet pelted down the corridor. The teacher seemed not to hear it. I thought he was used to concentrating in the face of many distractions.

'I don't think he's being bullied. Jack doesn't stand out enough, either in a bad way or a good way. He's a loner, but that seems to be out of choice. He's very quiet, very serious. He doesn't say much in lessons, but he listens. His work is adequate, as you know, although he doesn't try very hard. He gives the impression of absence. But mostly only mental absence, at least until this week. Has anything changed for him lately, at home?'

'His grandfather died, at the very end of last term.'

The teacher looked at me. He had a sympathetic, creased, battle-worn face. I thought he must be somewhere in his late forties. How many years of teaching Shakespeare did that mean he had notched up? Twenty-five, probably.

'Yes, I remember now. Does Jack miss him badly?'

I tried to answer as accurately as I could. 'Not in the everyday sense, because . . . well, he didn't live nearby. But now that he's gone, yes, I think so. It's another absence in Jack's life.'

I realised that I had dashed here in the hope that Mr Rainbird would be able to offer me explanations for the way Jack behaved and a suggestion for how to deal with him. But this was what he was looking for from me. I was his mother and he was only his teacher.

Mr Rainbird was tapping his mouth with the side of his thumb. 'What about his dad?'

'Tony remarried and had two more children. They live the other side of London. He sees Jack and Lola as often as he can, but he does have another family and a lot of calls on his time. Jack lacks a male role model.'

It was stuffy in the little room with the door shut and I felt hot.

Mr Rainbird half smiled. 'Some people would say that's no bad thing.'

I knew he said it not as a teacher and head of Year Seven, but as himself. I wondered if he was married and whether his wife was the sort who thinks all men are monsters.

I smiled back. 'In Jack's case, a father figure would be helpful.'

The root of Jack's problem was with me, but the root of *that* problem went back much further. Back beyond Stanley, even Tony. I could do relationships with women, I reckoned, but I got it wrong with men. From Ted onwards. The smile suddenly dried on my mouth. I blinked, afraid of another surge of irrational tears.

'So, what should we do?' Mr Rainbird asked. He was looking down at his hands and I knew it was to give me a chance to recompose myself. 'He can't afford to go on missing lessons.'

I stared hard at the pile of exercise books until I had my face under control. 'I'll go home and talk to him. I'll try and get to the root of this. And I'll make sure he comes to school on Monday.'

'I'll talk to him too,' he said. 'Maybe between us we can work out what the problem is. What do you think he's doing instead of being at school?'

I shook my head. 'I don't think he's doing anything. I think he's . . . just killing time.' He was waiting for this to be over, dreaming of when he would be old enough to change something for himself. I remembered how that was.

We both stood up and Mr Rainbird edged round his desk to open the door for me. In the confined space he had to reach past me and his shirtsleeve brushed against my shoulder. 'Are you all right?' he asked.

'Yes, thanks.' I wondered how distraught I actually looked.

'We'll speak again, then.' He didn't attempt any empty reassurances and he didn't make authoritarian demands. I liked him. We shook hands a second time and I retraced my path down the corridor and out to the gates. The school was quiet and empty now, the tide reaching its low ebb.

Jack was sitting in his accustomed place. There was plenty of evidence of toast, cheese, jam and yoghurt having been eaten. It was no wonder that he came home hungry. He would have had almost nothing to eat since breakfast because he went out with only enough money for a bus fare and a phone call home. We both knew that to take any more would only attract muggers. Jason Smith, he once told me, had had forty pounds in his pocket in school one day and made the mistake of mentioning it.

I made myself a cup of tea and swept up some of the food debris. I could feel Jack tensely waiting for me to say something. He had been waiting yesterday too, and the day before, and when I didn't the relief had allowed him to fall into a doze.

I turned off the television and sat down with my tea. 'I've just been to see Mr Rainbird.'

He flinched, just a little. I waited, but he didn't volunteer anything.

'I want you to tell me why you haven't been to school for three days.'

His face was a crescent of misery. I had been keeping my imagination in check but now it broke loose and galloped away from me. I pictured drug deals, the skinny shifty kids who hung around by the canal, a leering fat man beckoning from a doorway. The images catapulted me out of my chair and I grabbed Jack by the arms and shook him hard. 'Where've you been?' I yelled. 'Who have you been with?'

He stared at me. His eyes had rings under them and there was dirt and jam around his mouth.

'Where? Who?' I shouted again and my shaking made his head wobble.

'Nowhere,' he breathed. 'Just . . . nowhere.'

'You must have been somewhere.'

'I walked around. Sat on a bench. Then when it was time to come home, I came home.'

'For three whole days?'

He nodded, mute and despairing.

I sank back on my heels and tried to take stock. I wouldn't gain anything by allowing anger to balloon out of my fears for him. 'That must have been horrible. Much worse than going to school. You must have felt lonely.'

If he had let some pervert befriend him, if he had been sniffing glue out of a brown-paper bag, or stealing from Sue's Superette on the corner, or buying crack or other things that I couldn't even *imagine*, would he give me a clue?

He said, 'I watched the pigeons. They're filthy. Did you know that there are hardly any sparrows left in London?'

I closed my eyes for a second. I didn't know whether to be relieved or infuriated. 'Let's not talk about birds right now, Jack. Let's try to work out exactly what it is about going to school that makes you so miserable you'd rather sit alone on a bench all day.'

He appeared to consider the matter. I looked at the way that tufts of hair partly exposed the pink lobe of his ear and the prickle of recent acne along his jawline. In profile he resembled Tony, increasingly so now that his proper face was emerging out of the putty softness of childhood.

'I dunno.' The shrug again.

'Yes, you do. Is someone picking on you? A teacher? Other kids?'

'Not really. They think I'm sad. But I think they're even sadder.'

The rock of his unhappiness held glinting seams of mineral disdain. Jack was sharp-witted and he wouldn't have much time for losers, even though he might currently consider himself to be one.

'All of them? Everyone? Isn't there anyone you like or admire?'

'Mr Rainbird's okay. Most of the girls are just lame, they're always sniggering and whispering and fooling about. Some of the boys are all right. People like Wes Gordon and Jason Smith. But they wouldn't be interested in me. And the rest are dumb.'

This was the most information he had volunteered in about six months, since the end of the maddening old days when he used to respond to every remark or instruction with 'why?'.

I supposed Wes and Jason would be the cool ones, big, blunt-faced boys surrounded by hangers-on like those I had seen swaggering out of school this afternoon. I couldn't see Jack in their company any more than he could see himself.

I pushed my luck. 'Go on.'

His face contracted with irritation and his shoulders hunched up. It was just like watching a hermit crab pull back into its shell. 'That's all,' he snapped. 'You always want stuff. There's nothing, all right? I'll go back to school on Monday if that's what you want.'

'I want you to want to go. What I want isn't important.'

His head lifted then and he stared straight at me. It was

a full-on, cold, appraising stare that told me Jack wasn't my baby any more. 'Is that so?' he sneered.

I was still catching my breath when the doorbell rang. Jack turned the television on again and increased the volume.

It was Mel on the doorstep, with two carrier bags and an armful of red parrot tulips. I had forgotten she was coming. She took one look at my face. 'You'd forgotten I was coming.'

'No. Well, yeah. I'm sorry. I've just been having a set-to with Jack.'

'Do you want me to go away again?'

'Depends on what's in the bags.'

'Sashimi-grade bluefin tuna. Limes, coriander, crème fraîche, some tiny baby peas and broad beans, a tarte au poire from Sally Clarke's, a nice piece of Roquefort . . .'

I opened the door wider. 'Come right inside.'

Mel breezed into the kitchen. Her polished brightness made the dusty shelves and creased newspapers and sticky floor tiles look even dingier than usual. My spirits lifted by several degrees.

'Hi, Jackson.'

Jack quite liked Mel. 'Hi,' he muttered.

'I've come to cook you and your mum some dinner. However, that's going to be tricky if I can't hear myself think.'

'Oh. Right.' He prodded at the remote and Buffy went from screeching to mouthing like a goldfish.

Mel busily unpacked fish and cheese. 'Great. How's school?'

I tried to signal at her but she missed the gesturing.

'It's shit,' Jack said.

'So no change there, then.'

I thought I caught the faintest twitch of a smile on his face before it went stiff again. 'No. None.' He stood up and eased himself out of the room.

Mel started making a lime and coriander butter. I poured us both a drink and told her what had happened. While I talked

I cut the ends off the sappy tulip stalks and stood the stems upright in a glass jug. The orange-red petals were frilled with bright pistachio green. The daub of colour in the underlit room reminded me of Lola's jersey at the cremation.

'I'm worried. Really worried,' I concluded. 'I never get to the root of anything with Jack. He clams up or walks away or shuts himself in his room. I never know what he's thinking. What must it have been like for him, wandering around with nowhere to go and nothing to do for three days? Did he talk to the old dossers? I wonder how many weirdos tried to come on to him?'

'Worrying won't help,' Mel said.

'That's easier said, believe me. You don't know what it's like.'

She had been searching a drawer for some implement but now she slammed it shut. 'Thanks for telling me.'

'Shit. Christ. Mel, I'm sorry. I'm a thoughtless cow.' My face and neck throbbed with shamed heat. Mel didn't talk about it much any more, but her childlessness was still a wound.

'Where's your sharp knife? Oh, it's all right. I only want to trim the fish.'

'Sorry,' I murmured again. 'I don't know what's wrong with me.'

Mel put the knife down. She came round the worktop and wound her arms round me and I rested my head against hers. The touch was comforting.

'I think he'll be all right, Sadie. I've got no grounds for saying so, but I still think it. Trust me, I'm a City headhunter.' It was one of the things she often said, to make me smile.

'I do trust you. In spite of your utterly high-powered, bewilderingly incomprehensible job.'

'Good. Remember what Lola was like when we first met?'

'How could I forget?'

'Right, then.' She let go of me. 'Now, do the veg for me, please.'

I did as I was told, dropping the little peas and fingernail-sized beans into the steamer. 'Let's talk about something else,' I suggested.

'How about me?'

'Perfect.'

Mel shimmied the length of the worktop, rapping the knife point on jars and pans. 'I met someone.'

'No.' This wasn't exactly an infrequent occurrence. I already knew that Adrian's days were numbered.

She stopped dancing and held up her hand. I had been so preoccupied that it was only now I noticed that her face was as bright as a star. 'Yes,' she said. 'I really have met someone.'

While she told me about this latest one we finished off the cooking, stepping neatly round each other, tasting and discussing and amending, as we had done many times before. These were the evenings I liked best, the companionable times of making unhurried food in a warm kitchen while the light turned to dark outside. I laid the table with blue-and-yellow plates and put the jug of tulips in the middle. I lit a pair of yellow candles and the glow wiped out all the dust and shabby corners, and shone on Mel's star face and the flowers, and the photograph of the children and me that Lola had taken up to Ted's hospital bedside.

Mel flipped the tuna off the griddle. 'It's ready.'

I went to the foot of the stairs and called Jack. He appeared almost at once, changed out of his school clothes and with wet hair combed flat from the shower. He sidled to his chair and sat down. Immediately he started wolfing down the fish.

'Are you hungry?' Mel asked.

'Yes.' He glanced quickly at me. 'Didn't get anything to eat at lunchtime.'

'And why's that?'

'I should think Mum told you.'

'Yeah. Here, have some of these baby beans. So, who did

you meet? What amazing things did you do that were worth missing school for?' Mel leaned forward, pushing her coils of hair back from her face so that she could hear better, her eyes and all her attention focused on him. There was no censure, only friendly interest.

'No one. Nothing,' Jack muttered.

'Really? It sounds deadly boring.'

He nodded and went on eating. By the time the pudding came, he even joined briefly in our conversation. He talked slowly, as if he weren't quite used to the sound of his own voice, but at least he was speaking.

After we finished and he said goodnight, Mel and I opened another bottle of wine.

'Thanks, Mel.'

'Tuna was a bit overcooked.'

'I meant about Jack. Being so nice to him.'

'I wasn't nice, I was ordinary.' This was true. Mel had a gift for being ordinarily warm and inclusive. Tonight it had just seemed more noticeable than ever.

'You look very happy,' I said. 'This Jasper must be good news.'

'I am happy. I wish you were.'

I felt some of the protective walls around me shifting, as if Mel's darts might pierce them. I didn't like it.

'What did you mean, when you said your father was a con artist?'

What did I mean? There was the pressure inside me, building up inside my skull, threatening to break through the bones. 'Ted was a great nose, a fine perfumer, but that wasn't enough for him.' I chose the words carefully, biting them off with my tongue and teeth. 'He always wanted something more. There was so much yearning in him. He wanted to be rich and he never was. He wanted glamour but except for the illusion of perfume his life was humdrum. He thrived on secrecy, that nose-tapping and winking kind that men who think of themselves as men of the world go in for. To do with deals, scams, setting up little businesses. I think he must have lived through his fantasies and the reality was always disappointing. Women ultimately disappointed him. His daughter did, too.'

Mel leaned back in her chair. '*You* are his daughter.'

'Yes.'

'But you talk about the relationship as if it involves someone else.'

That was truer than she realised. Somewhere within the numbness around Ted's death there was raw grief, yet I could only touch the outlines of it. As if the bereavement didn't belong to me, but to someone I knew. As if I weren't entitled even to the painful connection of grieving and therefore the potential relief that lay beyond it.

'Mel, I'm not you. I didn't grow up in your family.'

'What about his house?'

'Still there.' Locked up, since the day of the cremation, with all his possessions inside it. Brooding, waiting for me.

'Are you going to go and sort it out?'

'Yes.' It came to me now that my reluctance formed part of the numbness. Of course I feared going back to his house and unlocking the memories, but sooner or later I would have to make myself do it.

Mel insisted, 'I'll come and help you. I'm sure Graham and Caz will as well.'

'Yes. Thank you.'

I knew I didn't want anyone else to be there, not even Lola and Jack. It wasn't just furniture and clothes and memories I had to deal with. It was the way the very scent of the place entered into me and shook my soul.

FIVE

I unlocked the front door of Ted's house and gently pushed it open.

The draught excluder caught on a heap of letters and circulars lying on the doormat, so I stooped down and cleared them out of the way. I was breathing hard. The air in the hallway smelled dense and mouldy.

In the kitchen I unlocked the back door to let in some air. The reek of mould was stronger in here. The silence pressed on my ears and in an effort to dispel it I rattled around opening cupboards and moving jars. There was the tin tea caddy from our old house, with pictures of the Houses of Parliament rubbed away where his thumb and palm had grasped it so many times. Inside, I knew, was the teaspoon with an RAF crest on the handle.

I lifted the lid off the breadbin and recoiled from the source of the smell, a puffy canopy of blue mould. Caz and Mel and I remembered after the funeral to empty the fridge and leave it with the door propped open, but we forgot the bread. Choking a little, I rummaged for a cloth and a rubbish sack. I went to wipe out the mould and the obscene furry nugget of bread that lay in the heart of it, but there was no point. I dropped the whole thing, bread bin and all, into the sack and firmly tied the neck. I was here to go through Ted's belongings. I didn't want to keep many of his possessions – there were more than enough memories already.

Upstairs there was the silence, even thicker and heavier. Ted's was a quiet road, and behind these closed windows nothing had moved for a month. I turned on the bedside radio but the sudden babble made me jump and I switched it off again.

The blue-tiled bathroom with worn blue candlewick mats was a comfortless narrow space that reminded me again of the dripping green box at our old house. Ted humming 'All Things Bright and Beautiful' as he shaved. Me perched on the edge of the bath watching him. Through adult eyes I could see myself, gazing, hungrily following his every move, trying by the sheer power of concentration to draw some attention to myself. It must have been infuriating for him.

There was a bottle on the wooden shelf over the basin. I reached for it, unscrewed the cap and automatically sniffed.

It was as if I had rubbed the green glass and whispered an incantation to bring the genie smoking out of its prison. The scent of his cologne rushed into my mouth and nose and eyes, and my obedient brain performed its trick of instant recall. The here and now dropped away, and Ted was standing beside me, in his prime.

He was wearing a dark blazer and a lightly checked shirt with a cravat, paisley-patterned. He was freshly shaven, with his skin taut and shiny where he had rubbed and patted it with the cologne. His thick hair was slicked back with some kind of brilliantine. I could see the tiny furrows left by the bristles of the old silver-backed hairbrush that he kept on the tallboy in his bedroom.

He winked at me. 'All ready, eh?'

'Are you going out?' I demanded.

Was this before or after my mother died? It must have been after.

I hadn't minded before about him being out of the house so much of the time. It was the normal state of affairs, and Faye and I were used to being on our own together. I remember watching and helping her to bake cakes. The first Victoria sponge that was all my own work was decorated with the wobbly word 'Dad,' piped in blue icing using a paper bag and a serrated icing nozzle. It was two days before he came home to taste it and the lettering had bled into the sponge beneath.

'I'm only nipping out for an hour or so,' Ted said.

I had heard that one before. I wheedled, 'Don't go.'

He only winked at me, impatient to be gone. 'Tell you what, I'll ask Mrs Maloney to come and sit with you.'

Mrs Maloney was a widow who lived a few doors away. Our north London outer suburban street was on a steep hill and the semi-detached, semi-Tudoresque little houses stood in stepped pairs in their strips of garden. Mrs Maloney's house was higher up than ours and I hated the thought of her looking down at our roof and the leggy rose bushes that lined the creosoted fence. She had wind, and was smelly and lugubrious. I hated being alone in the house, because of the spectres in the folds of the curtains and the whispers in the empty rooms, but I hated Mrs Maloney even more. She had to be fed tea and biscuits, and she sat in my mother's chair swallowing belches and asking me nosy questions.

'Can't I come with you?'

I remembered the day at Phebus Fragrances so clearly because it was so unusual for Ted to take me anywhere.

'Not this time, Princess.'

The doorbell rang, a long, shrill sound that meant the caller must be leaning hard on the button. Not all that many people came to visit us, not unexpectedly, and Ted and I glanced at each other in surprise. He went quickly to the bedroom window and looked down, making sure that he was shielded by the nets.

'Do me a favour, Sadie. Go downstairs and open the door and tell this man I'm out. You don't know when I'll be back. Right?'

I opened the front door. There was a man in a pale fawn coat with leather buttons that looked like shiny walnuts. 'Is your daddy in?'

I looked him in the eye. 'No.'

'When will he be back?'

'I don't know.'

The man stared at me so hard that it made me uncomfortable. But this wasn't the first time I had had to do something like this for Ted. I prided myself on being good at it. I made my face a moon of innocence.

'Right. Will you give him a message for me?' The man took out his wallet and selected a card, then wrote a few words on the back. 'Here you are. Don't forget, will you?'

I tried to read what he had written as I went back up the stairs. But Ted was on the landing, waiting.

He held out his hand. 'Well done, Princess.' He pocketed the card with barely a glance. 'Don't want people knowing where we are every hour of the day, do we?'

Once he had made sure that his visitor had really gone he went out himself, whistling. I had homework to do, and after that there was the television for company, and if I needed anything I could always run up the road to Mrs Maloney. But I could never fall asleep until Ted came home again. I lay on my bed, watching the ceiling and waiting until I heard his Ford Consul drawing up outside.

Next I heard his key in the lock, then low voices in the hallway. Sometimes on these late nights there would be a woman's giggle. Only then, when I knew that after all he hadn't disappeared for good and left me behind, did I close my eyes. If there was a woman, I pulled the bedclothes over my head and clamped my ears shut.

I screwed the lid back on the bottle and reached to replace it on the shelf. Then I remembered that I was here to sort out his belongings and dropped it into a rubbish sack instead. I still didn't like his cologne. Maybe it represented the way he wanted to be, or perhaps with his love of secrecy he just relished putting up another smokescreen. But to me it still smelled like a lie.

I cleared the bathroom cupboard of his smoker's toothpaste and indigestion tablets and corn plasters. I worked methodically, telling myself that these were only inanimate things, the inevitable remnants we would all leave behind, which would be cleared away for us, some day, in our turn. By our children and their children if we were lucky, by strangers if we were not.

Next I went back to the bedroom. I took his jackets and suits off their hangers and piled them up, thinking that maybe they would do for Oxfam. The cuffs were frayed and the trousers bagged, but they were all dry-cleaned and brushed. Ted had grown seedier in old age – he didn't bother to eat properly, preferring to smoke and nip at glasses of whisky, and he didn't get his hair cut regularly enough or trim the tufts in his nose and ears – but he was always a dapper dresser. I folded up his thick white silk evening scarf and put it aside, thinking that Lola might like to have it.

The shoes were lined up in a row on the wardrobe floor. The leather was split with deep lateral creases but they were well polished. I turned one pair over and studied the worn-down heels and touched the oval holes in the leather soles. I could see the pattern of his tread, and now that I listened I could hear his footfalls in the silence of the house. But I couldn't read the man any more clearly than I had ever done.

In the drawers of the tallboy there were socks and pants, and a coil of ties and paisley cravats. I put aside his RAF tie, frayed at the edges where he had tied the knot so many hundreds of times, and consigned the rest to the disposal pile.

I was up to my wrists in his old clothes now and the scent of him was everywhere, but I told myself it was just a job to be done. I kept at it and the pile of black rubbish sacks mounted up on the landing.

The bottom drawer of the tallboy was deeper than the rest. I opened it and saw that it was half full of papers. Reluctantly I knelt down and began to sift through them.

Most of the papers were old bills, but there was an address book with a brown leather cover, and an old-fashioned thumb index with black and red letters and numerals. I flipped through the pages, recognising one or two of the names, dimly remembering some of the others.

There was nothing hidden here. Ted was as inscrutable as he always had been.

In a creased manila envelope I found a handful of photographs. There was one of my mother and me, in the back garden of the old house. I was perhaps four years old, scowling under the brim of a sunhat and wearing a dress with a smocked front that I hated. Faye was characteristically looking into the distance away from the camera, as if she wished herself elsewhere. I had seen this picture before and almost all the others in the envelope, including one of Ted looking rakish and handsome in front of an MG. Somebody else's MG, although he managed a proprietorial air. There were also four or five photographs of women.

One of them caught my attention. She had a plump face with a round dimpled chin and her hair was arranged in a lacquered fringe in front and drawn up at the sides with combs. The lipsticked margins of her smile spread fractionally beyond the true contours of her lips, giving her a slapdash, come-and-get-me look. She had eyes that slanted upwards and this oriental aspect was emphasised by a thick line of black eyeliner that flicked up beyond the edges of her eyelids.

Auntie Viv.

Viv wasn't the first of Ted's girlfriends to be presented to me after my mother died. I could remember Auntie Joyce before her and possibly Auntie Kath as well. But she was one of the longer-lasting aunties and she was memorable because she was friendlier to me than any of the others.

I sat down on the green candlewick cover of Ted's bed. I was Jack's age again.

My father called upstairs to me. 'Sadie? Sadie, come down here and say hello.'

I came out of my bedroom. I had been reading *The Whiteoaks of Jalna* and wishing that Renny Whiteoak would come and take me away from Dorset Avenue, Hendon. There was a woman standing beside Ted in the hallway.

'Sadie, this is Auntie Viv.'

I didn't want any more aunts. I wanted my father at home, sitting with just me in the evenings to watch *Hancock's Half Hour* or maybe even helping me with my French homework. I wanted my mother back as well, of course, but even I, with my talent for wishing for what I was never going to get, knew that there was no point in dwelling on this one.

'Hello, love.' Auntie Viv grinned up at me. She was wearing a tight skirt with a fan of creases over the thighs, and high heels that tilted her forward and made her bum stick out. I noticed her teased helmet of silvery blonde hair.

'Hello,' I muttered.

Auntie Viv made me sit beside her on the sofa. Ted brought out the gin bottle and the best glasses with diamonds and stars incised on them.

'Give her a little one,' Viv suggested and, to my amazement, Ted poured me a small glass of sweet Martini.

'Cheers, love,' Viv said, and took a gulp of her gin and tonic. She scissored her fingers – red varnished nails, lots of rings – in my hair. 'Hasn't she got lovely hair? Is it natural?'

I thought this was a stupid question. I was twelve. As if I would be able to choose to have my hair permed or dyed or even set. And if I had, as if I would have chosen my side-parted, no-nonsense short wavy cut that I wore with a pink plastic hairslide in the shape of a ribbon bow. 'Yes,' I said stiffly, but I couldn't help yielding a little to Viv's admiration. They made an unfamiliar pair of sensations for me, the being admired and the yielding.

'Auntie Viv's a ladies' hairdresser,' Ted explained. 'We're planning a little business venture together. A range of hair-care products, exclusive, of course, but affordable too.'

'Shampoos, setting lotion, conditioner,' Viv said dreamily. 'Your dad's going to create them for me. My own range.'

'Really?' I asked. 'Will they be in Boots?'

Ted gave me one of his cold, quelling looks but Viv nodded. 'Of course they will. And in all the salons. With my expertise in the field of hairstyling and your dad's genius as a fragrance artist – he *is*, you know – we will be creating something every woman will want to buy and experience.'

I was impressed. Ted splashed some more gin into Viv's glass. They settled down for a business talk, but Viv told me that I should listen in. The ideas of the younger market were always important, she said.

I listened eagerly for a while. Viv had a lot of ideas for names and the shapes of the bottles and packages. She drew sketches in a notebook, tore out the leaves and handed them to Ted and me for our approval. The bottles were waisted and curvy, like Viv herself, and the colours tended to the pink and gold. She wanted to call the shampoo Vivienne.

Ted was more interested in formulations and how to buy in ready-mixed solutions for the various products to which we could then add our own fragrance and superior packaging. 'It's the way we'll make money, mark my words. Basic lines, but given an exclusive touch.'

They both drank a couple more large gins and I drained the sticky dregs of my Martini. 'Thirsty work,' Auntie Viv mouthed at me. The drink made me sleepy, and my arms and legs felt like plasticine when I shifted on the sofa. After a while Viv went into the kitchen, wobbling a little on her high heels, and made a plate of Cream Crackers with slices of cheese and a blob of pickle on top. Viv turned on the television. She chatted through the News, mostly gossip about her customers and questions about Ted's work. She sat close up against him and let one of her shoes swing loose from her nyloned toes. After we had finished eating she leaned her head back against the cushions and closed her eyes. Her hand stroked the nape of my father's neck.

'Hop off to bed, now, Sadie,' Ted said.

I began to protest, made confident by Martini and inclusion, but he fixed me with his icy grey stare.

'Goodnight, pet,' Viv murmured. 'See you soon.'

In the morning she was nowhere to be seen. While I made myself toast and a cup of tea before school I asked Ted, who was silently reading the newspaper, 'Will Auntie Viv be coming again?'

He looked at me as if I was mad. 'Yes, of course she will.' Then he refolded the *Daily Express* and went on reading.

That was the beginning of quite a good time. Ted was still out of the house a lot, maybe even more than before Viv arrived, but I assumed that when he wasn't at home with me he was with her. Viv was safe territory, I felt. She brought me her *Woman* and *Woman's Own* every week when she had finished reading them. She played about with devising hairstyles for me and chatted about lipsticks and clothes. One evening she brought a glass bottle with a bulb spray out of her handbag. She sprayed the insides of my wrists and showed me how to rub them together to warm the skin.

'What do you think?' Her face was pink with excitement.

I thought the perfume was wonderful. It smelled of cloves and carnations, and it made me think of velvet dresses and candle-light reflected in tall mirrors. Ted stood watching us, one hand slipped into his jacket pocket, one eyebrow raised.

'It's called Vivienne,' she whispered. 'He created it for me. Better than an old shampoo, don't you think?'

'Yes,' I managed to say. I glanced at my father but he was fondly looking at Viv. After that I always knew when Auntie Viv had been in the house. The perfume lingered in the cushions and curtains of the front room, and in the bathroom, and round the threshold of Ted's bedroom.

There were evenings at home when Ted and she worked on their hair products. Tubs of chemicals appeared on the dining table and I was invited to smell them. Mostly they reminded me of school soap. There were snippets of card and empty plastic bottles and colour charts too, and spiral-bound books of different kinds of lettering. I particularly liked the letters. I followed the extravagant squirls of the romantic typefaces with my fingers and measured the squared-off edges of the more brutal ones with my thumbnail. I found some greaseproof paper and laid it over the biggest, curliest set of letters. I traced off my name, Sadie Faye Thompson, but I got the spacing all wrong and the result looked amateurish and wonky instead of like a magazine headline. I tried again, this time ruling a pencil line and making sure the bottom of all the letters rested on it. I played about with the spacing between the A and the D and the T and the H, until the balance pleased me. At my elbow Ted and Viv were arguing because Viv thought it was taking him too long to produce her prototype shampoos, but I barely heard them.

103

After I had finished tracing the letters I shaded the back of the greaseproof paper with a soft pencil, like we did when we were tracing maps in geography lessons. I drew round the outlines once more to transfer my squirly name to a big piece of white card. Finally I found my colouring pencils and shaded the letters, some in blue merging into green and others in red merging into orange.

'Look at that.' Viv whistled when she saw the result. 'That's really professional, pet.'

I thought it would have looked better if I had done all the letters the same colour.

'Take all that stuff upstairs out of the way, Sadie.' Ted frowned. I could tell that he wanted to continue the argument with Viv without me listening.

I began to talk about my Auntie Viv to the other girls at school, boasting a little about how young and pretty she was, and showing them what she did to my hair. It was growing and she had cut a soft fringe instead of the way I used to wear it, pulled to one side with my hairclip. Once, I let myself make a slip, saying, 'My mum . . . well, Auntie Viv, that is.' I saw Jean and Daphne raising their eyebrows and smirking at each other.

The beginning of the end came on Viv's birthday.

I made her a card, using my special lettering. It said 'Auntie Viv' on the front with a red heart and the number 27 inside the heart. I knew how old she was because I asked Ted. Inside I wrote, 'Wishing you many happy returns of the day. With all my love, Sadie.' I wished I could have bought her a present but I didn't have any money, so I picked some roses from the garden, furled them in gold paper that I had kept back from the packaging samples and tied them with a ribbon. I was lucky that it was June.

Ted told me he was taking Viv for a night out.

'Where's the birthday girl?' he fretted while we waited. At last a taxi drew up outside.

Viv was wearing a short, tight dress in a patterned cream material. I started singing 'Happy Birthday' as soon as Ted opened the door, but then they were kissing each other and the sound sort of petered out in my mouth. She hugged me anyway, once they were finished, and I got the full blast of Vivienne.

Ted had a present for her. It was a big box done up with ribbons and shiny paper, and Viv fell on it with a little gasp. She shook it and held it up to listen to it as if it might be ticking, and then undid the wrapping, very slowly, to tease us.

There was a white box inside and a little pout creased her lipstick when she saw it. But she flipped off the lid and out of a nest of filmy tissue paper came a shoe. It had a silver heel like a real stiletto blade and the rest of it was exactly the same cream colour as her dress. 'How lovely,' she murmured. Then I saw the pout again. 'But darling, I thought it was going to be my shampoo and conditioner. You promised me they were going to be ready.'

'Try them on,' Ted ordered. She did as she was told, and I saw the shoes were a perfect fit. They looked much nicer with her outfit than the black patent ones she had been wearing.

I went upstairs, while they were kissing again, to fetch the card and roses I had hidden in my bedroom. When I came back Viv had pulled away from my father and was checking her reflection in the mirror that hung over the mantelpiece.

'Here you are,' I said.

'Look what she's done,' she cried to Ted. 'Isn't that the loveliest thing you ever saw?'

I saw his face as he examined the card. His mouth pursed and his eyes went flat. At first I didn't understand why he was angry, instead of being happy that I had done something to please Viv. But then it came to me, with a flash like a light going on and shining too brightly in my eyes.

Ted was jealous because she seemed to like my gift more

105

than his shoes. There was something else going on too, something even more complicated. Ted didn't want me making any offering to Viv that didn't include him. She belonged to him and I belonged to him, but that didn't mean that she and I could belong to each other. He wanted to keep us separate because that gave him greater power over both of us.

I blinked. I felt as if in a matter of seconds I had slid from being a child in the dark all the way into adulthood, with a view of an infinitely complicated new landscape. The transition made me breathless, but I was also strangely elated. It seemed that I had power too – the power to arouse jealousy. I smiled serenely at Ted, from within the shelter of Viv's scented hug.

'Very nice,' he said and put the card face down on the table. He shot his wrist out of his white shirt-cuff and examined his watch. 'It's time we were going, darling.'

'Oh, Ted.' Viv suddenly sparkled. 'I've got an idea. Let's take Sadie out with us tonight.'

'We can't do that.'

'Why not? She'd like it and so would I. It's my birthday, after all, so you should let me choose.'

Her pout was still pretty and seductive but with my new illuminated vision I could see that there was a steely core in Viv. I nestled against her, enjoying the sight of my omnipotent father's discomfort. I would still have sided with him in the end, in anything that really mattered, but I couldn't help being pleased and intrigued by the new perspectives. They exchanged a couple more salvoes, but it was clear that Ted was going to have to give way in the end.

Viv patted my bottom and giggled. 'Go upstairs and put something nice on, Sadie, and we'll hit the town.'

I didn't have anything that would have fitted Viv's notion of nice, or my own for that matter, but I did my best. When I came down again Ted was gloomily downing a gin and tonic and Viv had taken one of the roses from my posy, wrapped the stem in silver paper from a cigarette packet, and pinned it to her cream frontage. 'You look sweet,' she said to me. She took a zip purse out of her handbag, tilted my head to the light and applied a quick coat of mascara to my almost invisible eyelashes. A smudge of blue shadow completed the job. 'But you've got to pretend you're fourteen. Okay with that?'

'Now,' she told Ted. 'You can take your girls out and show them a good time.'

In the back of the Ford Consul, flashing past the houses in Dorset Avenue and the shopfronts of the Parade in the midsummer dusk, I felt as if I'd gone to heaven.

The evening, as it turned out, was closer to hell.

To begin with Ted was morose and Viv was determinedly, skittishly cheery. She kept winking at me through her cigarette smoke as if we were conspirators. The three of us sat at a round table in the corner of a place that was somewhere between a pub and a nightclub. It smelled beery and smoky. There were a lot of mirrors, and a long bar made of dark polished wood with dozens of bottles, and dark red curtains at the windows that shut out the remains of the light. In another corner there was a dais with a piano and a microphone stand. While Ted was at the bar a pianist came on in a dinner jacket. Ted and Viv had big glasses of gin, with big chunks of ice and little slivers of lemon in them. I had a smaller measure of sticky-sweet Martini. We all clinked our glasses and said cheers before we drank. I felt shy and sat well back in my seat to try to be inconspicuous. But I was happy too – a kind of shiny, explosive new happiness. I loved Viv and I wanted to grow up and be like her, and for the three of us to live together in a world that had mysterious and exotic places like this in it.

I sipped my drink and watched everything. Ted and Viv knew lots of people, Ted especially. Men came over to the table and kissed Viv, and then leaned over to murmur in Ted's ear. The women who accompanied them mostly had tight, low-cut dresses like Viv's, and back-combed hair and sooty mascaraed eyelashes. Viv laughed a lot and didn't seem to mind the teasing about being twenty-one again. Ted leaned back with his arm resting along the back of her chair and smiled and talked and smoked.

A woman in a shimmery scarlet dress came on to the dais and sang some songs. I remember 'Love Letters in the Sand'. Ted and Viv were drinking hard. Rounds of drinks were sent over by friends at other tables and Viv blew kisses at the men to say thank you.

I felt sophisticated and increasingly bold. I chattered too, mostly to Viv, although I began to notice quite soon that she wasn't really listening. After the singer bowed off the platform there was dancing. Some couples jived and other, younger ones swayed and wriggled on their own. I watched these with interest, wishing I could have a partner but knowing for sure that no one would ask me. Mostly, though, people sort of waltzed in unsteady clinches. Ted and Viv got up and danced together but then a man cut in on them and swept Viv into a showy routine. She threw her head back as he spun her round, but caught the silver heel of her shoe and almost fell over. When I looked for Ted I saw he was dancing with another blonde woman, holding her hips close against his with his hand on her bottom. Viv came back to our table first. She flounced down and made a 'so what' face in my direction, but without really looking at me.

When Ted came back she demanded, 'What's all that about?'

'All what?' he said coldly.

'That cow.' Viv sniffed.

'Don't be so common.'

The temperature of everything changed. From being the pouting belle of the evening Viv turned tremulous and uncertain. She pulled her chair tight up against Ted's but he was watching the dancers instead of paying any attention to her. I had a strange feeling gathering in the pit of my stomach that I chose to identify as hunger. I confided to Viv that I was hungry and she relayed this information to Ted. He frowned, having more or less forgotten that I was there.

'Davey'll make her a sandwich, won't he?' Viv asked tentatively.

Immediately, it seemed, a sandwich arrived in front of me. But time had started to do strange things now. It felt as if we had been sitting at our table for hours and hours, yet when I looked at the scenes around me they were blurred, as if everything were on speeded-up film. A thick blue canopy of smoke hung over the room, and the noise of shouting and the bursts of laughter rising over the loud music made my head ache. A woman nearby was sitting on a man's lap. Her skirt was hitched up and I could see her suspenders and a collar of white flesh bulging over her stocking tops. The man's hand was hidden in the dark recess under her skirt. I was horribly embarrassed and switched my gaze to the drops of drink spilled on our table. They glimmered like fat dark gems.

My sandwich was made of thick layers of ham. It was quartered, with the crusts cut off, and the quarters were held together by a toothpick with a paper frill on either end. There was a tomato, too, which had been halved by cutting it so that the edges made zigzags. I thought this was all very chic and appealing. I took a bite out of one of the quarters and chewed hard but the bread stuck to the roof of my mouth.

Viv and Ted had been talking in low, angry voices. Now she stood up and pushed away from the table. She stumbled but recovered herself and almost ran away towards the Ladies. Ted's eyes didn't follow her. Instead he leaned heavily towards me, the elbow of his blazer smearing the gems of gin. 'All right there, Princess? What d'you make of this, then?' His voice was slurred.

I tried to smile but I was distracted by how disgusting the

ham and the thick sludge of bread tasted. The noise in the room had become deafening. There were red faces looming everywhere, all gaping mouths and bristly hair.

A minute later, it seemed, Viv was back again. She had been crying. Her eyes were teary and smudged. She grabbed Ted by his sleeve and began pulling him to his feet. He jerked her wrist and she tried to slap his face. When she couldn't get her hand to connect she wrenched off her shoe and tried to stab him with the silver dagger heel. The red faces all turned in our direction. My head was swimming with shame and Martini fumes. I hated the bar and the people, and I was mortified to see my father and Auntie Viv fighting in public.

'I want to go home,' I blurted out. My words seemed to drop into a sudden pool of silence and the speeded-up film slowed to a dead stop. An age of time seemed to pass.

Then a woman at the next table leaned across to us. 'You take her home, Ted. She ought to be safe in her bed. What would Faye think of you?'

The mere mention of my mother's name in this place made tears run burning out of my eyes. Now Viv and I were both weeping.

'You mind your own business,' Ted snapped at the woman. But he and Viv let go of each other. Ted walked away and we followed him as best we could past the crowded tables to the door and out into the car park.

The cool air hit me in the face and made me so dizzy I almost fell over.

All the way home in the car my father and Auntie Viv shouted ugly things at each other. But every time I closed my eyes the car and the passing lights spun round so sickeningly, and I had to concentrate so hard on not vomiting, that I didn't care what else was happening. When we got inside the house I tried to hold on to Viv. I felt so ill that I wanted someone to look after me, but she pushed me away.

'That's enough of that,' she mumbled.

I managed to get myself upstairs and into the bathroom before I threw up.

Much later, when I lay shivering under the blankets, I could still hear the two of them storming at each other downstairs.

I only saw Auntie Viv two or three more times after that, then her visits stopped altogether. I missed her, and the *Woman's Own*, and my fringe grew too long and hung in my eyes. 'Isn't she going to come and see us any more?' I asked Ted at last.

'No,' he admitted. He looked depressed, but he tried to cover it up. 'Plenty more fish in the sea, eh? And she had no business acumen, you know. None whatsoever. Anyway, you're my girl. That's quite enough for me.'

This was blatantly untrue, of course, although I still wanted to believe him and was disappointed when the next auntie arrived. She was thin, and wore matador pants and black rollneck sweaters. Her hair was cut in a gamine crop and she called herself Maxine. She had a strong aversion to jealous, beady-eyed, twelve-year-old daughters and she didn't mind showing it. But, I thought, I wasn't a kid any more. Not after the sudden shaft of illumination that had come to me on the evening of Viv's birthday. I wouldn't let Maxine know that I cared about anything.

I put Viv's photograph back into the manila envelope. One of the other photographs, of a woman with windblown hair sitting on a stone wall, stirred a faint memory but I couldn't place her or recall a name. I put the envelope aside to be kept along with Ted's evening scarf and his silver-backed hairbrush and the address book. It didn't take me long to clear the rest of the room. Everything that didn't go in the rubbish bags or on to the Oxfam pile could be left to the house-clearance people. And once the house was empty, it could go on the market.

Ted's solicitor and I had already talked about his will. Half of his estate was to come to me and the other half was to be divided equally between Lola and Jack. Apart from the house, which was mortgaged, and a couple of thousand pounds in the bank, he didn't have anything else to leave.

In the living room I checked the bookcase. There were paperbacks of Ludlum, Higgins and le Carré, a few military biographies and popular history books and, lying flat on the bottom shelf under a pile of magazines, three volumes bound in dark-brown calf. They each had Ted's initials, ELT for Edwin Lawrence Thompson, blind tooled on the front. Inside were pages of notes, all in Ted's handwriting. The pages were dated, and a quick flip through them revealed that the time-span ran from the Fifties to the early Seventies.

These were Ted's fragrance notes and formulae. Some of them had the names of customers against them – occasionally Yardley or Coty, more often ET&P, which had been the name of his company. The P stood for Partners, although I wasn't aware that he had actually had any. One formula was labelled 'for Janice, August 1963', another just 'Linda'.

They weren't young any longer, these women of Ted's who had danced and kissed and promised all through his best years. Maybe they weren't even alive now. But the perfumes that he had devised for them were still here after forty years, perfectly preserved in the dense pages of notes. I read some of the scribbled lines. 'Amyl salicylate 600cc. Geraniol 100cc'. 'Give lift, 1% aldehydes'. The formula for Janice's perfume ran to thirty-five ingredients, Linda's had six more. It would take only Ted's deft work at the perfumer's organ of ranked bottles in the lab to bring them back to sparkling life again, the essences of Linda's and Janice's young selves.

I couldn't close my eyes and summon up the compound fragrance from the dry lists, as Ted had been able to do, or even capture the separate essences with their redolent names like frangipani, neroli and orris. But still the ghosts of his women and his work and Ted himself swam up at me, the thick drift of memory. My throat choked with it. This whole house was full of fumes, of too much scent and his deceiving cologne, and the spores of mould.

I snapped the book shut. I took the three heavy volumes with me, along with the silk scarf and the envelope of photographs, the old silver-backed brush and his heavy brass cigarette lighter. I dragged the sacks of rubbish out to the dustbin and parcelled up his clothes for the charity shop. But even when I had locked the door on the silence, even when I was back on the M1, I didn't feel any sense of relief. The pressure inside my skull was there again, and within my chest as if a dam might burst and release some black flood tide that would wash me away.

The image frightened me and the tightness got tighter. I took one hand off the wheel and sniffed at my scentless wrist. Then I gripped the wheel again and accelerated past a line of trucks, wanting to get home to Jack.

I was glad to be in before half past four, which was when he usually arrived home from school. When he and Lola were younger I had arranged my time at the Works so I could be at home as early as possible, and even now I didn't like to think of my child coming home too often to an empty house. Although Jack gave no sign that he welcomed my concern or my presence. The opposite, in fact.

He came in within fifteen minutes and sat down in front of the television. I made us a pot of tea and a plate of toast, and he devoured three slices of it with his eyes fixed on the screen. I tried to assess whether or not he had actually been at school all day, without asking questions that would make this too obvious. I knew, at least, that he had been there since the three days of bunking off, because Mr Rainbird had telephoned to let me know.

'Hello, it's Paul Rainbird here,' he said. He had a nice voice, on and off the phone.

'Is something wrong?'

He laughed. 'No, I just wanted to let you know that Jack's form teacher says his attendance is fine. And I wanted to ask if he seems any happier.'

'He doesn't seem any *un*happier.'

He laughed again, and he had a nice laugh too. 'We'll take that as a plus, shall we?'

'Yes, I think so.'

'Let me know if there's anything else you need,' he said, with a hint of ambiguity, before he rang off.

'What did you do today, Jack?'

A shrug.

'Did you have Biology?' Biology was the only subject for which he had any enthusiasm.

He gave me a dry look. 'It's Thursday.'

'Ah. Would you like some more toast?'

'No, but I'll have more tea, if there is any.'

Encouraged by the normality of this exchange I refilled our mugs and went to sit by him. The slope of his shoulders and his bony wrists made my longing to gather him up in my arms so strong that I had to clench my fists to stop myself. Recognising this by telepathy he sank deeper into his chair and drew up his knees as a rampart. It was one of the paradoxes of parenthood, I thought, that the demonstrative love I had yearned for as a child was utterly rejected by my own son.

'So what *did* you do?' Our conversations had deteriorated into a sort of contest to see how long I was prepared to go on asking questions and how effectively he could stonewall.

He gave an exasperated glance at the television. Then he sighed and slewed round in the chair to look me in the eye. 'Actually, I hung out a bit at dinnertime with Wes and Jason and people.'

'Really?' A pleased, bright smile creased my face.

'Yeah. I was telling them about cormorants.'

114

'Really?' The smile turned uncertain.

Jack sighed. 'Oh, Mum.' He sounded, all of a sudden, like Lola. He slid out of the armchair and picked up the precious pair of binoculars that Tony had given him for Christmas. He went to stand by the window that looked out on to the back garden and trained the binoculars on the roofs of the houses opposite. I should call Tony, I thought, and talk to him about the truancy episode. I doubted that Jack himself was giving anything away.

I cleared up the mugs and plates.

'I was up at Grandad's today. Sorting out his things.'

Jack continued his scrutiny of the pigeon population.

'I brought some bits and pieces back with me, I don't know whether you and Lola want to keep anything? They're in a box in the car. You could bring it in for me.'

He leaned on the table while I unpacked the box. My hands shook a little. He clicked the lighter once or twice but couldn't make it ignite, and glanced without much interest at the books of notes. I shook the photographs out of the envelope and spread them out to show him the picture of his grandmother and me in my smocked frock. The aunties' forgotten smiles beamed out of the sheaf at us.

'Some of Ted's girlfriends,' I said unnecessarily.

Jack picked up the picture of the woman sitting on a stone wall and studied it for a minute. 'She was at the funeral,' he said.

I remembered the woman in the dusty fur. I knew now why the picture had stirred a recollection. 'I thought I recognised something in the picture. What was her name?'

'Audrey,' Jack said.

That's right. 'You'll be his daughter,' she had said. 'I'm Audrey.'

Now Jack was flipping through the little brown address book. 'Here,' he said.

Sure enough, there was the name, no surname, almost the first entry. There was no address either. Ted must have known her well.

Jack said, 'Do you know what? She must live really near to us. Look.' The first digits of the telephone number were the same as ours.

'So she does. Well, did, I should think. She probably moved long ago.'

'You should call her and ask if she wants any of this.'

'Yes,' I agreed in surprise. 'Yes, I could do that.'

After Jack had gone up to his bedroom I rang Tony.

Suzy answered the phone. In the background I could hear a lot of children's noise. Their twins were nearly four.

'Hiiiiiiii, Sadie,' Suzy trilled. 'How are *you*?'

We exchanged brief polite remarks. Suzy always speaks to me as if I am deaf or mentally defective. I suppose it is because of the great difference in our ages, although she doesn't talk to Tony that way despite the fact that he is even older than I am.

'You want to speak to him?'

'Yes, please, if he's there. Thanks. Bye for now.'

He came on the line, his voice sounding exhausted and at the same time utterly familiar. 'Hello, Sade. Everything okay?'

I see Tony only rarely but I still feel that I know him better than anyone else. Even when I was leaving him for Stanley I still loved him in that well-rubbed, unsurprised and faintly exasperated way of long-standing couples and after Stanley left me I continued to feel exactly the same. It was as if the breathless, lurid and ultimately heartbreaking business of falling desperately in love had come and gone without in the least affecting my regard for my husband. It wasn't as brother-and-sisterly as it sounds, either, because we had always enjoyed ordinary but perfectly satisfying sex. (Better sex, in fact, than Stanley and I had shared, once the first terrible amazement

116

had worn off.) There was deep affection based on history and mutual regard and shared interest, and this, I suppose, is what most married love comes to in the end. I knew that I had hurt Tony very badly and I regretted it. And there are still some mornings when I wake up and am surprised all over again to find that he isn't lying beside me.

'I'm worried about Jack,' I said.

'Sadie, you're always worried about Jack.'

'Am I?' I never thought he was going to fall downstairs or choke or cut himself, the way I feared Cassie might.

'What's happened, anyway?'

I told him.

'Yeah, okay. That's legitimate worry.'

I felt a rush of relief at being able to talk to him. 'What shall we do?'

I could hear one of the little girls crying in the background and Suzy calling out, and then a crash that sounded like a large piece of furniture falling over.

Tony sighed. 'I'll talk to him. Is he coming to us this weekend?'

'If he wants to. Does that suit you and Suzy?'

'I'll check with her.' We always made our arrangements in this polite, considerate way. It was Tony's nature to be thoughtful and I did my best to be so because I was the one who had caused all this dislocation. He hesitated and then asked, 'Do you think it's anything to do with your dad dying?'

'Yes, partly.' It also had to do with other, longer-standing problems in Jack's life, mostly connected to me. In the pause while we both listened to the mayhem that was going on at the other end, I endured the familiar twist of guilt and regret at having left my husband.

'They're up late, aren't they?' I asked quickly.

He sighed again. 'Yes. I'll try and have a good talk to him, anyway. Listen, Sadie, I'm sorry I didn't get to the funeral. I know I should have done. But I really did have to be in Germany.'

Tony is an account director with a medium-sized ad agency and he travels a lot.

'It's all right,' I said gently. 'Ted wasn't there and he was the one who mattered.'

There was another brief silence. Both children seemed to be yelling now.

'Sadie?'

'What?'

'It may be the wrong time to say this. You won't want to hear it, anyway. But do you think you might be trying to love Jack too much? Do you think he might respond if you didn't crowd him so much? If you gave him some extra space?'

'Extra space?' I repeated. The words made me angry. 'What kind of a tired old cliché is that? I love him more than the world. There's nothing wrong with letting him know it.'

'I *know* how much you love Lola and Jack. But is your need to demonstrate it more about you and your history than about them?'

'That's crappy nonsense.'

'Is it?'

'What do you know, Tony, about how much space I do or don't allow Jack? You live out there in Twickenham, you see him every other weekend at the most.'

'The series of events that resulted in this situation weren't dictated by me.'

I bit my tongue, but in spite of my good intentions I still retorted, 'I *know* that, Tony, for God's sake. You can't resist a reminder, can you?'

'Look. I'm not reminding you or reproaching you. I don't want an argument.'

But we were arguing, nevertheless. My relief at being able to discuss our son with my ex-husband turned to anger with myself for the waste of all our joint history and achievements. If I hadn't run off with Stanley, would Tony and I be a solid couple like Caz and Graham now? And, more important, how much more comfortable would Jack therefore be, with himself and the rest of the world?

Even as I speculated, I knew that if I were to feel guilty for the rest of my life and regret my actions in every remaining minute of it, I still couldn't undo what was done.

I wondered if Ted had been thinking along the same lines while he lay in his hospital bed and held on to my hand.

I would never know, now. I was never going to be able to talk to him or even hear his voice again.

Tony's voice at the other end of the line almost made me jump. 'I've got to go and help Suzy with the girls,' he said. 'I'll give Jack a call and sort out about the weekend. I'm not supposing for a minute that my involvement will solve any problems for him or even answer any questions, but I'll do what I can. I'm sorry you have to deal with so much of this stuff on your own.'

'Thanks,' I said.

'I love Jack too, you know. And you as well, if that counts for anything.'

'Thanks,' I repeated, blinking at sudden tears. 'Bye, then.'

I walk across the kitchen and stand at the window looking at the empty roofline opposite. The pigeons have all gone home to roost. It's early May and the trees that line the garden walls are unfurling crumpled leaves from sticky sheaths. A luminously clear sky is fading into pale almond green behind the roofs and chimneys, and the rinsed clarity of the light reminds me of the evening over a month ago when Ted was taken ill and I was walking through the streets to meet Mel for dinner. I felt strong and lucky then, and rich in my children and my friendships, but now I am gripped by a dismal sense that I have reached the age of fifty and taken a series of wrong turnings.

I turn back and pick up the phone. Lola's network voicemail invites me to leave a message. Caz and Graham are visiting Caz's mother. And Mel's answering machine announces that she is unable to take my call. She is either out on the town with new Jasper or under the duvet with him, and I feel distinctly jealous. Intimacy is a fine thing, but some mindless sex would be welcome. I realise it's such a long time since I have enjoyed anything of the kind that I have almost – but painfully not quite – forgotten what it's like.

'Never mind,' I say out loud, and my voice breaking the silence underlines my isolation and makes me smile at the same time. I'm going to turn into one of those old ladies who talk to themselves. I've moved up into the front line for old age, now that Ted has gone.

I miss my father and I realise that I haven't even begun to mourn him yet.

SIX

We all had Cassie to kiss and cuddle and play with, at least.

Cassie soaked up our love, with no suggestion that there could ever be too much of a good thing. She didn't shut herself in her room, or give any of us cause to ask each other if she needed more space or less space. She ran away and hid, but she let us know where she was with squeaks and rustles if we took longer than one minute to find her. She held up her arms to tell us that she wanted to be carried, and when she was hoisted up she sat astride the bearer's hip and gave an angled-wrist wave like the Queen's.

I knew that if I crossed the yard from the bindery to the house at lunchtime, or at the end of a day's work, I could spend a few minutes drawing pictures with her or reading her a story. She divided her favours between her admirers fairly even-handedly but I liked to think that she was particularly attached to me. She called me Sadie-lady, after Evelyn warned her once when they very first moved in not to get egg on the lady's lovely coat.

Evelyn and Penny were both in the kitchen when I called in on the evening after my trip to Ted's house.

It had been another long day and Colin had only just gone home after a lengthy visit to check up on the progress of his book. I had given the job to Andy, who made up most of our

121

boxes. He had made a start on cutting the boards, but this wasn't nearly fast enough for Colin. 'My mum's waiting to see it,' he shouted.

'It'll be another week or so yet, Colin.'

'A week? It doesn't take a week to publish other people's books, I bet.'

'No,' I said irritably from behind my bench. 'It takes months to publish a real book.'

He ignored this. 'I don't like being without my recipes, you know. What if I wanted to cook one of them?'

'You could take it away with you right now,' Andy offered.

He wasn't enjoying the job – it involved a lot of work and the end result wouldn't deliver much satisfaction to the binder. The plan was to paste the greasy pages to sheets of stiff card, and the resulting sheaf of card would then be stitched and cloth-bound into a thick volume, which would have a substantial matching slipcase with Colin's name on the front. I had decided to give the job the full treatment, on the grounds that he would have nothing to complain about once it was finished. Andy took the view that as we'd never be paid for the work anyway, the standard didn't matter too much.

Colin certainly refused to listen to any discussion about money or even to consider an estimate. 'Don't be stupid,' he crowed. 'If I took it away you couldn't get on with publishing it, could you?'

I went to put on a CD, searching the rack for something very soothing for us all. I wasn't sorry when the end of the day finally arrived and I could make a ten-minute visit across the yard.

Cassie was sitting on her booster seat at the table, doing her favourite puzzle. Shiny painted fruits and vegetables had to be fitted into the right outlines in a wooden board. 'Here's the carrot,' she told me when I sat down next to her.

'So it is. What about the apple?'

We put our heads together and sorted through the shapes.

Evelyn was standing at the cooker dreamily stirring pasta sauce for Cassie's supper. She held her flowing velvet sleeve out of the way with her free hand while she gazed out of the window. "Lo, Sadie,' she murmured. She was wearing big silver hooped earrings that swung when she moved her head.

Penny was peering at her computer monitor by the front window. It was coming up to VAT time and she had insisted on doing the company books herself, but even though she was tapping away at the keyboard I could sense that her attention wasn't on the job. The atmosphere in the kitchen didn't feel comfortable.

Evelyn spooned the pasta into Cassie's bowl. We put the puzzle to one side and I laid her place with her spoon and fork. 'Looks *good*,' I told her. 'Can't I have some?'

She wagged her head from side to side and laughed. 'No.'

'One mouthful?'

'No*wuh*.'

There was burnished yellow late-afternoon sunlight sliding through the side windows. Evelyn curved her slender body against the door frame and gazed across the yard to where a seat stood against a whitewashed brick wall. In the intervals of Cassie's chatter I could hear that she was softly humming to herself. After a minute she drifted outside and sat on the bench with her face turned up to the evening sun. Penny's faux-intent rattling at the keyboard stopped at once.

I said, 'Pen, why don't you go and sit in the sun with Evelyn for ten minutes? Cassie and I are eating pasta.'

'Not you.' Cassie chortled. 'Mine.'

Penny took off her reading glasses and pinched her nose. She screwed her eyes shut and I recognised from the way her shoulders were drawn up that she was on the defensive. There was a small silence while Cassie stirred her food, then pinched a squirl between her fat fingers and fed it into her mouth. She glanced sideways at me to make sure I'd seen her and then smirkingly did it again.

'Yes, I think I will,' Penny said abruptly. She shouldered her way out into the yard and I saw her sit down next to Evelyn, who didn't move up to make room.

I concentrated on persuading Cassie to use her spoon. The child's soft chin and cheeks were coated with tomato sauce and there was a globule stuck in her black eyelashes. 'Mucky baby,' I told her.

'Sadie-la-aaaady,' she retorted and I took the opportunity to post a loaded forkful into her open mouth. Between her spoon and my fork, we emptied the dish. I had taken it away and replaced it with a pot of yoghurt when I saw Penny jump up from the bench and walk down the path towards the bindery. Her fists were buried in the pockets of her trousers and even though they were hidden from me I knew that they were clenched.

'I don't like that,' Cassie protested.

'Yes you do, it's strawberry. Your favourite.'

'Yucky.'

'Mucky yucky you.'

She stuck out her tongue. 'Poo.'

'Poo to you too.'

I took the yoghurt pot away and wiped Cassie's face clean. 'Shall we finish the puzzle?'

The cauliflower was always the last piece and her starfish hands were just pressing it into place when Evelyn came in again. Two patches of dull red showed high up on her cheekbones. 'Come on, Cass. Bathtime now,' she said. Without a glance at me she swept the child into her arms and carried her away up the stairs, her long skirt swirling behind her in a blur of colour and scent. The perfume was flowery and sweet.

Penny came in when she had gone and took a two-thirds-full bottle of wine out of the fridge. 'Drink?'

'Yes, a quick one.' I was thinking of Jack who would already have been home for an hour. Penny's hand was shaking as she sloshed wine into two glasses.

'What's wrong?' I asked about a minute later, when Penny had already drunk half of hers.

'Nothing's wrong.'

'Ah.'

From the time when we first met at college, and afterwards when the boys at her first job laughed at her and made leering remarks about rug munchers, it had been hard to get Penny to talk about herself or her feelings. Her square face flushed and she would try to change the subject, or else just walk away. Lately, though, since meeting Evelyn, she had been more open. Happiness had lowered her guard and softened the edges of her suspicion.

For this reason I pushed a bit harder now. 'Is it Evelyn?'

'What do you mean? Is what Evelyn?'

Her wine glass was empty so I filled it again. I hadn't touched mine yet. 'You don't have to keep everything to yourself, you know.'

Penny's laugh sounded more like a cough or a groan. 'You can talk.'

It was true. I hadn't spoken to Penny or anyone else about what was happening to me. I hardly cried for my father; it seemed that I couldn't. It was more that a cloud of grief loomed over me, like a storm that threatened but refused to break. I felt instead an arid, almost theoretical sorrow for Ted's absence, and my internal world was crowded with memories and dreams of him. Yet I was struggling all the time to keep him at a distance. I concentrated on the everyday, on Jack and Lola and the house, on work, on anything but my father and me. And I felt ashamed of these reactions, a complicated shame rooted in a sense of inadequacy that had stalked me almost all my life.

I said gently, 'We're not talking about me right now.'

Penny sighed. 'Evelyn wants another baby.'

I thought about it. I couldn't see that there was any problem in having a second Cassie for us all to lavish affection on. 'Well? There are ways of doing it, aren't there?'

Penny took a pot of pale-blue muscari off the windowsill and pressed the earth with her thumb. She filled a jug and watered the pot, leaving it on the draining board for the excess water to run off. 'She wants it to be Jerry's. So Cassie can have a real brother or sister.'

I had met Jerry when he called to see Cassie, although as she wasn't his only child and there were heavy demands on his time he had never been a regular visitor. He had a high, rounded forehead, a nose that ran in a straight line from that brow to its tip, and thick black hair that he wore in a helmet of tiny braids. He was six foot four and extremely beautiful. With such parents it was no wonder that Cassie was exquisite.

'That's not impossible either, is it?'

Penny gave the scornful laugh again. 'Can you see Jerry obediently doing the business and then popping round here with the result in a jam jar?'

'No,' I agreed, after trying to imagine this. 'So what does she want to do?'

'What she did to get Cassie, obviously. Start fucking Jerry again.' Penny didn't use words like that, or only very seldom. Her face was stiff and her body was rigid with the effort of containing her misery. 'I can't win, can I? If she can't have another baby she'll leave. If she goes back to Jerry I've lost her anyway.'

'Is that what she really wants, do you think? To start sleeping with Jerry again?'

126

'She says it would only be until she gets pregnant.'

'And you don't believe her?'

'I don't know.' She shook her head and I could see that she was losing the battle for control. Her mouth opened in an ugly shape and she squeezed her eyes shut against the pressure of tears. 'I don't know what I'll do without her. Without the two of them.'

I moved to put my arms round her. I cupped the back of her head with one hand as if she were Cassie and drew her forehead to rest against my shoulder. She sobbed just once, a terrible sound that seemed torn out of her chest as I rubbed her back and muttered useless soothing words. Penny's misery was so powerful it filled the room. I waited and went on stroking her, and I was thinking at the same time that even so much pain was something; it was living and breathing and it rolled over her like a breaking wave. I loved Jack and Lola, and I was anchored by affection for my friends, but it was a long time since I had known or even dreamed of passion like Penny's. I was dry and colourless in comparison. Maybe Tony was right, maybe I did channel too much of my leftover yearning towards Jack because I had nowhere else to direct it.

'Sorry,' Penny mumbled.

'It hasn't happened yet,' I told her.

'Not yet, no.'

'Give Jerry a few mags and a jam jar anyway. You never know.'

She snuffled with head still against my shoulder. 'I love her so much. It's stupid, isn't it?'

'I know. And no, it isn't. It's wonderful.'

'I think I'd like to talk to her on my own when she comes down again. Do you mind?'

I straightened her shoulders and rubbed away the tears from under her eyes with my thumbs. 'I'll see you tomorrow,' I said.

'Thanks, Sadie.'

I walked home along the canal. At the lock nearest to Penny's house two painted narrowboats were descending. There were people sitting on the roofs with their drinks and more people crammed into the little open apron around the tiller. Music and shouting and the steady throb of the engines echoed off the dripping walls of the lock and I could smell barbecue mingling with the thick water-green scent of the canal itself. There was the usual knot of spectators standing watching beside the wooden wings of the gates as the boats sank and the crew busily wound ropes round bollards and called instructions at each other. Above the lock fishermen were sitting with tubs of worms and cans of sweetcorn and greaseproof-wrapped sandwiches spread out beside them on the tufty grass at the water's edge. As I passed, one man hauled out a tiny silvery sprat and an intricate pattern of concentric ripples ruffled the khaki surface. I rounded a corner, and as soon as I was out of range of the lock I was all alone. The water was dusty here, covered with a powdering of pollen from the elderflower bushes sprawling over the towpath railings, and it looked solid enough to walk on. Behind my shoulder the gaunt cages of the gasometers netted the fading blue sky. I walked under the railway bridge where the light was dim and on the inaccessible opposite side I noticed the rocky no man's land where cardboard-box islands and stuffed supermarket bags indicated a dossers' camp. For the time being, it was deserted. Water dripped from the metal spars overhead and pocked the dark canal surface.

A commuter train rolled across the bridge and even though I had heard the same sound a hundred times before, the sudden thunderous boom and the rolling echoes made me jump and almost cry out. I quickened my step and walked out into the sunshine again. Ahead of me a pair of helmeted cyclists rounded a curve and swept past, gratuitously dinging their bells. I walked on quickly, with weeds and dry grass brushing my legs, wanting to get home.

Jack was in his usual position. We went through the regular question-and-evasion routine while I put together some supper, transferred wet washing from the machine to the tumble dryer and gave the ironing basket a shake-out. As I was putting knives and forks on the table I pushed to one side the small pile of Ted's belongings. The address book had been lying on top of the silk evening scarf and now it slid off on to the floor. I bent down to retrieve it, noticing that the floorboards under the table were dusty and well crumbed.

Jack was watching me. With his hair standing up in tufts and his wary but beady stare he reminded me of a small rodent. I felt ashamed of this thought as soon as it came into my head. I smiled warmly at him. 'Are you hungry?'

'Yeah. Are you going to ring her?'

'It won't be long. Ring who?'

'Grandad's friend. From the funeral.'

I looked down at the little brown leather book. An image of the old woman in the hat got mixed up in my mind with Aunties Viv and Maxine and Angela, their young mouths superimposing themselves on her zipped-up old one and their silly, gaudy girls' clothes fading into her dusty black. Yet I was sure – what was her name? Audrey, that was it – I was *sure* that Audrey hadn't been an auntie.

The stillness I had found in Ted's house thickened around me, even here in my own kitchen with the *EastEnders* theme tune gnawing at my ears. I had been intending to fill the fifteen minutes before supper with calls to Caz and Mel, but now I picked up the phone and flipped open the address book at A.

The ringing tone at the other end went on until I was on the point of hanging up again, but then a voice answered, 'Yes?'

Just that. It was her all right, I was sure of it, but I asked anyway. 'Is that Audrey?'

'Who's this?' the voice demanded.

'It's Sadie Thompson. Ted's daughter.'

There was a pause, and then a cool chuckle. 'Is it, now?'

I plunged on. I noticed at the same time that Jack was sitting upright in his chair, listening hard. I explained to Audrey that I had been clearing out the house, had kept some of Ted's belongings, wondered if she would like a memento of him. 'I think we're almost neighbours,' I finished up, disconcerted by the flat silence at the other end. 'I could drop round to see you, maybe?'

'All right,' she said, after another yawning interval. She gave me an address which was, indeed, only about ten minutes' walk away and I scribbled it on the kitchen notepad. We arranged that I would call in early on Tuesday evening of the following week.

Jack was still listening. 'I'll come with you, if you like,' he offered after I had rung off.

I gazed at him in delight. Mother and son, visiting an old family friend together and maybe sharing some reminiscences about Ted with her. That really would be something. 'Great,' I said.

The weekend came and went. It was an ordinary one, which could have stood as a snapshot portrait of my life in its crowded, detailed uneventfulness.

Lola came home, mainly for a twenty-first party on the Saturday night. She arrived late on Friday evening and filled the washing machine with her clothes. We sat together for an hour and shared a bottle of wine, and I listened and laughed while she talked about her escapades. There was a geography student who was really, really fit but he liked to go hiking in the Pennines at the weekends and she wasn't sure if she could handle this.

She spent Saturday afternoon on the phone and getting ready to go out. Whenever she put down the phone it rang again for her immediately, and quite often she was talking on the land line and her mobile at the same time.

I went to the supermarket, tried to do an hour's tidying up

in the garden, paid some bills and cleaned the kitchen floor. I was functioning normally, with exaggerated attention to routine, but the comforts of normality evaded me. The tasks I set myself seemed pointless and I felt stiff with loneliness.

In the evening I asked a neighbour's daughter, who was working for her A levels, to babysit Jack while I went over to have supper with Caz and Graham. They were having one of their combative interludes, and sniped at each other mildly about the food and which of them was busier with their work. The other guests were a couple I'd met several times and enjoyed talking to, and Graham's divorced male cousin who drank slightly too much and began repeating himself.

It was at least two hours before anyone mentioned property prices. Then Caz and Graham said they were thinking of maybe selling the house and moving to somewhere smaller because their boys would soon be leaving home.

'Don't bank on that, Mum,' the younger one retorted, with his nose in the fridge.

I looked around me at the shelves crowded with plates and jugs, and the curling snapshots pinned to the cork board, and the painted china cat I had given to Caz many Christmases ago because it looked like their real cat, long since dead. I had sat here hundreds of times, looking at these things in their places, and I didn't want my friends to move because I was afraid to lose what I knew. I wanted everything to stay the same and yet the ground itself seemed to be rippling under my feet.

'What do you think, Sadie?'

'It sounds like a good idea,' I said and the talk moved on.

After the other guests had left and Graham had gone to bed, Caz and I did the washing up and made a pot of tea. I knew I should go home too, but I wanted to stay here in the warmth of a safe place.

Caz saw me looking round the room. 'I know. It'll feel strange to leave this old house, but it's time we moved.'

I am much taller than she is. Caz colours her hair but I could see the grey and silvery roots at her centre parting. I wanted to hold on to her, to make a physical anchor for the two of us, but instead I asked abruptly, 'Are you happy?'

We have known each other for so long and our lives are so entwined in mutual ordinariness that we have stopped asking questions like this. Caz looked startled, but she considered her answer in her literal-minded way. 'Yeah, I suppose I am. You know, not in a fireworks sense, but it's enough. Content would be a better word. And you?'

I hesitated. A few weeks ago I would have smiled and said yes, of course. It would have been almost the truth, too.

'You don't seem very happy, at the moment,' Caz supplied for me.

'No,' I agreed. I had made mistakes with Jack and with Tony, but the roots of those mistakes went back much further, to when I was Jack's age myself. I was beginning to realise that Ted's death was shaking the walls that I had carefully erected round forty years of my life.

'What can I do?' Caz asked. Her hand rested on the teapot handle and her thin gold wedding ring caught the light. I had been her witness at the register office when she married Graham.

'Be my friend,' I said awkwardly.

Her face broke into her wide smile. 'You don't have to ask me *that*.'

When I got in at 1 a.m. Jack and the babysitter were sitting in silence at opposite sides of the room, staring at something unsuitable-looking on television. The sitter pocketed twelve quid and scuttled home across the street while I watched from the doorstep to make sure she got there safely. Jack hesitated at the foot of the stairs.

'You should be in bed,' I told him gently.

'You were late back.'

The words opened a window, one of those slits in time's continuity that take you back as fast as the olfactory nerve carries scent to the brain.

At Jack's age I had lain in bed night after night, unable to sleep. I would watch the lights on my bedroom ceiling and listen for passing cars. I was afraid that Ted wouldn't come home that night, or any night, and I would be alone. Panic shrank my innards and crawled along my spine so I gasped under the covers like a beached fish.

I tried to reach out to my son now. 'I don't want you to have to worry about me, Jack. I promise I'll always come back safely.'

But he didn't want his concern to show. He snapped, 'I don't worry. You're nearly always here, aren't you? I was just saying you were late.'

He turned his back and climbed the stairs. He was angry with the outside world for its indifference to him and with his home life for all its obvious imperfections, and I was the ready-made focus for his anger. His hostility made me tired. I didn't know how I was going to change anything for the two of us now, after so long.

Later, the noise of Lola coming in woke me up. I knew it was very, very late but I willed myself not to look at the clock and see the worst.

Neither child emerged from bed until lunchtime again the next day, and then they sat round in their night clothes eating cereal and yawning, and annoying each other.

'You must have been so wasted last night,' Jack needled. 'You knocked half the furniture over.'

'I wasn't.'

'It was *five* o'clock.'

'We were just chilling round at someone's place, okay? If you weren't such a sad specimen you'd know what it's like.'

'No he wouldn't, Lola. He's twelve, not twenty,' I said, but they both ignored me. In the end I left them to it and went over to Mel's house. There were cream-coloured vases of fat blood-red peonies on her tables and her polished oak floorboards with their overlay of pale rugs were completely free of dust. Mel herself was unmade-up and managed to look even better than with her painted-on public face. If I hadn't liked her so much I would have felt jealous of her. When she passed close to me I could smell her perfume, a strong, sweet waft of tuberose today.

Scents seemed to rise up all around me lately, as if by taking the lid off Ted's cologne bottle I had unstoppered not just his but a thousand genies. The woman friend of Caz's last night had been wearing a scent so thick with ginger and nutmeg that it had been almost culinary; this morning Lola smelt of patchouli overlaid with cigarette smoke. I was newly aware of other scents, everywhere I turned, nudging my memory and rubbing up against the boundaries of my consciousness, all of them tapping at the margins and searching for admission.

She gave me a cup of tea in one of her thin-rimmed white china cups and we sat in her sunny kitchen to drink it. I noticed that there was an empty champagne bottle standing on the floor by the bin and Mel's glance followed mine.

'Jasper was here last night. Do you know what? He *cooked* for me. He brought everything and I just sat here and watched, and didn't try to tell him what to do at any point. It was pan-fried brill, herbed crust, pak choi . . .' We caught each other's eye and laughed. 'And, as you know, it's the sexiest thing a man can do. Expertly cook for you and then feed you and then expertly take you to bed.'

So that was it; no wonder she looked so luminous.

'First time?' I asked.

She nodded. 'Definitely not the last. If I have any choice in the matter.'

We talked about it a little, but in much less detail than Mel usually went in for. She was protective of him and the newness of what was happening. 'It's really good,' she said disbelievingly. 'But I'm just going to wait and see what happens. Just straight. I don't want any games or stuff.'

I smiled at her. Mel was the Olympic gold medallist, the prime-time, turned-pro, million-dollar queen of dating game play and to hear her talking like this was something new. She reminded me of Lola, confiding in me about the geography student. I stretched my stiff knees under the table and thought I could hear them creak. 'Tell me more about him.'

He was forty-six, a bit younger than Mel, but not significantly so. He was a graphic designer, not loaded but not broke either. He was divorced, with an eighteen-year-old daughter who lived with her mother and he got on fine with both of them. He'd been involved with someone until recently, but it had fizzled out. Mel and he had met at a PR party, and he had asked for her number.

'He's not a loser or a loony, not a world-class bore, doesn't wear Y-fronts, doesn't pick his teeth. He's interesting, and funny, and interested. He's . . .' she hesitated and I waited for the punchline that would diminish him just enough to set up Mel's self-protection in advance. I waited some more and she sighed. 'He's lovely,' she concluded.

'That's good,' I said quietly. 'When can I meet him?'

'Soon,' she said and I knew she didn't want to share him with anyone just yet.

Back at home, Lola had packed her belongings into her car, ready for the return trip to Manchester. I stood on the front step, waving goodbye until the car was out of sight.

Afterwards I made Jack some supper, and checked and signed his homework sheet. He had done something, at least, but I knew it was only the minimum. I told him he needed an early night and he retired with his birdwatchers' diary.

I called Penny. We talked briefly about the coming week's

workload because it was easier this way than to do it within earshot of Andy and Leo. Then I asked her, 'How's Evelyn?'

'Um. Well, she talked to Jerry. He's asked us to a party.'

'What?'

'He says, so that we can all be friendly-style. I suppose it might help. You know he plays in a band?'

'No, really?'

'You'll come to the party, won't you?'

'Yes, I'll come,' I promised her.

That was the weekend. It was ordinary, like dozens of others. Nothing had changed since the evening a few weeks before when I walked through the spring dusk to meet Mel; the only real difference was that the real Ted had absolutely slipped beyond my reach. Until now I had always been able to tell myself that I would reach him some day, and set matters to rest between us, and so I had put off the moment until the opportunity was completely lost. Now I was left only with memories of him, and my mother, and unwelcome recollections of my childhood. The walls were coming down, and I was exposed to the cold and unexpected draughts of reality.

Was this grief? I wondered. If it was, it was an odd version of it because I was angry with my father and I thought I hadn't liked him very much in spite of the ties of blood. But still, and yet, the effect of his death was to make a subtle change in everything. It was as if I looked at my house and the canal towpath and Jack's face and my bench in the bindery from a slightly altered angle or through a clearer lens. Then there was the impression of perfumes, swirling in thick clouds just beyond the point where my olfactory nerve could detect them, like a thousand genies released from a glittering phalanx of bottles. And there was the urge to go back and break through the silence that lay like a blanket inside Ted's old house, to pull it apart and make a clamour with my demands and my questions. It was this, I knew, that drew me to the inimical Audrey. I wanted to know her.

I wanted to know what she knew.

On Tuesday evening Jack and I walked to her house. It was June, and the daylight streets were noisy with children wheeling in tight circles on bicycles and rattling over the kerbstones on skateboards. People sat on balconies outside their flats and spilled in crowds out of the open doors of pubs. The air was rank with the fumes of diesel and fast food, but there was still sweetness in it.

Turnmill Street turned out to be leafy and gentrified. Most of the early-Victorian houses were fully smartened up with crisp white paint and window boxes and brass or blue enamel numbers. There were too many cars for the available parking spaces. As Jack and I walked along, looking for number 27, a BMW glided beside us in search of a slot. But I knew which house was going to turn out to be Audrey's long before we reached it.

It stood almost in the middle of the terrace. The stucco of the gatepost was a scabby mess of rotting plaster reminiscent of peeling skin, and ivy crawled over the low wall of the garden and fingered the pavement. In the front garden itself, instead of clipped bushes and paving stones, there were an old bath and some geological strata of ancient sodden cardboard boxes. The house itself looked like a decaying tooth in the white smile of the terrace. Buddleia sprouted out of the walls where damp stains from the broken gutters marked the brickwork. The sills had once been cream-painted but were now cracked and blistered, and the windows were so nearly opaque with dirt that the loops of torn curtain inside were hardly visible.

Jack stood in the gateway, head cocked to one side like one of his birds.

'Shall I knock?' I murmured to him. There was no bell push and the door itself was an alluvial green that hadn't seen a paintbrush for at least forty years.

'Of course,' Jack answered.

I tapped and then, when there was no response to that, I hammered with my closed fist.

The door suddenly swung open and Audrey stood there. 'Oh, it's you.' She glared.

'Weren't you expecting us?'

'Kids come knocking and then run off.'

I glanced up and down the quiet, well-heeled street. 'Really? It doesn't look that sort of a neighbourhood.'

'They used to,' she said. The change of tense made me understand that she had lived here for many years, staying exactly the same while her surroundings had relentlessly risen in the world. 'Do you want to come in?' She addressed the invitation to Jack rather than me.

He was peering round us both, trying to see into the shadows inside. 'Yes, please,' he said smartly.

We followed her down a dusty hallway to the back of the house. In a long narrow room that looked out on to the back garden were a sink and an oven, a folding-leaf table and some upright chairs, two ancient armchairs, a radio and an old portable television set with its hoop of an aerial set at a hopeful angle. This was obviously where Audrey spent her time. More geological strata, this time made of yellowing newspapers, were built up on every open surface. And everywhere I looked there were cats.

'Do you like animals as well as birds?' Audrey asked Jack.

He nodded.

'He's Jack, too.' She pointed to an enormous black-and-white cat who occupied one of the armchairs. There was so much of him that rolls of fur seemed to spill off the cushions.

My Jack squatted down to the animal's level and stroked him. 'Is he the leader?' he asked.

'He certainly is. All the others have to get his say-so before they so much as yawn. Don't you, Mosh, eh?' She stuck out a foot and stirred an orange creature that was stretched out next to the oven.

'How many cats have you got?' Jack wondered.

'Eleven, last time I counted.'

I might as well have faded into the yellowish wallpaper. I looked round at the sediment of Audrey's life, trying to imagine her as she must have been thirty or forty or however many years ago it was, when Ted knew her. Without her lipstick and her strange funeral costume she looked less outlandish than she had done the first time I saw her. She had a strong-boned face with a slightly hooked nose and although her mouth was stitched with vertical seams now and there were deep creases at the corners, the lower lip was still full. I thought she would once have been beautiful.

'That's cool,' Jack said.

Audrey filled a kettle and lit the gas. 'What about you?'

'Cats? None,' he said.

Audrey and he were exchanging looks. 'I do what I want. I live how I like,' she told him. I had the sense that huge chunks of their conversation were taking place in some dimension to which I was not admitted.

Jack nodded and smiled, one of his rare, unconsidered flashes of real and admiring approval. Then he darted a glance at me. *Not like you*, the look said.

Audrey made a pot of tea. It took some rummaging in the backs of cupboards to assemble three cups, so it was clear that she didn't have many visitors. While she was busy with this I took Ted's silver cigarette case and the flashy 1950s cigarette lighter out of my bag and laid them on the table. They looked incongruous among the newspapers and dismembered biscuit packets.

'Have a Hobnob,' Audrey told Jack.

He settled back with his cup of tea and a biscuit, and one of the less characterful cats leaped on to his lap. Jack looked as thoroughly at ease as if he lived there.

'So,' Audrey said to me, having ignored me since I walked in through the front door. 'What exactly have you come for?' She pushed Jack-the-cat off his chair and indicated that I was to take his place. I started to say that I'd really just called to bring her something to remember Ted by, but she cut me short. 'I suppose by now you've seen his will?'

I nodded.

'Did he leave anything for me?'

'No.' Surprise pinched my throat but I managed to add, 'I'm sorry, were you expecting him to?'

Audrey shrugged. She spooned sugar into her tea and stirred. 'I thought he might have done the decent thing at the end. But I wasn't exactly expecting it, no.' I noticed that Jack was calmly gnawing the chocolate off his biscuit as if this turn in the conversation were entirely predictable.

'How did you and Ted know each other?'

'We met.'

There was a silence. Audrey's mouth folded into a smile and I could see that she was enjoying the mystery. I didn't like her and I didn't want us to be sitting there in her house among the softly decaying newspapers and fishy bowls of cat food. I thought she was like some rusty and cut-rate Mrs Danvers, holding the keys to rooms that had been locked up for too long. I was afraid of the lumber piled up within those rooms, but even so I was driven to open them up. How else, now that Ted was gone, was I going to learn anything more about him? 'And how did you meet?'

The folds of her smile deepened. 'In the usual way. And I lent him money to start up in business.'

Not another one, I thought. Ted's history was one long story of borrowing money to set up businesses. Even I, the hoodwinked and hidden-from, knew that much. If only his expertise as a businessman had matched his phenomenal memory for essences and the scale of his romantic imagination. 'You weren't the only one,' I said.

'He never paid me back.'

'You weren't alone in that either I'm afraid.' She was going to ask me for money from Ted's estate to settle some ancient debt.

Audrey suddenly struck an attitude on the worn mat in front of her gas fire, and the adjacent towers of newspapers and junk trembled.

'We were planning to conquer the world together. Paris, Rome, Rio, New York. Shops in the best quarters. Squads of technicians behind the scenes. Launch parties for our fragrances with jewelled flasks containing just a few drops of our golden liquid that women would commit murder to possess and lead men to their own deaths from desire. A life of rose petals and peacocks and diamonds, that was what Ted and I intended.'

Auntie Viv and her suburban dreams of setting lotions and conditioners had nothing on this. Audrey was slightly mad, I realised, or madder than just slightly so. And my son was looking at her with fascinated admiration.

Audrey bent one arm to her hip. 'And what did my money buy, you might wonder? *I've* no idea.'

I said, 'There isn't any money now, either. At least until his house is sold.'

Audrey gave a cackle of laughter. 'You don't say.' She wiped her eyes, seemingly in real amusement, then she sighed and sat down again. 'Oh, but they were good days, you know. The best. No one knew how to have a good time quite the way Ted

141

did. I remember once he took me to Paris. It was a big thing in those days, overnight on the Golden Arrow from Victoria and the sleeper carriages went down into the hold of the Channel ferry with everyone fast asleep all the way, except I was too excited to lie in my bunk. I pulled the blind up to look out and I saw the sailors working in their thick jerseys. And when we got there we stayed in a hotel that seemed all gilt and ormolu, and we went to a meeting with a fragrance house in the rue de Rivoli. Ted bought me a little suit, houndstooth check, specially for it.'

'When was this?'

Jack was less interested in these reminiscences. He stood up and sloped across to the back door. 'Can I go out in the garden?'

'The key's in the lock,' Audrey told him. He went outside and his shadow flicked across the dirty glass of the window.

'It must have been, let's see, 1958 or so.'

Before my mother died. Audrey saw me making calculations and coolly amended, 'Or thereabouts. I can't really remember. It's a very long time ago and Ted and I knew each other for many years.'

I said coolly, 'I didn't know you were a girlfriend of Ted's. I met most of them.'

Audrey sat up straight, drawing her knees and ankles together, and looking down her nose at me. My inference had offended her. 'I wasn't his *girlfriend*.'

'I see.' Although I didn't. 'Sorry.' She wanted me to think she had been a business associate, was that it? Travelling to Paris together to visit a fragrance house, Ted in one of his well-cut suits and Audrey in her little check costume. Now here she was, holed up with her cats in the dusty innermost recess of a decaying house while the rest of the world planted window boxes and put up roman blinds. And Ted himself was dead. It was a pathetic picture and I regretted my lack of warmth for her.

Then Audrey gave another cackle of laughter. 'You don't know much about your dad.' It wasn't a question. I could only shake my head in agreement. 'He never let the wind blow on you, my girl. Went to great lengths to shield you, he did.'

I looked her in the eye. Her gaze didn't flicker. There was nothing in the least pathetic about Audrey, I now decided. She had almost certainly told Jack the plain truth when she announced that she did what she liked.

'It felt more like neglect than shielding,' I murmured.

Audrey shrugged her indifference. 'I suppose it may have done. Does it matter, now he's dead and gone?'

I thought back to Dorset Avenue and the empty hours of waiting for Ted or of wishing, when he was there, that he wouldn't go out again so soon. I had never been interesting enough to capture his attention, never believed that I would be glamorous enough to do so, never even quite believed that I would grow up and out of my stalled adolescence. Ambergris, musk and vetiver. The words circled in my head like a spell and I thought of Ted's volumes of fragrance notes stacked where I had left them in my kitchen. The formulae for his spells. He had never tried to cast one for me. 'Yes, it does,' I said abruptly.

The back door creaked open again and Jack reappeared. 'It's amazing.'

'Thought you'd be interested,' Audrey remarked.

I looked from one to the other. 'What?'

'It's like a zoo.' Jack's face was shining. 'Come and see.'

The garden was maybe thirty feet long. All down one side there were rough hutches and cages made of wood struts and chicken wire, and inside the cages were rabbits and guinea pigs, most of them sitting vacantly in a slew of carrots and cabbage stalks. Jack tugged me along to the end of the line and showed me a hedgehog, and a small ball of russet-brown fur that turned out to be a sleeping fox cub.

'His mother must have been trapped or poisoned.' Audrey sniffed. 'I found him half dead near the bins beside the supermarket. Can't have him indoors because the cats'll polish him off. But I'm going to save him.'

I thought of the dog fox that I had seen near the end of my road, listening to the urban music and delicately scenting the night air.

The rest of the garden was a mess of bowls filled with scraps, bones, corn, vegetable peelings. The stink, on this warm evening, was noticeable. I could see over the top of a sagging larchlap fence the neighbours' clematis and Albertine roses, and I wondered what they thought of Audrey's reeking menagerie.

'I put out food for the foxes and hedgehogs,' she was telling Jack. 'Birds like it as well, of course. You see plenty of blackbirds and thrushes, the odd magpie and jay, as well as pigeons. They soon learn to beware of the cats.' The two of them picked their way between the debris and wandered along the line of cages together, and I leaned against the back wall of the house, watching and feeling left out of a club that I didn't want to belong to.

At last I had to tell Jack that it was time to go. He followed me reluctantly back inside the house and I showed Audrey the cigarette case and the other small possessions of Ted's that I had brought with me. She looked each one over and put it back on the table. 'I don't want any of these. I've got plenty of memories.'

Stung, in spite of my determination not to be, I packed the things back into my bag. 'That's fine, then.'

'Were there any photographs?' she asked.

'There was one of you. I should have brought it. You were sitting on a stone wall, it looked like a windy day.'

'Yes. Well, you'll be on your way, then?'

She accompanied us back through the dusty tunnel of the house and opened the front door. Bright, clean light streamed in.

'Come and see me again,' she said, but the command was issued to Jack, not me.

'Yeah,' he said. 'I'll bring your photo if you like.' We had got to the gatepost when he suddenly wheeled and ran back to the door. 'Wait. Wait a minute. You know at the funeral? You were wearing a fox fur, weren't you? I remember its eyes and the way its tail hung down. You like foxes, don't you, so didn't you think that was cruel?'

Sometimes Jack was like a little old man and at others he seemed hardly any older than Cassie.

'It was already dead when I got it, poor thing. I like to give it an outing now and again, particularly to funerals, so it can take a look at the world. Nothing wrong with that, is there?'

'No,' he agreed, apparently satisfied.

We walked home together. Audrey's tea had left a film on my tongue and I wished I hadn't drunk it. Whatever Audrey had meant to Ted, she made me feel uncomfortable.

'I thought that was quite cool,' was all Jack would say when I tried to press him.

Back in our house everything seemed clean and functional and cared-for, which was a plus at least. Then, over my shoulder, I caught sight of my rear view in the hallway mirror. My black T-shirt was a grey mat of cat hair.

Later, when Jack was in his room, I took the three volumes of Ted's notes down from the shelf and browsed through the pages once again, looking for Audrey's name. I couldn't see it. There were plenty of other names, and the formulae that had promised desirability and passion and dreams to so many women. The clouds of fragrance seemed to rise out of the pages, nudging and beckoning me.

SEVEN

The days of early summer gently trickled away, like dry sand through my fingers.

Jack went to school in the mornings, following protests that had by now become routine. Sometimes he came home much later than usual, telling me that the biology teacher had invited him to the first meetings of the school's new ornithology club. Remembering the brawling tide of children that had washed past me when I went to visit Mr Rainbird, I asked in surprise how many members the Bird Society had so far attracted. Jack scowled. 'Not many.' But no further information was forthcoming and I didn't press him. If things were even approximately working, I didn't want to start asking why or how.

I went to work every day, did whatever needed to be done there, saw Cassie if I was lucky and came home again. Colin's cookery book took handsome shape; I had persuaded the freelance calligrapher who sometimes worked for us to rewrite 'A Good BIG Dinner' and the rest of the headings in flowing script, as a favour in return for some work I had given her when she was broke. Leo and Andy did the paste-up between them and the folded sheets were made ready for stitching.

I didn't see Mel. She was busy at work and her limited free time, I guessed, was spent with Jasper. Caz and Graham were house-hunting. In the quiet evenings, when Jack had retreated from the supper table, I started at the beginning of Ted's first calf-bound volume of notes and began reading my way through them.

There were pages and pages of lists. The long chemical names, which I probably couldn't have deciphered anyway, were often confusingly abbreviated in Ted's pencil scribble. Only the old familiar perfume words leaped out at me – lilac, chypre, amber – as I frowned over the jottings and tried to imagine what he was imagining as he smelled and scrawled and worked his way towards a new fragrance. Here and there I found snatches of description that were oddly lyrical among the dry formulae. I began to understand the process, if not the inspiration behind it.

A commission might have come from one of the cosmetics houses, or Ted might have been working on an in-house project for ET&P, or he could have been privately creating a perfume for the latest Janice or Linda. Each time he had to give substance to an idea, and the way he began was by painting a word-picture for himself. Not of the potential customer or actual auntie, but of an abstract image. A sultry whisper in a crowded room, the flash of a peacock's tail, a meadow dreaming under the full moon were all examples from his notes.

I remember him sitting at the table in our front room in Dorset Avenue, staring through the dim net curtains at the unvarying vista of mock-Tudor gables opposite. The house was ticking with silence and I was – as always – greedy for his attention. I would play some game that would gradually encroach on the space around his armchair and try to engage him in it until he snapped at me, 'Be quiet, Sadie. Haven't you got anything to do?' It wasn't fair, I thought. *He* wasn't doing anything. But now I understood that he was thinking, trying to flesh out an image through that most incorporeal of means, perfume.

I have no idea how he set about it. How could a 'sultry whisper' be caught and translated and compounded via the orchestration of base and heart and top notes to make a fragrance that was finally packaged and sold as Whispering? I deal in solid forms myself and I work with my hands. The only abstracts I have to contend with are the curved or fretted spaces between letters, or the most pleasing balance between cloth and calf on a library binding. I turned the pages and my admiration for Ted's gift steadily grew.

He could take a brief and devise a perfume to order. On the one hand it was a dry and commercial business, to do with budgets and market positioning, but on the other it was pure romance. He could sell the formula to the client or he could make up the perfume himself in sufficient volume to retail it to the customers in his shop. Or, if he was in the throes of a seduction, he could mix just enough of the liquid to fill a single phial and present it to the latest of his women as if it were a bouquet of flowers. Except that this was a bouquet created with the greatest ingenuity and the caress of intimacy, and it would never fade because the formula was written out here in his notes.

No wonder my father had been so successful with that face-cupping and breathing-in routine. What woman could resist it? It was only a pity that his abilities as a businessman had come nowhere near matching his talents as a seducer.

In those quiet evenings that I spent reading my father's notebooks I realised how much I would have liked there to have been a perfume marked '*for Sadie*'. I searched all the way through, but there was no word-picture and list of ingredients marked '*for Faye*', either. I didn't know anything about my parents' courtship or their early years together: I wondered if my mother had once been breathless and flirtatious, and as mesmerised by Ted's charm as one of the aunties. She must have been, I thought. He must have held her face between his two hands and gazed into her eyes. I wished I could remember her like that, instead of as the turned-aside profile in the photograph and the muted but constant presence of my childhood.

If I had known I was going to lose her, I wouldn't have taken her for granted while I yearned for Ted's attention. I rested my fingers on the pages of notes. My poor mother, I thought. Ted's shadow overlaid hers now and his opacity obscured her for me. I couldn't reach back through the layers of years to touch her again and I knew I never would be able to.

Where are you? I whispered to her, but I heard nothing.

I tried to keep Ted in the back of my mind, fending him off. He was *dead*, wasn't he? I wanted him to go away and let me think for myself.

Near the beginning of the first volume of notes I did come across the description of a fragrance with no name. The first word Ted reached for in his word-picture was 'mystery'. Then, to enlarge on the notion he wrote 'multi-layered, teasingly complex. A veiled woman with the curves of her body showing through rich folds of velvet. Heady with smoke and incense.' I knew for sure that this wasn't a description of Faye.

I remembered that the word perfume itself came from the Latin *per fumare*, from smoke. And I thought I had read somewhere that the ladies of the harem would let their draperies billow over an incense burner, so they carried a drift of the fragrance with them wherever they moved. The idea of smoke and incense therefore went right back to the origins of perfume; I wondered idly if the roots of this particular creation were as deeply embedded in Ted's heart and imagination.

A long formula followed the description of the perfume, running to well over a hundred items. I scanned the list but couldn't begin to decipher what such a compound might smell like. No distinctive fragrance rose from the page to wind itself in my imagination, as it would have done for Ted. Then I noticed what I hadn't seen before. At the bottom of the last

149

page, the formula was labelled simply with a tiny pencilled 'A'. Maybe the initial stood for Audrey.

The reading and musing and the effort of comprehension that went with it brought yet more pictures of Ted into my mind, even though they were unwelcome.

Instead of seeing him standing by the chimney breast at home, in his cravat and checked shirt, with four fingers of one hand dipped into the blazer pocket, I saw him at his work. There was a stepped bank of bottles enclosing him in a semicircle. He was holding a paper dipper to his nose and smelling, with his eyes closed and his body completely still. His face was expressionless. He looked relaxed enough to be asleep, but at that moment no other world existed for him, only the tiny miniature landscape conjured on the tip of a paper strip. He was smelling not just with his nose but with his entire mind and being.

This image must have been locked inside me since the day I accompanied him to Phebus Fragrances. Or it might conceivably have dated from a later, very brief period when he had a shop in South Audley Street. I remember that there was a cubbyhole of a lab behind the showroom, where he worked on new fragrances to be sold over the counter. But this was at the height of Ted's grand period. He was busy playing the role of master perfumer who kissed the hands of Mayfair ladies and promised them the scent of desire itself, caught in a crystal bottle and named after them. I couldn't associate him then with the rapt and motionless man who brought every faculty to the point of concentration on a single scent. That version belonged to Phebus Fragrances and the days when Ted was learning his art from the old man.

The Mayfair shop was called Scentsation. I visited it probably only two or three times in the months that Ted owned it, but my memories of the place are vivid. The shop itself was a narrow corridor, no more than a few feet wide, but it was lined with mirrors set between dark, polished mahogany panels. The counter was mirrored too, and the floor was black marble tiles that were polished to a savage glitter. From the high ceiling hung a gilt chandelier dripping with crystal icicles and blazing with candle-shaped lamps. The little gold points of light were reflected and reflected again in the mirrors, so that the confined space became a magic box of illusion. You couldn't tell, without reaching out a hand to touch the cool glass, where reality ended and reflection began. To me, after the bus and tube journey down from our house in Hendon and the plunge on foot through the brick-red and grey canyons south of Oxford Street, it was an exotic and intimidating place. I was conscious enough of my school uniform with its cerise and chrome-yellow striped tie, skimpy navy-blue skirt and white polyester blouse, without the multiplied images of it and me offered by the mirrors. Everywhere I looked, there was a different unwelcome perspective of a lumpy schoolgirl with knotted hair and clothes that proclaimed her to be no one of any significance.

Then there was the scented air. The mirrored and panelled walls contained a faint breath of fresh flowers and warm aromatics, which conjured up worlds of glamour and privilege. In this perfumed and hushed atmosphere Ted worked with a sales assistant called Valerie. Valerie had a posh English voice, but when she spoke her name she gave it the French pronunciation, *Valérie*. She wore a little charcoal-grey suit with a boxy jacket and a tight skirt and pointy-toed shoes. Her hair was done up in a chignon finished with a black velvet bow. When she moved along behind her counter her fragrance, which was also the shop's, drifted a little more strongly in her wake – just like the harem ladies'.

On mirrored shelves under the counter and on glass strips against the mirrored walls, boxes and bottles of Ted's readymade fragrances were set out in precise rows or tidy pyramids. There was white-and-green packaging with white ribbon bows and the name of the shop was printed on them in elaborately curled lettering.

On these signature perfumes designed for his great Mayfair enterprise, Ted had bestowed oddly simple and rustic names. They were called things like River and Sky and Leaf and Rain. In those days they smelled just like scent to me, which is to say that I liked them while feeling entirely excluded from what they were supposed to achieve, but even then I didn't think the names sounded right for the hall of mirrors. They ought to have been more of the Ecstatic or Masquerade or Cause Célèbre variety, and there ought to have been more gold and shimmer about the packaging. It turned out that Ted was just a long way ahead of his time, of course. But it also meant that his Mayfair days of 1964 were short-lived.

He loved them, though, while they lasted.

I remember him in a grey suit with a chalk stripe and a pale, shimmery tie with a fat knot. I had called in at Scentsation for a reason, which was that I was going shopping. Daphne from school was having a record party for her birthday – singles piled up on her bedroom Dansette and maybe even some boys because, after all, we were fourteen at last – and rather to my surprise I had been handed an invitation. I knew the dress I wanted because I had seen it on my way down to the shop. It was made of blue-green satiny stuff with a moiré finish, and it had a smock cut and gathered cuffs that finished with a frill that would fall elegantly over the back of my hand.

I sidled into the shop and Valerie gave me a cool nod as she looked me up and down.

'Is my dad here?'

'Hello, Sadie. Just come from school? I'll see.' She knocked at the door that led into the smelling room and inclined her chignoned head to catch the response from within.

After a moment Ted materialised in his grey suit. He looked

surprised and faintly irritated to see me. 'Oh, Sadie. Yes, what is it?'

I looked from my father to Valerie and then back again. 'I want to go shopping. You know, Daphne's party. I told you, remember? And you said . . .' My voice trailed away, as it did too often when I talked to him. He had a way of waiting and listening that breathed impatience. What I had been going to add was that he had promised days ago that he would give me money for my outfit. But money was never an easy topic to bring up with him; it was something to be skirted around at best and preferably avoided altogether. He had probably only made the promise in the first place to keep me quiet at some other inconvenient moment.

I wanted the green-blue smock dress, though. I could imagine arriving at Daphne's in it and sophisticatedly picking my way through the groups of guests. Not for the first time I wished that Auntie Viv could at least have been around to back me up, if I couldn't have a mother like everyone else did. I squared up to Ted now. 'I've seen the dress I want.'

But he was already looking past me and out through the shop's tall, narrow plate-glass window. It had the word Scentsation lettered in a half-moon shape on the glass and just above the central T, like an exotic blossom balanced on a black stalk, I saw a woman's face looking in at us. She stood serenely for a moment and then strolled to the door. Ted was already there to hold it open for her.

The customer looked groomed and poised and rich. She had silver-gilt hair cut in a smooth bell that curved in to her jawline from beneath a neat pillbox hat worn perched on the back of her head. The hat was made from the same lavender-blue tweed as her suit, and her court shoes and handbag were fine grey suede. Under her arm, the woman carried a little white dog with the hair on its head tied in a topknot with a blue ribbon bow. I guessed that this vision exactly matched the way Valerie saw herself in her best daydreams, but by comparison Ted's assistant now looked over-made-up and her suit appeared cheap and crumpled next to the pale soft tweed. Valerie stood back against the shelves but I was trapped in the main part of the shop. I huddled against the mirrors to make myself as inconspicuous as possible, but then I moved my eyes and saw a little open-mouthed turnip face reflected from a hundred different angles. My hands, pressed flat against the mirrors, were leaving damp palm prints on the glass.

'Mrs Ingoldby,' Ted murmured.

'Hello,' the woman said carelessly. She put the dog down beside her slender ankles and the creature wandered straight over and began sniffing at my shoes.

'Can I help you with anything today?'

'I was thinking,' she answered, 'about the scent we discussed. My own scent. I would like . . . something *exotic*. But not, you know, obvious. A fragrance that will murmur my name, never shriek it.' She wasn't looking at any of us as she spoke. She was picking up green and white perfume boxes and little glass bottles, and putting them down again, haphazardly, after the briefest glance.

'Very well put,' Ted twinkled. 'If you would like to . . .' He gestured to the innermost corner of the shop where two fragile gilt chairs with green and white cushions were drawn up to a small table. Mrs Ingoldby swayed towards the nearest chair, high heels tapping on the marble, and waited while he drew it out for her. When she sat down Ted thanked her as if he were the one who had been given a seat. While the woman was settling her bag and gloves, and telling the dog to sit still and behave itself, Ted shot a glance over her head at me.

You, make yourself scarce, the look said. Don't leave your fingerprints on my glass, don't stand there with your reflection trespassing on my mirrors.

For a second I was frozen.

Ted drew out a leather-bound notebook from a drawer and uncapped his fountain pen. His eyes were fixed on Mrs Ingoldby again, now with a much friendlier gleam in them. 'Let's talk about exactly what you would like. Because I could create such a fragrance for you. Such grace and suppleness . . .'

'I'll come back later,' I managed to say, into the space between my father and Valerie. I marched out of the shop and into the street.

I stayed away an hour. It took me that long to walk up to Oxford Street again and check that my dress was still in the shop window. I even went inside, although I had nothing in my purse except my return bus ticket and I had had to rummage round the house to scrape together enough coins for that. There was one other dress exactly the same on the rail, in what I prayed would be my size. A gum-chewing girl who didn't look much older than me asked if she could help and I announced that I would be calling back later for *this dress*.

The girl took it off the rail and we examined it together. Four pounds, nineteen and eleven. 'Yeah. It's gear, i'n'it?' she agreed.

When I got back to Scentsation, Ted and Valerie were both behind the glass counter and Mrs Ingoldby had gone. Ted looked as surprised to see me as he had done the first time round – he must have forgotten my earlier visit.

'I want to buy a dress for Daphne's party,' I said loudly. 'I've seen the one I want and it costs five pounds.'

Valerie gazed tactfully out of the window. But Ted must have had some big success with Mrs Ingoldby because he walked to the till, rang something up and took a five-pound note out of the cash drawer. He folded it up and tucked it into the pocket of my school blouse where the fabric now strained over my breasts. I had grown a lot, lately. 'There you are,' he said.

I stared, surprised by his rapid capitulation.

155

'Go on.' Ted nodded towards the shop door. 'Get want you want.'

No wonder I still remember the day so vividly.

I bought the dress, hurried home with it, and when Ted came in later that evening I put it on and tried out a twirl in front of him. But he hardly looked up from the papers he had spread out on the dining table. He was impatiently reversing a pencil through his fingers as he raised an eyebrow at me. 'Very nice,' he said.

I went back upstairs, took the dress off the hanger and put it in my wardrobe to wait for the night of Daphne's party. I can't remember anything about the event itself, except that I didn't get off with Stephen Allardyce because that, of course, was Daphne's privilege.

One of the formulae in the notebooks, I supposed, would be for Mrs Ingoldby's perfume. I wondered if Ted's alchemy had restored her husband's flagging interest, brought her a new lover or simply made her feel more beautiful and desirable than all her friends – whatever it was she was hoping for when she came to Scentsation. In other words: if her perfume was a promise in a bottle, whether that promise had been kept.

I closed the current notebook. It was time to go to bed, but there was still a navy-blue light in the summer sky. When I went out into the garden there was the scent of honeysuckle from my neighbours' garden, but the city colossally overrode this rural whisper and crowded in on me more than it did in wintertime. The hum of traffic was louder and the noise of other people's living drifted out of open windows. I didn't mind any of this. It was comforting rather than intrusive to think of all the other lives going on around Jack and me. I stood outside for quite a long time, smelling the dusty, heavy sweetness of the air and listening to city music.

'Are you going?' Caz asked.

She was standing on a stepladder and opening the high cupboards in her kitchen. She would take a milk jug or a gravy boat from the piled shelves, look closely at it, and then reach down to put it with the small row of items she had decided to discard. Then she would change her mind and lean back down the steps to retrieve the jug and replace it on the shelf.

'How many milk jugs can one woman use, Caroline?' I teased her.

'Well.' She laughed and hesitated. 'You never know, do you? Three? Six? Vicars coming to tea and all that.'

'But you don't know a single vicar, let alone six of them.'

'And anyway they wouldn't all come to tea at the same time, would they? Unless it was a convention.'

'Or a comedy sketch.'

'And in that case they'd actually be actors or stand-up comedians. They'd be smoking roll-ups and talking about comic impact.'

'Exactly. And saying fuck a lot.'

'Of course. They certainly wouldn't care about whether the tea service matched.'

She clambered back down the steps and replaced the jug on the discard pile. It was a hot afternoon and her hennaed fringe stuck to her forehead in thick clumps. My shirt clung damply to my back. Caz and Graham had sold their house, for the asking price, to the second family who came to look at it. After three weeks' frantic hunting they had found exactly the smaller new place they wanted, and Caz was realising that they were actually going to move into it and also that if there was going to be any room for the four of them to live she would have to weed out some of their belongings. We were spending a Saturday afternoon sorting through cupboards together.

'So, are you going?' She meant, was I going to Penny's Evelyn's ex's party the next weekend.

'Yeah,' I said. 'I'll be there if I can get a sitter.' The neighbour's daughter was now in the middle of her exams.

'Matt or Dan could come over, I should think.'

I glanced out of the window. After a show of reluctance Jack had come to Caz's with me, but when Graham and the two boys suggested a game of tennis in the park his face twitched into an involuntary smile. 'Yeah? Doubles?'

Graham said, 'Men's four. We'll leave these two to their cupboards.'

They would be back soon and Caz was planning a barbecue supper in the garden. We had done a similar thing dozens of times before, although nowadays Jack didn't always want to join in. Lola adored Caz's boys, but Jack had become shy around them. And then when Graham and the two boys were together I sometimes saw Jack watching them with a deliberately blank expression that didn't quite conceal his jealousy. He would have liked to be playing football or fiddling with the barbecue with his own father, of course. And I wished it for him, too.

'They'll be back soon,' I said unnecessarily to Caz. I held up an oval meat dish with a hideous pattern. 'What about this?'

'Got to keep that. Wedding present.'

'Who from?'

'Can't remember.'

'Say goodbye to it, then.'

Jack and the others were indeed back within the hour. Matt and Dan lounged into the kitchen and went straight to the fridge. Jack sidled around the table in their wake and Matt flipped the cap off a chilled bottle of Beck's and handed it to him. Jack glanced quickly from me to Caz.

'Matt, he's only twelve,' Caz remonstrated.

'Ma, I was only twelve. It's a beer, not crack. And we had a hard game, Jackson, didn't we?'

Jack had flushed with pleasure. 'Cheers, mate,' he muttered and gulped at the beer. His Adam's apple bobbed in his skinny throat.

'Who won?' I asked him.

He twitched one shoulder at me. He looked small standing between Caz's big, fair-haired, sunny-faced boys.

'Jack and me did,' Dan said. 'He's a demon at the net. Just needs to grow another six inches or so.'

Jack aimed a weak punch at him, but he couldn't hide his pleasure. I tried to catch his eye and give him a smile but he was looking away. 'Can I watch TV?' he asked Caz.

'Of course.'

Later we sat out in the soft midge-furred evening watching Graham in his special barbecue apron flipping chops over on the grill. Jack hovered beside him, poking at the red coals with a pair of tongs and squirting water on the flames. He wouldn't yield his place to Matt or Dan, and even though he tried to look impassive I could see that he was enjoying himself. When the food was ready he ate eagerly. He didn't say much, but he listened carefully to the banter between Graham and his sons as if he were trying to soak up the essence of it, not the mere words.

When we had finished eating Matt and then Daniel stood up and said they would have to go. It was Saturday night and they had people to meet in bars, and then clubs to head for. They both touched Jack on the shoulder as they passed.

'See you later. Thanks for the game,' Dan said.

'Later,' Matt echoed.

'Yeah. See you.' Jack didn't smile but his eyes followed them as they left.

Graham said into the small silence afterwards, 'We should do it again. Make it a regular game. Don't you think so, Jack?'

Left here with the three of us, his quiet good mood seemed to evaporate. He shrugged. 'Maybe,' he mumbled on a downward note.

Caz and Graham both looked at me. They were trying to signal their reassurance, that they had been here with their boys too. Jack only glared.

I would have liked to sit out in the warm darkness, talking to Caz and Graham, and watching the red embers fade, but by ten o'clock I was driving home again with my silent Jack. I turned over in my mind the various ways I might initiate a conversation about our family and his dislocation from it. Or from me, if I was going to be honest. I slowed at the traffic lights and turned into the main road. The traffic was heavy. 'Jack? Will you try to tell me what I can do to make things better for us all? Because if you don't tell me, I can't help you have the kind of life you want. Can I?' I disliked the baffled, accusatory note that had already crept into my voice. I always heard it when I tried to discuss Jack's problems with him.

'What do I *want*?' he echoed and the sarcastic emphasis fully acknowledged the gulf between whatever it was he did want and the likelihood of him getting it. I remembered that perspective, of course.

'Yes,' I said firmly. He was twelve. At twelve, he was bound to think that he would be shuffled around between school and his mother's life for ever and would never have the chance to make choices or friends or a place in the world for himself. But he would grow up in the end, as Lola always said. I just wasn't sure how he and I would manage to hang on together until that day came.

I was expecting more silence. I would chip away with some more questions that sounded aggrieved even to my own ears and Jack would fend me off, then we would reach home and he would sidle away into his room. But then his head snapped round, so sharply that I thought I could hear his vertebrae cracking, and he was glaring full at me. I negotiated a broken-down bus that was wedged outside the bus lane and we moved forward in a slow stream of cars. Music pulsed out of most of them, the different tracks all welding together in a booming bass line that seemed to vibrate right through our silent vehicle. I gritted my teeth. Then Jack started shouting. 'I want to live in a family with my dad. I don't want to live with you always sighing and asking niggling questions like I don't know what you're trying to get at, right, just because I'm not the way you want me to be. I'm not what you and Lola want and that's too bad, and you're not what I want either, do you ever think of that? I want to do the stuff that I like. I don't want people to feel sorry for me and to look at me like I'm weird because I don't think I'm weird, there are other people like me, whatever *you* think. I like birds and animals, even Dad knows that, and Grandad did as well. Just because you don't care about the difference between a pigeon and a grebe it doesn't mean it's nothing, you know, it doesn't *mean* that. It's important.' He twisted round in the passenger seat and the rage came off him in waves that felt hot enough to scald and powerful enough to knock me sideways.

I tried to find a loose end in the tangle of words in order to pull at it. 'Nobody feels sorry for you. Do you mean Caz and Graham and the boys? Why should they? And you are what I want,' I soothed.

'That's a lie. What do you mean? You want me to be like Dan, or a girl like Lola. You can pretend and be all understanding and patient but I know the difference, I know what the truth is.'

He was right. I would have liked an easygoing all-rounder, like Caz's boys – anyone would. But if he had been a rebel, like Lola or even worse, I would have known how to deal with it. I thought I could have handled almost any other problem, but Jack's hostility entirely baffled me. I would have loved the attention and affection that I tried so fruitlessly to bestow on

161

him. But I was also aware that he was growing up with only one parent at home and in that I had replicated my childhood for my children even though it was the very thing I had wanted to save them from.

I tightened my hands on the wheel, and the sweat from my palms made it slippery. 'Do you want to go and live with your dad?' I asked.

I hated the idea, but if that was what Jack really wanted, I resolved, I'd go along with it. Whether Tony and Suzy would, though, was another matter.

'No,' Jack said scornfully. 'I want a family, not to have to live with one half or the other.'

'We have talked about this, haven't we? Tony and I don't live together, but it doesn't mean we don't love *you*, Jack. And you're not the only child in your position. Plenty of kids have divorced parents.'

The waves of his anger were subsiding. 'Yeah, yeah,' he sneered, which was no more than my platitudinous speech deserved.

I tried yet another line. 'I know I don't understand about birds. I wish I did. But you know other people who do, don't you? You go to Bird Club now.'

A black BMW convertible with the top down swept past and the blast of music buffeted my car.

'Yeah,' Jack flatly agreed. 'I go to Bird Club.'

'Let's have lunch,' Mel suggested on the phone a few days after this. I had missed her so much that just the sound of her voice made me smile. I agreed immediately and told Penny that I would probably be out for a couple of hours. She nodded without putting down her hammer and I glanced across the yard to the closed back door of the house. Evelyn and Cassie were nowhere to be seen. The next Saturday was the night of Jerry's party.

I saw Mel stepping out of a taxi as I walked towards the Thai café where we'd arranged to meet. She was laughing as she leaned in through the window to pay the driver and vitality seemed to bleed out of her and blur a little Mel-shaped envelope of air around her. I felt half as alive by comparison.

'You look good,' I understated. When she put her arms round me I smelled her perfume – spicy today with notes of cinnamon and oak – and I wanted to bury my face against her broad shoulder. I missed Lola and Jack's prickliness denied any possibility of contact, but was I *so* needy for physical warmth? It was no wonder I loved to sweep Cassie up and feel the india-rubber limbs and tiny bones suspended in my arms.

'You look tired.'

'Thanks.' But it was true, I was weary and for no reason that I could think of.

We had hardly settled in our seats before Mel announced, 'Jasper might join us for half an hour. He's at a meeting just round the corner.'

Instantly I realised that this lunch wasn't about me and Mel at all but about me-meeting-Jasper, and Mel had deliberately engineered it to happen in this low-key way because she hadn't wanted there to be any build-up to the encounter. That she had thought this much about it was significant because she had never been calculating about any of her previous lovers. Now I felt wrong-footed, and not just because I was wearing my work clothes, jeans and a grey T-shirt, while Mel was draped in taupe designer linens. I would have liked advance notice. I could have rehearsed myself into the right friendly frame of mind for meeting the man who was going to be my rival for Mel's affection and attention. I didn't *want* us to be rivals for her; it was just that this piece of calculation announced that we were almost expected to be.

'Here he is now,' Mel said unnecessarily, because I knew it was him as soon as the door swung open. Jasper was a big bear of a man with a head of thick greying hair cut modishly close to his skull. He was wearing clothes that made him look comfortable and didn't try to announce anything. His eyes searched the tables for Mel and at the sight of her his face broke into a smile as broad as a soccer pitch.

Mel almost disappeared in his arms. When she re-emerged, pink in the face, she made the introduction, mixing up her words as she did so, and Jasper took my hand in his. 'I've heard all about you, Sadie,' he said warmly.

I smiled back at him. That I hadn't heard many details about him told me more about Mel's feelings than volumes of words.

We sat down. It was one of those easygoing places with long wooden communal tables where the margins between groups of diners become blurred, and I realised that Mel had thought this out too. If the encounter were to be in any way awkward it would be easy to have a quick bowl of noodles and move on.

'I wanted you two to meet each other,' she said.

'I know. And now we have. I'm glad.' I smiled again.

Jasper and Mel were sitting opposite me. The food came, bowls of tom ka chicken soup, and Jasper politely waited until we had picked up our white china spoons before he began eating with obvious relish. He nodded appreciatively and dipped in his spoon again. Mel started talking about Thailand, saying that she and Jasper were thinking of taking a long holiday there. I couldn't actually remember Mel ever agreeing to take more than four consecutive days off work so I must have looked surprised. Jasper enjoyed scuba-diving, she explained, and he wanted to try it in Thailand.

'Mel would enjoy it too. Don't you think she would?' he said to me.

Mel protested, 'I'm a city girl. I don't do outdoor stuff, other than sitting on the beach. Anyway, I'd be scared.'

'I will look after you.'

'But I don't need looking after,' she told him.

They turned to smile into each other's eyes and I understood how far things had gone between them.

It was true that up until now independence had been Mel's mission statement, yet over our Thai lunch her face and all the lines of her body seemed to contradict it. She was doing it with humour and a twist of self-deprecation, but she was still *offering herself* to Jasper. She didn't need his care, or resent its availability. She just acknowledged his capacity and willingness to take care of her, and accepted it with grace.

Seeing it was like watching an entire romantic epic condensed into a five-minute playlet.

I thought that Jasper shrewdly took all this in, and his pleasure in it and in Mel herself was healthily touched with natural amusement. I guessed that Jasper was an optimist, one of those lucky souls who would always find joy in his surroundings.

'I'd forgotten that. Thanks for the reminder,' he said.

We all laughed now, and went on eating our soup. There was a sharp smell of lemon grass and hot peppers. It was sunny outside and light filtered through the windows of the café past glass vases of sprouting bamboo wands. The shadows of leaves stippled the wood floor and the scrubbed tables were decorated with rainbows that fell through the prisms of our water glasses. The tables were pleasantly full but not crowded and there was a low hum of conversation. The margins of Mel's linen top and Jasper's shirt softly fuzzed in the sunlight and I felt a flow of warmth towards the two of them. They were in love, and this seemed simple and at the same time magnificent. I was happy for their happiness and I thought, 'They've found each other. It seems so easy and logical, now it has happened.'

'And you, Sadie?' Jasper asked. 'What about you?'

He might have been asking about my holiday plans, or he

might have been asking something quite different because he had seen the softening in my face. I told him that I didn't know yet. Then I added without having given it an instant's prior thought, 'I might take Jack and Lola – they're my children – to the south of France. To Grasse, maybe.'

Recollection and longing struck me with such an unexpected jolt that I almost rocked in my seat.

When I was fifteen, I spent a whole summer near Grasse. It sounds unlikely, but I did. There was a square house set in fields planted with centifolia roses and jasmine bushes, and there was Madame Lesert. She was – I was told – an old business friend of Ted's, and he sent me out there to stay with her for reasons that I didn't and still don't fully understand. I do know that those weeks were a happy time for me, the best that I can remember between my mother's death and the year I met Tony. I arrived at Madame Lesert's house a troubled child, and by the time I left I had been thawed by warmth and simple affection. I have never been back there, perhaps because I didn't want to trespass on the perfection of the memory. Yet all of a sudden, sitting in a shaft of sunshine in a Thai restaurant, I was overtaken by a powerful desire to see Grasse again.

Mel and Jasper were both looking at me.

Jasper nodded. 'I should think they'd like that.'

I blinked, momentarily lost.

'Going to France,' he added.

I collected myself. 'Yes. Well, nothing's fixed yet.'

Jasper knew about Lola and Jack. He remembered what Mel had told him, but it wasn't so much that I felt unduly talked-about.

Jasper was easy to talk to and I liked the way he listened with his head on one side, paying full attention to the conversation. He had a hearty appetite and I liked that too. His movements with the cutlery and when he lifted his hand to the waitress to order coffee for Mel were precise. For all his bulk there was something neat and well-ordered about him. Jasper wouldn't be hasty or clumsy in anything he did.

All this time Mel and he sat close together, but not quite touching. I could sense how much they *wanted* to touch each other, and the resultant crackle of static across the inch of space between them was almost audible. I was envious, but benignly so. It would be wonderful if I could feel the way Mel so obviously did, but I no longer had any worries about rivalry. Maybe I wouldn't see as much of her as I used to and I probably wouldn't be her first resort as a confidante or adviser. But Mel and Jasper plainly belonged together and if I was going to be resentful of what was so natural I might as well resent the rain or leaf-fall.

Jasper looked at his watch. 'Back to work.' He sighed. He paid the bill for all of us, firmly rejecting my offer to go halves. 'Next time,' he said, with the easy certainty that there would be a next time, and many more after that for the three of us. I found that I was smiling at him.

He kissed me goodbye, warmly, on both cheeks. Then he wrapped Mel in his huge bear-hug again. We both watched him picking his way out between the benches and the shopping bags and bamboo vases.

'What do you think?' Mel asked, as soon as he was out of sight.

I was touched by how much what I thought mattered to her. 'I think he's gorgeous,' I said. He *was* gorgeous. I could very easily have fallen for him myself.

'Yes,' she agreed. Her face was smoothed out with happiness. 'Tell you what. Let's award ourselves an hour to go shopping. What do you think?'

I knew how busy Mel was and I knew she was making the offer in the same way that she had arranged this lunch and chosen the restaurant, because she had thought it out. She wanted me to know that there would still be time for the two of us, that she would see to it there was.

'I think we should,' I agreed. I had a job to finish by the end of the day but I could stay late and get it done. It was one of Jack's Bird Club evenings.

We walked down the street together. Mel put her arm through mine and the sunshine and the unusualness of being out at two thirty on a weekday afternoon made it feel as though we were on a little holiday. On the corner there was a clothes shop that we both liked and Mel stopped to look in the window. 'That would suit you,' she said. There was a red dress, sleeveless with a deep V front. 'What are you going to wear to Evelyn's party?'

'Evelyn's ex's party,' I said automatically. 'Are you going?'

'Yes. Penny asked me and Jasper's going to come too.'

'Good.'

We went inside and although I had no intention of buying a sliver of a fire-red dress to wear to Jerry's gig, I let her persuade me to try it on.

In the changing room Mel whistled. She lifted the hair off my neck and studied the effect. 'You've lost weight. It looks fabulous on you.'

'Mel . . .'

'Go on. Buy it. For my sake. Please.'

We were on holiday, almost. I bought the dress, which was expensive, and for some reason the memory of the blue-green smock that I had worn long ago to Daphne's – Daphne, I couldn't even remember her last name now – came back into my mind. I lifted my hand and sniffed at the veins of my inner wrist as if I were expecting to catch the ghost of perfume lingering there.

It was almost four o'clock when I got back to the Works. Andy and Leo were having their tea break, leaning against Andy's bench with their heads together over a motorcycle magazine. Penny was winding the handle of the big press down on a stack of freshly glued Law Reports. Bars of sunshine came in from the window overlooking the canal, and showed up the dust on bundles of leather and the rack of hand tools beside my bench.

I showed my carrier bag to Penny. 'Mel made me buy something to wear on Saturday night.'

She nodded and then caught the corner of her lip between her teeth. 'I'm not looking forward to it very much.'

I tried to convince her that she would enjoy herself, but Penny only nodded. I tucked the dress bag underneath my desk and started work again. I was wondering how it would be at the Works and across the yard if Evelyn took Cassie away.

EIGHT

'The party? Yeah, in the back there.'

The barman pointed towards the stairs at the rear of the pub and I eased my way through the crowd of Saturday night drinkers. At the door of the upstairs room a big man in a leather jacket grinned at me as he checked my invitation. 'Hello, there. You have a good time tonight, all right?'

The room was packed with people. There were white girls in skimpy T-shirts that showed their belly-button rings, black men with dreadlocks in rasta bonnets, tattooed people, smoke, earrings and studs and pins, and a blast of solid, sweaty heat larded with noise. At the far end on a low platform surrounded by music stands and stacks of amplifiers and instrument cases, a skinny DJ was working the decks. The band hadn't come on yet.

The first face I recognised was Cassie's because she was towering over everyone else. She was perched high up on Jerry's shoulders, swaying to the rhythm of her father's dancing and giving the crowd her Queen wave. Father's and daughter's foreheads had exactly the same commanding height and curvature. Cassie's eyes glittered with frantic excitement and she urged Jerry on by kicking her ankles within his clenched fists. The next person I saw was Graham. He was leaning against the wall with a pint in his hand, looking conspicuous in his weekend uniform of corduroys and a pressed shirt. I edged my way over to him.

'Christ,' he said. From this vantage point I could see Caz dancing in her intent way with a fat man I didn't recognise and just beyond her was Evelyn. Evelyn's hair was parted in the middle and fell round her face in Pre-Raphaelite waves. She was wearing a long skirt that swirled round her ankles and a tiny vest that revealed the wings of her collarbones and the fact that there was nothing but skin under the vest. She moved dreamily, with a smile curving her lips.

'Christ,' Graham muttered again. I took this as a general statement that he would prefer to be at home stoking the barbecue.

'Where's Penny?' I asked.

'She's here somewhere. You look nice in that dress. Let me get you a drink.'

'Thanks, Graham. I'll just go and see if I can find Pen.'

She was in the middle of the room, with Kathy and Dee who were two of her gay friends.

'Thanks for coming, Sade,' she shouted in my ear. Kathy and Dee draped an arm apiece over my shoulders and hugged me. They were both smoking and smelled very strongly of French tobacco.

'I didn't know you were going to bring Cassie.' She was the only child in the room. Jack was at home with Matt as babysitter.

Penny frowned. 'I didn't either. It came to her bedtime, but Evelyn announced she was coming with us because Jerry wanted her here. I said it was a ridiculous idea to bring a baby to a gig like this. Evelyn said it was too late to get a sitter. I said I would stay at home with her. Evelyn said if I didn't come I was being unsupportive and I didn't love her. I said – well.' Penny shrugged and lowered her hunched shoulders. Her face was contused with unhappiness. 'I said I loved them both and Evelyn said good, but Cassie is her daughter, hers and Jerry's, so she could decide whether to bring her to a party or not. That's more or less how we left it.'

Dee produced a glass of what looked like vodka and gave it to Penny, who drank most of it at a gulp. Alcohol had made her franker than she would normally be. 'It's only one night,' she said, looking at me for reassurance. 'It'll all be over tomorrow.'

'Of course it will,' I said. I patted her shoulder and left her with Dee and Kathy.

Graham gave me a glass of wine. I waved to Leo who was nuzzling his girlfriend in a niche beside the bar. Penny's friends and supporters were out in force tonight. I drank my wine, danced with Graham and then with Caz's partner who turned out to be a music critic with a mordant sense of humour. My ears got attuned to the noise and I began to enjoy myself. After a while I saw Mel and Jasper easing their way between the dancers to join us.

'I was right about that dress, wasn't I?' Mel crowed.

I looked down at myself. 'Yes, you were.'

Jasper kissed me like an old friend. Of course he was a good dancer, I discovered, when the time came for him to ask me. More drinks arrived. The DJ finally bawled that he was taking a break right now and we were all great and he'd be back later.

The band members were tuning up. I watched Jerry, minus Cassie now, as he adjusted the height of the mike stand and swung his hips to the music in his own head. Under the lights his skin shone as if it had been polished. Then, in the line-up behind him, I caught sight of someone else I knew. He fitted his lips purposefully to the mouthpiece of a trumpet and lowered it again to lean across to the trombonist standing next but one to him. It took me a second to place the man, because he was wearing a black T-shirt with a white Marilyn Monroe image instead of his schoolteacher's blue shirt, but then I had him worked out. It was definitely Mr Rainbird from Jack's school.

'All right, friends,' Jerry crooned into the mike. 'Here we go now. One, two, three.'

They launched raggedly into 'Mustang Sally'. I leaned back against the bar and laughed at the happy absurdity of it. It was Penny's Evelyn's ex's and Mr Rainbird's soul band. They had plenty of brass and enthusiasm, and Jerry's voice wasn't bad at all. It soon turned out that they had a wide repertoire, covering the standards from 'Knock on Wood' to 'Three Little Birds', and everyone was up and dancing. Mel inclined her head to mine and a spiral of her hair tickled my cheek.

'What do you think?' I shouted.

She rolled her eyes. 'The big time beckons Jerry.'

I danced with Jasper again, and with Andy who swam up out of the crowd, and with Dee who put her hands on my hips and ordered me to let *go* a little. It was a really good party. I was enjoying myself so much that it made me realise I didn't get out enough these days.

I caught a glimpse of Evelyn and Cassie. Evelyn was stooping right down, so that her spine curved to show the lovely long chain of bone, and her slender wrists crossed to hold Cassie's hands. They were twirling in dizzy circles and Cassie's head was thrown right back in the last transports of exhausted delight. I turned away again to talk and dance some more. A few minutes later I heard Cassie screaming. The sound was only just audible over the thump of music but I heard it as clearly as if the room were silent and deserted.

Frantically I pushed my way to the spot where I had last seen her. She was lying on the floor, her face mottled and her heels drumming. Relief brought my breath back. It was nothing more than a temper tantrum brought on by tiredness. Evelyn was stooped over her, and Penny was crouching beside Evelyn and trying to get past her to Cassie.

'What?' I asked Penny over the noise of Jerry's Desmond Dekker tribute number.

'She's tired. Not surprisingly.'

Evelyn was shouting at Cassie and pulling her upright. A

173

clearing had opened around us in the crowd but otherwise no one was paying much attention. Jerry at the mike had his eyes closed.

'No,' Cassie screamed and drummed her heels even harder.

Penny was trying to stop Evelyn hauling on Cassie. The two of them were facing each other off and when Cassie briefly opened her eyes to check what was going on she immediately saw it and screamed harder. Penny locked her arms round Evelyn who let go of Cassie to try to fend her off.

Seeing my chance, I stepped in and scooped the child up. Her body was rigid. 'Cassie! Cassie, it's all right, you're all right. Come to Sadie-lady.'

She took a deep breath to go on yelling but then thought better of it. She went limp and heavy in my arms.

'What are you doing?' Evelyn demanded, but not very aggressively. We were all pleased the tantrum had blown itself out. Penny's eyes met mine imploringly.

'I'll take her for a few minutes,' I said. 'You two go and, you know, have a dance. Enjoy the party. Cassie will be fine with me.'

Penny's arms were still round Evelyn. She murmured in her ear and stroked the waves of hair back from her cheek. Evelyn nodded, pouting a little, and let her head fall on Penny's shoulder.

I carried Cassie away towards a door at the side of the room. There was a green EXIT sign above it. As I made my way I saw that Mr Rainbird, resting for a few bars, was watching me go.

The door opened on to a fire escape. There was a metal platform from which a single flight of metal stairs led down to the alley alongside the pub. I let the heavy door swing shut behind us and the noise immediately diminished to muffled thudding. I held Cassie close to me as I sank down on the step. 'Here we are,' I murmured against her sweaty head. 'Here we are now.' She was drawing long, ragged breaths punctuated by hiccups. She snuffled a little and turned her face against my chest. My eyes stung and the complicated veins and ducts around my nipples ached with love. I hummed disjointed notes, deep in my throat, as much to comfort and reassure myself as her.

It was a hot June night. Even in my sleeveless dress the faintly stirring air felt warm on my arms. There was a stink of cats and of fried food from the pub kitchens downstairs. A door banged open below my feet and a kitchen porter slouched across the alley to toss a plastic rubbish sack into the overflowing wheelie bin parked against the wall. Cassie sighed and curled herself closer against me. Her breathing was even now and the hiccuping had stopped. I sat quietly, watching the cats around the bins and then looking up at the stars. Cassie fell asleep. The thudding behind my back stopped and after a few minutes started up with a different resonance. The set was over and the DJ had come on again.

The door behind me creaked open. A man's legs appeared at the corner of my vision and then folded as whoever he was sat down on the step beside me. I was briefly irritated at this intrusion into my communion with Cassie and the velvety night.

'Hello,' Mr Rainbird said. He rested his wrists on his knees and we gazed down into the rancid alley.

'I didn't know you were a musician,' I remarked.

'I'm not. I'm a part-time trumpeter in a pub soul band.' His voice was full of amusement, which made me think briefly of Jasper.

'Is she yours?' Mr Rainbird asked.

I laughed. 'Thank you, that's flattering. No, she's the daughter of my business partner's girlfriend. And Jerry,' I added as an afterthought.

'Ah. Right. I saw her on Jerry's shoulders earlier on. When I saw you carrying her out I thought maybe you and he . . .'

I really laughed this time and, turning my head, was surprised by how close Mr Rainbird was sitting. The step wasn't very wide. 'No,' I said.

'Right. Good. Jerry's probably not an ideal boyfriend. Or father, actually.'

There was a long but perfectly comfortable silence.

'Anyway. It suits you, sitting there holding her like that. How's Jack?'

'He seems okay. Thanks. He goes to school, very unwillingly. But on the other hand he stays late quite often, at Bird Club.'

'Bird Club?'

'Yes.'

After another silent interval I asked him, 'How do you come to be playing the trumpet in Jerry's band?'

'It's not a very interesting story. Shall I try to make up a more exotic one?'

'No.'

'All right. My girlfriend and I used to go out on Tuesday evenings to a jazz night in a club in Shoreditch. And at the club one night we were having a drink with a man called Phil who plays the trombone. I was telling Phil that I wasn't actually all that keen on jazz, it was Jane who was the real enthusiast. That's fairly unusual, you know. Real jazzheads are nearly always blokes. Of course you know that.

'Anyway, he asked me what kind of music I did like, which was quite polite of him considering I'd just dismissed the central passion in his life, and I told him I liked soul. And he said that was funny, because he was peripherally involved in the brass section of a soul band that some guy called Jerry was starting up, and I played the trumpet, didn't I? I agreed, for brevity's sake more than anything else, that I did play from time to time although I was pretty out of practice and really ought to give up before it gave me up. That sounded about right for the standard of the band, Phil said, and they were short of a trumpet in the line-up and why didn't I audition?

'So I went along to Jerry's place, which was swarming with musicians and thick with ganja. It was fun jamming with these guys, and Phil as well, and I ended up in the band. We play four, maybe five gigs a month and we don't get a lot of practice in. It suits me fine and I've been doing it for about a year.'

Cassie sighed and threw her legs out, and I gently shifted her weight so she lay on the side away from Mr Rainbird. This had the unintended effect of making us seem even closer together.

'Shall I take her for a bit?' he offered, with his shoulder touching mine.

'She's fine like this.'

'How's Lola at Manchester?'

'You've got a very good memory.'

'Actually, I've got a pretty lousy memory. I remember everything you said to me that day, though.'

It occurred to me, with a shiver of recollection about how it all went, that Mr Rainbird might be making a play for me in spite of the girlfriend with whom he went to jazz clubs. 'Lola's fine,' I said quietly.

'And Jack is coming on the school journey, isn't he?'

I had had to persuade him quite hard, but in the end Jack had agreed to go with the rest of the Year Sevens on the school holiday to Cherbourg. I sensed that there was an element of negotiation in his consent – if he went, it was on the understanding that I gave him leeway in other areas of his life – but I had yet to discover what the terms of his negotiated settlement might be. Therefore the prospect of the holiday gave me a slight uneasiness. 'Yes,' I said. And then, 'I'm going to take a few days off at the same time. I'm going up to Suffolk, actually.'

This plan took me completely by surprise. Jack would be safely elsewhere and I would have a whole week to myself, so I could easily slip away to Suffolk.

As soon as I had said it, the idea hammered in my head. Auntie Angela, one of the very few aunties with whom I had kept in touch in that we still exchanged Christmas cards, lived up on the east coast. She had sent me a note of sympathy and had written that she wasn't well enough to come to the funeral. If I went up to see her, I knew she would talk to me about the old days.

In all the years that had gone by, I had wanted to know less rather than more about our history: Ted's and mine, and Faye's. I felt damaged by it and wanted to rub it out, smoothing away the ingrained lines of bitterness. Memory was like having a bruise that didn't hurt, so long as you didn't press on it. But I was increasingly aware that Ted's death had changed all that. The scent of the past fumed around me as thick as mist, rushing from the olfactory nerve to flood the cells and chambers of my head. It teased my subconscious and made me give public voice to plans that I hadn't conceived even in my dreams. The trail was drawing me to Suffolk and reviving my memories of Grasse, and it seemed I had no choice but to follow where it led. My skin prickled and the hairs rose on my arms at the thought, and the faint but acrid odour of apprehension must have risen from my pores because Cassie stirred and began to whimper.

I'd forgotten, momentarily, about Mr Rainbird.

'To Suffolk? If I weren't escorting kids to Cherbourg I'd come with you.'

I was lifting Cassie to my shoulder and rubbing her back to soothe her but I did turn my head now to look straight at him. He had neat, unremarkable features and a mouth with a long top lip that looked tucked in at the corners, as though he were used to suppressing his amusement. There were fine laughter lines at the corners of his eyes too. He oughtn't to have looked distinctive, given the ordinariness of these separate components, but somehow they added together to make a good face. I wondered why I hadn't noticed this before.

He said quickly, 'It's where I come from. My part of the world, I mean. Near Ipswich. I could . . . I could have shown you some nice country pubs.'

I breathed in hard, making myself concentrate, and the distracting waft of perfume faded a little. 'That would have been nice. But Cherbourg beckons, doesn't it?'

'Oh God, yes. Trying to stop them doing all the things school trips are really about for just long enough to pick up some French vocabulary or a few cultural impressions. I shouldn't be saying this, should I?'

'It's nothing I don't know already. I'm Lola Bailey's mother, remember.'

'And Lola turned out fine. Much more thanks to you than to the school, I suspect.'

We both hesitated, but neither of us chose this moment to mention Jack. The bass vibration that shook the step and the closed door at my back had now stopped.

Mr Rainbird stretched his legs in the cramped space and eased himself to his feet. 'I've got to go and play the trumpet.'

'Thanks for keeping me company.'

'Sadie? May I call you Sadie?'

'Of course.'

'Shall I give you a ring?'

I remembered the evening in the new restaurant with Mel. I looked around my life that spring night and thought this is good, this is what I want – family and friends, work and the calm satisfaction generated by these things. But the weeks since then seemed to have stripped away several layers of comfortable, thick, nerveless skin. I felt exposed now, and shivery with a kind of feverish, naked anticipation. I guessed that I must look different to the world as well as feeling unfamiliar to myself, because I had never been asked out by any of Lola's teachers even though I used to spend half my life at the school, explaining away her latest transgression. But I did remember – of course I remembered – that this was how it went. You were asked for your telephone number. You gave it, or not, or you played a withholding game. It was that simple. Just as it had seemed, looking in from the outside, for Mel and Jasper.

Wait a minute, I wanted to say. My life's already overflowing. I like the idea, or at least the *idea* of the idea, but I've got something else to work out first. There's a scent to follow.

Mr Rainbird was looking down at me, waiting. Jerry would be back at the mike for the closing set. 'What about your girlfriend?'

'My ex-girlfriend. She's seeing a percussionist now.'

I laughed and so did he. I temporised, 'How about if I call you?'

'Okay,' he said at once. He took a notebook out of his pocket, scribbled down a number, tore out the leaf and handed it to me. 'Don't lose it.' These were the authentic tones of a teacher, but I didn't mind that. He opened the fire escape door and went inside.

I sat watching the cats but Cassie was restless now and after a minute or two she began to cry. It was almost eleven and I knew that the music licence only extended to midnight. If I took Cassie home and put her in her own bed, Penny and Evelyn could come back later to relieve me.

The atmosphere inside was even thicker, if that was conceivable and Jerry had cranked up the volume by another twenty decibels or so. Cassie flinched and whimpered, pressing her hot face against my neck.

'Where were you?' Mel asked as I edged around the room.

'Out on the fire escape with this one.'

'*And* the rather nice-looking trumpet player.'

Mel never missed a thing. And she was so happy, she wanted everyone around her to share the same happiness. My guarded instincts made me shrug non-committally as I kissed her goodnight. 'He's Jack's head of year. I'm going to take Cassie home and put her to bed. I'll call you tomorrow.'

Caz and Graham had gone. Penny and Evelyn were together,

at least, dancing in the thick of the crowd. Evelyn's eyes now had exactly the same overexcited glitter that Cassie's had held earlier.

'You're an angel,' Penny murmured. Her face was a solid dark red. 'I can't leave Eve here, can I?'

The bar downstairs was closing. I hurried through the knots of glassy-eyed people and their Saturday night swell of belligerence and out into the night. My car was parked at the corner and I lowered the sleepy child into the back, and trussed her into the baby seat I kept there for her. As soon as we were moving, under the glaring street lights and between the fluorescent-squared leviathans of the late buses, I felt calm and happy.

On this warm night the city seemed turned inside out. The pavements in front of smeared fast-food shops were crowded and when we slid past a scruffy slice of tree-lined green space there were dozens of people sitting or lying on the grass, and an icecream van as well as a hot-dog cart doing good business. An ambulance's blue light prickled in my mirror and I pulled in to let it sweep past. Faster-moving traffic instantly flooded into the space left in its wake. Faces loomed at my windscreen as I stopped at a crossing and I checked with my right elbow that the self-locking button was down. My car was a capsule of safety, weaving through the mayhem, with Cassie fast asleep in her seat.

I let myself in to Penny's house and carried Cassie upstairs. When she saw her bed she stretched her arms out, as if to embrace its security. Her head flopped on the pillow and she gave a sigh. I settled the quilt round her small shoulders and sat on the edge of the bed for a minute or two, in case she needed anything. But I thought she was already dreaming. I turned on her night light and before I drew her curtains stood looking down at a black angle of the canal. Three pale reflections of windows shivered on the surface; just beyond them the towpath was a faint streak of dusty earth that led past the dense darkness of undergrowth and disappeared into the utter black beneath a bridge. I drew the star-patterned curtains against whatever lay out there.

I rang Matt to tell him where I was and he said there were no worries, he'd go to sleep in Lola's room if he felt tired. I made myself a cup of tea and sat down at the kitchen table with the weekend newspaper supplements. It was 1 a.m. when I heard a black cab ticking outside.

Penny and Evelyn came in with a waft of smoky air and the exaggerated movements of people who have had plenty to drink. Evelyn came straight to me and put her hands on my shoulders, then leaned right down so that waves of hair flowed either side of my face. She smelled of the party.

'Fast asleep,' I said.

'There,' Evelyn said to Penny. 'I told you everything would be fine.' There was a smile of vindication in her voice, but at least it was a smile. Evelyn's mood had somehow swung into the benign sector in the intervening two hours.

'Thanks to Sadie,' Penny answered.

'Yes, thanks to Sadie.' Evelyn's fingers musingly stroked my hair. 'She is a heroine. Always a heroine, Sadie is.' She drifted away again, back to Penny, and curved the willowy arc of her body against Penny's hips. 'Hmm?' she murmured. The kettle was boiling but Penny ignored it, turning her face instead with blind relief to meet Evelyn's. Their lips just touched.

'I'm going home,' I said redundantly. Everything was all right here, for another night at least.

I turned the car round and drove to my own house. The television cast one baleful blue eye at Matt, asleep on the sofa.

NINE

There were three buses lined up at the school gates. Children swarmed on and off, yelling and shoving, while teachers counted heads against lists. Jack was already in his seat in the front bus. I could see him from where I stood with the group of parents who were still hovering between having said goodbye and actually leaving. He had hoisted his holdall into the luggage compartment, checked his backpack yet again to make sure that his precious binoculars were safe and submitted to my goodbye kiss by craning his neck to one side.

'Have a lovely time,' I told him. 'I'll see you in a week.'

'Bye, Mum.'

He climbed the steps without a backward glance. My heart ached for his solitariness in the excited mass of kids and I regretted having encouraged him to go on the holiday at all. A week could be a very long time to a lonely twelve-year-old, as I well knew. I hung around on the pavement, having half-conversations with the other mothers, just in case he decided at the last minute to bundle himself off the bus and come back home with me. But he sat with his head bent, apparently immersed in his book.

Finally the bus driver climbed into his seat. A teacher stepped off with a clipboard under her arm and the doors closed with a hydraulic swish. When the engine started up Jack's head lifted.

He searched for me in the crowd, then crooked his arm against the window glass to shield his eyes from the easterly sun. I stood upright and waved, with a wide grin pasted to my face. Jack smiled back with his arm still curled against the window like a shield. At the very last second, as the bus turned away at an angle, he used this shelter to touch his other hand to his mouth and blow me a kiss.

I watched until the bus lumbered to the end of the road and turned out of sight. Then I swung round and almost collided with Mr Rainbird. It was too late to compose my face.

'Don't worry. I'll keep an eye on him,' he promised.

'You don't need to do that. No, wait a minute. I didn't mean that to come out sounding ungrateful, I just hope he'll be all right and not need any special attention.'

Mr Rainbird had a clipboard too. The second bus noisily pulled away from the kerb.

'Did you lose my number?'

It was ten days since the party. The scrap of paper was still folded inside my wallet. 'No.'

'Well?'

'I . . .' There was too much memory and also too much present tense in my head. Jack and Lola marched in my thoughts alongside Audrey and Penny, and Auntie Angela who was waiting to see me up in Suffolk. My mind was already focused on the drive there. 'I'm sorry,' I said.

'Sir? Sir?' Two huge boys wearing barge-sized trainers were scuffling beside the third bus. I recognised Wes and Jason from Jack's form.

'Yes, what is it?'

'Sir, Miss Clarkson said we was on the wrong bus, yeah? But it's the only one left now.'

'Just get on it, then, and we'll sort it out later.' Mr Rainbird sighed and consulted his list.

'Have a good week,' I said.

'Thank *you*, Sadie. And the same to you. Don't forget our agreement, will you?'

Mr Rainbird was going to be persistent. I assured him I wouldn't forget and didn't add that merely recollecting didn't mean that I would actually ring. The doors had closed behind him too before I realised I was grinning. I was playing a withholding game, that was it. Whether or not I called this man in the end, I was still – after so long – back in the dance.

All these things – Ted's death, the crowding in of memories, my unlooked-for rebirth as a woman apparently desirable to men – these were all connected. The stopper was out of the bottle and the perfume was spilled. There would be no closing it up until evaporation was complete. The road outside the school was suddenly empty and quiet. I looked up past the walls of glass and concrete to the dust-white early-morning sky. It was going to be another hot day.

Later I drove up the crowded motorway past Colchester and on towards Ipswich. As I negotiated the bypass I wondered where exactly it was that Mr Rainbird had come from. Beyond Ipswich the route was quieter and I remembered that I was in no hurry. I slowed down to watch the unscrolling fields of sour-yellow rape and the flat meadows stocked with black-and-white cattle. I felt, and always do feel, a city dweller's sidelong, qualified appreciation of the open countryside. Five-barred gates seemed to beckon me into lush grass and down towards willow-fringed slow rivers, but I knew that if I did stop the car and try to step into the picture postcard I would find myself wading through cow-pats and nettles into a thick cloud of midges. I stopped in a village instead and sat on a bench outside the post office to eat a prepacked cheese and ham roll followed by a choc ice. The war memorial cast a finger of shadow over plump young mothers pushing babies in buggies to pick up older children from the gates of the primary school. I wondered how it would have been to bring up Jack and Lola in a place like this, and immediately my chest squeezed with a fierce, partisan affection for the grit and discord of the city.

At the end of the afternoon I reached the hotel I had booked. It was a red-brick battlemented place that faced in one direction on to the cropped fairways of the golf links and in the other over the crinkled sullen blue of the North Sea. My bedroom had twin beds with wooden headboards and candlewick bedspreads, and a dressing table made of the same shiny brown as the headboards, topped with a trinity of mirrors. I studied my greenish-tinted reflection from several angles, then rearranged the rose-patterned pin tray and powder jar on the glass-topped surface.

After I had hung up my clean trousers and put my folded tops in a naphthalene-scented drawer, I went out for a walk along the harbour wall. At the far end there was a Martello tower and I strolled with the elderly tourists and locals walking their dogs to look at the closed gate leading across a gangplank to a small, solid door. I would have liked to look inside the thick walls, but everything was locked up. I walked back even more slowly, past the yacht club where the dinghies were berthed in neat files. I was enjoying being alone. I could feel myself slowly uncoiling and expanding with the luxury of choice, the lure of my empty room.

I ate a solitary dinner and with the sound of waves washing on the shingle I slept better than I had done for weeks.

The next day I drove half a dozen miles inland to the village where Auntie Angela now lived.

Her modern bungalow was in a little close, with concreted paths leading up to each of the identical front doors. Angela's house had pots of salvias and busy lizzies on either side of the door, and vertical louvred blinds masking the picture window. I put my finger to the bell push and waited what seemed like a long time for her to open the door. At last she did appear.

'Good gracious,' Angela said.

We had kept in touch, but only just. It was twenty years since we had last met, a little while after Lola was born. Angela's exclamation meant that I didn't look like a young mother any longer, let alone the adolescent I had been when she first knew Ted. And on my part, if I had passed her in the street I don't think I would have recognised her. In the Dorset Avenue days she had been plump, with heavy white calves and soft dimply arms, but now she was hugely fat. Her face was a broad moon of flesh, with concentric circles wobbling round a tiny central boss of features.

'Come on inside, then.'

I followed her through the narrow hallway. She moved very slowly on twin pillars of fat, with ripples of it seeming to flow over the tops of her slippers. Her feet looked like flippers, too short to stop her toppling over. In her living room we sat down facing each other across the hearthrug, flanked by ranks of family photographs.

I knew that after Ted Angela had married a chef and they had had two daughters before the chef left her and emigrated to Australia. Angela had supported herself and the girls with hotel work, some of it quite probably in the place where I was staying now. Both girls had married and moved away, and Angela was left alone here. She had had a hard life.

'You've been quite a stranger,' Angela said.

The abrasive touch in this reminded me of Audrey. Ted must have liked his women to be cheeky, and it was just time's wear and tear that turned a pretty girl's taunting into sharpness.

'Well. I'm sorry about your dad,' she added more gently.

I rummaged in my bag. 'I thought you might like to have this, to remember him by,' I said and handed her a photograph that I had had copied and framed. It was of Ted smiling in his RAF tie and a blazer, taken some time in the late Fifties. He looked very handsome and wholly untrustworthy.

Angela studied it for a minute, then put it aside. 'Always a lovely boy, Ted was. A lovely boy.'

While she was in her kitchen making coffee I sat looking out at the deserted close and letting the image of my father as a lovely boy awkwardly settle over the different contours of my own picture. Angela couldn't manage to carry the tray so I brought it through for her while she shuffled breathlessly in my wake. She was doubly trapped here in her massive solitude.

We sat and drank our coffee: there were thin china cups and chocolate wafer biscuits set on a matching plate. My visit was clearly an event.

I told Angela about Lola and Jack, and she described her grandchildren and then talked about the years that had intervened since I had last seen her. The sound of her laughter came back to me through the thickness of time – it was a young girl's rushing giggle, held close in her throat as if she didn't want to let too much of her amusement be audible. None of the aunties ever stood a chance of taking Viv's place, but Angela had been one of the better ones. At least she didn't treat me as though I were a direct rival for Ted's attention and therefore an enemy. I tried to work out how long she had lasted. It might have been as much as six months, but she was definitely gone when I came back from my summer in Grasse.

Our coffee cups were empty and Angela had eaten the wafers. Her tongue flicked out to prospect for stray crumbs round her lips. The sun streamed into the room, filtered into stripes by the blind and I felt drowsy.

'Are you on holiday up here, then?' she asked.

'In a way,' I answered.

'On your own, are you?'

'Yes.'

She pursed her mouth so it turned into a little purple-red bud in the mottled plain of her face. 'You're looking for something.'

It wasn't a question so I didn't try to deflect it. In any case, in the silence of the bungalow with her girl's laugh in my head

I felt my defensiveness eroding. The quest was taking over; it was easier to say what I felt rather than try to hide it. 'It's more that I wanted to talk about him. I know it's too late to change anything now that he's dead, but I want to hear someone else's version of him.'

Audrey. You should be asking *Audrey* for this, a voice intoned in my head.

How was it that I could remember Angela perfectly well, and Viv and Maxine and all the others, and Audrey not at all? If it was because I'd never met her, why *was* that?

I told Angela, 'My memories are all distorted, you see. I'm angry with him because I think he neglected me but if I could see past that, if I could understand why, I might mind less.'

Psychotherapeutic jargon tried to crowd my tongue – to achieve closure, death's and the mind's door closing in synchrony, was that what I wanted? But the feeling I had now was too visceral to be manoeuvred with mere words; there was too much pain here, sharp blades of it sliding against my bones. I was afraid that I was going to cry.

Angela nodded. She sat with her bulk spreading across a sofa, her hands laced across her front. 'You were a funny girl,' she said.

I was surprised by my entry from the wings because I had been waiting for the spotlight to shine on Ted.

'You always seemed to be listening. Eavesdropping, was that it? Trying to get in on the fun?'

I thought back. Fun was more than I looked for. What I wanted was not to be excluded. Abandonment was what I feared most, not surprisingly. 'Yes, I suppose that's it, in a way.'

Angela said, 'I don't know what I can tell you, dear. Your father was just a boyfriend to me, you know. Older than anyone else I'd been with, a bit suave with his car and the scent and so on. He was lovely like I said, I always thought he was dead gorgeous. But wicked as well. Wicked in his ways with women, if you know what I mean, not because of what else he did. I never minded about that, it wasn't much anyway and I'd have waited for him longer than the six months or whatever it was. But he didn't want me when he came out. A clean break was what he was after. And then I met Michael and that was that.'

I was listening not just with my head now but with the whole surface of my skin, my new thinner skin. The drowsiness had gone and I sat upright, trying to sort meaning from the tangle of Angela's words.

'I remember you so well, back then. Fifteen, you were and your eyes big enough to see everything that went on but as innocent as a kid of eight. That was Ted's way with you. He didn't want you touched by all that.'

Apprehensiveness was gathering, crawling like nausea in my chest. 'All what?'

'What are you asking me?' Angela blinked, her eyelids like pale crescents of dough.

I spoke carefully. 'I don't know anything about this. What do you mean about not minding what he did, and waiting for him to come out, and my father not wanting me to be touched by it?'

A car had drawn up outside the bungalow opposite and a woman was lifting supermarket bags out of the boot. Angela's head had turned but I didn't think she was watching her neighbour. She was just working out the extent of my ignorance. 'You really don't know, do you?' she asked at last.

'No.'

'He sent you off to France.'

'That's right. It was you who took me to Victoria, remember, to the boat train.'

Ted knew about the boat train, of course; Audrey told me they went on it to Paris.

'Your dad asked me to.'

I could see that other Angela, nested like a smaller Russian doll inside the huge one she had now become. She was wearing a summer dress, shirt-waisted, with a pattern of leaves on the full skirt. She helped me put my suitcase on the rack, and handed me a two-page set of instructions about the journey ahead. I was terrified, but there was no point in begging Angela for a reprieve.

'It's all a long time ago,' she hedged.

I stared into her eyes. 'What is it, exactly, that I don't know?'

She looked straight back at me, making a decision. Then she said, 'Your dad went to prison. For fraud. He served three months of a six-month sentence.'

My first sensation was relief. I had been afraid of something much darker. Ted had always been a fraud; to hear that he had actually done time for it was only a confirmation. 'I see. How much more do you know?'

'Not much. He embezzled some money, not a lot, something to do with the shop he had in Mayfair.'

'Scentsation.'

'Daft name, I always thought.' Angela gave her girl's giggle again. 'He was caught and tried and found guilty, and that was the time I knew him. And when he was in prison he wrote to me to say it was finished.'

'I see,' I said again. The scale of his concealment was beginning to dawn on me.

The months leading up to that summer had no particular resonance. I remembered vaguely that Ted was busy and preoccupied. He was often absent and when he did come home late at night he was irritable, sitting with his piles of paperwork and answering in monosyllables if I tried to talk to him. But none of that was unusual. I fended for myself, doing my homework at the living-room table and making a sandwich for supper under the neon strip light in the kitchen. In the silent house the sound of the fridge motor shuddering into life could be startlingly loud. The fridge was usually almost empty. Evening after evening I would stare into the pastel-blue interior, willing it to fill itself up with food.

It was just before the end of the school summer term that Ted announced he had some business to do and he'd be away from home. He stood on the burn-marked half-moon hearthrug, rocking on his heels.

I left my seat, wanting to hold on to his arm and stop him going anywhere. I ended up hovering in front of him. 'Don't,' I managed to say. Floods of words built up in my mouth and even those couldn't convey what I feared, but all I could utter was a choked monosyllable.

Ted's eyebrow lifted and he gave me a quelling stare. 'Don't make a fuss, Sadie. It's all sorted out. You're going on holiday, to the south of France. What do you think of that?'

I'd never been abroad. I stared at him, mistrust forming like ice at the margins of a winter pond. 'Aren't you coming too? I don't want to go without you.'

He frowned. 'I can't. I told you, I've got business to do. But you'll be staying with a friend of mine. You'll have a good time, Sadie, believe me.'

I wanted to believe what he told me but I didn't trust him. I tried to mount an offensive. 'Who will I be staying with? Auntie who?'

'Madame Lesert,' he answered coldly and I withered under his glare.

I knew I'd never be a match for Ted because he had all the power. If I wanted anything from him, even money for my bus fares and food, let alone a new dress, I had to play by his rules and that meant doing what I was told. 'How long am I going for?' I whispered.

'I don't know yet. It could be just a couple of weeks, or it may be longer.'

He would have been hoping for a not guilty verdict, I now realised. Ever the optimist, my father.

So I went to France, the summer I was fifteen and stayed there for three months.

Angela saw me off.

Ted said a distracted goodbye earlier in the day as he detached my hands from the sleeves of his blazer. 'Don't be silly, Sadie. You're going on a top-notch trip that plenty of girls would give their eye-teeth for, and you're making a fuss about leaving home.'

I didn't care if I never saw Dorset Avenue again. It was Ted I was afraid to leave. There was no date fixed for me to come back and so I didn't know when I would see him again. It was like the other time, the one we now didn't mention, and I couldn't refer to that because it would only make him angry and he might be even less inclined to bring me back from the mysterious French exile.

I wrapped my arms round myself instead of him, containing my fears. I was wearing an angora cardigan that Angela had said I could borrow for my holiday, and the fibres were fluffy under my fingers. I kissed my father quickly on the cheek, wanting the separation to be over if it couldn't be avoided.

He gave me a wink. 'That's my girl.'

Now Angela leaned forward across the coffee tray and tapped me on the knee. 'Not upset, I hope?'

I shook my head experimentally. 'As you say, it's a long time ago. But why didn't he tell me?'

'I don't know, dear. Maybe you were the one thing he did have that he wanted to keep nice.'

Maybe, I thought.

'He wasn't a bad man, your dad, you know. He used to get carried away with all his ideas and he was so good at mixing his perfumes he probably didn't understand why he couldn't do some creative work on the money side as well. He couldn't charm the law the way he could charm me, though, could he?' Angela winked at me.

'Thank you for telling me,' I said.

I wanted to get away from here so I could weigh up what this new information meant. A con artist, my father *was* a perfumer and a con artist. That was how I had described him to Mel and it turned out to be closer to the truth than I knew.

I looked at my watch.

Angela shuffled to the door with me. She put her wide arms round me and kissed my cheek. I kissed her back, feeling the powdery softness of her skin.

'I was always fond of you, Sadie.'

Angela had remembered my birthday until I was well into my twenties. She had noted all my changes of address since then and her Christmas cards still arrived faithfully every year. To me she had been just one of the procession of aunties, a better than average one it was true, but still one in a long line. I had meant more to her, perhaps simply because of my vulnerability that summer. The thought made me draw further inwards. I didn't want the child I had left behind to be exposed to Angela's pity. I didn't even want to see myself in that light.

I rested my hands on her arms. My fingers seemed to sink down and down into the flesh.

'I know, Angela. Thank you. I'll try to be a better friend from now on.'

I made her promise that she would come and stay with Jack and Lola and me in London. In the autumn, maybe, when the cooler weather came, she said. Travel was too much for her when it was hot. She stood on the doorstep watching as I drove away.

I reversed my route back to the coast and parked the car facing a wide shingle beach. I walked to the water's edge and turned towards the sun, stepping aside from the waves and following the spits of hard wet sand that lay between the shining stones. I was thinking that I could go back to London and resume my life. I could take the view that Ted was gone and I had grieved for him in my way, after a fashion, but now it was time to move on.

That wouldn't be the truth, though, and I had an appetite for the truth after so long.

I didn't know why Ted had concealed so much from me. I didn't even know what had made him so harsh in his handling of a child. *He wasn't a bad man, you know*, Angela had said. *He didn't want anything to touch you. He wanted to keep something nice.*

I was harsh in my response to him too, because that was the adult way I had learned to contain the past and its deficits. All I had seen was his selfishness and his charm, that poisoned and perfumed chalice, directed everywhere and at everyone except for me. But it was possible that what Angela said was true and, given this new chink of insight, I began to think that maybe he had loved me in his own way and had done his best to protect me. The search I had involuntarily embarked upon was a way of finding out what had really happened between us. And when I had done that, maybe I would be able to forgive him.

I walked on, following the curve of the beach. I began thinking again about Grasse.

I reached the Gare du Nord in Paris at midday the next day and climbed awkwardly down from the high carriage with my suitcase bumping my shins. I hadn't slept on the ferry crossing – there had been no sleeper berth for me and I was afraid to close my eyes in the crowded lounge. For two frozen minutes I stood looking at the unfamiliar signs and listening to station announcements that I couldn't understand. Then a woman who looked a little like Valerie from Scentsation appeared. She said in strongly accented English that I must be Sadie

Thompson and I was so relieved to be rescued that my eyes filled with tears.

The Frenchwoman told me that she was a friend of a friend of my father's. She took me to a café near the railway station and bought me steak frites and a salade verte. The food was better than anything I had ever tasted, but I was queasy with fatigue and loneliness, and couldn't eat much of it. I remember spelling out the names of the Métro stations in my head and thinking that the curved shapes of the signs and the curled lettering were so beautiful and exotic compared with the workaday London tube.

At the end of the afternoon there was another train and a night in a stuffy couchette before I looked out of the window in the pearly morning and saw the Mediterranean for the first time. At Nice station Philippe Lesert was waiting to meet me. He took my suitcase as if it weighed nothing and opened the passenger door of a dusty 2CV for me. We drove away from the startling blue-whiteness of the coast, where the light was so strong it hurt my eyes, past farms and flower meadows and little houses with ochre tiled roofs. The road was quiet and dappled with the shade of mimosa trees.

At last Philippe pointed out medieval Grasse on its hill ahead of us, but we turned aside before we reached it and came to a house set in fields full of flowers. The house was ugly, too tall for its width and with a shallow grey roof like an afterthought, but it had pistachio-green shutters and tubs of marigolds, and kitchen herbs at the back steps. Philippe stopped the car on a patch of dusty earth, then opened the car door for me again, just as if I were someone who mattered. I stepped out and the cool, elegant scent of jasmine folded itself around me. The waves of perfume filled my head with wonder and I said in amazement, '*Oh.*'

'Is strong, yes?' Philippe laughed.

Mr Phebus had given me a jasmine dipper to sniff, all those

years ago, but I didn't remember it having the sweet and bell-like clarity of this perfect fragrance. This was Valerie and Auntie Viv and Mrs Ingoldby refined and softened and purified until it was the very essence of unattainable loveliness.

Philippe spoke a little English. He was eighteen, three years older than me, and he had one of those thin, mobile, olive-skinned French faces. Because of the suitcase-carrying and door-opening, and also because of the way he talked to me as if I were one of his friends and not just some inconvenience of a strange English girl, I already thought he was wonderful.

'You smell at dawn, when we pick flowers. Then, ah.' Philippe blew on his fingernails and shook his hand as if it were burning. His eyebrows made black circumflexes. '*Voilà, maman, la petite est arrivée.*'

Madame Lesert came down the steps. She was wearing a coarse apron and wiping her big hands on a cloth. She was short, not much taller than me, wide-hipped with thick, strong legs and feet sheathed in dusty clogs. Her corrugated grey hair was tied up under a printed scarf. I learned later that she was a widow who ran her husband's fields of flowers grown for the perfume industry with autocratic efficiency. Philippe was her only child and she was protecting his birthright. She patted my shoulder in greeting. '*Alors, Sadie, bienvenue.*' She pronounced it Sad-eee. '*Tu as faim?*'

She didn't speak a word of English. All through the weeks that I lived under her roof her remedy for my shyness and melancholy and homesickness was food. *Tu as faim?* I can hear her voice now, and smell her thick vegetable soups and good roast chicken.

I had been travelling for over thirty-six hours and Angela's angora had moulted over everything I was wearing. I nodded and managed a watery smile.

She took me upstairs to my bedroom. It was at the top of the tall house and it had a wide view over the fields. There was an iron bedstead, and a china ewer and basin on a wooden stand, and as I looked around I was so interested in it all that I forgot my misery for a minute or two. Madame left me to unpack my few clothes and I put them away in an old-fashioned clothes press, then Philippe called to say that le *déjeuner* was ready. I sat opposite him and next to Madame, and we ate tomato salad that tasted of pure sunshine. They must have seen how exhausted I was, because they didn't ask questions or bewilder me with information. They ate slowly, exchanging a few calm words, and I knew at once that this was how they always behaved together and that I was accepted. I listened and watched the sunlight on the bare stone floor and felt some of the stiffness leak out of my body.

That night I slept on a feather mattress with my head on a strange, long, hard French bolster, and I woke up the next morning just as it was getting light. I could hear voices and people passing outside so I left the warmth of my feather nest and pattered barefoot over the bare floorboards to the window. I unhooked the shutters and leaned out. The sky in the east was shell-pink, lined on the horizon with unearthly green. There were twenty or thirty women fanning out between the jasmine bushes. They wore headscarves and aprons like Madame Lesert, and some of them had babies tied in shawls on their backs. Round their waists were sacks with wide open mouths and they moved up and down the rows of bushes, picking off the white starry flowers and dropping them into their sacks. They called out to each other in different languages, not French. I learned later that these were Italian and Portuguese migrant workers.

And the scent.

I understood Philippe's quaint gesture now. The jasmine perfume was strongest at dawn and it rose up to me at my window in great billows of voluptuous sweetness. I knew, as I had never grasped before, what perfume meant.

The flower pickers looked to me like something out of a picture in a book or at an art gallery. Their brown hands flew, but the scene was static, even timeless. In my ignorance, I still knew that I was watching a scene that had been the same for hundreds of years. The nape of my neck prickled at the thought.

I sat at the window for a long time, until it was fully daylight and I realised that I was hungry.

Tu as faim?

Breakfast was bread and honey that tasted of lavender. Philippe broke off chunks of his bread and dipped it into his flat bowl of milky coffee. I thought this was a very strange thing to do, and it would have been frowned on at home, but I copied him and he grinned encouragement at me.

I soon discovered that the days followed a very simple routine and I loved that after the uncertainty of life at home with Ted. Madame Lesert and Philippe were always up before it was light, because that was when the pickers came chattering down the track to the fields. Once the sun had heated up and the jasmine's unearthly perfume began to fade, they gathered at rough tables under a sun awning. Philippe and Madame weighed each picker's sack and wrote the figures down in a notebook. Afterwards Philippe carried out jugs of coffee and unmarked bottles of red wine, and Madame and I brought baskets of bread and tomatoes and cheese. I listened to the incomprehensible chatter and the laughter that went with it as the women ate and drank. I used to wonder how such brown, gnarled fingers could be so dextrous and quick with the tiny stars of flowers. The women who had babies with them unhooked their aprons and calmly breast-fed in the shelter of a folded shawl.

After the pickers had streamed away again down the track, Philippe loaded the morning's harvest into a little grey three-wheeled truck and drove the sacks away to the perfume house up in Grasse. While Madame frowned over her figures and accounts, I cleared the remains of the pickers' breakfast and attended to the chores she had shown me how to do. I swept the stone floors and sprinkled them with water to keep the dust down, and washed and dried dishes. I fed the hens and brought in the eggs, and watered the herb garden. None of this felt remotely like work, here in this sun-washed, cheerful place. I felt as though I had walked into a book, one that I might have found in the school library and sighed over for a life that was so picturesquely different from my own.

Later in the day there was cooking. I watched Madame making bread and chopping vegetables for soup, and putting a chicken in a pot to cook slowly for the evening meal. She taught me how to knead bread dough, how to slice onions with my fingertips folded out of the way of the sharp blade, how many handfuls of rice and dried pasta would make enough for our dinner, and which herbs to pick to flavour which dishes. I watched and listened, greedy for her company and approval as much as for her delicious food. She noticed my interest and responded by teaching me new tricks; under her supervision I made a thick vinaigrette dressing that glossed the salad leaves, an omelette from our own eggs that puffed golden on the outside and melted within.

'*Bien fait, chérie*,' she would say, nodding at my efforts. Philippe was a good son, but I think she must have enjoyed having a girl in the house. At first we could hardly exchange a word, but with raised eyebrows and smiles and gestures we still managed a conversation that satisfied us both. After a little while I acquired a few French words and stock phrases, and whenever I used them she would puff out her red cheeks in admiration and reinforce my feeble efforts with a voluble response.

In the afternoon heat, she used to sit in her armchair in the coolest corner of the kitchen and listen to music on her radio. I preferred to wander outside and marvel at the sensuous ripple of the sun on my skin and hair. I used to sit with my back against the house wall and my legs stretched out in front of me, idly watching the lizards run over the stones and the butterflies settling briefly on the rosemary bushes. I turned brown and stood taller because I wasn't hunched up inside myself in anticipation of the next surprise I would have to deal with. With the exception of Sundays every day at the Leserts' was exactly the same, purposeful and yet tranquil, even down to the never-ending sunshine.

On Sundays there was no jasmine picking. We put on neatly pressed clothes instead of everyday ones and went to mass in the little church in the village. Madame and Philippe knew every single person in the congregation, and the ritual of handshaking and kissing afterwards seemed to go on even longer than the service itself.

The only other break to routine came when we drove in the 2CV up the steep road to Grasse. Madame liked to go to the market for the few items of food that she didn't produce herself, and she would walk around the stalls with a wide wicker basket, frowning and testing the lemons in her capable fingers or sniffing the saucisson that the stall-holder held out for her approval. Philippe showed me round the old stone ramparts of the town and we leaned shoulder-to-shoulder and gazed southwards at the distant blue arc of the sea, or peeped into the dim interior of cafés where old men hid from the sun with cloudy glasses of pastis lined up in front of them. When I became more confident about the pattern of the ancient, narrow streets I liked to wander about on my own, making chance discoveries. The best was the flower market, in a tiny sunken stone square in the very centre of the town. The tiers of blooms scorched my eyes with their brilliance and their scent seemed even stronger through being contained in this austere, shaded space. After the market Philippe drove us home again, with me crunched up among the shopping in the space behind the two canvas seats. Madame kept up a disparaging commentary about the price of her purchases and the acquaintances she had bumped into.

In the evenings after dinner, which was eaten early because we were such early risers, she would sew or frown over the newspaper for an hour and then, by nine o'clock, she would be getting ready to go up to bed. Sometimes Philippe used to comb his black hair back from his handsome face, slip his pack of Gitanes into his shirt pocket and disappear with a wink at me. I knew he would be going to meet a girl but even so I couldn't be jealous. For the first time in my life I felt an utterly benign and selfless love: if Philippe was happy, it was enough to make me happy too. That, and the mere fact of his existence in the first place. A special smile from him, a teasing joke, a goodnight kiss on one cheek and then the other, that was all I looked for.

On some other wonderful evenings he used to take his fishing rod out of the corner and raise a circumflex eyebrow at me. I would jump up and follow him along the track and down between the willow trees to the khaki-coloured river. He taught me how to fix the bait to the hook, smiling when I recoiled from the maggots in their nest of meal. He put his arms round me from behind and guided my wrists as he tried to teach me to cast, but I was hopeless at it. How could I concentrate, when I could feel his laughing breath warm on my neck and his heart beating against my spine? I preferred the safer option of sitting beside him while he fished, watching the water as the twilight gently thickened around us. I can't remember whether we ever caught a fish, but I can see the lines of his profile and smell the French tobacco on his clean breath.

I didn't hear from Ted, but Madame assured me, with Philippe's help, that he was occupied with his business and all would be well. And because I was happy with the Leserts I accepted what I was told and didn't try to speculate any further. Life in the fields seemed so timeless that I half believed nothing could change and that I would stay here for ever.

But it did change, of course. The jasmine harvest ended and I was no longer woken by the pre-dawn voices calling outside my window. Philippe worked long hours among the bushes, pruning and tying back the new growth. A letter came with an English stamp and, after she and Philippe had conferred over it, Madame called me and said that in one week's time my father would be waiting for me at home.

I felt a leap of joy and relief, and at the same time sadness at the thought of leaving the Leserts. 'Can I come back and visit you again?' I begged.

'*Bien sûr, chérie*,' Madame said.

Exactly a week later Philippe took me and my suitcase to the station. It was an affectionate but unemotional parting from both my friends. They were secure in their routines among the flowers and the summer had been ordinary for them except for the presence of an English girl who had, in the event, fitted in quite well. I don't think they ever guessed how momentous it had all been for me. I didn't expect letters from them and there were none. I knew they weren't the letter-writing kind.

When I finally reached Dorset Avenue again, Ted was at home. I put my suitcase down, feeling almost shy at seeing him.

'Good Lord, Sadie,' he said. I wanted to hurl myself against him, and hug and be hugged in return, but he held me at arm's length so he could look at me. 'How tall and brown you are. I'm not sure I'd have recognised my little girl.'

I bit my lip. This was a compliment, but it emphasised the extra distance that the summer had put between us. 'I'm still the same,' I mumbled. Ted looked thinner. 'How are you? Where have you been?' I blurted out.

'Around and about,' he said, in the voice that told me not to ask any more questions. I followed him through into the kitchen and put the kettle on. I opened the fridge to look for milk and found that it was empty.

So there was an entirely new perspective to the picture, like one of those images that can be either a candlestick or two facing profiles, depending on how you look at it. I had been banished or I had enjoyed the best summer of my life. Ted had abandoned me or he had tried to save me from the humiliation of knowing my father was in prison.

I had walked a long way down the glittering beach. I turned and faced out over the waves. Ted felt very close at hand now. I couldn't *see* him because his shape, the genie that had escaped from the bottle, was changing all the time. I couldn't fix him, or the past, or even myself without finishing what I had begun.

But my face was wet with tears at last and I could hardly see the way as I walked on, leaving my solo footprints in the sand.

TEN

Most of Turnmill Street looked tranquil and prosperous in the afternoon sunshine. Pools of shade from the tidy trees spilled over the parked cars and clipped hedges, and there were tasteful white or silvery themed flower displays in tubs and window boxes. A trio of small children in private-school uniforms was being shepherded out of a people carrier by a young woman who was probably their nanny.

The flakes of paint and ancient plaster from the façade of Audrey's house drifted across the cracked path and fell on the deposits of litter in the garden. I banged on the door and waited, then stooped and tried to peer through the letter box. When I straightened up to knock again the door did its trick of swinging open without warning and Audrey confronted me.

'Yes?'

'I was just passing,' I said with approximate truth.

'Yes?'

'And so I thought I'd call, on the off-chance that you might be in.'

Her full lips crimped as if to acknowledge a glimmer of humour in this but the amusement was private, not to be shared with me.

'May I come in?' I persisted.

'All right.'

I followed her down the hallway again and into the narrow

room at the back of the house. It was hot with the sun streaming full through the murky windows and the close air was thick with the usual smells of cat food and animal breath. I glanced out at the double row of cages in the garden, and the cabbage stalks and bread crusts scattered between them. Next to my shin Jack the cat was ripely occupying his favourite armchair. Several other cats prowled or basked in the vicinity.

'Push him off there,' Audrey said, but I chose an upright chair at the corner of the table.

'I've been up in Suffolk for a few days,' I said conversationally, when Audrey had taken the armchair instead and hoisted Jack's bulk on to her lap. A jet throttled back overhead, and I thought it must have drowned out my words because she made no response. I handed over the box I had carried in with me and said more loudly, 'I've been in Suffolk. I picked masses of these at one of those farm places so I brought some for you.'

In the box were a punnet of strawberries and some broad beans still in their swollen pods. The four days I spent alone in the country had given me plenty more time to think as I walked on the shingle beaches or browsed along the bean rows at the Pick Your Own. I decided that if I came to see Audrey again, in the two days remaining before Jack came back from France, without cross-examining her exactly I might still discover more about Ted and the past. His absence now seemed to swell in my mind with each day that he was gone. I was beginning to believe that I had constructed my own version of our joint history. Maybe I had built up a carapace of resentment that was just beginning to crack open. Angela's memories of a lovely boy were increasing an already giddy sense of dislodgement.

'Suffolk?' Audrey murmured, rather as though I had said Lhasa. She poked her earth-rimmed fingers into the strawberry punnet and fed herself a couple of the fat berries.

'I went to look up Angela. Do you remember Angela, who was one of Ted's girlfriends?'

'Yes,' she said. Just that, no more.

'Were you friends? Do you keep in touch with her?'

'No.' The negative did for both parts of the question. When I was walking and making plans up in Suffolk I had let myself forget quite how unforthcoming Audrey could be.

'I had a long talk to her and she told me some things I didn't know about Ted. Something quite startling, in fact.'

Audrey's head turned and Jack stopped his rhythmic kneading of the bobbled fabric of her trousers. Two pairs of eyes regarded me flatly.

'I didn't know that he had been in prison,' I said.

'And were you surprised to hear it?'

I noticed that Audrey betrayed no surprise whatsoever. I had been right to deduce that it was Audrey I should be talking to about the past. Whoever she was and whatever she had been to Ted, she knew much, much more than she was so far prepared to give away.

My father was a perfumer and a con artist. You would have liked him.

'No,' I said. 'Not really.'

'I see.'

The cat, sensing that some moment of drama had passed, resumed his kneading. Another plane roared overhead. When the wind blew in a certain direction they came right over my house too, a mile or so distant in a straight line from here, but I didn't normally register their passing. So I was listening harder than usual, without knowing what it was that I wanted to hear.

'I brought you this, too. You asked if there were any photographs.'

I handed over the same picture of Ted that I had given to Angela. I had searched my house for the photograph of Audrey herself, the young woman sitting on a low stone wall with the wind blowing hair round her face, but I'd been unable to find it with the others I'd brought back from Ted's. I thought it must have fallen behind a piece of furniture or else I had allowed it to be swept up in a pile of papers, and I was ashamed of my carelessness. Audrey took the other picture and looked at it for a long moment. Then she put it down carefully, in a way that told me she would pick it up after I had left and stare at it much longer and harder.

'Why have you come? Not just to drop in an old photograph and some Suffolk farm produce, I imagine?'

I sat forward on my upright chair. I found myself thinking that I had nothing to hide from Audrey, or to be afraid of in her house, and then wondered why I should imagine that I might have. It was sad here, among all the lumber and decay, and with loneliness hanging like a blanket at the windows, but that was all. There was nothing sinister. What I did fear was what Audrey might force me to confront within myself.

'Since Ted went,' I explained, 'since he died I feel him in my head all the time. He's gone and I never asked enough questions about him while he was still alive, and I never talked to him about what put us apart from each other. You know that about us, don't you? You know that we weren't good friends even though we only had one another? My mother died. You know that, too.'

Audrey inclined her head very slightly. Her thin grey hair was pulled back from her face, showing her bones. Her ringless hand, netted all over the back with dark veins and sinews, stroked the cat's fur, head to haunch, head to haunch, in long deliberate sweeps. *How* did she know, exactly? My knowledge of her was almost non-existent, apart from what she had told me herself. All I could be certain of was that her name appeared in Ted's old thumb-indexed address book, he had saved a photograph of her that was now lost, and that in her turn she had cared enough about him, or about *something*, to appear at his funeral decked out in her dusty fox fur.

I looked at her, trying to catch a smile in her eyes in order to return it. But Audrey's face was closed tight and the only emotion I could discern was anger. Ted had borrowed money from her and had never returned it, and therefore it was hardly surprising that she felt no warmth towards him or me. Yet somehow I didn't think this was the whole story. I was also sure that whatever the story might turn out to be, Audrey was at the heart of it.

I plunged on, talking almost at random in the hope that the flood of words would carry me towards what I wanted to say. 'Now he's gone I catch the scent of him everywhere. Can you understand what I mean by that? I used to think I didn't love him. My memory tells me I didn't, but there's a much deeper sense than memory that suggests I must have done. Still do. His presence catches me unawares, the way smelling a familiar smell immediately takes you straight into another place before you can even formulate a thought.

'I've come here because I don't know much about Ted's life. He hid everything from me, even a prison sentence. But if I can find out some more about those days when he and I were living in Dorset Avenue together, from the time my mother died until I grew up and left home, I might understand more about who he really was and why we lost each other. It might help to exorcise the past.'

Audrey shifted the cat's weight and it flexed its claws in warning across her knees. 'I thought you were going to say exorcise *him*.'

'No, I didn't mean that.'

I wanted to return the genie to the bottle, perhaps. The little crystal bottle with the dried brown residue of the last drop of perfume, caught like a tear at the bottom. I gathered my resources for a further admission. 'I thought he didn't love me.'

I had barely time to register what a wail of bitterness this sounded before Audrey snapped back, 'Did it occur to you that he thought just the same about you?'

I stared at her in astonishment. I was going to say, no, that couldn't be possible. As a child I had hung around, on the margins of Ted's life, longing for attention from him or even attention by proxy from the aunties. He couldn't possibly have imagined that I didn't love him and crave his affection.

But then I thought, it's like Jack and me. Ted and I couldn't be more different as parents and that was what I had intended for the whole of Lola's and Jack's lives, and still intended for the future. Yet with some part of myself I was also afraid that Jack didn't love me. However much I tried to hug him close to me, however hard I tried to compensate for having left his father, he pulled away from me and withdrew into himself. I had broken up his family and, whether he did it consciously or otherwise, he made me pay dues for that. Had I made Ted pay, too, for Faye's death and what came afterwards?

It's a cycle, I thought. Ted's mother and father had both died before I was born. I would never know the truth about them now, but they had created the child who became my father and in my turn I had my troubled relationship with my loved son.

Then I told myself it's *not* a bloody cycle. It stops right here. Jack and I would be all right and, much more important, Jack himself would be all right. I would see to that.

I said, 'I hadn't seen it in exactly that light. But maybe you are right. I'd like to know more and try to understand these things better.'

There was a moment's silence in which I thought Audrey might relent and talk to me. Her hand lifted in mid-stroke while she considered the options. Then she smoothed the cat's fur even more deliberately and the creature closed its eyes in supine contentment. 'I was your father's business partner for a few years. He borrowed money, put it into a shop, lost it, never paid me back. He made promises, which he always broke. What else are you expecting to hear?'

'Was it because of your money that he went to prison?'

'Didn't *Angela* tell you about that?' Her voice had a harsh edge to it now.

'Angela said she didn't really know or care about what he'd actually done. He was inside for three months, that's all, and before he came out he ended it with her.'

Audrey shrugged. 'It wasn't to do with my money.'

'Whose was it, then?'

'Why are you so anxious to know all this? I can't help you, anyway. It's nearly forty years ago.'

I took a deep breath. I was getting angry myself now. 'So who can help me?'

'You could try the Public Record Office, I suppose. If you really want to know.'

There was nothing to be gained from this. Audrey didn't want to tell me about Ted and I wasn't going to be able to cajole or disarm her. But I couldn't stop myself from asking one more question. 'Did you know my mother and father before she died?'

'No,' Audrey said. Her wide mouth puckered, the vertical creases round it deepening as she bit off the monosyllable.

'But you said . . .'

'I don't remember dates. And I don't remember a whole lot of other things, nowadays. Do you know how old I am?'

The question was delivered with all the go-on, be-amazed quavering bravura of a pub granny. But in spite of the livestock, and the detritus of her house, and the impression she gave of being an eccentric recluse, I didn't believe that Audrey was even briefly forgetful, let alone senile. She was too cunning, and too careful, and the anger I glimpsed in her was much too fresh.

'No,' I said.

'And I'm not going to tell you,' she wound up triumphantly. The cat bounded off her lap and headed for one of the rancid bowls lined up by the back door.

I picked up my bag and stood up. 'All right,' I conceded. 'Thank you for the chat, anyway.'

'And thank *you* for the vegetables. From Suffolk.'

Neither of us mentioned the photograph.

'I'd better go. I've got things to do at home. Jack's been in France and he's coming back the day after tomorrow.'

'That's right,' Audrey agreed.

I was on my way down the dingy hall towards the brightness of Turnmill Street before the oddness of this properly struck me. I let myself out and closed the peeling green door behind me.

That's right, she had agreed in a placid voice as if she were the one who knew about Jack's movements and I the one who was asking for confirmation.

I walked past the line of shiny cars to where I had parked mine, my mind running on the implications of this. I thought about it as I drove and by the time I reached home my suspicion was hardening into a near certainty.

'What's happening, Mum?' Lola asked when she called me that night. I tucked the handset under my chin and talked as I unloaded the dishwasher. We usually spoke to each other every two or three days and she had already heard about Angela and my days in Suffolk.

'Let's think. Work's pretty busy, we've had a big job on for Quintin Farrelly. I'm doing a bit of cleaning up in the house before Jack gets back. I called in to see Audrey and took her a picture of Ted.' Life was going on as I usually lived it, more or less.

'Yes?' Lola waited. I loved the sound of her voice and the image of her student room with its photo collage on the wall and her mess of clothes and books and the flame of a scented candle reflected in the dark window glass.

'That's all.' I smiled. Telling her anything else meant telling everything and although I didn't want to conceal from her the way I had started thinking about Ted, I wasn't ready to confide even in Lola yet. 'What about you?'

'Oh, Mum.' There was a gurgle of laughter and excitement in her voice. 'Sam and I went out last night.'

Sam was the geography student who liked hill-walking. Lola had been trying to decide whether or not to fall for him for weeks now.

'Uh-huh?'

'Yeah.'

'And?'

'He's fabulous.'

We both laughed.

'I'm glad to hear it. You deserve fabulous at the very least. Are you happy?'

'Yes, Mum, I am.'

We talked for a little while about Sam's perfection before Lola said she had to go because he was waiting to meet her.

'Call me on Sunday night, then? You'll be able to speak to Jack then as well.'

'Has he enjoyed himself?'

He had called me just once, using the phone card I'd presented him with. He hadn't exactly been forthcoming about Cherbourg, or anything else. 'Your guess is as good as mine, Lo.' I didn't mention what Audrey had said and the suspicion that had hardened in my mind.

'Yeah. And are you okay, Mum? I want *you* to be happy as well, you know.'

'I am.'

'I love you, you know.'

'I do know that. I love you too,' I told her as we rang off. Lola was so very easy to love, with her sunny self-assurance and her certainty that the world would treat her as kindly as

213

she deserved. And, like Mel, she was so happy that she wanted everyone around her to enjoy the same state of grace.

I finished swabbing down the work surfaces, scoured the sink and then dialled Mel's number. She answered at once and in the background I could hear the watery tinkle of ambient music. The candles would be lit in her pale-toned apartment too. I'd got it all wrong, I thought, spending my evening solitarily shining the kitchen taps.

'Is Jasper with you?' I asked. I didn't want to sound envious, but I probably did anyway. I would have liked very much to be with someone like Jasper tonight.

'No,' Mel said.

I heard a match strike and then an inhaled breath.

'Sadie? Are you there?'

'Of course I am. Is something wrong?' It can't be going wrong already, I thought.

'I'm scared,' Mel said.

'Why's that?'

'I'm afraid of wanting him too much. I'm afraid I'll love him so much that I'll die if some night I wake up and he isn't here. I told him to stay away for a few days, so I can slow everything down.'

I could imagine how it might feel. Mel was so used to being in control of her own life and the men she spent her time with. She had been so certain that none of them would ever measure up to her father, let alone assume a bigger role. This late exposure to the paradox that love made you cravenly vulnerable as well as invincible must indeed be frightening.

'Can you understand what I mean?'

'Yes,' I said, thinking of Stanley. For a while, after he had gone, I did indeed feel that I would prefer to die rather than live without him.

'I don't think Jasper understands.'

'No, perhaps not. But aren't you putting yourself in a lose-

lose situation, Mel? You're afraid of the loss so you go right ahead and precipitate it, have I got that right? This way you end up without him, whereas the other way you never know. And I can't see Jasper going down a similar route. Can you?'

She laughed now. 'No. He's so positive.'

And confident, I thought. That was one of his attractions. 'Listen to me. This is my advice. Go ahead and risk it. Open your heart up to whatever is going to happen. It might be the greatest passion since Antony and Cleopatra.'

'Or whatjacall'em, thingy and thingy in *Sleepless in Seattle*.' Mel had a surprising fondness for soppy films. When she was ill, she liked to lie in bed and watch *Love Story*. I had always thought that she allowed herself to be sentimental in her imagination and stayed tough in real life.

'Or on the other hand it could just break your heart. But it's better to have tried it, isn't it, than never to have been there at all?'

It was so easy to give advice, I thought, and I was the worst exemplar of what I preached. What passionate risks did I take nowadays, in my tidy life with my anxieties about children and work, and my safe web of old friends? And yet my skin did feel thinner now, and the scented fumes were rising in my head. Maybe everything was changing. Maybe I wouldn't be content any more to let Mel do the living, with her red lipstick and electric hair and appetite for everything that was new, while I sat on the sidelines safely and watched her.

Mel sighed. 'I know all that, Sade. But I'm still scared.'

'If you weren't afraid, it would mean that he wasn't important enough to you anyway.'

'Yes,' she said then. 'That's true, I do know it's important. I know he is. I'm going to call him now.'

'Good idea.'

'Thanks, Sadie.'

'You're welcome,' I said.

The next day was Saturday. I moved the furniture around in Jack's bedroom and hoovered in the corners before pushing everything back into place again, and I pinned up the corners of his curling bird posters, and dusted the books and encylopaedias. In the evening I went to the cinema with Caz and Graham, and we came back and ate a late last scratch supper in their old kitchen. All the china ornaments including the painted cat had been taken off the shelves and packed in boxes, and there were dark rectangles on the walls where pictures that were so familiar that no one ever spared them a glance had once hung. They were moving out in three days' time and they were both tetchy with the strain of it. Everything was changing.

On Sunday afternoon I drove over to school to collect Jack. I hung around with the other parents for the inevitable half-hour before the delayed buses finally turned the corner. The previous week's scenes reversed themselves as shouting children poured down the steps and struggled round the piles of luggage. Jack was one of the last to emerge. I skipped through the crowd and put my arms round him. He wriggled away after the briefest submission to my hug and a just discernible returned pressure.

'Did you have a good time?'

'It was okay.'

The other families were dispersing with their chattering kids. I carried Jack's holdall back to where I had parked the car. I didn't see Mr Rainbird anywhere.

Back at home, Jack glared at his sparkling bedroom. 'It's all moved around in here.'

'I had a clean-up. I didn't throw anything out or anything, I just dusted.'

He whirled round to face me. 'Don't touch my stuff.'

'Jack.'

'I don't want you fiddling with my things. This is my room and you should leave it alone.'

216

I closed the door, although of course there was no one else in the house to overhear anything. 'Let's talk about this.'

'No.' He had already taken his binoculars out of his backpack. He unbuttoned the leather case and rubbed his thumb over one of the knurled screws with his eyes fixed longingly on the window. He wanted to resume his study of the pigeons and not to have a confrontation with me. I sat down on the bed and let a minute of silence tick away while Jack fiddled with the binoculars and birds sat on the roof ridge opposite like a feathered jury.

Now was as good a time as any, I thought. Otherwise we'd settle back into our routine of question and non-answer. I said quietly, 'Let's not talk about dusting, then. Let's talk about you and me.' He kept his head turned away and I couldn't tell if he was listening. 'You see, I'm afraid of things going wrong between us. If we don't talk to each other about anything at all, except to ask if supper's ready or to argue about house cleaning, the silence will just grow and get deeper, and in the end we won't know how to break it, ever. You can tell me to leave you alone or ask me to go away, if that's how it's got to be, but I'm still your mum, Jack, and I care about you more than anything in the world.'

He went on fixedly not looking at me.

'It's all right to talk to you like this, isn't it, even if you won't answer? There are some things I want to tell you that might help you to understand why all this is important. One of them is that I was very unhappy when I was your age. Your gran died – you know that – and there was Grandad and me left in the house on our own. Just like this.' I made a gesture that took in the two of us and the four walls. 'Only Grandad was never there for me to talk to.'

'Why?'

The monosyllable took me by surprise. He was listening, then.

'He went out to work. He had to do that, of course. He had girlfriends, and he liked to go out and enjoy himself with them. It didn't suit him to have a child to look after and he was selfish about his own pleasures. And I was jealous and therefore probably quite demanding.'

That was a fair summary, I thought. I didn't want to demonise Ted in his grandson's eyes.

'There were other things too that I didn't understand so well, to do with money. He borrowed money from people and didn't pay it back, and when they came looking for him he used to disappear. I'm only just beginning to understand that he behaved like that probably, but I'll never know for sure now, to protect me. I never realised that he didn't want me to be, what's the word, tainted? But the sad thing is that I would much rather have known what was happening to him and been allowed to know him better. What happened was that we drifted further and further apart as I grew up, and even right at the end, when he was lying there in the hospital in Bedford, we couldn't connect with each other again.'

Jack said nothing.

'I wanted to tell him that I loved him and I didn't manage it. So I'm telling you now that I love you and I always want to be here. If you'll let me.'

I was going to break the cycle somehow. I wished I could have sounded more eloquent, but too much language might have edged Jack further away.

Jack still said nothing. The assurance would never spill from him with Lola's ease, I knew that. But he couldn't make himself speak at all and I felt his confusion and also his stubbornness. I knew I *was* the enemy to Jack. Maybe the best thing I could do for him was accept it and not mind too much.

'You're always here, Mum,' he said. He made a little enclosing movement with his hands to indicate that I fenced him in with my anxiety and possessiveness. Perhaps Tony was right and I did try too much. So did parents always get it wrong, however hard they tried? I wondered. Or was my family alone in this?

I smiled and stood up. 'And always will be.'

He took up his binoculars again in evident relief. 'Am I going to Dad's next weekend?'

It was the weekend he was due to go, according to our usual arrangement. 'Yes. If you want to, of course.'

He nodded. 'Yeah. I do.'

'Good.' I kissed the top of his dusty head quickly, before he could avoid it. 'Let's unpack your things and put them in the machine. I'm making penne with tuna for supper.' One of his favourites.

'Okay.' He sighed.

The damp clothes in his bag smelled of sea water, and a scatter of sand fell out on the carpet as I unfurled them. After some prodding Jack admitted that they had had sailing lessons in the harbour, and long hikes with map-reading tests, and that Wes and some of the others had got drunk on red wine bought at the Hypermarché. 'Dean Gower puked up in the bunk room,' he said. 'It was all red.'

'Lovely.'

'Mr Rainbird cleared it up. He was okay about it.'

'Was he? What was the best bit of the trip?'

'There was a huge colony of nesting guillemots on some cliffs right by the centre.'

The next morning Jack went to school without a word of protest. He said he would be late back, because he was going to Bird Club.

I put the finishing touches to Colin's book. It looked extremely handsome in its fat red slipcase with his name blind tooled on the spine and front. Penny was working on a stack of Law Reports and Cassie was perched on a stool at the end of her bench. She had a pile of Duplo bricks spread around her and banged at them busily with a small wooden hammer. 'My work,' she said seriously. 'I'm busy, thank you.'

Penny told me that Cassie's childminder was ill and Evelyn couldn't miss her morning's class. She was training to be a reflexologist. I said it was lovely to have Cassie with us while we worked, which it was, but I looked around from my job every twenty seconds to make sure she hadn't picked up a stray scalpel or decided to eat glue.

At midday Colin arrived. He bustled in with his raincoat done up to the neck, even though it was a warm day. 'Is my book ready at last?' he asked. I had telephoned his mother only an hour earlier to say that it was waiting for him.

'Here you are,' I said and put the heavy volume into his hands. Penny and Cassie both watched as he took the book out of its case, pursing his lips as he checked his name and flipped the thick creamy pages. The magazine cuttings each sat in a specially cut pocket, grouped into menu sections and titled in flowing sepia calligraphy. He looked at every page, breathing through his mouth as he slid the greasy cuttings in and out of the pockets and squinted at the titles.

'What do you think?' I asked.

At last he nodded. 'It looks very nice,' he said and a smile briefly transformed his face. With his thick features and unlined skin, he looked disconcertingly like a plump schoolboy when he smiled.

'I hoped you would be pleased,' I said.

'Yes. Yes, I'm quite pleased, as a matter of fact. My mum will like it.'

'What's this man?' Cassie asked loudly.

'This is Colin,' I told her. 'He's a customer of ours.'

'Colin,' she repeated.

Rather surprisingly, because he rarely betrayed any interest in anyone or anything except his own concerns, Colin immediately tucked his book under his arm and strode round to Cassie's side of the bench. Penny and I took two steps closer to her.

'What's your name?' he asked her.

She told him in a clear voice. Evelyn was an unconventional mother but her methods meant that Cassie was used to adult company and questions.

'Do you want to see my book?'

'Yes, please. It's red,' Cassie said. She reached out to touch it as soon as he placed it on the bench but he hoisted it out of her reach.

'No dirty fingermarks, thank *you*.'

She rested her chin on her clenched fists and looked at the pages with obedient interest as he turned them over for her. Penny and I shrugged at each other behind his back.

'Writing,' Cassie said, pointing at the titles with her chubby finger.

'Yes, it's writing,' Colin agreed. 'Now I can get on with my cookery. It's been quite a nuisance that it's all taken so long, I can tell you, but I suppose it was worth it in the end.'

'I've got my book.' Cassie offered him one of hers.

'That's not quite the same,' Colin said, but quite kindly. 'Well, now, I'd better get home because my mum's waiting to see this.' He tucked the book into its case and slid the whole thing into a plastic supermarket bag that he drew from inside his mac. 'I'll be off, then.'

I handed him a sealed envelope. 'Our invoice,' I said discreetly.

He frowned and drew himself up. 'What's this?'

'It's our bill. For binding your recipes.' I had given some thought to this tricky question. In the end I had arbitrarily decided on £110. This didn't reflect anything like the amount of time spent on the job, but I felt that on the other hand it wasn't an insultingly low figure and it also represented the payment we might reasonably expect actually to get from him.

His frown gathered intensity as he ripped open the envelope and unfolded the single sheet of paper. 'What's this?' he repeated.

I explained again. Cassie was watching with great interest but Penny had suddenly got very busy with her Law Reports.

'A hundred and ten *pounds*?'

'That's right.'

'Books don't cost that much. I know that perfectly well. Do you think I was born yesterday? Hardback books cost fifteen or sixteen pounds. The ones with pictures cost maybe twenty-five. I looked in Smith's, you know.'

'Yes, but that's . . .'

'You're just trying to take advantage, aren't you? But I'm no fool, you know. Oh no.'

'*Oh* no,' Cassie agreed, wagging her head just like Colin.

He took out his wallet and counted out two tenners and five pound coins. 'There you are. That's for you.'

'Thank you,' Cassie prompted me.

I bit the insides of my cheeks. 'Right, Colin,' I managed to say. 'Thank you.' I took the money to the till and rang up the sale while he tore the invoice into quarters and dropped it on the counter.

'I know what's what. I'm not one of these people who can't even speak the Queen's English, am I?'

He took his book and sailed to the door. 'Bye, Cassie,' he said, ignoring Penny and me. 'I'll be seeing you again.'

'Bye-bye.' Cassie beamed and gave him her wave.

Penny and I kept our faces straight until the door closed behind him. Cassie gazed at the two of us and then happily joined in the laughter.

'I think you should be glad of the twenty-five quid,' Penny gasped. 'Andy and Leo bet me a fiver you wouldn't get anything out of him at all.'

'He's a funny man,' Cassie said.

'He certainly is,' I agreed.

Quintin Farrelly came in at three o'clock to pick up six rare books that I had restored and rebound for him in full calf. He paid up immediately and in full as he always did, and I wished we had a few more customers like him, as I always did.

After he had gone Evelyn put her head round the door. 'I'm back,' she told us. She was wearing a tiered gipsy skirt and pointed-toe cowboy boots.

'Mummy,' Cassie shouted and slithered off her stool to run to her.

With Cassie in her arms Evelyn wheedled, 'Pen, why don't you stop for half an hour and have a cup of tea with me? I really want to tell you what happened in class.'

Penny hesitated and I said, 'Let's shut up early. We've got Colin sorted out and Quintin's cheque to put in the bank.'

I had something I wanted to do, too.

I walked home beside the khaki canal water, but of course our house was empty when I reached it. Jack had told me he would be late because of Bird Club. I left the house again and drove straight to Turnmill Street. I had to park at the very far end because the road was lined with cars and I was still sitting in the driver's seat when I glanced up and saw Jack in the distance. He walked straight up to Audrey's house without seeing my car and turned in at the gate. I couldn't see her front door from this angle but he stood on the step for only a few seconds.

Ever since Audrey had said *That's right* I had been guessing that Bird Club was a fiction and this was where he was spending his after-school hours.

I locked the car now and took five steps towards the house before I stopped. I tried to reconcile uncomfortable feelings: I didn't want Jack to have secrets from me, any more than I wanted to keep what I knew from him. I was jealous of Audrey because my son chose to spend his after-school hours with her and unhappy, but not very surprised, to discover that he needed to lie about his whereabouts.

I walked another ten paces, then stopped again. I didn't like the picture from any angle.

A woman pushing a double buggy gave me a hard look as she passed. I walked on down Turnmill Street and came close to Audrey's peeling gateposts. I had intended to knock on her door and ask if Jack was there. I would be brisk and friendly but I would make it clear that I wanted to know whom my son visited after school and why neither of them had told me about it. Now I couldn't ask the question because I already knew the answer, and I would seem to be spying on my child even if it had come about by accident.

I don't like secrets, I was going to say, but a cold fingertip of memory pressed at the nape of my neck and I shivered. I hated secrets; Ted had concealed himself from me within the tissue of secrecy and the musty, guilty smell of that place made sudden tears sting at the back of my eyes. If I tried to confront Audrey now, with her anger under its thin veil and her air of knowing more about my life than I knew myself, I might reveal too much of myself to her.

I wheeled round yet again and made my way back towards the car. I felt cowardly in my retreat and also lonely, but this time I kept on walking. I would go home and wait until Jack appeared for supper.

While I waited I peeled potatoes and transferred clothes from the washer to the dryer. I sat at the kitchen table and wrote a shopping list, then turned on the six o'clock news but didn't listen to the headlines. At last I heard Jack's key in the lock. His bag thumped on the floor of the hall and his trainers dragged down the stairs to the kitchen. He went to the fridge and took out a carton of orange juice while I sat at the table and waited.

'Hi, Mum,' he said in the end, registering my failure to ask how his day had been and whether he was hungry. Then he looked at me. 'What's up?' he asked.

While I told him he stood with his head hanging, nudging at the corner of the fridge with the toe of his trainer. 'You shouldn't have been watching me,' he said.

'I'm sorry it looks like that. I didn't intend it to happen that way, but if you hadn't been going to Audrey's without telling me it couldn't have happened, could it?'

'No.'

'Why didn't you tell me?'

He glared at me. 'Because I didn't want you to know, all right? I like it at Audrey's. I feed the animals and play with the cats. We don't say all that much, if that's what you want to know. Audrey's quite quiet. She lets me just, like, be there.'

Unlike his mother.

'Anyway, it's only going round to some old friend of Grandad's. It's no major deal, is it? There's a whole lot *worse* things I could be doing.'

'I know that. I just wish you didn't have to tell me you're somewhere when in fact you're somewhere quite different.'

He held his head up now. 'Yeah. Well, I knew you wouldn't want me going there. I'm not sure why and it doesn't really bother me all that much. And you didn't have to go and find out, did you?'

He was right, in part. Jack was intelligent and I felt a distinct surge of admiration for my son's reasoning. It was Audrey who was the problem.

I cooked supper and we sat at opposite ends of the table to eat it. Jack read a bird book and I frowned at the *Evening Standard*. There was a lot of coverage of pending tube and bus strikes. When he had cleared the table and put our plates and cutlery in the dishwasher, Jack said he was going to bed. He gave me an awkward kiss but when I tried to catch him in a hug he stepped out of my reach.

I waited until I was sure he was safely in his room, then dialled Audrey's number.

The abrupt way she said 'Yes?' was becoming familiar.

'I want to talk to you about Jack.'

'Is that so?'

I had tried to make my voice sound neutral, but hers was spiky with hostility.

'I know that he was at your house today, Audrey. I think he's been visiting you quite a lot lately, hasn't he? And I wanted to try and work out, with your help I hope, why he feels that he has to lie to me about it. He's been telling me he goes to an ornithology club at his school.'

'How much working out does that require?'

'Why my son lies to me?'

'Why he prefers you to think he's elsewhere, rather than at my house.'

I took a breath to keep my voice steady. 'Perhaps you could tell me why you let Jack spend his afternoons with you under false pretences? I might not have made any objection, yet you both assume that I would, and you cut me out right from the beginning. I don't think it's correct for you to establish a relationship with him that's based on a falsehood. I don't . . .'

'Why does what's *correct* matter so much to you?'

'Because I'm his mother. It's my responsibility to teach him to tell the truth. I try to give him the right guidelines.'

Audrey sniffed. 'You like control, Sadie. You like your child to be where you want him to be and act the way you want him to act, and reflect the happy family glow right back at you. And if you understood that, you might get a bit closer to knowing why Jack doesn't want to be at home and doesn't tell you where he is. He doesn't care to be controlled by you or anyone else. I didn't know he was lying to you, as it happens. He didn't volunteer the information and I didn't ask him. But I can't say I'm surprised to hear it. How did you find out where he was today?'

'I saw him arrive. I was parking my car at the end of the street, on my way to see you.'

'And now you know. Does that make you feel better?'

I couldn't fathom Audrey's hostility. I wasn't an enemy. Why was she determined to make me into one?

'No,' I said. I had been imagining that Jack and I were just at adolescent cross-purposes, as Lola and Caz and Graham also believed. I thought I could put matters right between us by an effort of will. But now an abyss had opened up and as I peered down from the edge of it into windy darkness I was afraid that I might lose him altogether.

'I'm sorry for assuming you were party to the lie,' I managed to say. Actually, I thought that Audrey was likely to have understood the situation perfectly clearly, but I still shouldn't have made the accusation.

She ignored the apology anyway. 'What are you going to do, then? Forbid him to come round to my place?'

'I don't think I can do that, can I? I could ask you to make sure that your influence on him is a positive one.'

Audrey gave a derisive hoot. 'Jack's old enough and more than intelligent enough to make his own judgements about influence, don't you think?'

Her aggression stung me. 'Why are you being so bloody unhelpful? I don't understand what's the matter with you or what makes you so hostile, but if you want to stay in touch with my family, for Ted's sake or Jack's or your own, you could try to see my point of view. My concern's for Jack.'

'You're a priggish woman, Sadie, do you know that?'

'Maybe I am,' I breathed.

'Goodnight,' Audrey said calmly. And she hung up.

I walked around the kitchen, steadying myself. The waves of anger slowly subsided as I made myself a cup of tea and sat down at the table to drink it. My next instinct was to call Mel or Caz and summon their support in refuting what Audrey had said. But I knew I should deal with this alone. I sat for a long time and tried to disentangle the threads of truth from the mess of resentment.

I did need to control my life, because I had grown up in confusion. Lola had rebelled against that control in all the usual ways, and Jack was choosing to make his protest in a different but equally characteristic manner.

I was a bit of a prig, with my ideas about duty and truth. Audrey was right about that.

And I also loved my children. I would hold on to that.

ELEVEN

On the following Friday evening I drove Jack over to his father's house in Twickenham. As soon as Tony opened the door to us he held out his arms to Jack and they stood under the porch swaying together in a long hug.

'Go on in, son,' Tony said when they finally broke apart. He kissed me lightly on the cheek as I edged into the porch too.

'Bye, Mum,' Jack called and vanished into the house.

'Are you coming in for a drink?' Tony asked. 'Suzy's just putting the girls to bed.'

Past his shoulder I could see toys and shoes and an overturned tricycle blocking the hallway, superficial evidence of the close chaos of life with small children. I smiled at him. 'I won't, thanks. I've got to get back.'

'Okay.' My ex-husband looked relieved and also embarrassed by his relief. Suzy and I didn't have much in common except Tony himself, and our encounters were always slightly uncomfortable.

'Is everyone well?' I asked.

'Yeah, fine. I'll bring him back on Sunday evening, then.'

'Thanks.' I nodded. This was our usual arrangement. 'Have a good time.'

Even after all these years, it felt strange to be walking away from Tony. The sound of his voice and his silhouette against the lighted hall were so minutely familiar. I knew just what it would be like, if Suzy and the twins were to be somehow dematerialised, if I were to go inside now and sit down to family dinner with him and Jack. I knew what we would talk about and what Tony's responses would be to my remarks, and the exact way he would sit on the sofa after dinner and go through some papers from work.

As I drove back across London in the dusk I was thinking that was why I wasn't in the house in Twickenham. I still loved Tony and I knew his face and the shape of his hands and the weight of his body as well as I know my own. We met when I was still at art college. I went to a party, wandered into the kitchen in search of something to drink and there was Tony. He was standing at the sink washing glasses, smoking a cigarette between clenched teeth and talking volubly out of the other side of his mouth to a girl with spiky eyelashes painted on her lower lids.

'Here's a glass,' he told me, squinting through the smoke and handing one over, 'and there's the Vino Collapso. Pour me one as well, will you?'

It wasn't love at first sight. We moved in the same circle and kept bumping into each other. In the end he asked me out and on our first date he came to pick me up, at exactly the appointed time, in his Triumph Herald. He was already working in advertising. He drove me home again afterwards, too. He was never late, never cancelled, never kept me guessing. And very quickly, amazingly, he did fall in love with me. I was wary to begin with and then I eagerly gave way. Tony offered me delicious safety and the reassurance of unconditional love after Ted's shiftiness, and I grabbed hold of him.

It was only much later that I discovered safety wasn't what I wanted after all.

Stanley, on the other hand, was a showcase of theatrical attitudes and unpredictability. On Valentine's Day he carved our entwined initials into every stripped pine floorboard and door panel in our living room, and a month later he completely forgot my birthday. He could be dazzlingly generous, as when he saw me longingly stroke a cashmere sweater that I couldn't afford and came home the next evening with the same sweater in six different shades, and as mean as the time he made me pay exactly half the cost of the petrol we used to drive up to Sunderland to visit his mother.

Ted adored him. Of course he did, because they were so alike.

'He's a bit of a shyster, you know, your boyfriend. But he's bloody good fun.'

He was very disappointed when Stanley left me but there had also been more than a whiff of male solidarity.

'Damned shame. But then, you are a bit older than him and you have got two kids. I suppose that's not what a chap like Stanley really wants, in the long run, is it?'

Tony and Stanley were the male polar opposites that drew my wavering compass needle, after I left Ted behind. Once Stanley had gone I was trying to make up to Lola and Jack for the dismantling of their family and there hadn't been much time or space left over for lovers. I had had plenty of good friends instead.

But I still felt twenty-seven under the skin, whatever the external evidence might suggest to the contrary. It wasn't too late.

When I reached home I wasn't ready to go straight inside. I strolled up our street past the area steps and lit basement windows to the Tesco Metro near the tube station. As Jack was going to be away I hadn't bothered with the weekend shopping and there was no food in the house. I bought chicken and some cheese and salad, then walked a little way along the high street. There was a noisy, turbulent atmosphere of Friday night festivity, with City boys in shirtsleeves outside

231

bars and barelegged girls lurching along the kerb. Crawling buses belched out fumes and the air stank of diesel and frying onions. In an hour or so, at closing time, all this would probaby turn ugly. I peeled away from the crowds and made my way back home through the quiet side streets.

Once I was inside I didn't cook even the simple meal I had planned. I shoved the food haphazardly into the fridge and turned to the telephone instead. Caz and Graham were in the new house and I planned to go over in the morning to help with some unpacking. Mel and Jasper had gone to Paris for a long weekend and Lola was with Sam. The world seemed as crowded with couples as the Ark.

Without giving myself time to think further I opened my purse and extracted the folded piece of paper with Mr Rainbird's telephone number written on it.

'Hello. It's Sadie Thompson here,' I said when he answered.

'Yes, I recognise your voice.'

I rested my forehead on my free hand, wondering what I thought I was doing. 'How are you?'

'Very well, thank you. I'm just doing some marking.' We listened to the distance between us and tried to work out what to say next. It was a long time since I'd done anything like this and I was relieved when he took the initiative. 'I was wondering if you would like to see a film or have dinner with me?'

'Yes, I would, thank you. Maybe both? We could go to the cinema and have dinner afterwards, perhaps?' This is right, this is how it goes.

'Are you by any chance free tomorrow evening?'

'Well, yes,' I said. 'As it happens, I am free.'

'I'll come and pick you up. Would about six suit you?' He spoke quickly, as if I might change my mind otherwise.

I gave him my address.

—⁓—

'Jack's head of year, eh?' Caz said. We were taking her milk jugs and meat dishes out of their packing case nests and putting them away.

'Mm.' I unwrapped the china cat and put him on the mantelpiece. He looked dusty and displaced in this new setting, and I ran my finger consolingly down his painted back.

'What's he like?'

'Rather crumpled, quizzical, sympathetic. Like an English teacher, in fact. One of the kids got drunk on the school trip and threw up everywhere. Jack said Mr Rainbird cleared it up and was quite nice about it.'

Caz straightened up from her packing case and blew upwards so her fringe lifted off her forehead. 'God. Grab him.'

'Caz, we're going to see a film together. He hasn't asked me to marry him.'

'Would you like him to?'

I started a laugh but it got caught in my throat. 'No. Not at all. I'm an independent woman. I'm happy to stay the way I am.'

Caz raised an eyebrow. 'That sounds like Mel's mantra. "Men, who needs them? Use 'em and lose 'em." '

'And look what's happened to *her*.'

Caz nodded. 'Yeah. Well, Jasper's a bit of a dish, isn't he? Your Mr Rainbird seems all right, too. It's nice for some, I must say. Here are you and Mel, both of you going out to dinners and having an exotic time and the possibility of interesting sex. I'm jealous.'

We both looked out through the patio doors into the small garden where Graham was irritably stowing garden tools in a lopsided shed. I was reddening with embarrassment at the mere thought of having sex with Jack's head of year. Then my eyes met Caz's and we laughed, duly acknowledging but not needing to calibrate the prolonged and intricate compromises of marriage against the daily tiny exposures of being single.

'I'm not going to sleep with him. Anyway, would you really want to swap places?'

'No. I couldn't deal with all that business of having to wear matching underclothes,' Caz said.

Mr Rainbird rang the doorbell at four and a half minutes past six. I invited him in and he followed me down the stairs to the kitchen.

'You look . . . very nice,' he said.

I felt flattered, because he clearly meant it. 'Thank you. So do you.'

He was wearing a black linen jacket over a plain T-shirt and the crisp line over his ears and at the nape of his neck suggested that he had just had a haircut. He patted his elbows. 'The other jacket's the corduroy one with leather patches.'

'Really? I think of you in the Marilyn T-shirt.'

'That's just my gig outfit.' He looked pleased that I remembered, though. I gave him a glass of wine.

'Where's Jack?' he asked.

'Gone to his dad's for the weekend.'

'Ah.' I couldn't tell whether he was relieved at this news. 'What will he think about me taking you out like this? Does he know?'

I liked the way he chose to bring this up immediately. I had been asking myself the same question and the answer was almost certainly horrified. 'No, not yet. But I'll tell him all about it tomorrow.'

Mr Rainbird nodded. 'I'll hope for a good report, then.'

We drove to the local multiplex in his car, a green Morris Minor estate complete with timbered sides. I admired it and he grinned.

'It belonged to my dad. He was going to sell it, but I wouldn't let him. I swapped him my Honda in the end, just to keep his in the family. I'm not very interested in cars, I just like this one.'

'So do I. Is your dad still alive? What did he do?'

'Yeah, he is. He was a teacher, too. Physics. And my mum

taught home economics. It was DS, domestic science, in those days.'

'I remember.'

'She died last year. I miss her, but not as much as he does. They were married for fifty years and they were always each other's best friend. I remember you telling me that Jack's grandfather died last term. Was that your father?'

'Yes.'

He waited, but when I didn't volunteer anything he didn't press me any further. We negotiated a skirl of traffic at the roundabout and failed to overtake a bus that greedily straddled the outside edge of the bus lane.

'Not much power under her bonnet,' Mr Rainbird said fondly.

I enjoyed not being the driver and therefore not having to search for a parking space once we reached the cinema. I sat comfortably in my seat instead, and gazed at the late shoppers coming into the car park with their Debenhams and Dixons bags.

There was a choice of three films and rather than the Mel Gibson war epic or the family special effects movie we settled unanimously on the starry adaptation of a Booker prize-winning novel. Mr Rainbird bought the tickets and I judged that it would be inappropriate to offer to pay for my own. We rejected popcorn, also unanimously, and settled into our seats. I often went to the cinema with Lola and Jack, or with Mel and it felt different to be sitting with my arm almost touching Mr Rainbird's.

I liked the film, but I couldn't have answered many questions about it afterwards. I was smiling as we walked out at the end with all the other couples, blinking slightly in the glare of lights and threading our way through the press of people waiting for the next screening.

Mr Rainbird lightly touched my elbow. 'I thought we might eat at Casa Flore?'

This was an excellent choice, our neighbourhood non-pretentious old-fashioned Italian restaurant. Even Mel approved of it.

It was full, but he had booked a table. We sat opposite each other in a corner between the Technicolor painting of the Amalfi sunset and the shell sculpture that doubled as a wall lantern.

'Jack seemed to enjoy the Cherbourg holiday,' Mr Rainbird said, looking at me over the leather-bound menu.

'Did he?' I was pleased to hear this. 'He didn't have a lot to say about it when he got home, except for the guillemot colony on the cliffs and someone throwing up in the bunk room.'

'Yes, that last was definitely the highlight of the trip for most of them. He didn't say much while we were there either, but he was part of it all. Jack's an observer but he's not an isolate. And he's very knowledgeable about birds.'

'Thank you for looking out for him,' I said.

'It was a pleasure,' Mr Rainbird answered and again I knew that this was the truth. There was an openness about him, a transparency that didn't in any way suggest simplicity.

We ordered our pasta and scallopa Milanese, and when they arrived I was surprised to get the full brandished-peppermill and bella-signora treatment from the waiter, a first in all the times I had eaten here with Lola and Jack or Caz and Graham. Either I was more attention worthy because I appeared to be half of a couple, or I just looked different tonight.

We discussed the film. Mr Rainbird had read the book, which I had not, and he knew all the author's other books as well, and he talked about them in a way that made me want to read them too. I thought he was probably a very good teacher. We went on to talk about what we had both been reading lately, and then I told him about the business of bookbinding and how the physical shape and form of a book could affect my response to it. I mentioned Colin's volume of recipes and the way that a carrier bagful of greasy magazine clippings had become something quite imposing.

He laughed at the story but then he said, 'It was generous of you to do all that.'

'I couldn't afford to do it too often. Penny and I don't have a very fat profit margin.'

Mr Rainbird smiled. 'Just the same, it sounds to me as though you have the balance of your life about right.'

'In most things,' I agreed. 'And you?'

A small silence shivered between us, made more noticeable by the clamour of the restaurant. There were things he could have said that might have made him sound needy or lonely or anxious, or on the other hand smug, but he didn't utter any of them. 'More or less,' he agreed.

I wanted to hear some more. 'You said you'd split up with your girlfriend?'

He looked as if he didn't mind me bringing it up. 'About six months ago.'

'How long were you together?'

'Ten years. God, that's a long time, isn't it?'

'About two-thirds as long as I was married to Tony. Did she leave?'

'No, I left her. We both knew it wasn't working any longer. But when it finally came to separating she wasn't very happy.'

I liked the strength of mind that his decision implied. I know it takes courage to walk out of a long relationship. Thinking of Tony and me, and of Stanley from whom I hadn't heard in years even though I had once imagined that I couldn't draw a single breath apart from him, I asked, 'Did you have someone else?'

'No. I still don't.'

I found myself looking as if for the first time at the shape of his face. There was a new noise in my ears that I identified as the circulation of my blood. The sudden awareness that I was attracted to someone – to *him*, to Jack's English teacher – was so startling that it left me without anything to say.

Then he added, 'I think I talked too much, when we were sitting out on the fire escape the other night. You made it seem easy to talk.'

'Do you wish you hadn't?'

'I might have wanted to give a better impression of myself, first off.'

I smiled. 'Don't worry about that.'

'I suppose the fact that you're here now means I needn't.'

We had shared a bottle of Montepulciano and had become absorbed in our conversation. I saw his hand lift slightly from where it rested on the tablecloth, as if he were going to cover mine with it, but then decided that this wouldn't be the right move after all. He lifted the wine bottle instead and poured the last drops into my glass.

'You were going to Suffolk. Did you enjoy it?'

'Your part of the world, I remember. I went to visit an old friend of my father's. I wanted to talk about him to someone who knew him.'

'My father and I talk about Mum a lot. Just remembering her. The way she said things, like she always used to say braces and belt, not belt and braces. She used to cut the crusts off sandwiches and slice them into triangles, even if it was only for me. So I know what you mean.'

I almost thought, no you don't. But it wasn't so easy to dismiss Mr Rainbird. He might also be easy to talk to.

'Did it help?' he asked.

'I'll tell you about it. Some day, not tonight. I mean, it's not anything enormous. Just the past, you know.' The past, that inaccessible territory.

'All right,' he said easily.

We had finished the wine and drunk our coffee.

'Shall we go?' he asked.

I nodded and he called for the bill. I offered to pay half but he shook his head.

'It'll be my turn next time, then.'

'I'd like that,' he said. We seemed to have passed the point where it was necessary to negotiate whether or not there would be another evening. In his quiet way, Mr Rainbird was just as confident as Jasper.

Outside there was still greenish-blue light in the sky and I could hear the last calls of birds going to roost in the trees of the green opposite Casa Flore. It was mid-June, another warm city night.

'Come and look at something,' Mr Rainbird said. He crooked his arm and without thinking I slipped mine through it. He wasn't much taller than me and we walked easily in step, shoulder to shoulder.

He guided me through the traffic and we crossed the corner of the green, then turned down a street diagonally opposite. I was thinking of all the similar little networks that made up London's vast nervous system, when Mr Rainbird stopped at the entrance to a narrow alley. There was a tall iron gate blocking the alley itself, but another one just wide enough for pedestrians stood open at the side. He stood aside to let me through. On the other side of the gate I felt the pressure of cobblestones through the thin soles of my shoes.

I had known about this turning, of course, and had glanced down it in passing, but this was the first time I had walked along here.

There was a perfect double row of tiny houses, each with its miniature square of front garden separated from the alley by a low wall. The houses had little gables surmounted by Gothic lace ironwork and the tiny double bay windows were capped with an exuberant finial of wrought iron. Down the centre of the street stood a row of lampstands with curved brackets and iron stems twisted like barley sugar. The gas mantles had been replaced by electric bulbs, but their light was still appropriately yellow and dim.

I knew that these were almshouses, built a hundred and fifty years ago by a philanthropic Victorian ironmaster for poor but virtuous women of the parish. It wanted only a few inches of snow to make the perfect Christmas card scene. The white flowers of nicotiana and tumbling Iceberg roses shone through the dusk instead and I half closed my eyes to make snow of them.

We walked slowly to the end, admiring the perfection.

'How many poor but virtuous live here now?' I wondered. The alley was gentrified to the point of caricature and the almshouses probably changed hands for half a million apiece.

'Oh, I expect there may conceivably be virtuous lawyers and television executives and bankers.' Mr Rainbird laughed. 'But definitely no poor ones along here.'

We were just turning back again when there was a sudden scuffle. The end of the alley finished in an even narrower short cobbled passage, just wide enough to admit a person, leading out to another ordinary street. Two dark figures burst from the passage mouth and ran headlong towards us. They were wearing hooded tops and their feet and hands seemed freakishly huge. Mr Rainbird pulled me aside and stood in front of me, but one of the runners knocked him as he pounded by and we both staggered against the wall of the nearest garden. Mr Rainbird caught me and I heard myself give an involuntary squeak of fear. Then the runners were gone out of the gate at the other end, leaving the echo of loud laughter in their wake.

'It's okay, they're just kids,' Mr Rainbird said. I stood still for a second longer, my head close to his chest, imagining that I could hear his slow, steady heartbeat. He was used to the behaviour of huge children, of course, living as he did in the tidal waves of them at Jack's school. I detached myself carefully, breathing hard. The sudden eruption of threat in this enclave of prettiness had frightened me more than I wanted to acknowledge. There I had been, thinking of the city as a vastly amorphous but basically benign organism; now there seemed to be only a thin veneer of order crusted over a boiling crater of unrest. I shook my head to dispel the unwelcome idea.

'Are you all right?'

'Yes,' I said. The alley was quiet again, with its lighted windows just showing behind good curtains and the white glimmer of flowers in the dark. We walked back to the car and Mr Rainbird drove me home. The pavements surged with people all the way and the roads pulsed with steady gouts of traffic.

'I'll call you,' he said, when we drew up outside the house. He kissed me lightly on the cheek.

'I'd like that,' I said.

I noticed that he waited while I fumbled with my keys and let myself in, and only drove off when the front door shut safely behind me.

The house was very silent and empty. I went round methodically switching on lights and drawing the curtains, with unease crawling in my veins. It was gone eleven but I was sure Penny would still be up. She answered her phone on the second ring.

My anxiety irrationally focused on Cassie. 'Is everything all right?'

'It's late, Sadie.'

'Is Cassie asleep?'

'Yes, of course she is. Hours ago.'

I exhaled with relief. 'Good. That's fine. And what are you doing?'

'Just reading. Evelyn's out somewhere with Jerry. In the interests of "establishing a better relationship", as she puts it, which I interpret as finding out whether or not she really wants to have another baby with him and therefore whether or not to sleep with him. For purely mechanical purposes, of course.'

I heard the desolation in my friend's voice and at the same time a distant police siren. In my mind's eye I saw the blue light needling its way up the high street.

'Penny, there's nothing you can do about it.'

'Nothing short of going round to his place with a paring knife and slicing his obtrusive balls off, you mean?'

'Short of that, yes. I meant more that Evelyn will do what she wants to do' – of course she would – 'and all you can do is wait and let her know that you love her and Cassie. Evelyn's not a fool,' I concluded. I meant that she knew how much Penny loved her, but also that she would make the inevitable calculation about who was better placed to look after her and her child.

Penny let this pass. 'We've got Cassie, at least,' she said.

I thought of her childish fragrance under the quilt in the top bedroom and the cat's-cradle structure of the gasometers outside her window. 'Yes,' I agreed. 'Goodnight, Pen. I just wanted to know you were there. And to let you know that I'm here.'

'Thank you,' Penny said.

I went round the house turning off the lights again. I made a cup of tea and took it upstairs, sitting on my bed to drink it with my knees drawn up against my chest. I wanted to draw everyone I loved best closer to me and I went through their names and faces in my mind like an incantation to ward off the unease. Jack and Lola, Tony, Mel, Penny and Cassie, Graham and Caz. And then, when I switched off the light and lay in the darkness, Ted was there, more strongly than ever, giving off his mixed scent of breezy citrus and male pheromones and indifference to my younger self.

All right, you too, I murmured. Wherever you are.

⸺⁓⸺

With the daylight, I forgot about my anxieties. Tony brought Jack home again at five o'clock in the evening. As soon as

Jack came into the house I could feel his resentment gathered inside him like a black ball. Tony followed behind, accepting my invitation to come in for a cup of tea. Downstairs in the kitchen, Jack was already glaring into the depths of the fridge.

'Did you have a nice weekend?'

'There's no cheese spread.'

'No,' I agreed.

'I'm going upstairs.'

'Don't you want a cup of tea with Dad and me?'

'No.'

'Jack . . .' Tony remonstrated but I shook my head at him.

When Jack had gone I made myself busy with cups and Marmite toast, which was what Tony and I always used to eat for Sunday tea. He laughed when he saw me taking the jar out of the cupboard. 'You're such a creature of habit, Sadie.'

'No, I'm not. Not any more.' I didn't really know whether I was or not. Habit seemed to have been forcibly taken away from me in the last few weeks.

I laid the tray and carried it over to the stool next to the sofa where Tony was sitting. He moved up to make room for me and I sat down next to him. It felt normal to be sitting knee to knee, passing cups and plates. Comfortable, even.

'How was he?' I asked.

'Moody, I suppose that's the word.'

'No, really?'

'Oh, come on, Sade, don't be sarky.' Tony chewed his toast. 'Is it girls, do you think?'

'No, I don't. Listen, I wish it was anything half as normal as that. I wish he had any friends at all, let alone a premature interest in the opposite sex.'

'He's twelve. I was interested in girls when I was twelve.'

'I know, Tony. You're not Jack, though, are you?'

'I wish I *was* twelve again.'

I laughed and he shrugged in protest. He was much more

243

creased and tired-looking than he used to be, but otherwise Tony was always the same. He was good-humoured, fundamentally optimistic and admirably loyal, even to me.

'How's work?' I asked.

'Oh, God. The toy account. The client changes his bloody mind every two hours. I've got to go to Germany first thing in the morning. What about you?'

'Quite busy. We could always do with some more, though. I would be happier all round if Jack was a bit easier to deal with.'

'He'll be all right in the end.'

'And you know that's what Lola says too. She'll be home next week.' I was happy to think that there was a whole long summer of her company ahead.

'She told me. We had a long talk on the phone yesterday.'

I nodded. Lola and her father had always managed to sustain a relationship separate from me. In the beginning, when everything about our divorce hurt more than it did now, I had felt jealous of their continuing closeness and affection but now it reassured me.

'Sadie, what's up?'

Tony pushed my hair back behind my ear and turned my face towards his. We didn't touch each other any longer, except ritually on meeting and parting. Now the friction of his fingertips made me jump and then shiver, and there was the raw feeling again, as if I had lost a layer or two of protective epidermis.

'Nothing. Why?'

'How much do you miss Ted?'

Was it missing someone who was dead, this feeling that the world had altered and that the old perspectives and measuring devices were no longer quite true or reliable?

'A bit.'

'Yes. You know, I wish I'd been at his funeral. I keep thinking about it, regretting that I wasn't there.'

Ted had never really liked Tony. He had thought my husband was dull. 'Your accountant' he had called him wilfully, because he knew well enough that in those days Tony was a junior account handler in an ad agency. 'He *looks* like an accountant,' Ted would say and shrug.

'Ted wasn't there himself,' I said. It was true. He had been entirely absent from the proceedings.

'Even so. I wish I had been.' Tony put his empty cup back on the tray and dotted up the last crumbs of toast with his forefinger before licking it clean. 'Well. I'd better head for home. I've got to finish the presentation for tomorrow, and Suzy's had a long weekend with the girls.'

'Of course. Thanks for having Jack. He misses you. Not that it's your fault,' I said hastily. 'I didn't mean that, it's just the way it is.'

Tony hugged me. 'Don't worry so much.' We liked each other, Tony and I, and there were times when I did wish we were still together, living in a comfortably battered house like Caz and Graham, mildly bickering, complaining about one another and yet vegetably entwined like ancient tree roots.

He called goodbye upstairs to Jack on his way out.

Jack appeared at the head of the stairs, his small figure outlined against the light in the stairwell. I could see the conflict between his wish to run downstairs to his father, and his anger with him for leaving and me for always being there. 'Bye,' he said. He turned away again before the door closed behind Tony.

He claimed that he had homework, so I let him eat his supper in his room.

Mel called much later, to tell me about the pictures she and Jasper had looked at together and the dinner up in Montmartre with all the lights of Paris laid out just for them.

'How wonderful,' I said.

'It was.' Mel chuckled. 'Weird, isn't it? I looked at him across the table and I thought, it's you. After all this time, it's *you*.'

'You're not afraid any more?'

'I'm still scared, yes.' And it was true, I could hear the shiver of it in her voice. 'But if it's so valuable, how could I *not* be frightened of losing it all? When I stopped seeing him I realised that I couldn't bear not to be with him. My skin felt cold. My heart seemed to beat less regularly. It's as physical as that, but it inhabits every corner of my mind as well. I didn't know that this is how it feels to be in love.'

Mel sounded humble, even awed – my dismissive, comical Mel who had always been so certain that she would never love anyone as much as she had loved her daddy.

'That's how it happens,' I said.

We made a date to have dinner together later in the week.

'Suzy makes bacon in the mornings,' Jack said at the breakfast table. His eyes looked small, as if he had slept too much.

'Really?' I wasn't going to rise to that one. I was writing overdue cheques for the telephone and electricity, to stave off the threatened disconnections. 'What have you got on at school today?'

He didn't answer.

'What time will you be home?'

A cunning look crossed his face. He poured milk into a bowl, slopping some of it on the table as he put the carton down. 'Why? Will you be here?'

'You know what time I usually get in. I have to work, Jack.'

'Suzy doesn't.'

'Well, bully for her.'

'I'm going to Audrey's after school.'

I put my biro down in the clutter covering the table. Jack

took a slow spoonful of cereal and deliberately, sloppily chewed on it while he stared defiance at me.

'What about your homework?'

'I'll do it there. Audrey helps me. She's at home, isn't she?'

'Okay.' I found the envelope for the electricity bill and stuffed the counterfoil and my cheque into it. There was no point in arguing this issue. Let him go to Audrey's, if that was what he wanted. 'Make sure you're back for supper.' I got up from the table to search for a stamp. 'And it's time to go to school now.'

He made no move. Perhaps I was getting tired of loving Jack too much.

'I don't want to go.'

'Don't, then,' I said. I found the stamps and put the letters into my bag.

By the time I was ready to leave the house, Jack was there before me.

'Say hi to Audrey for me.' I smiled.

He shrugged and hoisted his bag on to his shoulder. I watched him as he trailed away up the road and turned the corner.

As I drove to the Works I was thinking that I could turn the Audrey situation round, if I was clever enough. I would talk to Lola about it when she came home.

Two days later she was back. The house filled up with her smoky scent and her discarded clothes and mini-discs and used ashtrays. She washed all the clothes she owned, then left them damp and creased in the ironing basket while she wore mine, and she took the phone handset off its cradle and put it down where I couldn't find it on the rare occasions when it did ring for me. She poured us glasses of wine and sat on the kitchen sofa with her feet tucked under her while I cooked, talking about Sam and her life, and asking me questions about mine.

'Has he called again?'

'Once, but I was out,' I said. I had mentioned the Mr Rainbird evening to her and she had been predictably fascinated.

'Zoe Slavin from school was completely in love with him, you know,' she confided. 'And she wasn't the only one.'

'Lo, I don't want to hear.'

'Oh, don't worry. He wasn't at all sketchy around us girls. Not like Mr Allan.'

'I'm pleased to hear it.' I hadn't told Jack anything about my date with his head of year and I couldn't imagine how the right moment was going to present itself, given the current climate between us. To change the subject I said, 'I've had an idea about Audrey.' Jack was spending more time at her house now than he did at home and Lola was concerned too.

'Oh, yes?'

'We could demystify her, in Jack's eyes.'

'And how shall we do that?'

'By making her a part of the family,' I said. 'She's obviously important to Jack. And she was an old friend of Grandad's. So it would be appropriate, wouldn't it, to ask her over to Sunday lunch?'

'You could try it.' Lola grinned. 'You could certainly try and see what happens.'

TWELVE

We sat in another new restaurant, Mel and I. This one had been Mel's choice. It was very smart and much more expensive than the places we usually went to. 'This is my treat,' she said, as we settled at our table. 'I wanted to come here first with you.'

It was one of Mel's gifts to make you feel that you were the very person in all the world she longed to be with at that moment. I badly wanted to see her too – it seemed a long time since I had last had her to myself.

She fitted well in these surroundings. There were pale cream walls, leather seats and as a centrepiece a six-foot flower arrangement featuring tropical leaves and blooms like exotic birds. The tall glass windows were partly frosted but they gave enough of a view of the street to make the diners feel a privileged, soft distance from the real world. Black-suited waiters with proper French accents brought us menus and good bread, and blue glass bottles of mineral water.

'How lovely.' I sighed. It had been a long day, one of those days when I felt that I had worked hard and achieved nothing. I had made a stupid mistake in setting up some type and hadn't checked it before finishing a title, and I had had to re-cover a complicated book as a result. There was a tube strike, one of a series that had blighted the early summer, and we had both had to fight our way here through hot seething streets. But in the restaurant's plush calm it was easy enough to forget all this.

'And how modish,' Mel said, after studying the menu. 'Everything's retro.'

The food was old-fashioned French. I ordered frog's legs because I was so surprised to see them and Mel chose an endive salad with Roquefort. Neither of us wanted to forgo having the côte de boeuf with sauce béarnaise to follow, so we both ordered it.

'And it's got to be a serious burgundy to go with all that, don't you think?' Mel was looking at the wine list.

'You *are* pushing the boat out.'

She debated her choice with the sommelier at some length and then made the decision. This was my friend at her eager, hungry, inquisitive best, enjoying her surroundings and opportunities, and I loved watching her.

'It's because I'm so happy. I want to wrap my arms round everything. I want to lick this butter and kiss the greeter and go over there and snuffle up the scent of those over-the-top flowers.' Her eyes travelled over my face 'Is it all right to say that to you?'

'Yes.' Of course it was, even though I felt a little current of jealousy riding in my veins.

'I'm still scared too, I told you. I went through this stupid pantomime of "give me space, I don't want to feel so much" but then I knew I already did feel so much and it was physically painful not to see him. Then we went to Paris and it was wonderful.'

'Yes.'

'Sadie, he wants me to meet his daughter.'

'That's good, isn't it?'

'Yes, it's good.'

Her agreement still left a curlicue of doubt hanging in the air.

'Mel, she's his. You'll like her – love her – for that reason alone. And there's no chance that she won't love you back as soon as she sets eyes on you.'

Our first courses were reverently placed in front of us. With the point of my knife I carved the muscles of my frog's legs off the little bones and took a slippery mouthful. The taste of garlic and butter reminded me of the long-ago summer in Grasse when I had first tasted food like this. When I first realised how good food could be.

'Can I try some of that?'

We traded forkfuls.

'This is serious cooking.' But even though she was eating Mel was also listening intently to what I said. This was one of the foundation stones of our friendship – we ate and talked, and told each other what we were thinking. 'I'm sure you're right. I hope his daughter and I will like each other. But, you know.'

I did know. I had been Mel's friend through the last throes of her longing for a baby, and I had seen the sadness that descended on her when she accepted that it was finally too late. She felt her own emptiness so profoundly: the prospect of meeting Jasper's daughter, the loved child of a woman he had once loved, would be disturbing, however welcome the idea might also be.

She hesitated, then said, 'There's a part of me that mourns, how sad, how wasteful for the two of us not to have found each other until now, when it's too late for us to have our own child together.'

'Does he want one?'

Mel shook her head and the black curls fanned out round her face. 'No. He says he's already got everything he wants in the offspring department, in Clare.'

'Then he's lucky.' I wondered briefly if Mr Rainbird hoped for children of his own, after spending his working life surrounded by other people's. 'And nothing has really changed for you about a baby, has it? Except that now you have the consolation of loving Jasper and being loved by him. I know you *do* love him. I've never seen you look or heard you talk this way before.'

'It's because I know it's serious. I'm taking it so seriously. Plenty of men I've been out with before now had kids and I never paid much attention to that.'

'No, you didn't. This is different. Go and meet Clare. She'll be someone new to love even though she isn't your own child, and maybe there's some way she can even become a kind of substitute, in time, in a small way.'

It was easy enough for me to say, because I had known the absorbed intensity of pregnancy and the intimacy of feeding my babies, and because Lola and Jack were within every fibre of me then and now, and always would be. Mel had never known this connection and it was wrong of me to envy her even a little bit for what she was enjoying today.

'Thanks, Sadie.' She was smiling, her red lipstick a generous slash of colour against the tasteful monochromes of the restaurant's decor.

I did love her. Her friendship mattered to me more than almost anything else in the world. 'You're welcome.'

'I don't want to talk about myself through the whole of the next course as well. It's your turn now. Tell me something.'

On that night when Ted was taken ill, I had deflected her questions about him, and Mel had noticed that I did so and minded that I withheld something of myself from her. I wanted to offer her something now to make up for that, but there was also more – the thought of confiding in her about my father had become inviting rather than impossible.

At lunchtime today, after I had made the mess of finishing the book and before I set to work again to repair the damage, I picked up the Works telephone and dialled the number of the Public Record Office in Kew. Penny had gone across to the house and closed the yard door behind her. I guessed she was having one of the urgent, muttered conversations with Evelyn that were becoming more and more frequent. Andy and Leo were both out and I was on my own in the bindery.

Once I had pressed the right buttons in response to recorded instructions about how to access records, I was connected to a real person. His voice was surprisingly warm. I explained to this stranger with the attractive voice that I wanted to try to find out about someone who had once served a prison sentence. How could I discover what his crime had been and the circumstances surrounding it?

The Records man cleared his throat. 'Well, now. Was this person tried in the High Court, or the Crown Court? We only hold High Court records here and those are closed for seventy-five years.'

'I don't know,' I confessed. Maybe Audrey knew that the trial was in the High Court, or maybe she just assumed that all criminal records would be kept in the same place. I gave him the meagre information that I did possess.

'Hm. It doesn't sound like the Old Bailey to me. I'm telling you this personally, you understand. You'd have to try the London Metropolitan Archive for Crown Court archives. Or you could go to the British Library and look up the *Times* index, you could probably find out from that what court this person was tried in.'

This all sounded remote from Ted and his doings. I tried to imagine going through ledgers or, more probably, reams of microfilm in search of his name.

'But I'll tell you what I'd do, if I were in your place,' my new ally said.

'What's that?'

'Where did your friend – I mean, this person – live?'

'Hendon,' I told him. Dorset Avenue: Tudorfied semis, suburban gardens, the length and breadth of respectability.

'You know the date. I'd go to the archives and look up the local newspaper. It would be reported there.'

The *Hendon & Finchley Times*. Mrs Maloney always read it. 'You're right,' I said. 'Of course it would.' I thanked him for his help.

'All in a day's work,' the official said. 'Good luck. I hope you find what you want.'

I could imagine this much more easily, how I would turn the pages of big bound volumes of newsprint, with their reports of Princess Margaret's party-going and Helen Shapiro's concerts, and local events like school summer fêtes and flower shows, until I stumbled across a picture of Ted. Maybe it would even be the one that I had had copied for Angela and Audrey.

'Do you remember I told you that my father was a con artist?'

'A perfumer and a con artist,' Mel said, leaning back in her chair.

'It was more true than I realised. I found out some more about him,' I said. 'He went to prison.' I told her about going to Suffolk to see Angela.

'Does knowing that make you feel any different?'

I considered briefly. 'No.' I wasn't shocked or dismayed, which is what Mel was meaning.

'And so what is it that you do feel?'

This made me think more carefully. 'In the dark,' I said at length.

That was just what it was. Ted had put up so many smoke-screens. It can't have been just my mother and me he hid from, but his other women too and his creditors, and the consequences of his doings that were ranged around him in a circle like so many precariously vertical dominoes.

When I was a girl Ted had always seemed to be so strong and so self-confident that I bought into his image without questioning it. (I wasn't alone in that, of course, as the list of aunties demonstrated.) As an adult I thought I saw through him, yet even while I was convincing myself of this he still made me angry and sometimes intimidated me, which was a measure of his lasting power over me. And now, behind the puffs of coloured smoke that drifted at the far end of the hall of mirrors where my father dwelt, I was beginning to think there had only been a void. There was nothing solid there and perhaps nothing so very significant to hide either, except my father's fear of being exposed for what he really was.

It was fitting that his great gift was as a perfumer, the creator of illusion, and it was sad that even his gift had come to almost nothing except some old-fashioned and mostly forgotten fragrances, and three volumes of notes.

I looked into Mel's face across the plates and glasses, with the muted noise of the restaurant like a shell held to my ear.

For the first time I felt pure sympathy for him, and it was like having a hand pushed deep inside my chest cavity. Poor Ted, I thought, with the fingers tightening round my heart. He had been on the run for the whole of his life. He had juggled so hard, for so long, and the fear of dropping those spinning balls must have been ever present. He had been dextrous enough to go to *prison* and still manage to keep the whole episode from me. All the Ted of my childhood, the RAF slang and the blazers and the cars and the shop in South Audley Street and the vanishing acts, both real and emotional, had only been balls in the air.

'You can turn the lights on, you know, if that's what you want,' Mel said, cautiously.

'I know I can.' If finding out the bare biographical details meant anything, when the reflections of coloured smoke made such elaborate pictures.

I told her about my call to the Record Office and the newspaper idea.

'Are you going to pursue him?'

Pursue was an interesting word for her to choose, I thought. It made Ted into a fugitive little figure, running away from me through the smoke into the inaccessible past.

'Maybe. Just a little way.'

'Shall I come with you?'

She was offering to stand by me, if I needed to look at anything that might be difficult to confront alone.

'I don't know. I'll ask if I think I need you, but I'm not used to going public about my life. I felt ashamed of being different from other kids so I put a lot of effort into pretending to be the same as them, and when I couldn't do that I kept quiet. It's not like your family, is it?'

'Not superficially, no. But my father was so powerful, his influence hobbled us all. Look at me, I'm only just finding out how to fall in love with a man who isn't him. We're our fathers' hostages, both of us.'

She put the last morsel of beef into her mouth and leaned smilingly back in her chair. 'And listen to me, I'm talking about myself again. That's enough about me. What do *you* think about me?'

This was one of Mel's favourite self-knowing jokes and it did have bite because she was interested in herself. She had all the self-confidence that came from being her daddy's princess, and I enjoyed the privilege of it at second hand by watching the sureness it gave her. With the added charge of being in love, Mel shone as brilliantly as the midday sun reflected off a sheet of mirror glass. I could see the diners at the other tables covertly glancing at her, wondering who she might be.

'I think you could ask for the pudding menu. I'll tell you after I've eaten the tarte tatin.'

Mel ordered us a glass of Barsac apiece to go with it and we toasted each other.

'To many more dinners,' she said. 'Even when we're old and grey.'

'Especially when we're old and grey. I'll tell you what I think. That you're the best friend any woman could have. Let's drink to friendship.'

Mel squeezed my hand. 'Thank you, Sadie,' she said. 'You too.'

She paid the hefty bill with a reckless flourish. 'Thank *you*,' I responded.

I made my way home through the chaotic streets. There were no taxis anywhere, the tube entrances were still barred and the two buses that swayed past were crammed to the doors. In any case, I was happy enough to walk. I was full of rich food and I was peering through the mildly distorting golden lens of plenty of wine. I felt buoyed up by the evening and by having opened a small chink for Mel to look into. It hadn't been so difficult after all.

'To friendship,' I repeated aloud, to the cats and the parked cars, as I finally waltzed round the corner into my street.

As the next few days turned out, it was just as well that I had the dinner with Mel to buoy me up.

Lola was working for an employment agency as a temp receptionist because it paid better money than bar work, but it also meant that she had to be up, washed, dressed in a skirt and decent shoes, and out of the house by eight thirty every weekday morning. She wasn't prepared to curtail her nightlife, however, and so she was always tired and hung-over and irritable. Her mess erupted out of her room and exploded in unpredictable corners of the house, and I found my best shoes and my Nicole Farhi shirt wedged under a half-full suitcase on her bedroom floor. She emptied the fridge of food even faster than Jack could manage to do it, and left the debris all over the kitchen floor and worktops. 'Sorry, Mum,' she groaned disarmingly when I yelled at her. 'I'm just *so* busy.'

'This is what life is, Lo. You go to work, you fit in everything else when you can. And you don't have to go out every single night.' I could hear the carping, killjoy note even as the words came out of my mouth. Did I really not want my twenty-year-old daughter to enjoy herself and to go out as often as she had the energy for it? 'Well, it's what my life is,' I added ruefully.

Lola put her arms round me at once and I breathed in patchouli and cigarette smoke and elastic skin.

'Poor Mummy. Come on, don't cook. Let's go out and have supper together. We can drag Jack with us. Let's have a family date.'

'Are you treating us?'

'Um. I don't get paid until next week, it's something to do with the accounts people. Can you lend me the money?'

I had to laugh.

Jack was sleepwalking through the last days of the school year. He spent most of the after-school hours at Audrey's and in the limited time he did spend at home he either lay on his bed or glowered at the local bird population through his binoculars. He hardly ever spoke to Lola and me except to snap at us.

I telephoned Audrey and held out an olive branch. 'Why don't you come and have a family Sunday lunch with us? You've been so hospitable to Jack and Lola and I would love to see you here.'

'Why?'

'Well . . .' Her lack of social emollience disconcerted me, but perhaps I usually erred on the side of being too conciliatory. 'Because we would.'

'All right. I'll come on Sunday, then.'

I told Jack about the arrangement and he whipped round at me with fury glittering in his face. 'Can't you just leave me alone?'

'It's only lunch, Jack. You're spending such a lot of time round at Turnmill Street I thought it was fair to invite Audrey back here.'

'You just have to own everything, don't you? You can't let me have anything to myself.'

I tried too hard; Tony and Mr Rainbird had both seen that. But I had been balancing equations in my mind ever since Ted died, trying to work out via the past what the exact margins were between loving my son and loving him too much. I was tired of the battle with him, but I still couldn't see how to care for him less openly while I had my different memories. 'Okay. I'll call her and cancel,' I said.

I didn't want to be vanquished by Audrey in any kind of contest, let alone one that centred around Jack, but I didn't want him to see me caught in a playground squabble with her either.

'No. Don't be stupid. She already thinks you're weird enough.'

'*Audrey* thinks *I'm* weird?'

'Oh, Mum.' Jack sighed. 'Just forget it, okay? Like you said, it's only lunch.'

Sunday with Audrey kept its place in the diary.

I did some research into summer holidays. In the past we had been to a cottage in Cornwall, to Wales and the Lake District and, when we had a couple of fatter years at the Works, to an apartment on Skopelos and then a *gîte* in Normandy. This year, with the genie out of its bottle and all the smoke and scent swirling around me, I really did want to go back to Grasse.

There wasn't a lot of money in the budget, but after hunting for a day or two I found a site between the town and Cannes that offered camping, caravans and some farm buildings converted into holiday lets. I remembered a golden countryside of olive trees and vineyards and ochre-walled houses with clay tiled roofs. Lola refused to have anything to do with tents and the caravans, even in the brochure, looked hideous. I agreed that the apartments looked like the best option.

'Is there a pool?' Lola asked. 'Any bars, or clubs?'

'There's a pool at the site, look,' I said, showing her the picture. 'There are plenty of bars in Grasse and clubs in Cannes, I'm sure. Although it must all be completely different from the way I remember it.'

'Okay,' she said.

Jack just shrugged. I booked the first two weeks of the school holidays and considered us lucky to have found somewhere in the south of France that I could more or less afford.

I also spoke to Mr Rainbird.

'It seems a very long time since we saw each other,' he remarked, after we had exchanged the initial courtesies.

'I know. I'm sorry.'

'Shall we remedy this?'

I hesitated. 'I'm not sure how to tell Jack.'

'How to tell him what, exactly?'

'Um. That I'm dating his head of year.'

'Just that would do, wouldn't it?' There was some amusement in his voice but also the faintest edge of impatience.

'Jack and I aren't having a particularly easy time at the moment. He's angry with me, for all kinds of reasons, most of them justified.'

'Sadie, kids are often angry. Do you want us to go out again?'

I listened to his breathing. 'Yes.'

'Okay. Good. So do I.'

But. I waited to hear what the *but* was going to be.

'So, if what you're saying is that before you and I go any further you want to find the right way to tell Jack that we're going to the cinema, I'll just wait for you to do that and then call me, shall I?'

No but at all.

Mr Rainbird, I thought, you're quite a class act. It was a second before I caught myself giggling. I said with the vibration of laughter in my throat, 'Yes, please. I promise I will.'

'Goodnight then,' he said and I could hear that he thought all this was quite funny too. I liked the fact that he didn't take it too seriously, but that he didn't entirely make light of it either.

Lola was in, for once. I had thought she was absorbed

in the television but she looked up immediately. 'Was that him?'

'Yes.'

She grinned. 'Good for you, Mum.'

I went back to Ted's notebooks and reread the entries for the spring and summer of 1965, just before he sent me to Grasse. Nothing looked much different, at least to my inexpert eye. There were the same lists of natural and chemical ingredients, occasional names and the jottings from which everything else sprang. Maybe Ted's writing was more hurried, maybe there was less fluency in the expression of his ideas, but there was nothing to indicate that he was about to go to prison. Then there was a gap of almost four months, from the middle of July to the end of October. The last formula before the lacuna was labelled 'MAL'.

When the notes did resume, in November, there was a difference. The new formulae were short and to my eye they looked ugly because the ingredients were all of synthetic origin with no natural oils or extracts. Ted's scrawl was careless and I imagined that I could read dismissiveness in every stroke of his pen. The heading they came under was R & J.

I remembered the time very clearly.

I had a job in the Christmas holidays of 1965, working for Restall & Jackson, who were also Ted's new employers. This cash in hand was the first money I had ever earned and the half-crowns and ten-shilling notes in my purse seemed to generate raw heat that I warmed my hands on while I waited to catch the bus from Hendon to work and back again. 'Christmas shift temporary hands' Ted's bosses called us and we were a strange collection. There were Jamaican women whose bright clothes seemed to bleed colour into the clammy winter atmosphere, thin and anxious white mothers in headscarves, and gangs of careless teenagers who smoked in defiance of the signs that decorated the factory floor. I was the youngest faceless possessor of a pair of hands, but not by very much. There were two sixteen-year-olds, one of whom was visibly pregnant, but they popped bubblegum and shouted taunts at the tattooed machine minders and ignored me. No one else paid me any attention either, but I didn't care. I was doing something, getting paid for it and I was out of Dorset Avenue for hours at a time.

Ted had got me the job, of course. 'It'll give you some cash, Sade,' he said. 'Things are a bit tight all round and anyway we need some extra hands on the line this time of year.'

I knew that things were tight, as he put it. Our house was cold, and we had run out of even basic supplies like detergent and tea.

'We'll soon be flying on two wings again,' he told me and winked. 'Since I was away on that job I haven't had a chance to get properly organised.'

Away on a job, that was where he now claimed to have been all summer. I believed him, queasily, with an underlying sense that whatever else there was to know I wouldn't like and so it was better not to ask. I had been 'learning French, on a valuable cultural exchange', which was how my absence during the first month of the school year had been explained at school. All the alliances in the new form had been made by the time I got back, and the loose friendships I had cultivated with Daphne and the others the year before seemed to have been forgotten. There was some interest to start with in the details of my exotic summer, but the truth was that I had little to tell even though I tried hard to embroider the story of Philippe. Some of the girls giggled and whispered about me but I closed my ears and ignored them, and they soon found some other misfit to focus on.

So I didn't mind feeling isolated among the other temporary

hands, because I was used to solitariness. The best thing about working at Restall & Jackson, even better than the money, was Ted's proximity. I worked early or late shifts and so we didn't very often catch the bus together (the car had long gone), but at least I saw him every day. I knew where he was and the absence of anxiety – the gnawing fear that one day he would simply be gone and this time would never come back – was better than a coal fire or a steak and chips dinner.

The factory was housed in a big metal shed near Wormwood Scrubs, on a flat, windy piece of ground near a railway line. Litter caught in bare bramble arches, the puddles were like dead eyes and there was always the sound of shunting on the sharp wind. It was a long, cold walk from the bus stop and even inside the metal walls of the factory it wasn't noticeably warmer. I could see my breath condensing while I performed whatever repetitive task the fat foreman set me to do.

Restall & Jackson manufactured cheap toiletries, and we temporaries were there to fill the extra bottles, and pack boxes of shampoo and bath oil and body creams ready for vans to take them out to the Christmas trade. The factory floor was a series of big metal vats where paddles restlessly stirred vanishing ellipses into thick seas of lotion. The base material always seemed the same, a whitish runny fluid that the machine-minders poured into the vats from big unmarked drums. Other jars of ingredients were mixed in until the floor manager indicated that the resulting compound was ready for bottling.

Sometimes I stood on the automated line, watching the robot lines of empty jars as they shuttled into position under the nozzle to receive their ration of pink or yellow or pale-green sludge. I had to check the fill levels and push rogue bottles back into the endless procession. At other times I was on labelling. There was a rudimentary machine that slapped gummed squares on to the prone bottles as they shuttled along the line. The products were the cheapest, and the matching labels were crudely printed lettering decorated with coarse line drawings of lavender or roses or ferns. I thought how easy it would have been to design better-looking packaging and passed the time by dreaming up artistic ideas.

Sometimes shorter runs of the product had to be hand-labelled and I would stand with two or three of the other temporaries, working through a pile of labels and an army of blank bottles. Or I would be given a plastic jug and a crate of empties and told to hand-fill a couple of gross of bottles from a barrel of scented stuff. The worst job on the line was packing finished product into cardboard cartons. The boxes were flat-packed and had to be made up by hand, and the rough card edges cut my inexperienced fingers. The stretching and reaching with handfuls of bottles was physically tiring, and it didn't leave me with enough energy even to daydream. I listened to pirate Radio Caroline – I had no choice, it blasted through the factory on speakers and the line workers sang along and shouted over the noise – and tried to let the day pass as if I were watching it from somewhere outside myself.

Ted was the Restall & Jackson in-house perfumer. 'A gifted nose, with a West End reputation.' That's how I overheard Mr Eddy Restall describe him to a visiting buyer who was being shown around the factory. The buyer raised his eyebrows and glanced back over his shoulder to where Ted was working. The offices were up a metal staircase from the floor, with dusty windows looking over the line, but Ted's cubicle led straight off the floor. He wore a white overall and sat at a bench surrounded by his perfumer's organ, the stepped semicircle of brown bottles. Usually he was frowning and writing notes, with his mouth twisted as if there were a smell he didn't like right under his nose.

I knew that the dirty-floored cubicle, with its flimsy metal cabinets and filthy enamel sinks stained with green dribbles like snot, was a long way from the swooning elegance of Scentsation, even from the real old business of Phebus Fragrances. But I still felt stubbornly proud of my father's gift. It was just too rarefied for this tin shed, that's all.

When he wasn't scribbling Ted unlocked his cabinets and mixed drops of liquid from phials and bottles. The floor manager would collect a full jug of synthetic perfume compound from him and tip it into one of the vats where the paddles blended the scent into the sea of lotion. The perfume element was a tiny proportion of the total volume but I thought that was no great loss in any case. All the Restall & Jackson products smelled more or less the same. They were sweet, with a powdery chemical after-note; old ladies' smells, cloying and sickly. These were the formulae that Ted jotted down with little jabs of his pencil, labelling them R & J. Old Man Phebus must have trained him too well for him to fail to keep a record of the fragrances he created, even these, which he plainly despised.

I didn't ask him any direct questions about what he was doing there. I knew better than that, and in any case I understood without being told that he had to work himself back, in some way, after the summer. He won't be there long, I assured myself, not long at all.

For two weeks, until the day before Christmas Eve when the last van full of packed cartons pulled away, I had my father in the corner of my eye, and my brown-paper envelope full of coins and the occasional folded banknote.

On Christmas Eve Ted went out to buy groceries and I used some of my earnings to buy a little tree that I stood on a table in the bay window of our front room. The decorations were kept packed in cotton wool in a cardboard box that lived the rest of the year in the cupboard under the stairs. It was labelled 'Xmas decorations' in my mother's handwriting and I thought about her as I hung the glass balls and wound the tinsel round the spiky, resinous branches and waited for Ted to come back. I would have liked to sit with my father that evening and maybe talk about her, remembering the Christmases we had all spent together even though they were fading, blurring too fast in my memory through lack of visiting. But Ted put on a crisp white shirt and his RAF tie, and announced with a smile that he was going out for an hour or so. He had recovered his gloss and vigour. He even looked taller than he did when he was at the factory, sitting hunched up in his white coat.

'Don't wait up.' He winked at me. 'Why don't you pop up and say hello to Mrs Maloney?'

I watched television instead.

For Christmas, I gave him a book of art nouveau poster illustrations. I loved the colours and the sinuous forms, and I thought Ted would too, although he didn't seem very interested in looking at them. My present was a five-pound note folded in an envelope.

I watched quite a lot of television that Christmas.

A month later Ted had a new job with a small independent fragrance house. Restall & Jackson was never mentioned again and it was only now, turning the 1965 pages, that I thought of the tin shed and the vats of sickly-scented coloured sludge.

On the Friday morning before Audrey was due to come for lunch, I drove to the newspaper library. The archive was housed in a north suburban street, not so very far from Dorset Avenue itself, and I followed a route that was so familiar that I didn't have to think about which way I was going. I passed a hardware shop, once owned by the father of a girl I was at school with, and noticed that it was now a video store. The cinema had been turned into a bingo hall in the Eighties but was now empty and boarded up and there was a huge supermarket and DIY store complex on a triangle of land where there had once been some ramshackle garages and a dance hall notorious for Saturday night hooliganism.

I was already waiting in the lobby when the library staff opened the reading room. A leather-bound volume of the *Hendon & Finchley Times* was put on the desk in front of me. I sat for a moment staring at the dull red leather binding, and noticing the worn corners and the uneven gold-tooled printing of the volume's dates. A bulk job, quickly done, I judged. But it must have been nice steady business for whichever bookbinder had had the contract for binding all these papers for library use. Everything was put on film these days, of course.

I opened the cover and glanced automatically at the marbled endpapers.

Then I looked at the front page of the first paper: HENDON SCOUTMASTER'S HIGH AWARD. CHIEF RABBI VISITS KINGSBURY.

It was like peering into another century rather than a mere forty years back. The yellowed pages were limp and the paper fibres seemed to have sucked up the type, turning it soft and muzzy. There were interviews with local girls who looked forty but were in fact eighteen, and who had 'passed with flying colours' the selection tests to become air hostesses. Every wedding in the borough seemed to be covered in minute detail. There were women's features about choosing dainty gloves and hats to get ahead in, and I read incredulously that 'gay bachelors have had their day. Now it's gay spinsters and gay wives.'

Those were the days when gay had nothing to do with damned homos, as Ted used to grumble in his old age. I was still smiling at this when I turned another page and saw it, next to EDGWARE BRIDE'S SATIN GOWN.

HENDON MAN GUILTY OF FRAUD.

I knew immediately that this was what I had come to find, but I read the paragraphs about the satin bridal gown and the three bridesmaids, and the groom's sister who had flown from New Jersey to see him wed, before I turned to the story about my father.

His case was reported in some detail, although there was no photograph.

The Middlesex Quarter Sessions chairman, W. H. Gascoigne QC, had found Ted guilty of a 'particularly low type of offence'. He was accused of obtaining the sum of £344 8s 8d by virtue of a forged receipt of purchase.

I read more quickly, with a prickling of discomfort at the nape of my neck that spread up and over my scalp like a too-tight cap.

Ted had undertaken to supply Messrs Bourne & Hollingsworth Ltd with an exclusive sample range of fine fragrances under the Scentsation trade name and he had presented his financial backer, a Mrs Caroline Ingoldby, with a receipt for the purchase of perfumery materials in connection with the manufacture of the said fragrances. She had advanced him the money in good faith, because she was an admirer of the accused's perfumery products and believed that they might have a joint business future. The delivery date for the consignment of perfume had not been met, however, and when the store had insisted on receipt of the goods or cancellation of the contract, Thompson had applied to Mrs Ingoldby for further funds to solve 'unforeseen production problems'. Mrs Ingoldby had become suspicious and had caused the original invoice to be examined. It had proved to be a forgery.

Thompson had claimed that he had some business debts and had 'robbed Peter to pay Paul, as it were'. He had every intention, he said, of fulfilling the order to the department store and settling his financial shortfall from his share of the resulting profits. He pleaded guilty to the charge and expressed his sincere regret for the matter. Mr Gascoigne took the view that it was particularly reprehensible of the accused to have preyed upon a woman's innocent trust. He therefore sentenced him to six months' imprisonment, also taking into account an earlier offence where Thompson had been found guilty of embezzling some funds from a previous employer and had been fined.

I read the article carefully, twice over, but there were no capillaries of ambiguity running through the *Hendon & Finchley Times*'s blocky prose.

Everyone I knew back in those days must have known. Mrs Maloney, Daphne and Daphne's parents and the other girls in my class, and Miss Avery my headmistress and the other teachers, they would all have read or heard about my father going to prison. I sat in my library seat with the other readers coughing and shuffling around me, thinking that I didn't care about this, either in the present tense or on behalf of the child I had been then. But what did strike me was the strength of my determination not to confront the truth or any shading of it.

I had seen but somehow managed to ignore the other girls' whispers and the sympathetic but speculative glances of the teachers. Angela had said nothing to me either at the time or afterwards. Mrs Maloney must have made knowing remarks with her mouth pursed and her eyes darting but I had squeezed her insinuations out of my mind.

I didn't want to know what Ted had done or where he was, and therefore I had remained completely ignorant. I had even believed the preposterous story that I was going to France in order to learn the language and experience another culture, when I hadn't been away on holiday since before my mother's death and Ted showed no other particular concern for my school progress.

Such tenacity betrayed the understood fragility of my world.

If I mistrusted Ted, if he let me down as he so easily might, I had no one else to turn to. And so what he did had to be right and what he said had to be true. From my adult perspective, the mental contortions that this must have involved felt utterly exhausting.

A perfumer and a con artist, I had told Mel, and the

admission rose straight from a deep well in my consciousness. I *had* known, really, all along.

Other memories gather, and they are so unwelcome that I have to open my eyes very wide and stare hard at the window and the square of sky beyond. I don't want to cry here, in front of the readers and the handlers of newspaper archives who trundle the volumes to the desks in wheeled trolleys.

I straighten the rippled pages of newsprint and carefully close the cover. I place the card that indicates I have finished with my volume carefully on top and collect up my belongings. Outside, the air is gritty and there isn't a breath of wind. I can look down on the tube tracks through a chainlink fence and while I stand and try to collect my thoughts a tube train rattles into the station below me and foreshortened commuters step out on to the platform. A sluggish tide of people washes up the steps as the train jerks forward again.

My car is parked across the road. I slide into the seat, noticing with surprise how much unexpired time still remains on the ticket. It feels as if I have been away for much longer.

I drive back along the familiar route, noticing automatically more changes that don't really make the old neighbourhood look different, not thinking, not weighing up yet whether I am relieved to have unpicked a piece of Ted's history or whether the reflections and the illusions are still more vivid because he has made them so.

THIRTEEN

It was the third week in July and the leaves on the trees in our road were already browning and crisping at the edges with the heat and the lack of rain. In spite of this, Audrey was wearing her fox fur. I opened the front door on Sunday morning and there she was, standing on the front step with the dusty pelt fluffed up around her chin. I knew that she didn't leave her own house all that often, and I was aware that I should probably have offered to go and collect her in the car. Too late, I had a mental picture of her solitary figure marching up the street with the fur drawn on like a suit of armour.

'Hello, Audrey. Come on in.'

She peered past me into the hallway. I could hear Lola laughing as she talked to Sam on the phone.

'Quite a big house, this,' Audrey remarked. She had a good look into the room that led off the hall, then craned back her head to see up the stairs.

'Is it? I suppose it is.'

'Must cost a fortune to heat it.'

The fox's glass eyes unwinkingly regarded me. There were beads of sweat breaking through the face powder on Audrey's top lip and I wondered why we were discussing central heating.

'Oh, it's not too bad. Shall I take your fur?'

'No, thank you.'

'Come on downstairs, then. I thought we might have a drink in the garden before lunch.'

Jack was hovering in the kitchen. I had been feeling nervous on his behalf, anticipating how it might be for him to encounter Audrey on his own tricky ground rather than in the safety of Turnmill Street, but I saw now that there was no need for anxiety. He gave Audrey a quick, relieved smile and she tapped him reassuringly on the shoulder. The complicity was all between them and I realised that I was the one they were mutually wary of. I went to the fridge and took out a bottle of white wine.

Lola came in and Audrey's glance travelled over her fringed miniskirt and suntanned bare legs.

'We met at the funeral.' Lola smiled.

'That's right. Aren't you cold?'

I steered everyone out into the garden and we sat down at the table in the shade of the neighbours' cherry tree.

Audrey sipped at her wine, pursing her full lips as if she disapproved of the taste of it. 'You're pretty well set up here,' she said, looking around at the overgrown garden and the rear wall of the back extension, which urgently needed repointing.

Her comment irritated me. But the dilapidation on my patch was, admittedly, nothing compared with the state of Audrey's own house. I thought of the loneliness like a blanket at its windows and remembered that Jack and Lola and I were a family, even though we might not always function as such as smoothly as I wanted. I felt a spasm of sympathy for Audrey and consequent shame at my own possessiveness. If Jack kept her company from time to time, it was the last thing I should mind about. 'We don't have a menagerie in our garden, though,' I said brightly.

'Do you remember the cub?' Jack asked me.

'The cub?'

'The first time we went to Audrey's there was a fox cub.' He was amazed that I actually didn't remember.

'Really?' Lola was interested. 'A baby fox? How cute is that?'

'Oh, yes,' I recalled too late. There had been a bundle of russet fur in one of the cages.

'Well, Audrey fed him on milk and scraps and stuff, and he got bigger and bigger and really strong. We used to shut Jack and the other cats in the house and let him out in the garden, and he ran around and sniffed everything but he still went back in the cage every time for his food. Then we let the other cats out, except for Jack because he's like the leader and the most threatening, and the cub was well big enough to stand up to all of them. There was some snarling and spitting and stuff, because they were used to seeing him in the cage and then he was out in their territory, but basically they left him alone. Then we decided it was time for Jack and him to go head to head.'

Lola was looking from her brother to Audrey and back again, and I could see her interest. 'What happened?'

'We opened the cage, right? And the cub came out and went straight up to Jack and sniffed him. Audrey thinks it was because he never had his mother to teach him what to be afraid of and so he'll go for anything. Jack hissed and fluffed his fur up, right, like cats do, and the cub ran and Jack sprang after him and then they did this sort of fight and the cub nipped the back of Jack's neck, behind his ear. You never heard such a noise of yowling and yapping. Audrey got them apart and the cub ran back in his cage and Jack sort of slunk into the house.'

'One-all draw.' Lola laughed.

I was enjoying Jack's story, or rather I was enjoying hearing him tell the story, but I also noticed Audrey's stillness. She sat with her glass of wine on the table and her hands resting beside it, just listening and watching Jack.

'Yeah. And since then, they totally ignore each other. The cub's taller than Jack now, anyway. We leave his cage open all the time and he spends less and less time there. He'll be making his own way soon.'

273

One more urban dog fox to go foraging through the dustbins at night, I thought.

'That's really sweet.' Lola sighed. 'I must tell Sam about it.'

'Audrey sort of rescued her fur, as well, you know,' Jack told her.

'I was wondering about that.' I saw that Lola, my barefaced girl, was actually blushing as she glanced at Audrey.

'It was dead already when she got it, right? So she looks after it and takes it for outings now.'

Lola nodded her head, in all seriousness. She was drawn to Audrey too.

I studied the other woman's face, noticing again the remnants of beauty in the bones and mouth. She sensed that I was looking at her and her eyes hooded over like one of her animals' as they briefly met mine, and slid past me to the garden wall and the pattern of leaves, then away in an arc to rest on Jack again.

'Are we ready for lunch?' I asked. To my annoyance I sounded like some 1950s hostess. Jack sniggered with embarrassment and Lola murmured, 'Chill, Mum.'

We moved inside and arranged ourselves at the table. It had occurred to me that with her enthusiasm for animals Audrey might be vegetarian, so I had made a tomato and feta tart, and a dish of roasted vegetables.

She sniffed at the creamy and crimson runny innards of her slice of tart. 'What's this?'

I explained and she sniffed again. 'I see.'

'Is there something you don't like, Audrey?'

She chuckled. 'I was expecting roast beef and Yorkshire. Or a nice bit of lamb, maybe. That's what Sunday lunch means to me.'

'Oh dear. I thought you might not like eating animals.'

'Why not? Animals eat each other.'

Jack corrected her earnestly. 'Not herbivores. Sheep and cows are herbivores, actually.'

Audrey favoured him with a benign glance. 'Proper animals, then.'

'There is a natural food chain, you know,' Jack told me. 'Carnivores have their place.'

'Next time, I promise Beef Wellington.' I smiled.

Audrey tilted her head to indicate that next time was still a matter for consideration by her and nibbled cautiously at her feta tart.

Conversation over lunch didn't exactly go with a swing. I tried everything I could think of, from transport politics to Greenpeace to Jack's interests inside and outside school, without much response from Audrey. Jack and she made asides to each other, to do with conversations they had had on other occasions and opinions they both held that weren't – I gathered – necessarily to be shared. Lola discreetly raised her eyebrows at me, but she was insulated by her own ever-pressing concerns and also by what seemed to be a sneaking interest in and even admiration for Audrey.

In spite of her reservations about my food I noticed that Audrey cleared her plate quite quickly and allowed me to top up her glass more than once.

I removed the first course and served the pudding, a lemon polenta cake that was one of Lola's favourites. She gobbled up her helping and eased away from the table. 'Mum, is it okay if I go to meet Jules? Leave the clearing up, I'll do it later.'

I nodded. Lola asked Audrey as she said goodbye if she could come round some time to see the fox cub.

'If you make sure you ring up first,' Audrey told her. 'I don't like unexpected callers.'

Jack scowled at his sister's retreating back. He didn't want to be left at the table on his own, caught between me and Audrey, but I thought it would do him no harm to stay where he was and see it through. I was telling Audrey that we were going off next week on holiday, to stay near Grasse.

'Grasse?'

'Yes. Ted sent me off there to stay with a friend of his, that summer when he was, er, away.'

I looked at her and waited, but she said nothing.

'I thought it might be interesting for Lola and Jack to see something of the industry. To give them an idea about their grandfather's world.'

I waited again, but in the silence that followed Audrey only moistened the tip of her little finger and pressed it to the last remaining crumb of cake on her plate. She transferred the crumb daintily to her tongue, a surprisingly pink and smooth tongue. She reminded me of one of her legion of cats.

'Would you like another little helping of my polenta cake?'

'No, thank you. Too much foreign food doesn't agree with me.'

'I'll make us some coffee, then, shall I?'

Jack began to collect plates and even went so far as to slot a few haphazardly into the dishwasher. The angle of his shoulders and the way his head hung told me how uncomfortable he was. I should have risen above my feelings and let his friendship with this prickly old woman run its natural course without intrusion from me.

And yet the circumstances gnawed in my mind.

Audrey's hostility rose like a rank scent between us; I could smell it even now as I ground the coffee and laid out cups, and watched Jack showing her a new postcard picture of a buzzard in flight that I hadn't seen yet. It went beyond what could be rationally explained by our few meetings, even though I had been clumsy, and she had called me a prig and we had quarrelled. It was true that my father had taken and then lost her savings, and that some of her present difficulties might be caused by that, even though it had happened so long ago – but then surely it should be possible for her to say so and even to ask me for some recompense?

I thought the truth must lie elsewhere and that it might turn out to be something much less fathomable. And her attachment to my son did disturb me. There was an excluding, her-or-me, combative element to it that made me afraid for all three of us.

I carried the coffee tray to the table.

Audrey accepted a cup and dipped her head to smell it before taking a swallow. I saw the muscles of her gullet move under the crêpey skin of her throat. 'That's very good,' she said and I found that I was disproportionately pleased with the note of approval. I settled more comfortably into my chair.

Audrey reached down for her cracked old brown leather handbag. She opened the clasp and began fishing round in the contents. 'Since you're taking such an interest in your father, this late in the day, I thought you might like to look at this,' she said. She passed a little bottle across the table and I took it in the palm of my hand.

It was a beautiful *flacon*, made of smoked glass and shaped like a teardop, with overlapping petals of silver and mother-of-pearl cupping the base. The stopper was a smaller fluted teardrop of glass set in a silver collar. There was no label, no marking of any kind. When I held the bottle to the bright light coming from the garden I could see a brown residue of dried perfume trapped within. I touched the glass stopper, testing the fit. I could just feel the minute frictional resistance of ground glass against ground glass.

'Go ahead,' Audrey commanded.

Jack was bored by this. He left the table and wandered across the kitchen, then stood in front of the fridge and fidgeted with the magnets that held lists and reminders pinned to the door. Something escaped a magnet's hold and fluttered to the floor.

I withdrew the stopper and sniffed. The perfume, whatever it had once been, was dead and gone. All I could detect now was a faint powdery whiff of roses. *Roses de mai.* 'What is it?' I asked.

277

'One of your father's fragrances.'

'What is it called?'

'Innominata. Nameless, if you like.'

There were spots of colour showing through her face powder.

'Did he create it for you?'

Yes, of course he did. The face-cupping routine.

Audrey nodded. Then her mouth crimped with a mixture of pain and triumph that made me uncomfortable. There was too much here that was too complicated and I didn't want any of it touching Jack. I really should have left well alone, I thought. My need to explore the past had a forensic feel to it now and I might want to forget the truth as soon as I had uncovered it. I recapped the perfume phial.

I tried to tell myself that I was being fanciful. Audrey had been in love with Ted and he had taken advantage of her, like plenty of others. It was Audrey herself who was making me uneasy, not my father's past history. 'Why Nameless?' I asked, for the sake of something neutral to say.

'Because it suited me,' Audrey snapped. Jack half turned from the fridge in surprise. There was a small silence in which I could hear water dripping in the sink and a jet passing overhead.

I handed the bottle back. Ted's handwritten volumes of formulae were on a shelf upstairs. If the one labelled 'A' was really hers, it could almost certainly be recreated. The brown smear left in the bottom of her teardrop, Ted's promise in a bottle, could be made to live and breathe its roses and neroli and sandalwood once more.

If that was what she wanted.

'When did he make it for you?' I asked.

'Nineteen fifty-six.'

It was a very precise answer, given that she had claimed to be so vague about dates. The timing was right for the position of the formula in Ted's chronology of perfumes. It would have been during his rise to eminence at Phebus Fragrances. Just before or even at the same time as the business trip to Paris, when he bought the little checked costume for Audrey to wear.

Another thought came to me. 'I found a photograph, among his things.'

'You gave it to me.'

I frowned, and then remembered that she must mean Ted's film star picture. 'No, not that one. This one was a picture of you. You were sitting on a wall somewhere with the wind blowing your hair.'

The date of that would be about right too. Audrey's hair and her clothes looked as if they belonged in the mid-Fifties.

Jack dropped something on the worktop behind me and I heard the scuffle he made to mop up a spill.

I added, 'Only I'm afraid I've stupidly gone and lost it. I'd love you to have had it.'

'I have got it.'

I frowned again.

Jack sidled round into my field of vision. 'Er, Mum? I gave it to her. You know. I thought it wouldn't matter. It was only an old photo.'

Audrey smiled with the corners of her mouth tucked inwards. She was pleased with this evidence of Jack's concealment. It linked the two of them against me, like his sneaking away to Turnmill Street after school.

I kept my voice light. 'Well, that's fine. It's Audrey's picture. You should have mentioned it to me, though, Jack. I was worrying about how I could have been so careless with it.'

'Sorry,' he muttered.

'More coffee, Audrey? I've got my father's volumes of notes upstairs, with all his formulae written out. We could look through them and see if we can find your perfume.'

Audrey's tongue touched the outer corner of her mouth,

where face powder still clung to the dark hairs of a faint moustache.

'It's just a bottle of scent,' she said. 'What would I need scent for, these days?'

I didn't quite believe in her dismissal. If it was just a bottle of scent, why had she taken the trouble to bring it to show me?

'Jack? You know those books of Grandad's? Will you bring them down for me?'

He slouched away. Given the pace at which Jack usually moved, it would be several minutes before he reappeared.

'I took your advice,' I said smoothly, 'and looked up Ted's record. It turned out that the local paper was the simplest way. The *Hendon & Finchley Times*.'

Her face still did not flicker. 'So now you know your father was a criminal. Does it make anything any different?'

'No, not really.' As I had told Mel, I was in the dark. I was sure Audrey could have illuminated matters for me, but I was just as sure she was choosing not to. The scent of her hostility, drifting between us again, was much stronger than the faded residue of roses caught in her little *flacon*.

Jack came back with the books. I opened the first one and turned the handwritten pages, searching for the long formula labelled 'A'. 'Here it is.' I pointed. And Audrey leaned forward to look, then reached into her handbag and brought out a pair of spectacles. There, I thought. You do want to see it, don't you?

But after a moment's scrutiny she took off her glasses and sat up straight. She drained the last of her coffee and replaced the cup firmly in its saucer. 'It doesn't mean a thing to me.'

The ambiguity was deliberate, of course. Either she couldn't decipher what the list of essences meant, or she was pretending indifference.

I closed the book and put it aside. So Ted had created a perfume for her, but not for my mother or me. I knew and

Audrey knew, and there was more triumph than pain showing in the pucker round her mouth. She was formidable, I suddenly thought. There was a steely strength in her that I hadn't fully appreciated and my pity or sympathy or whatever it had been was misplaced. She would have been a match for Ted. More than a match, probably.

'It's been very interesting,' Audrey said. 'And now it's time for me to get home. The animals don't like to be left for too long.'

'We must do this again.' I smiled at her. Jack fidgeted near my elbow, indicating his displeasure at this suggestion. 'And I'll give you a lift home.'

Audrey stood up and adjusted the hook that fastened her fur. 'I'll walk, thanks. I'm used to walking. Maybe you'll keep me company, Jack?'

'Okay,' he said quickly.

I couldn't find any reason for protest. I went with them to the front door and Audrey's stiff bearing indicated that I shouldn't try on anything as bogus as kissing her goodbye. We nodded at each other instead. I watched them part of the way down the road. Neither of them looked back. Jack was chattering as he hopped along beside Audrey's dusty figure, and she bent her head to listen to him, then nodded and laughed. I could see the fox tails swinging as her shoulders shook.

I didn't try to guess what they were laughing about. I went back inside and cleared the table and loaded the dishwasher. Then I sat outside in the shade of the tree and tried to read the Sunday papers.

Audrey wanted Jack's company but she definitely didn't want it in the context of his home and family, or particularly me. My plan to defuse her appeal to Jack by drawing her more closely into the circle didn't seem to have worked and when I considered it now it seemed in any case like a cheap manoeuvre. I refolded the newspaper and read about the developing transport crisis. There were more tube and bus strikes forecast for the coming weeks. I was glad we were going to France to be in the sun together, the three of us.

Lola came home before Jack did. She sliced leftover polenta cake and fed it into her mouth, scattering crumbs. 'I thought she was quite interesting, Mum. A bit scary, maybe. And she wasn't giving anything away, was she?'

'No,' I agreed.

'Was she one of Grandad's girlfriends?'

'She claims not.'

'Oh, well.' Lola yawned. 'It's all a long time ago. Jack can't come to any harm round there, anyway. Just let him do what he wants.'

I didn't have much option. He shrugged off my questions (of course), when he did come home, late for starting his homework. 'Oh, I just hung out. I fed the cub, played with the cats, not much.'

'Did Audrey enjoy her lunch with us?'

'She thought the food was funny.'

'I don't suppose she eats like that very often.'

'No, she thought it was *funny*.'

Maybe that's what they had been laughing at.

I didn't see Mr Rainbird in the press of children and teachers when I collected Jack and his folder of artwork and other belongings at the end of term. I called him that evening instead. 'We're going to France for two weeks' holiday,' I explained.

'I hope you'll be impressed by Jack's command of the language, after Cherbourg.'

'I'm sure I shall be. I wondered if you are still interested in us going out together?'

'Sadie, I thought I'd made that clear.'

'So how about the Tuesday evening after we get back?' I gave him the date.

'I'll just consult my diary.' Our passports and air tickets and the booking confirmation for our apartment were laid out on the table in front of me and I slipped them into a folder while I waited. 'That looks good to me,' he said.

'I'll look forward to it,' I told him. And it was true.

We flew to Nice. The airport was being rebuilt and the white light reflecting off raw concrete made us all blink. The air was so heavy I felt we had to wade through it like water and when I tried to catch the ozone sparkle of the turquoise sea all I could smell was dust.

We queued for and finally collected our rental car. Lola did her best to navigate the route towards Grasse while I struggled with the unfamiliar controls of the Renault. We stalled once at a roundabout and the driver of a Dutch pantechnicon shouted soundlessly down at me from behind his high windscreen. Everything seemed to have changed. The coast was ribboned with huge motorways and the sea was only intermittently visible between ziggurats of apartment blocks.

'You're in the wrong lane, Mum,' Lola yelled. 'Look, there's the sign for Grasse.'

Jack hunched in the back seat with his face turned towards the hills. They were beige and grey humps rising out of the haze.

This wasn't the introduction I had wanted them to have. The scent of flowers and the cool, dewy mornings I remembered had nothing to do with this traffic and the vistas of cranes and building sites. 'We just need to get off the motorway,' I muttered, hunching over the wheel as the trucks and tourist buses thundered past.

We turned inland, and Cannes and its islands in the shimmering bay lay directly behind us.

'I remember this,' I suddenly said.

As we drove up the broad valley I did remember the shape of the landscape. I could see Grasse on the hill, and the outline of the higher hills beyond was familiar against the sun-drained sky, but everything else seemed to have changed. Where there had once been meadows there were now rashes of white and ochre villas, and huge traffic roundabouts, and building sites that heralded new Casino supermarkets and more fuel stations and a drive-thru' McDonald's. Up the gentle slopes of the valley the developments had spread until there didn't seem to be a metre of space anywhere that wasn't a road or an apartment block or someone's fenced-off patch of garden. Jack and Lola had gone quiet in the heat.

'Soon be there,' I said brightly.

The campsite was up a winding road on a steeper section of the hillside. There were mimosa trees overhanging the gate, some of the branches still plumed with powdery dead flowers, and banks of nettles beyond the driveway. I understood, when the concierge showed us to our apartment in the converted barn, why the place was cheap. But to my relief there was a wide view of the valley that reduced the sprawl of building to toppled white sugarcubes and there was even a grey-blue smudge of sea on the horizon. The immediate area was planted with vines and olive trees, and the middle distance was punctuated with dark cypresses. Lola flung her suitcase on her bed, took out her bikini and went straight to the pool. The water had a greenish tinge, but there were plenty of bleached sunbeds lined up round it. Four boys who had been half-heartedly playing water volleyball stopped to watch her as she settled down to read.

Jack took possession of his cupboard of a room, meticulously laying out his binoculars and notebook, and a guide to the birds of the region. I kicked off my shoes and sat on our tiny terrace, listening to the woodpigeons in the trees and letting the sun soak into my bones. When I closed my eyes the scent, a mixture of baked dust and thyme and the faintest suggestion of flowers, was more familiar than any landscape could be.

'Mum, is this compulsory?'

We had spent four days sunbathing and eating and reading – at least Lola and I had, while Jack flitted under the trees or sat on a rock with his binoculars – and now we had driven up into Grasse and found a parking space among the lines of glittering cars in the square. I thought we should visit the Museum of Perfume.

'Yes,' I said. It wasn't much of a link to their grandfather's history and I was making it for them rather late in the day, but it was better than nothing. And so they semi-obligingly joined the crowd of tourists to be shown round the old copper stills with their preening swans' necks, and the baskets of paper rose petals, and gazed at fake jasmine flowers pressed into white paste that was supposed to be animal fat, once used to absorb the intense floral scent from the blooms.

'Ugh,' Lola said faintly.

At the end of the tour we came to a mocked-up perfumers' organ in a mocked-up lab. There was even a waxwork perfumer in a white coat, sitting at the centre of his bank of bottles and holding a fan of paper scent dippers to his nose. He didn't look like Ted – he was wearing pince-nez and a luxuriant moustache but I could see my father just the same. There he was with his hair brushed and brilliantined back from his forehead, his cravat, the paisley one, and I smelled the citrus lie of his cologne.

That's my girl, eh? Why don't you pop up to see Mrs Maloney?

I don't want to. I want to be with you. I'm afraid that if I don't watch you you'll die, or go away and leave me again.

285

'Mum?' It was Lola at my elbow.

The museum's folksy re-creation of Ted's trade was nothing like Restall & Jackson, or Phebus Fragrances, yet it conjured him up so strongly. This was the closest I had felt to his physical being since the night before he died, and the memory and the simultaneous knowledge of his absence brought with them a wave of grief so sudden and so painful that I almost stumbled.

'Mum, what's the matter? Are you feeling all right?'

'Yes. I was thinking about Grandad.'

'Come on outside and let's sit down.'

I was blinded by the sunlight in the museum's little courtyard. Jack and Lola took an arm apiece and guided me to a chair. I wanted to hug them close against my heart; I was thinking it was too late for Ted, and me and I must never let it begin to be too late for the three of us.

Lola brought me a plastic bottle of mineral water and I took a sip. Jack sat on the kerb at my feet and stared at my knees, rather than take the risk of looking up into my face. I stroked the stiff wedges of his hair and for once he didn't pull away. There were geraniums in tubs flanking the door we had just emerged from and a scatter of crimson dead petals like flakes of blood on the paving stones.

'I'm fine,' I said.

'I often think about him,' Lola told me. 'The things he used to say. He's still here, in a way, if we remember him, isn't he?'

'That's good. I'm glad you do,' I managed to say.

'I do as well,' Jack muttered.

After a minute or two, the startling pain subsided to an ache.

'We shouldn't have come here, Mum. I didn't know it was going to upset you.' Lola glared at the Museum's door, as if the curators were responsible.

'It was right to come.' Here and to Grasse. Both were right. I felt as if a river that had been dammed might start to run again with clear water.

'Can we go and get something to eat?' Jack muttered.

We walked down to the old stone-flagged flower market that I had loved so much when I was fifteen and ordered crêpes and salad at a restaurant in the shade of the stone arches. There were citrus trees in pots against the medieval walls, and a view down steep steps to an alley snaggled with iron balconies and washing lines. Even in the middle of the day it was cool here out of the sun.

'It's beautiful.' Lola sighed. 'You're right. I'm glad we came. Are you okay now, Mum?'

I smiled at her.

Later, while they were eating ice cream, I slipped inside the restaurant. There was only one public telephone at the campsite and no phone book. But here, right at the back next to the *toilettes*, I found a telephone cubicle complete with a dog-eared local directory. I riffled through the pages, certain that I would find nothing. Yet here was the name, clearly listed and a number right here in Grasse.

Philippe Lesert.

I dialled the number and a woman's voice answered. Yes, he was at home.

Of course he was – it was the hour for *déjeuner*.

I gave Mme Lesert my name. A moment later Philippe picked up the phone.

'*Oui?*' It was a heavy, rather tired-sounding voice. I began my careful explanation of who I was but he interrupted me in disbelief. '*Sadie? C'est toi?*'

'*Oui, Philippe.*'

We laughed at one another's surprise. I tried to explain and apologise for my long silence and sudden reappearance, but Philippe wouldn't hear of it. 'And you are right here in Grasse?' he repeated.

'Yes. Yes, on holiday with my children.'

'We must make a rendezvous, please. I should like very much to meet your husband and family.'

287

'Only my son and daughter.'

I learned that Stéphanie Lesert was a writer of children's books and was so unfortunately busy this week that Philippe could not ask me to their home. But, perhaps, I would be willing to meet him for lunch?

We made a date for three days' time.

'Who were you talking to, Mum?' Jack wanted to know.

'An old friend. Someone I knew the first time I came here.'

Jack and Lola made the face they always made at each other following any suggestion that their mother might have had a life that pre-dated them.

'Are we ready to go?' I asked. '*Tu n'as pas encore faim?*'

'Why do you keep saying that, Mum?' Lola groaned. 'It's really annoying.'

'It's what my friend's mother used to ask me.'

I was wondering if Marie-Ange Lesert might still be alive. I hadn't found an opportunity to ask Philippe in the course of our short conversation.

Two more days passed. It was hot and windless, and I sat on the terrace with my book and stared out over the built-up valley towards the sea. Lizards ran over the baked stones and bees hummed in the clumps of red clover along the margins of the campsite. I thought I could just make out the position of the old farmhouse and when I borrowed Jack's binoculars to look more closely I saw a grey smudge that I was sure must be the tiled roof.

Lola had made friends with the volleyball boys and went down with them to the beach in Cannes. Jack didn't want to go to the beach. He wandered through the tinder-dry woods and up the steep incline at the head of the valley to sit on the rock ridge at the top and watch birds. The other families at the site played noisy ball games together and lit barbecues, or loaded up their cars with elaborate picnic equipment before driving off for long days beside the sea, but it was as if we three were on separate holidays within the envelope of a family trip. Yet it was a solution of a kind, I decided, since even Jack seemed reasonably content. His luminous white skin turned blush-pink and then developed a faint glow of colour.

On the third day I drove to meet Philippe for lunch in a restaurant up in the old town. When I walked into the dim interior a man stood up at a corner table. 'Sadie, I would have known you anywhere.'

He kissed me on both cheeks and held my hands between his. I wasn't so sure that I would have recognised him. He was still slim but his black hair had turned grey and there were deep vertical lines at the sides of his mouth. He was smaller and much sadder-looking than I remembered. For all Philippe's gallantry, I guessed that if he were being truthful he would have said the same about me.

There was a bottle of champagne in an ice bucket beside the table and Philippe poured me a glass. 'To nineteen sixty-five,' he said. I echoed the toast and we drank.

The lunch was like any other reunion between two people who haven't met for almost forty years. There were points of recognition so intense that it seemed as if no time at all had intervened and there were huge chunks of separate histories to sketch in. Philippe told me he had sold the family land, most of it for real estate development. There was no money to be made from growing flowers for perfume; synthetic perfume essences are produced in labs using coal tar and petroleum, and where real flowers are used they are mostly imported from India or Egypt or Thailand. A tiny soupçon, he said, of *jasmine de Grasse* might be added if the accountants' figures allow for it.

Philippe now worked as a marketing director for one of the big perfume houses. He spread his hands and his eyebrows made the circumflexes I recalled so vividly. 'I am all to do with figures and product these days, and nothing to do with the land or with flowers. Maman was the last of us to live the old way.'

Marie-Ange Lesert had died nine years ago. After that, Philippe sold the remaining few hectares of cultivated land to one of the last three jasmine farmers left in Grasse. 'It's all gone, everything that you and I remember,' he said. His dark eyes were so shiny that I thought he was about to cry.

'And I do remember it so well,' I said. Madame with her red, brawny arms and her feet in clogs, the smell of cooking and jasmine and roses, and the calm welcome she gave to a withdrawn English teenager. I would never know, now, what her link had been to my father. She must have loved him in some way, for some reason, and she had taken in his daughter out of love because I had felt it all round me in the old farmhouse.

The champagne was going to my head. 'You were the first love of my life,' I told Philippe. 'Did you know that?'

He inclined his head, smiling. 'One should always notice these things. And not act on them, in your case. You were far too young and a guest besides.'

I found that I was blushing.

I told Philippe about how I loved paper and print and old books, and he listened and watched my face.

'I think you must very much resemble your father. You have the same vitality of intention, the devotion to your materials and methods that a perfumer must have.'

The warmth that suffused me wasn't just because of the champagne. Was I like Ted? I was startled to realise it, but I was flattered by the comparison. 'Do you know anything about him? Do you know how your mother and he were connected?'

He spread his hands. 'I'm so sorry, no. I never thought to ask maman. But this is why you are here in Grasse, isn't it? Now he is dead and you are mapping his history, because it is a way that you can make him live.'

'Yes.'

'I remember the same, when maman died. There are all her boxes of papers and her trinkets at my house, and I keep them for no reason except – *ha* – they were hers. Stéphanie thinks I am a little crazy, but then her parents are both still alive. She is not yet in the forward line and she doesn't see the dark so much ahead of her.'

There were crumbs scattered over the white cloth and a crumpled paper napkin next to my empty coffee cup. We had finished the champagne and we were the only diners left in the restaurant. I was thinking about Jack and Lola, and the brightness they spread through my life. 'It isn't all dark.' I smiled.

Philippe covered my hand with his. 'No, of course it is not.'

He called for the bill and when he had paid it he asked, 'Would you like to come and pay a little visit to the old place?'

'Yes. I'd like that very much.'

We drove in Philippe's BMW down the hill from Grasse to the valley road and turned right across the valley floor. The road was lined with villas and pizza parlours and opticians' shops but Philippe cut through the traffic and turned left at a roundabout, and we came past a stretch of scrubby land on a road that was suddenly rural.

'Oh, look,' I said in surprise.

'You remember.'

The dusty road made an elbow bend beside a broad khaki-coloured river fringed with willow trees. It was where Philippe and I used to go fishing on limpid August evenings. There was a dilapidated wooden gate and a broken wooden sign that I didn't have to read. The house was exactly the same, too tall, blinkered with green shutters and set in a patch of trodden dust edged with nettles and clumps of goosegrass. There were still apple trees against a low stone wall, but the ramshackle construction of old packing cases and wire netting where Madame Lesert had kept her chickens had been replaced with a modern corrugated-iron henhouse.

The flower field had shrunk to a tenth of its old size and now it lay within a corral of holiday homes and garden swings and swimming pools. But some of the jasmine and centifolia roses still flowered, and the scent of them was the same as it always had been.

I had been happy here, and the warmth of the place and its people had offered me reassurance when I needed it. The Leserts had given me the resolve to go back to London and my life with Ted.

Philippe and I stood quietly, separately thinking about our separate might-have-been. We were turning away to leave when two boys on Mobylettes came bumping down the track. They were wearing leather jackets and fluorescent trainers. Philippe raised a hand to them in greeting. 'They are the sons of Michel, who bought the land from me. But I don't think these two will be stepping into his shoes.'

Neither of us spoke of it, but it seemed unlikely that there would be flowers growing in these fields for another generation. We drove back up the hill together without looking back. Philippe and I said goodbye on the steps of his office. He kissed me and rested his hand for a minute on my arm. 'Don't leave it for another forty years, please, Sadie.'

'I won't,' I promised him.

Jack and Lola were both waiting for me back at the apartment.

'So, Mum, how did it go with the French love interest?'

They were exchanging the look again.

'It wasn't like that at all,' I protested. I kept the truth, which was that it could have been, entirely to myself. It was a fresh, revitalising piece to add to my happy memories.

On the last day Jack and I went for a walk together, up the hillside to his lookout place on the ridge of rock. It was early in the morning, still cool with a hint of mist and the resinous scent of pine in the air. Lola was sleeping off her final night out with the volleyball boys and their friends.

'Okay,' Jack said and sighed when I asked if I could accompany him.

I scrambled up the steep ravine in his wake, my progress noisy with the snap of dead twigs and the rustle of undergrowth. Jack had the ability to move as quietly as a shadow between the fibrous tree trunks. I was breathing heavily and sweating in spite of the cool air when we emerged from the trees. A curve of sundried grass rolled upwards to a crown of bare rock, with a backdrop of harebell-blue sky. Jack had his head tilted back as he scanned the horizon. His binoculars swung round his neck.

'What can you see?' I asked.

His shoulder twitched. 'I saw a stonechat. And there were some crested larks.'

'Are those uncommon?'

The question wasn't even worth a second shrug.

More scrambling brought us to the rock band and Jack sprang straight up the sloping ledges to the ridge summit. I followed more carefully, testing the outcrops of stone before trusting them with my weight. I am not good at heights and I didn't look down until I was sitting at the top next to Jack.

The view was worth the climb. Beneath was the carpet of real estate, spilling all the way down to the sheet-steel glimmer of the sea, and to the left were the medieval towers of Grasse rising out of fields of olive trees. But beyond the ridge, in contrast to all the small-scale urban tangle, another landscape was revealed. There were peaks and jagged towers of rock here, grey and ink-blue in the shadows, and ochre or silver or warm peach in the strengthening sun. Birds wheeled round the exposed faces and traced punctuation marks against the sky. I turned my back on the valley and watched. Jack was completely still, but I could feel the thread of his concentration like a wire under tension. For maybe fifteen minutes we sat there until my attention began to wander.

I was shifting my position, realising how hard the rock was under my haunches, when Jack drew in a sharp breath. He jerked upright with his binoculars raised. I followed the direction of his gaze. Two huge birds soared across the rock face, quite close at hand. I saw the flash of white tails banded with black, domed heads briefly etched against the stone as they wheeled and rose again. Their wings were great broad spans, the tips heavily fingered. They lifted lazily and majestically above the cliff and into the blue space above. I watched until they were no more than black dots in infinity and my eyes stung in the bright light. Jack stood for seconds more, straining forward as if he could catch them.

As he lowered his binoculars again, he gave a deep sigh. And when he turned his face to me his eyes were shining with rapture.

'What were they?'

'They were golden eagles,' he whispered. He looked incredulous and enchanted, as if he had been given the best present of his life. I was about to ask more questions but I managed to stop myself, to let him savour the moment in peace. The sun beat down on the tops of our heads.

After a moment Jack slipped his binoculars into the case. I understood that this had been the best moment and any other sightings could only be an anticlimax. We reversed our route down the rock band and he held out his hand to help me. I followed him down the slope and into the welcome shade of the woodland.

'Have you seen a golden eagle before?'

His eyes were still brilliant as they held mine. He was breathing hard, as if he had been running. 'You only get them in the north of Scotland.'

'Did you know they were here?'

'No. I didn't really expect it. But you get . . . what is it? A feeling that something's going to happen? Not with your brain, but under your skin and down your spine?'

'A premonition.'

'Yes,' Jack said happily. 'A premonition, that's it.'

We made our way on down the dry earth channels left by the winter rain. The hill road that led down to the campsite was in view before he looked back again. 'Thanks, Mum,' he said.

Lola was sitting outside, drinking coffee and yawning. Her legs and arms were silky brown and above the neckline of her T-shirt I could see the white lines left by her bikini straps. 'Where have you two been?'

'Jack will tell you.'

'You'll never guess.'

Lola looked fondly at him while he spilled out the story, and I sat and listened and watched the two of them.

It had been a good holiday, surprisingly good. Even if we hadn't followed the nuclear families' pattern of picnics and barbecues and ball games.

FOURTEEN

'What are you afraid of, exactly?'

Mr Rainbird and I were sitting in the Italian restaurant, at the same table as before. As we took our places I was already thinking of it as ours, even though we had been here together exactly twice. We had been talking about our separate past lives, lightly enough but with that undercurrent of comparison and recognition that means you are probing for common ground, terra firma on which something new but solid might be constructed.

'You have a fortified air. As though the drawbridge is permanently up.'

As I considered the idea I felt tired, and I knew it was from the effort of preserving my independence and security. This meant, of course, that I was always fearful of the opposites, as Mr Rainbird had correctly guessed.

Ted had never been dependable, nor had he made our joint lives secure.

'Against all invaders?' I chose to be flippant because I was disconcerted by his acuity. He knew I was being evasive. 'That's how it appears, yes.'

'Are you a marauding party?'

'Given half a chance, I would be.'

I drank some wine to cover my faint embarrassment. But it was also one of the things I liked about Mr Rainbird: that he admitted to his interest in me without appearing to think it was anything to be surprised or bashful about. I was defensive in my response for all the usual reasons, like fear that this was a routine he went through with every female between sixteen and seventy, fear that I might succumb and then discover that I had managed to misread the signals and fear that if he was really interested in me and only me there must be something seriously wrong with him. Yet now, sitting watching him eat fegato alla Veneziana, I understood that there was nothing wrong with him at all. His shirt collar was frayed and he looked a little seedy, as if he could do with some ironing and some more proper food, and a lot more regular company, but he was a good man. I smiled unguardedly and he caught the smile and flashed it back at me. Then we both looked down at our plates as if our food had suddenly become the most interesting item in the room.

Whatever the outcome, I thought, flirting with Mr Rainbird was the nicest thing that had happened to me since we had come back from France.

It was, in fact, the only nice thing.

Penny's and Evelyn's relationship had evidently taken a serious downward turn while I was away. On my first day back at the Works the house door stood wide open but there was no sign of Cassie, even though I was used to her running to find me after I had been away. *Sadie-lady? Sadie-lady!* There were no toys lying around in the yard and none of Evelyn's discarded espadrilles, or scarves, or gossip magazines were visible either.

'Where's Cassie?' I asked. Andy and Leo were both at their benches.

Penny didn't look up from gluing a binding. 'With her mother.'

There was a scissoring snap as Leo brought down the guillotine blade on a stack of card.

I got on with my work and waited until eleven o'clock when the men took their mugs of coffee outside into the smoky sunlight for ten minutes. 'What's happened?'

Penny did lift her head now. There were deep lines round her eyes and at the corners of her mouth. 'She's living with Jerry again.'

So the room at the top of the old house was empty; the star-patterned curtains staying open at night on the view of the canal and the gas cylinders.

'Why?'

'Partly because she wants to get pregnant. Partly because she's not sure about being gay. Or she's not sure about being gay and with me. Or something.'

'Is it the end?'

'I don't know. She says not, but you can never rely on what Evelyn says. I'd have them both back any time, Sadie. In fact, I'm not sure how I'm, you know, going to go on without them.'

There was so much pain in her face that I could hardly look at her. I went round the end of my bench and put my arm round her shoulders.

Penny sagged and let her forehead rest against me but she stood up straight again a second later. She looked suddenly as she used to while she was working in her first job with the mocking boys: mute and stony, with the old defences in place. Penny was pulling up her own drawbridge again. 'I will, of course. Go on, I mean. What else is there to do?' She turned away from me and put another set of stitched Law Reports on to the pile for gluing.

'It may still work out,' I said, forcing conviction into my voice. 'Evelyn loves you in her way, and Cassie adores you.'

If the future, without the little girl's warmth and laughter in it, was a bleak prospect for me, it was a thousand times worse for Penny.

'We'll see,' my friend said.

Andy and Leo came in, shuffling awkwardly, knowing that everything was wrong and afraid, as young men are, of what might be required of them if they had to help out.

Life was no more comfortable at home either.

Lola had decided that she was going on holiday again, with Sam this time, right at the end of the summer and she needed to earn the money to pay for it. She was doing full-time reception work and a part-time bar job as well, so we hardly ever saw her.

I was seeing plenty of Jack, though and he was impossible. It was as if the holiday in Grasse, and especially the glimpse of the golden eagles, had opened a window that he couldn't bear to have closed again. He roamed sullenly around the stuffy house, kicking the doors open and shut, or staring through the windows at the heat-heavy sky. 'London's a shithole,' he snapped, when I tried to talk to him. 'It stinks. Why do we have to live here?'

The long holidays were always a problem for Jack because he didn't have any friends. It was difficult to come up with ways to entertain a solitary child who lived in the middle of the city and whose only real interest was birdwatching.

'Because we do. It's where I work,' I said as patiently as I could.

'Well, I hate it.'

'You'll grow up and then you'll be able to choose where you live.'

Everyone grows up in the end, even though at Jack's age I had found that just as hard to believe as he did now.

And London did stink that August.

It was very hot, a windless and humid heat that left the exhausted streets hazed with dust and clogged with litter. The leaves turned brown and drooped from motionless branches.

Their sticky exudations coated the cars and attracted a further coating of dirt, so the fuming traffic seemed composed of endless furred metallic segments, like some great worm dug out of the earth, and left exposed and stewing under the white sun. The traffic was worse than I had ever known it. The transport strikes had become so frequent that they ran into one another, and no one ever knew whether it was worth plunging into the suffocating Underground to try for a tube, or if it was better to stand outside in the heat, gazing down the lines of gridlocked cars in the hope that a bus might materialise in the grimy distance. The shortest car journeys became voyages of endurance that might extend to an hour or longer, and if you tried to walk anywhere the soles of your shoes stuck to the smeared pavements and the sun fried the top of your head.

The heat didn't engender any sense of lassitude, though. Instead, the whole city seemed to simmer with rage and aggression. As I sat in the car, trying to get to or from the Works, I listened to the radio news reports of street violence breaking out in Brixton and Homerton and Goldhawk Road. Whenever I set out on foot, even if I was only going as far as the high street, people pushed and jostled each other on the pavements as if they would shove the next person to cross their path straight into the gutter. Crowds of shiny, heat-reddened faces surged past, and there was a mingled smell of sweat and desperation in the air. Anger seemed to gather in clouds in the doorways and to seep from the very cracks in the brickwork until a miasma of threat hung everywhere.

Down by the canal, all along the towpath, there were gangs of kids circling on bikes and dully taunting one another, and sleeping dossers stretched out like corpses in the rank weeds. There were even jams of boats, waiting their turn for the locks, loaded with sun-scorched people who had come out in search of tranquil water and were enraged to find only more confusion. Boomboxes competed to send up the loudest, most distorted snatches of music.

I hurried along beside the oil-slicked water, head down to avoid making eye-contact with anyone, stepping over empty cans and spilled fast-food cartons. Under the bridges, in the brief bands of shade where dripping water echoed, there was an illusion of coolness before the sun struck me full in the face again.

For the first time in my life I felt afraid of London, of my own place.

Jack started spending more and more of his days at Audrey's.

In spite of my misgivings, I was glad that he was somewhere, doing something, with somebody.

That evening, when the time came for me to leave to meet Mr Rainbird for dinner at the Italian restaurant, Lola was due back at any minute but hadn't actually arrived yet. Jack was sprawled in the stifling kitchen watching television because I insisted that he come back home from Audrey's by six o'clock every evening.

'I've got to go,' I told him, 'or I'll be late. Lola'll be back soon. Will you be okay?'

He didn't look at me. 'Yeah. Where're you going?'

I could have told him, but I chickened out. I didn't have time to go into it now; I would tell him later that I had been on a hot date with his head of year.

Actually, strictly speaking, Mr Rainbird wasn't even his head of year any longer now that Jack was moving up into Year Eight. I would find a way to make a joke out of it. Jack would groan, and then maybe even laugh.

'To have dinner.'

'Who with?'

'Just a friend. Listen Jack, have you seen my keys anywhere?'

He wanted to know who, I could tell from the way his slouch had turned into a sideways lean, but he didn't want to betray interest.

'Nuh.'

'Thank goodness, here they are. Will you ask Lo to ring my mobile as soon as she gets in?'

'Yuh.'

I felt the accustomed twist of guilt as I left the house. I shouldn't be going out to have a good time, should I, and leaving my child on his own? I knew this, surely, better than anyone else?

Lola called as I was walking down the street to the restaurant. There was a group of young men lounging against the window of a bookmakers' just ahead and I turned aside to shield my phone from their view.

'You'll stay in the house with him?'

'Yeah. Okay.' Although Lola didn't sound delighted at the prospect, on a rare night off. 'Have fun, Mum, all right? Don't do anything I wouldn't do.'

'Plenty of scope, then.'

After this ritual exchange I dropped my phone back into my bag, zipped the bag up and held it tightly under my arm. I could feel six pairs of eyes on me as I walked on, but I didn't look round and I told myself that I was imagining things. As soon as I pushed open the door of the restaurant I saw Mr Rainbird, at the corner table, waiting for me.

When we had finished dinner and spun out two cups of *espresso* apiece, what seemed like a long time but also a matter of mere minutes later, he drove me home. Darkness had brought no relief from the heat; if anything, the night seemed even more oppressive than the day that had gone. Neon adverts and shop signs bled colour into the bruised air and the day's noise lay trapped under the weighty sky.

'What a hell's kitchen,' Mr Rainbird murmured, as he tried to nose the bonnet of the Morris into an unrelenting stream of traffic coming at us from the left. I was well fed and relaxed with red wine, and I watched the shops and houses and cars sliding by with calm detachment.

I had told him that Jack didn't yet know who I was out with and he sighed, signalling dismay and also definite disapproval, but when we reached home he parked the car a tactful distance from my front door. He switched off the engine and the lights and we were left cocooned in the smell of creased old leather as the ticking and whirring sounds of motorised action gradually subsided. A memory of Ted's Ford Consul floated into my head but I closed my eyes and dismissed it. Mr Rainbird took me in his arms and kissed me.

It was a nice kiss. I hesitated and then I kissed him back. Our tongues touched and seemed to match. I relaxed, but what I began to feel was the opposite of relaxation. I put my hand on his arm, then moved it along his shoulder until my fingers touched the nape of his neck, under his surprisingly soft hair.

It was Mr Rainbird who pulled back. When I opened my eyes I caught the glimmer of his smile. 'I think we should call it a night, Ms Thompson.'

Anxiety and pre-embarrassment crawled along my spine, and I sat upright. Had I misread the signals after all?

Then I saw that he was teasing me, but with affection and also a definite shading of regret. He had a better sense of time and place than I did, that was all. 'Too old for snogging in the car?' I smiled.

'Nope. But, you know.' He nodded in the direction of my house.

'Yes. You're right. Thanks. And thank you for a wonderful evening.' I meant it.

'I'll call you tomorrow,' he said.

He sat there until I reached my doorstep. I waved to him and slipped my key into the lock.

The hall lights were all off, but I knew at once that there was someone watching me in the darkness. 'Jack?'

It was like the night when I came back from dinner with Mel to hear the news about Ted. I groped along the wall and found the light switch. I jumped at the sight of Jack standing motionless at the head of the stairs. He was staring down at me, his eyes wide and dark.

'What are you doing?' Alarm made my voice sharp.

'Where have you been?' he countered just as sharply.

'I told you. Having dinner. Where's Lola?'

'In her room.'

'Okay, Jack. It's time for bed now.'

He didn't move.

'Jack.'

'So did you have a good time?'

The tone of his voice warned me, and I saw now that his face was taut and waxy with accusation. I sighed. 'Yes.'

'I asked Lola who you were with.'

Lola had known. I hadn't asked her to keep my arrangements to herself, not specifically, because I couldn't have expected one child to keep a secret from the other. I had just assumed and hoped that Jack wouldn't be that interested, and even as I was making these rapid calculations I recognised the scale of my mistake. At Jack's age I had been more interested in my father's doings and whereabouts than anything else in the world, as a matter of self-preservation. Ted was all I had. It shouldn't come as a surprise that Jack felt the same about me.

But Jack surely wasn't as isolated as I had been? Or so aware that his small niche in the world was precarious?

Another set of blind assumptions, I realised. I couldn't know how Jack felt: only how I wanted him to feel. There was a big difference.

'You should have told me you're going out with a *teacher* from my *school*.' He made it sound like some perverted act.

'Yes, I should have done.'

'I hate being treated like a kid. I hate secrets,' Jack blurted out.

Of course he did. So did I. I knew the insecurity that untruths bred, so how could I inflict the same on my son?

I put my bag and car keys down on the table in the hallway and climbed the stairs towards him. He shrank back against the wall, his eyes burning and his mouth twisted. I was the enemy.

'Jack, I'll tell you everything. *Please* let me tell you.'

He was backing away from me, retreating towards his room. I followed with my hand stretched out to him as if I were trying to soothe a frightened animal, one of Audrey's menagerie. Jack reached his bedroom door. He half sat and half fell against his bed, lifting an arm to ward me off. 'Go away.' He was close to tears now.

'Jack, it's okay. Listen.'

Even up here, the air smelled and tasted of melting tarry streets. There was a coat of fine grey dust covering the floor and the shelves, as if the city itself were stirring under the stained pavements, smoking and giving off clouds of ash, as threatening as the caldera of an active volcano.

'Listen,' I repeated as softly as I could. 'It's not a secret. I like your teacher and I think he likes me. I'm sorry you felt excluded. I was afraid that you would be embarrassed and I was trying to find just the right time to talk to you about it.'

'Embarrassed.' Jack repeated the word flatly. Then he swung round to stare out of his window at the orange-black sky. 'Suzy's pregnant again. She's had tests. It's a boy.'

I caught my breath in sympathy. This was very hard. Tony's other family and therefore his competing love for people who were nothing much to do with Jack was all too obtrusive. My son had taken the birth of the twins hard enough, those dear little scarlet-faced babies with their tiny clenched fists and black eyelashes, but at least he had been able to tell himself that they were only girls. *He* was Tony's son.

Now there was fresh unwelcome proof that Tony and Suzy had sex with each other and as a direct result he wouldn't be the best-loved boy any longer. There would be a younger and probably more satisfactory claimant.

On top of this, tonight, there was the possibility that his mother and his teacher were also thinking about having sex. Might even, for all Jack knew, already actually be having unrestrained and completely inappropriate sex, all over the place, in the same world that he had to live in.

Even his sister never stopped talking about her miraculous new boyfriend and all his virtues.

Embarrassing barely described it. Everyone Jack knew was about to have even less time to devote to him. He was a lonely misfit at school and he needed reassurance and security at home, so life deftly handed him the opposite.

'How do you know? Are you sure?' I was grasping at straws, but maybe there had been a mistake.

'Dad rang. He wanted me and Lola to know first. *You* know.' Jack made an angry face. I did know. Tony always tried to do the right thing in these matters, whatever was considerate, even to me as well as to his older children. Sometimes they appreciated his concern, at others it was too much. They needed accessible reasons to be angry with him from time to time, just as they were often angry with me, and Tony made it more difficult for them to find any.

'Yes. So where's Lo now?'

Jack did the shrug. 'Told you. In her room.'

I listened to the sounds of the house. There was no muffled bass thud of music vibrating through the floorboards. Lola had retired to bed and probably pulled the covers over her head. She would be upset at Tony's news, too. That explained why she hadn't emerged to see me. Lola's sadness and jealousy wouldn't last long because there were too many other things going on in her life, but they would be real enough tonight.

I sat down on the bed beside Jack. I hugged him, only briefly because he kept his spine rigid and his head turned away, but at least he didn't actually push me aside. 'I'm sorry about Dad and the new baby. But I suppose we should have been expecting it.'

'Why? Isn't four kids enough?'

'I expect it was Suzy who wanted another.'

'Hm. Do you know what? They're going to call it Hugo. *Hugo*,' he repeated in disbelief.

'Are they really? Well. At least being called Hugo is one thing you don't have to cope with,' I said.

I might have been mistaken but I thought I saw the beginnings of a smile, before Jack remembered that he didn't do smiles.

I looked at his bedside clock. 'It's midnight. Time we went to bed. We can talk more tomorrow.'

He turned his head. 'What did you talk about to Mr Rainbird?'

'Quite a lot of things. About when we were young, like you are now. He told me about his mother and father. His mother especially. She died last year and he misses her.'

'Did you tell him about Grandad?'

That was a sharp question.

'Not as much.'

'Are you going to see him again?'

'Yes, I think so. Would you mind that?'

The shrug again. 'It's quite weird to think of teachers having parents like normal people.'

'Mr Rainbird is a normal person.'

'I'll take your word for it,' Jack said and I laughed.

'I love you best in all the world,' I told him truthfully. He made no response to that.

Outside Lola's door I stood and listened for a long minute. I could see in my mind's eye the long curve of her back under the duvet and the threads of hair spread over the pillow. I tapped gently with one fingertip and whispered, 'Lo?' When there was no answer I knew she was asleep. Lola wouldn't hear me without answering.

I went quietly along the landing to my own room. It was stuffy, although the windows were open. A car passed outside and the headlights swung briefly over the ceiling. When I lay down, I tried to dismiss the day. It had been too long and too complicated for me to try to set it straight before I slept.

In the morning Jack croaked from under the covers that he was going to Audrey's. All I could see of him was stiff hair and a pale crescent of forehead.

'Are you sure?'

There was a holiday play scheme, if all else failed, that Jack grudgingly agreed to go to because one of the leaders shared an interest in ornithology. If it was one of his days for going there I would drop him off on my way to the Works.

'Yeah.'

'Not to the scheme?'

'No.'

'I'll see you later, then.'

Lola was already downstairs, late for work. She was standing in her underclothes, alternately gulping instant coffee and eating buttered toast with one hand and jabbing the iron over a skirt with the other.

'I'll do that for you.'

'Thanks.'

She chewed and stared into space. Her face was still shuttered with sleep.

'News about Dad and Suzy,' I began.

'Yeah. Well. It's up to them, isn't it?'

'You weren't upset?'

'God, Mum. What would be the point?' She had been, in other words, but didn't feel like discussing it now.

'None, really. Jack minds, though, doesn't he?'

'Jack needs to get a life.'

I opened my mouth to defend him, but Lola was irritable and in a hurry, and I could tell that the heat outside was already building up into another testing day.

I said instead, 'He'll grow out of it.' Lola acknowledged my use of her mantra with a twist of her buttery lips. 'Here you are.' I turned her skirt the right way out and handed it to her.

She pulled it on over her hips and yanked at the zip. 'Gotta go.'

'See you later, then.'

I drove to work, trying not to fume at the traffic.

Penny and Andy were already at their benches. It was Leo's day at college.

In the middle of the morning Colin appeared at the front counter. We all tried to ignore him but he rapped on the countertop with a coin. 'Shop!' he called briskly.

'Hello, Colin,' I gave in.

'Nobody working here today?'

'Three of us are working, if you look closely. We're pretty busy.'

He hoisted a bulging carrier bag and dumped it on the counter. 'Got another book. I want to discuss it with you. The last one was nice, but I can think of some improvements.'

I put down my job and walked to the front of the shop. Colin had actually shed his raincoat, presumably as a concession to the heatwave, but he was still wearing a grey hand-knitted jumper with the front zip done up. There were pearly drops of sweat on his top lip and on his forehead. He smelled sharply unpleasant and I resisted the impulse to take a step backwards.

'I'm afraid we're not scheduling any new work at the moment, Colin.' I met his eye, resolving that I wouldn't be backed into any corners.

'That's rubbish.'

'It's not, actually. And we lost money on doing the last book for you, you know. By rights we should have charged over a hundred pounds for binding your recipes.'

'I paid you. What's wrong with my money?'

I sighed. A typical Colin not-quite sequitur. 'Nothing. Except that there wasn't enough of it.'

He pursed his lips and looked cunning. 'I'm on benefit, you know. I'm not one of your la-di-da types with posh cars and big houses and money to throw around on a lot of nonsense. *Oh* no. I'm on the sick. Under the doctor, up at Homerton. I have to watch what I spend.'

'I understand.'

'Good. So.' He began shovelling dog-eared magazines out of his carrier bag and as they spilled over the counter I scooped them up and tried to force them back at him.

'Colin. Listen to me. We can't do any more for you.'

I thought he hadn't heard or wouldn't listen because for several more seconds we continued our tussle. Then suddenly his arms dropped to his sides and magazines slithered off the counter and rippled to the floor. His thick lips parted as he stared at me.

'I'm sorry,' I said. My voice sounded reedy and was followed by a long silence. I heard a small clink behind me as Andy put down one of his tools.

'I don't want there to be any trouble,' Colin said.

I couldn't tell from his nasal tone whether he was conciliating or threatening. 'Of course. Of course not,' I soothed. 'Nobody mentioned trouble.'

I became suddenly and acutely aware of how many dangerous instruments surrounded us. There were knives for paring leather and long needles for stitching bindings, and the great curved blade of the guillotine glinted only a metre away. The benches were strewn with hammers and mallets.

My skin prickled. I wanted very much to get Colin out of

here. I smiled and put my hand to his elbow. 'We've just got a lot of work on right now and we can't handle any more even from our best customers. Phew. Isn't it hot in here? Let's collect up your things, look, and go outside. We can chat out there, can't we?'

He took the carrier bag when I held it out and stowed it under his arm, the movement releasing a powerful wave of stale-sweat stench. With his head bent, Colin meekly allowed me to steer him out into the yard. The sun's force was like a battering ram. Since he seemed submissive I led Colin on towards the street entry at the side of Penny's house. When I glanced back I saw that Penny and Andy had moved as one to the bindery door, to keep me in sight.

'You've already got your beautiful book,' I reminded him. 'Your mum must have been impressed with that.'

At the gate, Colin pointed down the road. 'There's my bus.'

'Don't miss it. You never know these days when there'll be another one along.'

He hesitated, then looked at the back door of the house. 'Where's that kiddie of yours?'

'She's not mine. She and her mum moved away.'

Colin peered down at me. His moist lower lip protruded and he looked genuinely concerned and upset. 'Oh, dear. That's a pity. You must miss her.'

'Yes. Quick, here comes the bus. Bye now, Colin.'

He shambled into the middle of the the road, first causing the bus to brake and then taking the opportunity to wave the driver in to the stop opposite the house. I waited until he had lumbered on board and the doors had hissed shut behind him.

Penny and Andy watched me come back down the yard.

'Was it just me, or did our Colin seem rather sinister today?' I asked.

'It's the heat. Makes everyone weird,' Andy judged.

We went back to work. The tasks I had to complete were

unenticing and the atmosphere in the bindery was depressed. Penny hardly spoke at all and Andy objected to whichever CD I chose to play. The scorching day dragged and I was relieved when it was finally time to go home. I was looking forward to spending the evening with Jack. We were going to talk about his father and the new baby, and I'd tell him about Mr Rainbird and me so that he wouldn't need to feel that I was keeping secrets from him.

I got in at ten past six to find the house empty and close-smelling. I went round opening the windows and the garden doors. The air outside was no fresher than what had been trapped inside, but it seemed worth making the exchange. At half past six I went out and sat in a deckchair in the garden to wait for Jack. I had a slight headache so I leaned my head back and closed my eyes.

I am in a narrow cul-de-sac and I'm looking for something. I don't know what it is but my whole body strains with anxiety as I search behind piles of rubbish and cardboard boxes. Grey and black cats slink along the oozing walls and although I can't see them, I sense that there are other animals here too, wild animals who have made their lairs inside the boxes. Suddenly there are people standing at the mouth of the cul-de-sac and when I see them I remember that what I'm hunting for is my mobile phone, because I need to call Jack and Lola. But now I have to avoid the men, because they are going to rob me and I won't be able to ring my children. I summon up all my strength and charge forward, straight at the people. As I start running I feel the wild animals at my heels, their low bodies hugging the ground and their red tongues showing. Ahead of me I can see the men's faces and they are smiling because I'm plunging into their trap. They have the knives from the bindery. Then my phone starts ringing.

—⁓—

I opened my eyes. My mouth was dry and I was stiff from having curled at an awkward angle in the deckchair. My headache was worse. As the dream receded I realised that the ringing was from the house phone in the kitchen. I stumbled inside to answer it and as I mumbled 'Hello?' I saw the digital clock on the oven showing five past seven. I must have slept for nearly half an hour.

'Sadie?'

It was Mel. We had only seen each other once since Grasse.

'Yes. I was asleep in the garden.'

Mel began to talk, but I had to interrupt her. 'Actually, Jack should have been back an hour ago. Can I call you later when I've got him home?'

'Sure,' Mel said warmly. 'Just let me know everything's okay.'

I dialled Audrey's number. I hung on and on, listening to the ringing tone. I would let it ring all night, I decided, if that was what it took.

'Yes?'

'It's Sadie here. Is Jack still with you?'

'Yes.'

'Can I speak to him, please? And he's supposed to be home at six every evening, Audrey.'

The only answer was silence. I heard Audrey putting the receiver down and walking away. I chewed at the corner of my mouth as I waited.

'Mum,' Jack said at last in a heavy voice.

'Do you know what the time is?'

'What?'

I lifted the hair off my collar, feeling the sweat on the exposed skin. Jack sounded as if he didn't have any idea of the time, barely even knew who I was. 'Jack,' I said clearly. 'I'm coming in the car to pick you up. I'll be there in ten minutes.'

'Mum . . .'

I replaced the receiver. Two minutes later I was driving towards Turnmill Street.

At Audrey's peeling front door I stood and waited to be let in. I banged with my fist on the blistered paintwork and when nobody came I crouched down and peered through the letter box. It gave me a view of the murky hallway and its piles of junk and the door that led into her back-room sanctum.

'Jack!' I shouted, but nothing stirred.

Under the trees of Turnmill Street the shadows were powdery with dust. Two girls walked past Audrey's gate, looking curiously at me. Their heels clicked on the pavement as they passed out of sight beyond the neighbours' privet hedge. I banged and shouted again through the letter box. Then I saw Audrey emerge and walk very slowly up the hallway. I straightened up at once but the letter box gave a tell tale rattle. The door jerked open.

'Didn't you hear me knocking?' I asked. 'I've come to pick Jack up.'

Audrey looked pale. Her hair hung in grey wisps beside her jaw. She hesitated, then half turned away from me. 'Jack?' she called, into the dim house. 'Jack?'

I saw him backlit against the yellow glow from the end room, but he didn't come any closer. I had no choice but to slip past Audrey into the hallway. I negotiated the lumber that blocked my path to Jack and when I reached him I saw that his face was swollen and shiny, and his eyes were puffy with crying.

'What's wrong? What's happened?'

Jack's mouth twisted as he bit his lip, trying to hold back more tears. I could sense Audrey close behind me and the shadowy house rearing above us. 'The cub's dead,' he whispered.

'The cub?' I repeated stupidly.

He couldn't stop himself crying and it was to Audrey he looked for comfort, not me.

She put me firmly aside. 'Come on.' She took Jack's arm. 'Come on now.'

'He was run over. We let him out in the garden just like always,' Jack sobbed. 'And then he wasn't there and he didn't come back, and when we went to look we found him lying in the street. He was squashed.'

The fox cub, of course. The ball of fur I had seen curled up in one of Audrey's animal cages, that was all, nothing more serious than that. Relief flooded warmly through my veins. 'Oh dear. That's very sad.'

Jack flung himself as far from me as possible in the confined space. 'Sad? Is that all you can say?' He hid his face against Audrey and wept, while she stared coldly into my eyes and stroked his hair as if he were one of her cats. I felt wrong-footed and excluded from the symbiosis of their grief.

I said as gently as I could, 'It's time we went home now.'

He didn't even look round. 'I'm not coming. I want to stay the night here.'

Audrey's glance glittered like chips of ice. I kept my dismay at the idea submerged as far as possible. Jack had never stayed with friends overnight, at sleepovers or birthday parties. Apart from the Cherbourg trip, he had always been with me or with Tony.

'You haven't got any pjs here, no toothbrush, nothing. You can stay another time.' I was getting this all wrong, I knew, but I had no idea how to make it right. The feeling of confusion and powerlessness was horrible.

He shook his head violently.

Audrey said to me, 'I can sort him out some things.'

I glanced up the cobwebbed stairs. It was very likely that there would be a well-aired bedroom up there with clean sheets on the bed and a brand-new toothbrush still in its packaging. 'I'd rather you came home, Jack.'

315

'No,' he snarled.

This wasn't just about the fox cub, of course. It was because of Tony's new baby son, and Lola and Sam, and me and Mr Rainbird. Audrey's house had become a retreat from all of this and the drama of the cub's death made him feel even more part of it.

'Come with me,' I said. 'Now.' I took hold of his hand and tried to draw him away from Audrey but he snatched himself out of my grasp with a strength that surprised me.

'I. Am. Staying. Here.'

My hands fell to my sides. Audrey had never taken her eyes off me. I could not stand here and do battle with her for possession of my child. I'd have to back down temporarily and do it as gracefully as I could.

Just for one night.

I took a deep breath and smiled. 'All right. You can stay with Audrey until tomorrow morning. I'll bring some clean clothes and pick you up in time to go to play scheme.'

Jack rubbed his eyes with his knuckles. Audrey's full mouth loosened and curved with triumph.

There was much more to this for her than a night's sleepover. The depth of rivalry between Audrey and me went way back into history, the thick roots twisted in the earth of the past and Ted's devious doings, and I'd have to dig those roots up somehow and dismember them.

'He's twelve. He can make some of his own decisions,' Audrey said in her superior way.

No he can't, I thought. I couldn't, at his age. I was in Ted's power and in his thrall, and I don't seem to have escaped even now. His hand reaches out and clutches me and you too, Audrey. But I didn't say anything. I hitched the strap of my handbag over my shoulder and felt in my pocket for my car keys. 'Goodnight, Jack,' I said softly.

'Say goodnight,' Audrey told him while I waited.

'Night, Mum.'

'I'm sorry about the fox cub.'

'Okay.'

I walked down the hall and then looked round. Jack had already withdrawn to the back room and Audrey stood guarding the door.

'I'll be here to pick him up at nine o'clock,' I said. I let myself out into the stifling night before she could try to contradict me.

I drove home and sat at the kitchen table for a long time, watching the green numerals of the oven clock precisely totalling the minutes and hours. I didn't ring Mel, or Caz, or anyone. I just sat, with my hands loose in front of me, waiting and thinking. I wanted to seize Jack and bodily carry him out of Audrey's ambit, but the fact that I couldn't do that didn't mean that I wouldn't bring him home. Here, at home with me and Lola, was where he belonged.

FIFTEEN

In the morning I stood on Audrey's step with a carrier bag containing Jack's clothes for the day. I knocked and called and knocked again but the only response I got was from Audrey who finally spoke up from the other side of the closed door. 'Jack's staying here with me and the animals.'

'He can't.'

'Why is that, if it's what he wants?'

'I don't know that it *is* what he wants.'

I wrestled in my mind with lurid images of drugging or hypnotic suggestion, while behind me the morning business of Turnmill Street went on regardless. A gaggle of children from one of the houses opposite was shepherded into a 4 × 4 and driven away by a woman in white plimsolls and tennis shorts. The postman worked his way along the street, but didn't turn in at Audrey's gate. A young man came out of the house next door and stared at me over the sagging wall. He had a tan and taut biceps, and a vest cut to show them off.

'Hi. Do you know your neighbour?' I asked, hoping that I might recruit some support or at least glean some useful information.

'Not really. She's eccentric. Are you a social worker? Or Environmental Health? We've been complaining about all the rubbish and the animals.'

'No, I'm not.'

Another young man came out, this one wheeling a mountain bike. 'Is something wrong?' he asked.

'No.' I smiled through my teeth. 'I'm a family friend.'

'Family? That's great. Maybe you can get something done.'

They embraced each other and the cyclist pedalled off.

I called again through the letter box. 'Audrey? I just want to talk to him for a second, please. I won't make him come out if he doesn't want to.'

Minutes passed, then Jack came into view. Against the light coming from the back of the house I couldn't see his face clearly, but he didn't look as though he had been drugged or hypnotised, nor did he even appear to be particularly forlorn. He seemed calm, with Jack the cat rubbing and twisting round his ankles like a plush cushion on legs.

'Mum, what do you want?'

'To talk to you. Don't make me do it through this slot.'

'I want to stay here because Audrey and me are both unhappy about the cub dying, and you're not bothered, are you? What else would I be doing today anyway?'

'You'd be at home. Where you belong, with me and Lo. And I'm sorry the cub got run over too. I'm just less sad than I would have been . . . oh, if something bad had happened to you, or Lola, or Dad.'

Lola had come in very late and gone out early. I told her that Jack had insisted on staying at Audrey's. 'Then let him,' she said.

Jack stood on one leg to allow the cat more twining space. 'You've got to go to work, haven't you?'

'Yes,' I admitted. There was always that pressure.

'I'm staying here,' he repeated.

I considered the situation. There wasn't anything I could do, for the time being, short of breaking the door down. The paintwork wasn't in good shape, but the door itself was heavy and the lock and hinges were sound enough. Jack was apparently well and comfortable, and probably enjoying the sense of power that defiance gave him.

'All right. See you later.'

I marched down the path and back to where I had parked the car. It took me nearly an hour to reach the Works. A truck had shed its load at the Highbury roundabout and the resultant chaos had added to the usual congestion, so the streets for miles around were set solid. When I finally slammed across the yard I saw out of the corner of my eye the lacy and ruffled hem of a skirt and the curled toe of a babouche slipper. When I looked, there was Evelyn sitting sunning herself with her long fingers wrapped round a glass of orange juice. Her hair tumbled prettily round her face.

'Hi, Sadie.' She sighed in her soft voice. 'How're you doing? Everything sweet?'

A familiar one-legged teddy bear and some crayons and paper were lying on the bench beside her.

'You're back,' I said unnecessarily. I was already tending towards the house door, hungry for the sight of Cassie.

'Last night.'

'And Cassie?'

'Yes.'

There she was, in her booster chair at the kitchen table, squeezing raisins between her fat fingers as if she had never been away. Her face turned towards me like a flower. 'Sadie-lady!'

I scooped her up and swung her round. She threw her head back and laughed with delight, and the weight of her in my arms and the sticky scent of her neck when I kissed it made me realise how much I had missed her. Evelyn was watching us from the doorway.

'Play. Let's play,' Cassie imperiously demanded with her hand snatching the air in the direction of her toys.

'I've got to work, Cass, or Penny'll want to know why.

Tell you what, though. I'll come across at teatime and read you a story. I promise.' And how simple that was, I thought, compared with my negotiations with Jack. I was going to put her back in her chair but Evelyn said she would take her.

As I passed the child over, Evelyn's hair caught between us and briefly lifted off her face to reveal a shiny red and purple swelling over her cheekbone and under her eye. I glanced away at once but she knew I had seen it. She shook her head so that the masking curls fell free again and drew her lips up into a bright little smile. 'Clumsy, aren't I? I walked smack into a lamp-post when I'd had a couple of drinks,' she said.

I nodded sympathetically, accepting the lie while I wondered with a beat of horror if there had been any threat to Cassie.

Penny was busy at her bench but she looked straight across at me when I came in. The lines of misery round her eyes and mouth were all rubbed out.

'So,' I murmured.

Andy and Leo waved vaguely to me, then bent their heads to indicate that they were elaborately absorbed in their separate tasks.

'I'll look after them. I won't bloody well let anyone lay a finger on either of them now or ever again,' Penny swore in a low, fierce voice. 'He'll have to kill *me* first.'

'I hope not,' I said.

At lunchtime I told her about Jack and Audrey. We sat in the shade of the bindery wall because it was far too hot in the sun. My thin skirt stuck to my bare legs and sweat glued my hair to the back of my neck. When I closed my eyes, thick gold and purple patches swam behind my eyelids. 'What shall I do?'

'I'd say don't force the issue. But I'm not really the best person to advise you or anyone else, am I? Given the state of play in my own life.'

'Are they going to stay?'

'I hope so.' I understood how much of an understatement

that was. 'Because they can't go back to Jerry.' But Penny held up her hand to indicate that we were discussing my concerns now, not hers. 'Have you talked to Graham and Caz? Or Mel? Whatever happens you're not on your own. You've got all of us to help you out, remember.'

I was glad of Penny's assurance. She knew the core of isolation and the chill that went with it, because it was hers too. Caz and Graham didn't because their roots were so closely entwined, and Mel had never experienced it because the warmth of her family always insulated her. As I considered loneliness that wasn't so much about feeling lonely as managing your life alone, I was watching the iridescent sheen on the wings and bodies of flies settling on the stones of the yard. I couldn't remember another summer as hot as this; even the one I had spent in Grasse long ago seemed degrees cooler in comparison.

'I do remember,' I said gratefully to Penny.

As soon as I reached home again I called Tony. He was still at work, preparing to pitch for a new account, and it took some persistence to break through his PA's resolve that he shouldn't be disturbed. I imagined him in his shirtsleeves at a desk piled with storyboards and charts and scripts, as I had often seen him when we were married. Poor Tony, I thought. He had plenty to deal with.

'Sadie? Hello?'

'Congratulations,' I said.

'Thank you.' His tone didn't give much away. 'Is this just a friendly call? Because I'm quite tied up, actually, Sade.'

'No, it's not really about that.'

He listened while I told him what was happening. 'Who is this Audrey, exactly?'

'An old friend of Ted's. Not a girlfriend, she claims.'

Tony chuckled, his affection for Ted sounding only faintly

touched by weariness. 'He doesn't let go, the old boy, does he? Even though he's dead there are still plenty of surprises.'

'Yes,' I said. Ted could always be surprising.

'I'll be through here in an hour. Do you want me to go round to this house, wherever it is, and try to talk to Jack?'

'I think what's set this off is partly to do with you and the new baby. It being a boy, you know. Not only that, of course. There's plenty of other things that are going on in his life to make him unsettled. But it's never that simple with Jack, you know?'

'So what can I do?'

I sighed. 'Nothing, probably, right now. I just wanted you to know where he is. Because you're his father.'

As always there was that connection, even though I had severed the other ties. Silence hung between us now, weighted with concern and on my part at least, regret for a lost possibility more than any faded reality. Tony and I couldn't discuss regret either, nor even refer to it, because it was much too late and neither of us could allow the intimacy that talking about such things would call up. Intimacy existed, bred by all the years we had spent together, but it was kept in abeyance.

The thought made me profoundly sad. The denial seemed to parallel the state of affairs between Ted and me, and to presage the likely future with Jack as well. I held the receiver so tightly that sweat sprang from the palms of my hands.

'Thanks, Sadie,' Tony said gently. 'You can count on me. You as well as Jack. And try not to worry. He'll come home when he's ready.'

Would he? I was afraid that he might never want to come back, that I had lost him without knowing what was happening and that it was now too late for me to make amends. I tried hard not even to admit to the much darker, Gothic fears that went with the shadowy depths of the house in Turnmill Street.

'I'll keep you posted,' I said at last. 'Tell Suzy I'm pleased about the new baby.'

'I'll do that.'

Later, I stood yet again on the step at Turnmill Street. There was no response to my knocking. If anything, Jack's resolve to stay put seemed to be strengthening. All I could think of was how much I wanted to get him home again, yet I had packed a bag with some more of his clothes and the other belongings I thought he might need. I didn't want to allow the possibility of his staying here tonight, let alone any series of nights to come, but I wanted him to have the comforts he might need from home if he did stay, if it did come to that.

There were so many contradictions in my mind, it was hardly surprising that they were reflected in Jack.

I could only guess, but perhaps part of Jack also wanted to emerge from the house and be driven home. Maybe he felt that matters had already gone too far for that, though and he'd have to stick to the route he'd chosen in order not to lose face to Audrey, or to me. Maybe Audrey was cajoling him into staying put. Maybe he was simply glad to be at Turnmill Street instead of at home. Maybe he just wanted attention, from me or his father or from a world that didn't seem to acknowledge his desires. And perhaps this rebellion meant that his bewilderment and disappointment with life were finally taking pointed and aggressive shape.

I knocked as hard as I could, then leaned forward so that my forehead rested against the door. The flaking paint crackled, just audibly. I could also hear the throaty calls of pigeons roosting close at hand and the rumble of traffic. In my mind's eye I saw Jack and Audrey sitting in the back room, among the cats and piles of newspapers, gazing at each other with wide eyes and holding their breath until the knocking should stop. Suddenly, hot anger flashed through me.

I hammered until my fist throbbed and yelled, 'Audrey! I

want to speak to my son. Open this door immediately or I'll call the police.'

The door opened an inch and I peered into the gloom. Audrey was there.

'Tell him to come out right now.'

It was too dark to see her face properly.

'He doesn't want to.'

'I've had enough of this.' I pushed hard at the door, getting my shoulder up against it. Audrey resisted with surprising strength and the door almost slammed in my face before I could shove back again. I heard a rattle as she swiftly slotted the chain into place and blocked the door's inward swing. Now I was securely locked out.

'This house is my property,' Audrey said calmly through the gap. 'And Jack's my guest. Why can't you let him be? We're watching *Animal Hospital*. I'll tell him to phone you later.'

I took a breath. This exchange was so rationally irrational that it sounded surreal.

'You don't own him, you know,' Audrey added. A smoke-grey cat appeared in the narrow slice of hallway and stared up at me with yellow eyes.

'Listen to me, Audrey. Nobody owns anybody else and I wouldn't claim that they do. I am Jack's mother, though, and I'm responsible for his safety and his well-being. And a lot of other things besides, but let's keep it simple for now. I'm not convinced that he's safe with you, especially since you seem to need to lock him in.'

'The chain's to keep you out, not him in.'

'I don't want my son locked in a stranger's house.'

Audrey snorted. 'I'm not a stranger. I knew his grandfather for nearly fifty years. And if he wants to take a break from life with you maybe you should ask yourself why, instead of coming round here and shouting at me. There's no need to worry. I'll take good care of him.'

'Let me talk to him.'

'We're watching *Animal Hospital*.'

'Bugger *Animal Hospital*.'

I could almost hear Audrey pursing her lips. I'd uttered a profound blasphemy. 'I'll see that he calls you later,' she repeated. The door was closing again and I had to accept that the score now stood at Audrey and Jack 2, Family 0.

I called into the crack. 'Jack? Can you hear me? I've brought some clothes and your GameBoy and your CD player. Is there anything else you need before you come home tomorrow?'

There was no answer.

'Open the door please, Audrey, so I can hand you the bag.'

'Leave it on the step. I'll pick it up when you've gone.'

As I reached the gate the door flew open, the bag disappeared and the door slammed shut again.

I drove home through the dark-blue August twilight. I was angry and shaking from my confrontation with Audrey. I had been made to feel powerless in relation to my own child and I vowed that wouldn't continue. If I was going to have to fight to bring Jack back, then so be it.

When I pulled up I saw that most of the lights in our house were on although Lola had warned me it was one of her bar-job nights. I let myself in and the smell of soy and ginger wafted to meet me, with the sound of voices. In the kitchen I found Caz sitting at the table with a glass of wine. Graham and Jasper were leaning against the counter also holding glasses of wine, and Mel was stirring the contents of a frying pan.

I blinked. 'It's not my birthday, is it? I wasn't expecting a surprise party.'

'It wouldn't really be a surprise party, would it, if you were expecting it?' Graham remarked reasonably. Caz shushed him and came round to me with a drink. I swallowed a gulp and Mel blew me a kiss.

'Penny called me. She said you're worried about Jack and

from the sound of it I don't blame you. I rang Caz, and we thought we'd all come round and cook some food for you and have a case conference. Lola let us in before she went to work. Penny wanted to be here too, but she's got some stuff to deal with herself tonight.'

'She has.' I sat down. My legs felt shaky and the wine hitting the lining of my stomach made me remember that I hadn't bothered to eat for a day or so. 'Thank you,' I said. Caz patted my shoulder.

I looked round the circle of faces in the candlelight. The door to the garden stood open and moths fluttered at the night's edge. I was glad to see everyone and I was touched by this demonstration of friendship, but I also felt that what was happening was between my son and me, and I should be able to sort it out for myself.

At the same time it occurred to me that the person I really wanted to talk to about it all was Paul Rainbird. I put this startling realisation to the back of my mind for proper consideration later.

Jasper was sitting opposite me. He and Mel kept looking at each other, as if to check one another's reaction to what the rest of us were saying. He said suddenly, 'Clare didn't speak to me for two months after her mother and I split. Not a word. I thought I'd lost her for good.'

'What happened?' Caz asked.

'We made it up in the end but it took time. Then she was very possessive of me for a while and hostile to my girlfriend. She went in for a couple of heavy relationships herself and they both ended badly.'

'And now?'

'We like each other again.' Jasper looked less confident and more troubled than I had seen him before. 'At least, I like her. Love her very much.'

The eerily positive picture of his family history had been

327

painted for Mel in the early days of their relationship, I understood. Nothing was really that simple. Not with all the stepped and paralleled and severed relationships that lay behind most of us.

Mel gathered her hair in a tight fistful and held it away from her face. 'Kids, eh?' Her laugh was shaky.

I was thinking that we couldn't solve one another's problems. But we could draw comfort from comparisons, and we could get together and drink wine by candlelight. This would be my family, when even Jack and Lola had moved on and become absorbed in the joys and demands of their own families.

At that moment the phone rang and I got up to answer it.

'Hello, Mum.' Jack's voice sounded small and clear. Audrey was true to her word, then.

'Hello. Hold on for a minute, I'll take this upstairs.'

I replaced the handset and went up one flight of stairs to the living room. As I picked up the phone again I saw how much tidier the place looked than it usually did, as if neither of my children lived with me any longer. 'Are you there, Jack? What are you doing?'

'Not much. We've been watching TV. I fed the cats and the rabbits. It's so hot.'

'Do you want to come home? Shall I come round and pick you up?'

'No, Mum.'

There was a silence. I wanted to extend the conversation but I wasn't sure what to say next. In the end I went for the obvious. 'I miss you. Is there anything you need?'

'I'd like my binoculars. And my bird book. It's on my table in my room.'

'Jack. You're not *staying* there.'

'Yes, I am.'

I bit back the sharp contradiction. If I was going to fight,

I would have to use more subtle weaponry than a telephone slanging match. 'I'll bring them tomorrow.'

'Thanks,' he said, still in the same small but clear voice. He sounded older, as if he were discovering unexpected resources within himself.

'Anything else?'

'No. Who's there with you?'

'Just Caz and Graham and Mel and Jasper.'

'Oh. That's nice.' After another small silence he said, 'Well. Goodnight, then.'

'Goodnight. I love you, you know. You can call me as soon as you want to come home, any time, even if it's in the middle of the night.'

I wondered if Audrey could overhear what he was saying. Reluctantly I said goodnight again and then he hung up.

Mel was coming up the stairs as I made my way down. 'Jack?' she asked me.

'Yes. What are they doing downstairs?'

'They're fine.' Mel steered me back into the living room and we sat down on the sofa. Her face was shadowed with concern. 'I met Clare, you know.'

I exhaled. 'I'm sorry. I should have asked you about it. It's just that with all this . . .'

'I didn't mean that. Meeting her gave me a new perspective, that's what I want to say. Because I wanted so damn much for her to like me, I felt disabled. None of the usual strategies was going to work, just because I knew they were strategies and I felt ashamed of employing them. You know . . . no asking her leading questions about herself, no going for easy girlie ground to make her think I'm her friend. I just wanted to be honest with her, and the sheer *effort* it took made me suspect that I go about the rest of my life in a mere cardboard two-dimension.'

I smiled. 'Mel, you're the most three-dimensional woman I know.'

329

'Wait. I'm not fishing for compliments. I got it all wrong anyway. When I met her, she was very cool. Not unfriendly, but holding herself in reserve. And I was second-guessing so hard, trying to be so not over the top, so *limpid* that she could see straight into the real me, that I forgot to be anything natural at all. We were like a pair of icebergs sailing past each other. Jasper said afterwards that I seemed strained.'

'Did he?'

'It was so important, to me and to him, and I was trying too hard *not to try too hard*.'

I was laughing now, in spite of wanting to take all this seriously.

'No, listen. I'm telling you this because of Jack and you. Trying to make a go of it with Clare made me aware how difficult all this must be for real parents and I've never understood that before. I assumed that liking each other came naturally, after the breast-feeding and before the grandchildren. It was how it happened in our family, but that was luck, wasn't it?'

'More like good management.'

'It's such a labyrinth. With kids the more you want something to work, the harder you're likely to try and the more awkward and seized-up the relationship gets. Is that right?'

'Yes. Like handling pastry too much. You can work at it, and go on working and hoping to make it better until you bring it to the point of ruination.'

Mel ran her fingers through her hair until it crackled. I thought that if I turned off the lamp I'd see a wild halo of blue sparks.

'My God, that's frightening. I was scared to death of Jasper's Clare and she's a nineteen-year-old girl. It must be even more complicated with Jack, when you love him so much. And for Jasper, with Clare. I can imagine it, even though I've got none of my own.'

I noticed that Mel's way of speaking about it had changed.

She still lamented her childlessness, but the raw edge of agony seemed to have melted away. That was what falling in love with Jasper had done for her.

At the same time, I was thinking yes, that's right. I've got to find a way to lay off Jack, just as Tony and Mr Rainbird told me, and now even Mel is circuitously telling me. But abandoning him to Audrey and Turnmill Street isn't the way.

Not abandoning him, however hard he insists on the opposite, that's the right way. He's pushing me, to see what I will do. He may not even know it himself but he's testing my allegiance and that's good. When I was Jack's age I hadn't owned even a fraction of the confidence it would have taken to test Ted.

I groped for Mel's hand and held on to it. We sat and looked out at the windows of the houses opposite ours and the yellow bloom of the nearest street lamp. I wondered if the dog fox was delicately stepping somewhere beyond the circle of light. 'Clare is scared too,' I said. 'She's afraid you'll turn out not to be good enough for her father. She's afraid you might have hoodwinked or hypnotised him. Or that he'll love you too much and therefore love her less.'

Mel drew up her knees and rested one cheek on them, looking hard at me. 'You've been through all this.'

'In a way.'

We squeezed each other's hands.

'It doesn't stop, does it?' Mel murmured. 'Learning and loving.'

'No. Even though we're as old as we are. Fifty outside, twenty-seven within. It doesn't stop.'

'Good,' she said.

We found that the party in the kitchen had changed gear. The table had been cleared and the dishwasher was humming. The three of them had drawn up their chairs, there was another full bottle on the table and Graham was shuffling a pack of cards.

He looked at us over the top of his glasses. 'We thought we'd make a night of it. What'll it be? Gin rummy? Pontoon? Or a couple of hands of poker?'

'What's the time?' I looked at the oven's green digits.

'Oh, come on. How old do you feel?' Mel demanded.

'What the hell,' I said and took my place.

We played pontoon for 50p stakes and I'd already lost £3 by the time Lola came in. She was wearing her bartender's black T-shirt and trousers, and her hair was knotted on the top of her head. She looked tired but wide awake, rather than tired and three-quarters asleep as she did in the mornings.

'This looks good to me.' She poured herself a drink and sat down to join us. 'Mum, what's the news on Jack?'

'Still at Audrey's.'

'Uh-uh. What are we playing? I'm in.'

'Aren't you tired?'

'I'm not ready to go to bed.'

'Let her play.'

I forgot about Jack for an hour. I lost another fiver, and drank some more wine and laughed a lot. Mel was always brilliant at cards because she wanted to win, and in contrast Jasper turned out to be even less concerned than I was.

In the end Lola was the overall winner because luck had been on her side, as always. She raked a pile of coins into her pocket and beamed around the table. 'A lot easier than bar work,' she said.

As the others left we all agreed that we should do this more often. It had been a good evening, against the odds: I felt the warmth of it around me as I locked the front door and turned off the lights.

Lola slipped into my room while I was getting ready for bed. 'Are you really worried?' she asked. She wanted to pitch her own anxiety by estimating mine, so I smiled and shook my head. Looking down, I saw that our bare feet were exactly the same shape. I remembered how amazed I had been, on the day of her birth, by the wrinkled crimson perfection of hers.

In the morning, I had a red-wine hangover. I left the wine glasses and debris from last night littering the kitchen table, and hunted for Jack's bird book and binoculars. Lola had already gone to work. Outside, the sky was white and the sun's glare made my eyes throb. The drive to Turnmill Street took longer than it had done last time, and I reflected that I would soon have to abandon my car and walk everywhere because it would be quicker.

At Audrey's front door I banged and shouted, and waited before banging again. The street was quiet, the patches of shade under the trees looking inviting from where I stood on the scorched doorstep. I was bending down to peer through the letter box when I heard a car draw up. A door opened and closed, and there was a chatter of voices broadcast over some radio static. When I turned, a young policewoman was coming in through Audrey's gate. She was in shirtsleeves, with a radio transceiver clipped in her top pocket. I saw the chequered band round her hat and the sun glinting on badges and numbers. Fear stiffened my back as I stood upright. Why were the police here?

'Good morning,' the WPC said pleasantly.

'Is something wrong?' I asked.

'Is this your house?'

'No. No, it isn't. My son's . . . staying here.'

'I see.' She was looking at the filthy windows and the debris scattered in the garden. Her radio chattered again. 'We have had a call from one of the neighbours. Somebody has been seen several times, shouting and hammering at the door. And there is a child on the premises who doesn't usually live here. Is that right?'

The relief I had briefly felt now shifted into anger. I turned my head to stare back at the shiny windows and padded curtains and trim hedges of Turnmill Street. Self-satisfied, bourgeois, rising-property-values bloody place, I thought, my sympathies suddenly with Audrey. Some busybody had it in for her because her paintwork and ideas about garden maintenance didn't conform to local standards. 'That would be my son, yes,' I said pleasantly.

'Shall we just have a word with him, then?'

This put me in a difficult position. I could knock on the door, but the policewoman and I might well stand here hoping for a response until the sun fried us both to a crisp. I decided that candour was the best resort. 'I don't honestly know about that. He's being a bit rebellious. He's a teenager, you see. Well, almost a teenager. He's decided to stay here with, with . . .' My voice trailed away. I realised I didn't even know Audrey's surname. 'A family friend. He's upset because his fox cub died. And he won't come out, which is why I have been banging on the door, actually.' I knew that this sounded unconvincing.

The driver of the panda car was now coming to join his companion. As if to embody the cliché, this one looked even younger, barely older than Jack himself. I could distinctly see the pimples on his jawline. I stood on the doorstep between them and noticed that a couple of passers-by had stopped to watch what was going on.

'His fox cub,' repeated the policewoman. 'Your son is twelve?'

'That's right.'

'Let's see, shall we?'

She rapped smartly on the door and the second officer moved in to back her up. I was edged sideways off the step. I was sweating with embarrassment as well as from the morning's sickly heat.

The door opened at once to reveal Audrey. She looked smaller and frailer than she usually did. Her eyes travelled straight from the police to me and I knew she would assume this was my doing. I'd threatened it, but I hadn't ever meant it.

'Good morning,' the policewoman said again. 'Are you all right?'

I realised with a small shock that they were just as prepared for her to be a thuggish twelve-year-old's hostage as they were for Jack to be a helpless kidnap victim.

'Yes, thank you. Is there some problem?'

'We understand you have a young man staying with you? This lady's son?'

Audrey's cold glance rested on me. There could be no doubt in her mind now that I was responsible for this invasion.

'Audrey, I . . .' I began.

'That's correct,' Audrey agreed, cutting me short.

The police radios clattered on and the knot of bystanders was growing. The mountain bike man from next door was looking on from his doorstep.

'Where is he now?'

She lifted her chin. 'Well, he's here, isn't he? Jack!' she called into the dim recess of the house.

The police and the neighbours and I formed an audience round the front door. Two cats slunk out, twisted between our legs and stepped daintily among the fossilised cardboard boxes.

His feet and legs plodded into view at the head of the stairs. We all craned forward. Jack came down slowly, reluctantly, one step at a time. His face, when I could see it, was a troubled mask.

'I didn't call the police, Jack. One of the neighbours did,' I told him.

'What's going on here?' the WPC asked.

He shrugged. 'Nothing.' He wouldn't look at me.

The officers were losing interest. No one was hurt or being held captive in Turnmill Street. It was that great waster of police time, a domestic, and the radio clamour announced that there were bigger scenes brewing elsewhere. I could tell they were already preparing to withdraw when Audrey made the tactical error of protesting too much. 'It's the summer holidays, isn't it? What harm can it do, if he wants to stay here with me?'

The policeman spoke for the first time. 'By rights, he should be at home with his mum.'

'I'm fine here,' Jack mumbled. My heart twisted with sympathy for him because he couldn't be seen to lose face by coming with me, nor did he want to reject me under the gaze of the police and the band of spectators. I would have given anything for this scene not to be happening.

'You're not a relative, are you?' the WPC asked Audrey.

Audrey glared. She was angry because she had given away her advantage. Her thin grey fingers wrapped round the edge of the door, making it into a shield. 'I am his grandmother.'

My breath caught under my sternum. Audrey closed the door, gently but firmly.

The officers turned to me. 'His grandmother? On your husband's side, is that?'

I found my voice, after a moment. 'I'm divorced. It's a fantasy. My husband has never set eyes on her.'

They glanced at each other but they were moving, off the step and past the cats and the geological strata of decaying cardboard. They had had enough of this.

'I think your lad'll be back home as soon as he gets tired of all the attention,' the WPC said, kindly enough. They peeled away to the panda car, settled themselves inside and cruised off down the street. The onlookers were dispersing because there was no drama here. No visible drama, at any rate, although a new and fearsome thought was making the sweat turn cold on my back. I shivered as I walked away to my car.

If Audrey was claiming to be Jack's grandmother, there

could be only one possible connection between her and Ted and me.

No. No, that wasn't even a possibility.

Mr Rainbird said when I called him, 'Damn. I've got a gig with the band tonight. But listen, why don't you come along and we can have a drink or something to eat afterwards? I know it's not exactly an irresistible proposition, but maybe if you're not doing anything else?'

His honesty disarmed me, as it always did. It was Friday and Lola had gone up north to stay the weekend with Sam. 'I'll come.'

He gave me directions and I promised to be there for the second set.

When I arrived, the pub was hotter than a Turkish bath. The heads bobbing between the bar and the bandstand were damp and there were dark T shapes marking people's clothes. The smell of sweat and beer filled my mouth.

Jerry was singing 'Destination Anywhere'. He stood up on the low stage with the pub's red and blue lighting throwing purple slashes across his handsome face. The colours reminded me of Evelyn's bruises and I looked away before he caught my eye. I felt that I was betraying Penny and Evelyn and Cassie just by being here and watching him.

Mr Rainbird saw me and smiled when he lowered his trumpet.

I searched for a space at the bar and bought myself a drink. The ice cooled the back of my throat and I rested the frosted glass against my forehead. This was the first empty moment of the day and even in this inferno I was glad of an interlude of peace. I stopped thinking and let the cold fingers of vodka slide along my veins.

The music was good, if you didn't have to try to talk against it.

I closed my eyes through 'Try a Little Tenderness', then opened them for long enough to get my glass refilled.

By the time I have downed this one, after a couple more songs, my arms and legs feel as though their wiring has been severed. My spine loosens and I lean back, hitching my elbows on the bar and watching the musicians. I try to cut Jerry out of the picture, and find that I can do this surprisingly well by closing one eye and moving my head, then doing the same with the other eye. He leaves a Jerry-shaped cartoon space at centre stage. Mr Rainbird and the trombonist play their good meaty brass section, and tonight there is even a pair of girl vocalists who press their red lips close to the mike.

The music and the heat wash over me in big, lavish waves. I am smiling and clapping along with everyone else.

By the time the set ends I have finished my third icy drink. The band plays 'Wait 'til the Midnight Hour' for the encore and I am sorry when we have clapped and stamped our way to the final bars. The bar staff are calling time and the pub doors stand wide open as bouncers try to funnel people out into the street. A faint breath of cooler air just fans my face.

Then Mr Rainbird is standing right in front of me. 'Shall we go?' he says.

We are walking down the street together. He puts one arm round my shoulders. His trumpet case is in the other hand.

It feels so cool out here, after the heat of the bar. Sweat dries under my arms and in the small of my back. I feel light-footed and light-headed as we walk along together. The pavements under our feet are sticky. I can hear and feel the faint suction as well as the click of my heels and the soft padding of his rubber soles.

It's nice, walking like this, in step and with the music still in our heads. We are humming the same tune and just moving together, in no particular direction and in no hurry. Even the noise of the traffic seems muted. The trees are limes dripping sap, and wide horse-chestnuts, and London planes with their fantastically patched and mottled bark that makes me think of maps of exotic lands. Under one of these Mr Rainbird stops and puts down his trumpet case. He stands in front of me and a street lamp throws his shadow across my face.

He puts his hands on my shoulders and looks down at me. Then he kisses me, and after a minute I lock my arms round his neck, holding him close, tipping my head back and opening my mouth to his.

When we move apart we do so very reluctantly.

He says, 'Sadie, would you like to come home with me?'

I think about this and the thought makes my veins feel as though they are running with honey, not vodka and ice.

I begin composing a sentence. 'Mr Rainbird . . .' I say by mistake. Of course I know his name. It's just that up until now, in my head, he has stayed partly connected to school and Jack and a public role, and I have used this to keep my distance from him.

He puts one finger over my lips, silencing me. 'I have just asked you to come to bed with me. It's all right to use my first name.'

Laughter begins in the pit of my stomach and bubbles upwards. Somewhere a thread is severed and his teacher persona drifts away out of my consciousness.

'It's Paul, by the way,' he adds considerately.

'I know,' I insist, but I can hardly get the words out. Suddenly we are both laughing so hard that we have to hold each other up. I laugh with my cheek against his shoulder and he cups my head with his hand, so I can hear the gusts of laughter rising in his chest.

SIXTEEN

You don't forget how to make love, I discover, any more than you forget how to laugh. It's just that lately I haven't been doing enough of either.

Tonight, though, goes some way towards making up the shortfall.

I lie in Paul Rainbird's arms, salved by slippery skin against skin, after an interlude of eager touch and taste that has made me cry and laugh, with my eyes shut and my mouth open against his. My heartbeat slows and steadies, and I imagine that it matches his, beat for beat. I can tell from his breathing that he is still awake and listening, like me, to the night noises from beyond the open windows. There are sirens, speeding cars and slamming doors, voices shouting in the distance and footsteps closer at hand. The city is simmering, threatening to boil over, but this room contains its own tiny calm world. I feel as though I am lying stretched out on a smooth, sun-warmed rock. Paul's fingers twined in my hair are like strands of seaweed, anchoring me close to the murmuring sea. Everything is clean and salty. In here the night noises are as distant and unthreatening as the cries of seabirds. Gulls, terns and guillemots, Jack would say.

Even the thought of Jack slides through my head without making me need to roll on my side or draw up my knees to ease the stab of anxiety.

Paul's room is white-painted and neatly arranged, like the rest of his flat. There are belongings laid out, lines of books and a few framed photographs, but they have an almost marginal air, as though he doesn't look at them with full attention. The place gives an impression of being only half occupied and I sense that it also stands as a metaphor for his life.

'I'm always waiting and watching for something to happen,' he told me earlier. Then he added, 'Maybe something has, now.'

'Does it annoy you when people ask what you are thinking?' he asks. I can hear his voice outside us both, in the common air, but also the matching vibration from within his ribcage. It's like being given a private piece of him that seems more intimate than sex.

'No.' I smile. My mouth pulls minutely against the skin of his chest.

'So what are you thinking?'

'About how tender this is. And how natural and important it feels for skin to touch skin. It's as though some vital element that's essential for us to be happy can only be absorbed directly through our pores.'

'An osmotic process.'

'That's right.' A memory is stirring insistently in my mind. 'I was thinking of my father and mother, too.'

The old man is still stalking me. But suddenly my mother is there with him, as if this act of pairing with Paul has opened another door, allowing couples instead of just broken-off individuals to pass through the eye of memory's needle.

'Go on,' he says. He settles his arms round me.

'We went to the coast for the day. It must have been Brighton, I think. I can remember walking on the pier and seeing the sea a long way down through the chinks in the decking.'

It was a bright, windy day. Strands of hair blew across my mother's face – light-brown hair the colour and softness of

341

mouse fur. (Did I think that then, or am I overpainting the shade and texture now?) She laughed with her head back, picking the threads away from her mouth. She was wearing lipstick, which she didn't usually do, a wide belt that emphasised her hips and canvas peep-toe sandals powdery with whitener. She looked pretty, but my father was the magnificent one.

He was tall and his laugh was as loud as the waves breaking under the pier columns. The other couples and families who passed turned to look at him but he didn't notice them. He only noticed us. 'My two princesses,' he said.

I had been walking between them, holding their hands. I must have been six or seven. I wanted them to swing me, but my mother said I was too big and heavy for that now.

'How about this, then?' Ted asked. He took hold of my wrists and in a single smooth movement he lifted me up above his head and dropped me on to his shoulders. The suddenness of it and the height took my breath away. Speechless, I knotted my fingers in the brilliantined crest of his hair and he gripped my ankles. My white socks emerged from the collars of his big fists and I knew I was safe.

'Are you ready?' he called back to me.

'Yes, yes.' I was ready for anything, up here, with a giant's-eye view of the pier's smooth decking pointing away to the horizon and the sun-flecked sea stretching on either side of us.

'Then let's go.'

He started to run. 'Ted! Ted, be careful.' My mother's voice behind us, thin and anxious, was snatched away by the wind rushing past. I could feel the heat of my father's shoulders directly under my thighs and calves, and the texture of his skin and the hard bone of his big skull beneath my fingers. The lemony, salty scent of him seemed right, then; it was only later that it was all wrong.

'Giddy-up!' I shouted and squeezed my knees against his neck. People were looking at us and I was amazed to tower so high above grown men. We ran along the pier, galloping like a horse and rider all the way to the railings at the end where fishermen were tethered to the water by curved lines. Ted was panting and sweat flattened his thick hair. At the far end he whinnied just like a horse, pawing with his feet and tossing his head before swinging me up into the air. His mouth was red and his teeth were so white by contrast, and his moustache prickled my cheek when he kissed me. Then he set me squarely down on the dull decking. Faye was a long way off, walking towards us with her skirt blowing round her calves.

Ted winked at me. 'We could win the Derby, you and me, eh?'

'Again,' I begged, but I knew that it was a once-only joyride. And I also knew not to push my luck with further demands, not with Ted.

When Faye caught up with us we sat down in a glass-and-wood shelter that blocked out the wind. Ted bought dishes of cockles from a kiosk and I pulled a face at the vinegary sliver of chewy rubber and sand. They both laughed at my disgust and I got a Wall's neapolitan ice cream instead, a crystalline pink and brown and white block wedged in a rectangular cone. My parents lit cigarettes, my mother cupping her hands round hers while Ted flicked his shiny lighter to it like a kiss. Watching him, full of pride, I wanted to tell the people who passed that he was an artist who wove dreams for ladies, using the petals of roses and the mysterious clouds of musk and amber and vetiver.

I remember driving home through the dusk. It must have been one of Ted's prosperous times. Other families' cars were beige or dusty black, but ours was bright yellow. It had leather seats, very dark red. 'Ox-blood red,' my mother said. Ted drove one-handed, with the other arm curled round the back of her seat.

Of course she was my mother. I know it, as surely as I know

that Lola and Jack are mine. Whoever Audrey is, there is no blood connection between the two of us.

'I don't know what made me think of all that,' I tell Paul. I am drowsy with the sudden, surprising, sexual intimacy where there was none before. Sleep is coming at me in big waves now. He strokes my hair and I fall asleep.

In the morning, I woke up with his arms still round me. It took me a few seconds to work out where I was and whose unfamiliar room I was lying in. Paul's face was creased with sleep and his hair stuck out in rakish wings.

'Hello,' I said.

He sat upright and rubbed his face, and I could see full consciousness coming back. I watched to see if realisation was going to be followed by a flicker of dismay, but all I could see was happiness faintly shaded with uncertainty. 'Are you all right with this?' he asked, meaning the room and the bed and what had happened here.

'Yes,' I said. 'If it's all right with you.'

He kissed me. 'Better than that.' He beamed.

We lay down again and he ran his hand down over my ribs, into the hollow of my waist, over the swell of my hips. I put my fingers to his cheekbones and the angle of his jaw, mapping his face.

We stared into each other's eyes. I kept telling myself, Jack is at Audrey's and Lola's with Sam. The absence of responsibility made me feel lightweight, as if I might drift upwards away from the sheets and pillows, if I didn't have Paul Rainbird's arms and legs to hold me down.

Later, we got up and padded around in his kitchen. It was oppressively hot outside, I could tell from the slow shuffle of a woman crossing the street with a bag of shopping and the drooping branches of the plane tree opposite. Paul had given me a clean T-shirt to wear and I sat on a stool watching him make coffee and toast. The details of someone else's kitchen – the layout of cupboards, the design of mugs and location of the coffee jar – were all interesting, clean-edged, like on the first morning of a holiday. He gave me the choice of honey or Marmite, then put the coffee pot on the table between us. 'How's Jack? Is he at his dad's this weekend?' he asked.

'Um, no.' I told him what was happening.

I remembered the first time I talked properly to him, in his room at school after I'd found out about Jack's truancy. I had liked the attentive but undemonstrative way he listened then, and he was still listening to me now. He didn't try to propose solutions or tell me that everything would be all right, or that I was worrying too much or not enough. He just gave me his full attention.

'I wanted to tell you about it. My good friends came round the other evening and we had a conference. They were very supportive and I was grateful, but I was thinking that you were the person I really wanted to talk to.'

'Because I was his head of year?'

'No. Because you're you.'

'Really?'

There was a hesitancy about him and a reluctance to take anything for granted. At some point he had drawn back his antennae and retreated into himself, maybe after his long relationship had ended. He was waiting and watching, perhaps, but without much expectation. I recognised the remains of damage in him and it touched me. And it also struck me that I didn't want to be toting the remains of mine around any longer, any more than I wanted to be Paul's aide in shouldering or smothering his. That was the past and we were free of it. We had the luxury of choice and I knew that to choose was to be whole.

I touched his hand across the table top. It was an ordinary morning, a baking August Saturday in the inner city, but something out of the ordinary was happening. 'Yes. Tell me something, Paul.' It seemed to be the first time I had used his name. 'Didn't you want children of your own? Don't you still want them now?'

'I did, with Jane. She did, with me. But the time was never right for both of us at once, so it never happened. I don't regret it now because I think we'd have split anyway.' Tactfully he considered what he was about to say, then said it regardless. 'And so as far as the present goes, I teach enough kids from fractured families. And from non-existent families. I see what it's like.'

'Like Jack.'

He laughed. 'Not much, no. On another scale, actually. On completely another *planet* from Jack. Some kids – not all the ones from problem backgrounds, of course, but some of them – are like a different species.'

'I can hardly imagine.' I already admired him for doing his difficult job; now I knew the colour of his voice a little better and the dryness of his understatements, I had a glimpse of just how difficult it might be. I remembered the tides of children I had seen pouring out of the school. They had been menacing enough.

'I try to teach them *Macbeth* and creative writing, and the unfashionable difference between an adjective and an adverb, yes. Mostly it's utterly pointless. They're angry, some of them, and violent because of their anger, but it's bred out of deprivation and neglect and brutality that you and Jack could hardly conceive of. So no, I don't yearn too much for fatherhood. I fear the responsibility of it.'

He spoke simply, almost flatly. Another siren ululated in the middle distance. Then he added, 'Very occasionally you do get through to one or two of them. One of them says, Yes, I see. Or, I liked that, sir. And you know they'll remember whatever it was you were trying to convey to the rest of the mob, long after they've left school and gone to work. Maybe even until their dying day. That compensates for all the rest of the mindless argy-bargy that teaching's about nowadays. It comes close to having one of your own, I'm pretty sure. There was a moment with Jack, in fact.'

'Was there?' I was startled.

'I gave him a poem to read. About a bird.'

'What was it?'

'"The Windhover".'

I'd never heard of it. In front of Paul I was slightly ashamed of the fact that, to me, books had always represented calf bindings and coloured endpapers, and tooled or carved designs in all their sumptuous variety and possibility, rather more than windows into an infinity of knowledge.

'Jack told me he didn't understand most of it and that didn't bother him. But it described what the bird in flight looked like and, because Jack knew all about that, he felt that he could trust the poet for having got that much right. And he said the words and the rhythm also made him feel what it was like to *be* a bird in flight. He decided that the point of a poem was to tell you something you knew, and then to use that to introduce you to something you didn't know and were pleased to find out about. I thought that was quite impressive.'

So did I. Warmth spread along my spine and filled my throat, and I recognised the feeling as pride. I was proud of Jack, just as I had been when he stood up to talk at Ted's funeral.

'Thank you,' I said to Paul.

He fidgeted a little, as if my gratitude made him slightly uncomfortable. 'Just doing my job.'

'And doing it well,' I persisted. I found myself wanting to chip away at his self-deprecation. I suspected that he was a brilliant teacher, I knew that he was a pretty good trumpeter and I had just found out that he was surprisingly good in bed. The last thought, unexpectedly coming into my mind, made me blush.

Paul took my hand and held on to it. 'What do you want to do now, Sadie? Would you like to spend the rest of this lost weekend with me?'

I totted up my responsibilities. I had to keep in touch with Jack and I had to let Lola know where I was. That was all. 'Yes, please,' I said.

While Paul was in the shower, I took out my mobile and rang Lola.

'You're *where?*' she demanded, on a rising note of disbelief.

I repeated myself, taking a certain saucy pleasure in surprising her so completely. Safe, predictable, dependable Mum had taken a giant step off the beaten track. Lola had obviously never considered that I would actually do such a thing, even if invited. My role was to be flattered but to decline gracefully. To be suitably maternal, not unsuitably wanton. Ah, but it's wasted on the young, I thought.

'God, Mum. You and Mr Rainbird. I can't believe it. You got large and then stayed the night with *Mr Rainbird*?'

'His name's Paul.' I stood looking out of the kitchen window at an unfamiliar view.

'I know that. What was it like, anyway?' Her voice had changed. There was respect in it and a new note of complicity, and definitely a touch of pique. Stanley, I remembered, was a long way in the past for Lola.

'Fine,' I said equably.

'Fine? My mum goes to bed with one of the teachers from school and all she says is *fine*, like we're talking about having supper with Mel or going to the twenty-four-hour Tesco?'

We were both giggling now. 'How's Sam?' I asked.

'Oh, fine as well. I feel a bit tame, if you want to know the truth, compared with you.'

'Lo, I've got to go.' I felt a little guilty, talking about Paul while standing in the middle of his kitchen. 'Don't worry about me. I'll call you tomorrow.'

'I hope you're using a condom,' Lola said smartly as she rang off, echoing my often repeated warning to her.

Paul reappeared in jeans and a white T-shirt, his hair damp from the shower and sticking in dark feathers to the nape of his neck. 'Everything okay?'

'I was talking to Lola.'

'Ah. Should I worry about this?'

'Not at all,' I reassured him. Jack was enough to worry about.

We walked in the park and ate a picnic of takeaway sandwiches in the shade of a huge horse-chestnut tree. Paul threw crusts for the pigeons. They strutted on gnarled feet and rushed at each other with beating wings to defend their pickings. All around us were couples lying openly entwined on the grass, and babies in buggies shaded by little frilled parasols, and groups of noisy softball players, and odd-looking solitary men wearing too many clothes who watched the nearly naked girl sunbathers. This afternoon's benign version of the city was much more familiar to me. It was the place where Penny and Evelyn cycled to the farmers' market with Cassie in her seat on the back of Penny's bike, where winter rain pocked the windows and where the slow queues at the bus stops and checkouts were silently long-suffering. The recent threatening version was hatched out of the weird, prolonged hot spell. The heatwave had lasted so long that I couldn't imagine proper rain ever falling again, rather than a few drops spat out by thundery clouds that wouldn't yield a proper downpour.

In the early evening, when the metal disc of the sun slid to a lower angle but the air still seemed to heat your lungs as you sucked it in, Paul and I drove to Turnmill Street. Sullen faces loomed out of the crowds at crossings and mutinous gaggles kicked at tin cans spilling from litter bins. Every surface, flat or vertical, was stained with unidentifiable blotches of putrescent liquid and masked with dirt.

We parked the car and walked slowly towards Audrey's house.

Jack had withdrawn from both versions of the city. Refusing to engage with either, for the past five days he had barricaded himself inside the shadowy house with Audrey and the cats and hedgehogs and rabbits for company. Part of me couldn't blame him. He knew what it was like to be a bird in flight and to be bound to such a breathless, dirt-marked, sullen earth must be agony for him.

Paul stood quietly by the peeling gateposts while I performed the now familiar ritual of banging on the door and shouting through the letter box. Nothing stirred inside the house and no one answered, although I was certain that they were both in there.

I put down on the doorstep the box of fresh fruit and vegetables, and some of Jack's dwindling supply of clean clothes that I had brought with me. I called goodnight to Jack through the slot, told him to telephone me if he needed anything and retraced my steps. Paul and I walked in silence back to the car.

'Let's go home to my house,' I said, as we drove away. He put his arm round my shoulders and I thought again of my mother and father in the canary-yellow car with the ox-blood leather seats.

I opened the windows into the garden and we sat under the tree and watched the light fade. I didn't want to talk and Paul understood that without my having to explain it. When it was fully dark we went upstairs together.

I woke twice in the night, soaked in sweat and confused to find a man's body in my bed. I fell uneasily asleep for the third time and was gripped by a nightmare.

I am in a closed space, with no space beyond it. The walls

squeeze me and I know with complete certainty that there is no calling for help because there is no one to hear. I am alone, and the desolation of it wrings tears out of my eyes and a terrible wail from my throat.

I woke up, still hearing the wail. I was tangled in the bedcovers and I fought to free myself.

Paul sat bolt upright beside me. 'You are safe,' he said. 'You are safe now.'

He held me until the nightmare released its grip, then he went into the bathroom and came back with a cold sponge. He wiped my face with it and stroked my throat. The gentleness soothed me.

'I'm sorry,' I mumbled.

'It was a bad dream. Everyone has bad dreams.'

We lay down again. It was still dark but I could hear the tentative notes of the day's first bird singing. Soon the big jets coming in from Hong Kong and Singapore would begin to drone overhead.

'Talk to me?' Paul asked.

'What about?'

'Tell me why you have bad dreams. Tell me what's the worst thing that ever happened to you.'

'That sounds like some party game gone badly wrong.'

I knew that I was pulling up the drawbridge while Paul lay still and waited. But the nightmare's desolation clung around me and I found myself wanting to push it away and not be alone any more. I made myself speak and it came out sounding as if my voice was rusty from lack of use. 'My mother died,' I said slowly.

That was just how it was. One day she was there and the next she was gone. There had been no interlude of illness.

'What happened?'

'A cerebral haemorrhage, I believe.'

—w—

I came home from school one afternoon and instead of my mother waiting for me with a glass of orangeade or a cup of tea, I found Mrs Maloney. She told me that my dad would be home soon and in the meantime why didn't I sit quietly and watch the television?

I asked her where Mum was and she said I was to be good and my dad would tell me all about it.

I didn't ask any more because I already feared what I must hear.

After a long hour he came in and told me she was dead.

I tried to be brave and not to ask too many questions, because that was plainly what was expected of me.

The time afterwards, after she disappeared, is distorted in my memory. She was so conclusively absent, but her absence also seemed to have a retrospective, cumulative quality to it, as if she had actually begun to fade before that time and had been slowly but surely dwindling towards her own vanishing point.

And after her death, instead of being comfortingly present Ted became less and less accessible. From a mature viewpoint I could excuse his absence from me as to do with his own grieving, but as a child I took it personally.

As he receded, so my demands increased. I feared that he would disappear as abruptly as Faye had done, so I clung about him, watching him for signs of fatal illness, checking that he wasn't preparing to go out and leave me. He didn't fall ill, although the amount he drank took its toll, but he went out very often.

My watchfulness very soon began to annoy him, so I tried to pretend I wasn't worried, didn't notice whether he was there or not. I had no idea where he went, or what could be more important than him and me, but I came to the conclusion that whatever was wrong must lie within me, because after all he was glorious and gifted Ted, and I was just Sadie.

All this was in the days before the first auntie made her

appearance, of course. Mrs Maloney was supposed to look after me, but I hated her smell and her lugubrious manner, and the way she snooped around our house when Ted was out and we were alone together. I was supposed to go to her house for my tea after school and wait there until he came back, but then he often left me stranded until nine or ten o'clock and sometimes I had to stay the whole night.

I had my own doorkey to our house, so after a while instead of going to Mrs Maloney's I began to let myself in and to comfort myself with orangeade and tea and biscuits, like Faye used to prepare for me. I'd sit at the table in the kitchen and do my homework, with the radio on, just as I used to do when she was still there. It was lonely, but better than being in the other house.

Mrs Maloney came to look for me one afternoon and tried to tell me off, but I stood up to her. I said I wanted to be in my own home and she could tell my dad if she wanted, or we could keep it just between the two of us. I knew that he paid her for minding me and she didn't want to lose the money. Ted had enough to worry about, I told her righteously. Did she want to make matters worse, for no reason, when I was perfectly all right where I was?

That was how we left it for a while. If he was early, Ted used to come in and find me watching television, or else I would be in bed pretending to be asleep and waiting for the sound of his key in the lock. He didn't seem to notice that I wasn't at the other house, where I was meant to be. 'How's my Princess?' was his invariable question that didn't require an answer.

I learned how to cook some rudimentary meals for myself, how to wash and iron my school clothes and even do some lopsided mending. Mrs Maloney got her pound notes and the time slowly passed.

One evening Ted said he had to go away on business for a few days.

'How long for?' I asked at once in my suspicious but trying-to-be-careless way.

'I told you. Just a few days.'

'When?'

'Next week. You'll be fine with Mrs Maloney, Sadie. Don't make a great song and dance, now.'

I lay awake at night praying that he wouldn't go, but he did.

I let myself into our house on the first day he was away and scented the cold, unused air. There wasn't much food, but I made myself a kind of meal from bread and tinned meat. Then I tucked some blankets around myself and sat down to watch television. Mrs Maloney came and knocked at the door.

'Go away,' I told her. She had a key, but I slid the bolts.

Her angry voice came through the door. 'Just you listen to me, you little madam. Your dad's gone off with his fancy woman and he'll be back when it suits him. You're to do as you're told and come with me to my place, do you hear?'

I didn't know what a fancy woman was, but I could guess. The thought made me feel sick. I didn't want to listen to Mrs Maloney's insinuations and I didn't want to sleep another night between her sticky sheets or eat her pallid food or listen to her bathroom noises. I didn't want to stay in this ghostly house either, with the void of my mother's death and Ted's absence lurking in every shadow and in each fold of the curtains, but it was less of a bad thing.

'Go away,' I repeated.

When she went, at last, I crept upstairs and lay under my bedcovers. I was shivering so hard I thought my jaw would crack.

That was the first of nine days.

That was the worst time.

I went to school and came home again. In between times I bolted myself in and waited.

I watched television, read books and slept as much as I could, which wasn't much. The silent house was full of noises.

I heard my mother's voice calling me. I would hear Ted's key in the lock and I'd jump up and run trembling to the front door, only to find that there was no one there. In the darkness there were footsteps coming closer and I cringed under my covers for fear of burglars. I feared the ghost at the head of the stairs and the little black faces in the curtain folds, and the skeleton hands that rapped against the closed wardrobe doors. My whole body ached with the effort of listening and trying not to hear.

Mrs Maloney realised I wasn't going to do what she told me and because she was lazy she soon stopped trying. She covered herself by knocking perfunctorily at the door whenever she passed and, I supposed, by noting when the lights went on and off. 'Sadie Thompson,' I could hear her complaining within my head, 'you're a naughty, wilful, disobedient girl. No wonder your mother died, the poor creature. Behaving the way you do, you deserve it and everything else you've got coming to you.'

I closed my eyes and rocked myself under the bedclothes.

I ran out of bread and milk, and then everything fresh. I found some sixpences and shillings in a dish in Ted's bedroom, mixed up with his cuff links and collar stiffeners, and took those to the local shop. It didn't feel like stealing and anyway I didn't care.

As the days crept by I felt odder and odder. For a whole weekend I didn't speak to anyone. A single hour seemed to stretch out to the length of ten. I talked aloud to myself and the sound of my own voice made me jump. Something had happened to the Ascot heater in the bathroom, because the blue crown of gas jets no longer appeared when I turned on the taps and the water stayed cold.

When I went back to school on Monday morning I knew that I looked strange. The girls started whispering about me but no one spoke directly to me. I was hungry and cold all the time, but the sight of school dinners made me feel sick. None of the teachers noticed, though, and I was grateful for that.

I began to wish I had stayed with Mrs Maloney, anything would be better than the silent chamber of horrors that our house had become, but it was too late for that. I wasn't going to go knocking at her door and ask her to take me in.

I was afraid Ted would never come back. I was sure he was dead. He had gone beyond my reach, just like Faye.

Then, on the evening of the second Friday, without any warning, I heard his key in the lock. I knew with a heart's leap that this time it really was him, not just my imagination or Mrs Maloney trying to get in. I ran to the front door and dragged back the bolts.

Ted was there, with his leather suitcase in his hand and the waft of his cologne coming at me. The scent stuck in the back of my throat and I nearly gagged. He was frowning. 'Hello, there. What's this, Sadie? I thought you'd be up the street.'

'I . . . I just wanted to be home for a bit.'

'Come on then, let me get inside.'

I was blocking the doorway. I jumped aside, pressing myself close against the wall.

He went upstairs with his suitcase and even from the back he looked tired and older than the nine days' difference. I heard him using the bathroom and turning on the taps. 'Damn pilot light's gone out,' he said, crossing the landing once more. A few minutes later there was hot water again.

When he came downstairs I went and stood in front of him. 'Where have you been?'

His eyes were narrow and wary but his mouth looked as if he was hurting.

'I thought you weren't coming back,' I persisted. My voice was thin and accusatory.

'What's this? I told you I'd be back. Mrs Maloney was here to look after you.' He was blustering. We both knew he had done wrong to leave me. Ted wouldn't admit it and I didn't know how to press him. He was too powerful and I was afraid he really would leave me if I made myself difficult. My mouth worked but no words came out.

Ted patted my shoulder. 'Are you hungry? Shall we get fish and chips?'

I was ravenous and suspicious. 'Can I come with you?'

'I insist that you do.'

We drove to the chippy in the car. There was a black hair comb on the passenger seat, looking as if it had dropped out of someone's handbag. I scooped it into my hand and kept it hidden, and while Ted was ordering our dinner I dropped it into a bin.

We sat at the kitchen table to eat our supper straight from the newspaper, looking out of the window at the wilderness my mother's garden had already become.

Ted wiped his moustache with the back of his hand and smiled at me. I thought he must be pleased to be home. 'So. How's it been without your old dad?'

'I was lonely.'

'Mrs Maloney took good care of you.'

There was no room for contradiction. And now that he was back, the nine days seemed to fade, becoming a time I didn't want to reach into. 'Did you get your business done?'

'It was so-so, old girl. Swings and roundabouts, you know.'

We finished the last few chips and then watched television together. I kept glancing at him out of the corner of my eye, trying to gauge how he looked, until I realised he had dozed off with his mouth hanging open.

For a while after that my father seemed subdued. He was at home more in the evenings and I began to relax, although I was never quite off my guard. Mrs Maloney and I operated a sort of armistice because neither of us mentioned what had happened, to Ted or to each other. I knew now that she didn't have any power over me and never would do. I had learned a bitter independence.

Then, within a matter of weeks, Ted introduced me to the first auntie.

I often wished that I could discard my unwelcome independence and be mothered again, especially by Viv, but it stubbornly remained a part of me. In the Scentsation days and until I went to Grasse it stood me in good stead. I never trusted Ted again, not really in the recesses of myself, although I wanted to and tried to, and although I loved him, in my way. I was quick to place my trust elsewhere, as soon as I thought I was grown up. I gave it to Tony, then I made the mistake of falling violently in love with someone else. My family, Jack and Lola, suffered from the mistakes I had vowed never to make.

'That's it, really. That's all that happened,' I concluded. But I turned my face against Paul's shoulder and he held me to him.

'I see,' he said.

'What?' I asked, not making the connection. Or not admitting it.

'I understand now why you're so upset about Jack.'

'It's quite different,' I protested.

'Yes, of course,' Paul gently agreed.

The nightmare's miasma had receded and my limbs were beginning to feel heavy. I closed my eyes experimentally, then found it was difficult to open them again.

'But it touches quite a lot of chords, doesn't it? Jack running away from home and locking himself in a place where you can't reach him?'

'I don't know how to deal with it. I love him so much, he must know that, but I don't know how to get to him.'

'We'll find a way,' Paul said.

I adored that *we*. I hadn't heard it like this, spoken in the vulnerable small hours by a man I trusted, since Stanley left.

On the Sunday morning, it was my turn to make the coffee and toast. Paul's eyes rested on me as I trod the overfamiliar route between toaster and kettle and fridge, and just once he put out his hand to stroke my hip as I brushed past him. The single touch made me shiver with recollection and anticipation. I bumped against the counter and almost spilled the milk.

'Lola said I'm making her feel a bit tame.'

'Sex is too good for the young,' he said calmly.

'My thoughts exactly.'

He carried the breakfast tray out into the garden for me. It was a very still day. I peeled an orange and left the thick curl of skin on my plate while I divided the segments, pulling the last strips of curdy pith away from the flesh before I offered one to him. He took the crescent and ate it as I absently arranged the others like the petals of a flower.

'What shall I do?' I wondered, but I was asking myself rather than him.

'I did have an idea, after you fell asleep last night.'

He had been lying awake, thinking about me.

The happiness that the notion gave me was out of proportion to the casual admission and I thought, how desolate have I really been, and for how long? I smiled at him. 'Go on.'

'If Jack won't come out and you can't get in, maybe you should move the goalposts. Doing something always feels better than doing nothing, don't you think? Maybe you should let him know that you're close and that you won't ever give up or let him go, however hard he tries to make you?'

I knew he had put his finger on something. Jack was testing me, to see how long and how hard I would hang on. It wouldn't be the right response to shrug and back off, leaving him at Turnmill Street with Audrey to come to his senses or to grow up or climb down or whatever the well-meaning advice might be. My son was challenging me. The world seemed indifferent to him, his father's new family was an implicit rejection. Lola was absorbed elsewhere. It was as if he were saying to me, *Don't let me down. However hard I push you, don't show me what I fear, which is your rejection or your indifference.* I was his only anchor and he was using Audrey to pull on my chain. Although probably he didn't even know it.

'I think you're right,' I said.

'So let's go and show Jack we're with him. We can't go inside the house in Turnmill Street, but we can take his family to Turnmill Street. Let's have a picnic in the garden and sit there while the sun shines. Deckchairs, Sunday papers, sandwiches, that sort of thing. We can chat to the neighbours, make friends with the cats.'

'Isn't that setting a siege?'

'Not at all. Just joining in the fun.'

'What if Audrey calls the police?' But she wouldn't do that. She knew she was on tricky ground after our last encounter with the law. 'And if you're there, won't that make Jack more hostile?' Even though it was Mr Rainbird who had introduced him to 'The Windhover'.

'If you sit there alone, Sadie, you're going to seem – well, lonely and accusatory and maybe even desperate. If we're together it's a party. You're letting Jack know that you've got a life of your own that has a huge space in it for him. And that's the truth, isn't it?'

I nodded. It was the truth. I wanted Paul to be there and there was also a touch of anarchy to his proposal that appealed to me.

'Let's do it.'

There was a strip of shade beneath the wall separating Audrey's rubbish-tip garden from the next-door rectangle belonging to the two young men. We sat in the folding chairs that I had hauled out of my cellar. Paul read the *Observer* with close concentration while I flicked through the supplements. I knew we were attracting attention, from inside and outside the house. As they parked their cars or walked past with shopping bags, neighbours glanced across and then looked more closely. If I happened to catch anyone's eye, I nodded and smiled. Nothing moved behind Audrey's shrouded windows, but I knew she and Jack were watching.

When lunchtime came Paul strolled round the corner to a bakery and coffee shop, and came back with a brown bag. We were eating our picnic when the people from the other side emerged from their house. They stood and looked at us.

'Hello?' the woman said pointedly. She was wearing pearl stud earrings and a blue sundress, and her husband was in salmon-pink Lacoste.

Paul and I introduced ourselves and I explained about Jack and Audrey, as lightly as I could.

'We heard that the police were here,' the woman said. I wondered if she was the one who had called them.

'Yes. No need for that, of course. Jack's just going through one of those adolescent phases. Audrey's a sort of family friend.'

'Is she?' The man looked at us and then into the garden, as if to say that I must be a fine friend.

The woman clearly felt this was too confrontational. She said quickly, 'Anyway, we know all about adolescent phases. I'm Gilly, by the way, and this is Andrew.'

I told them our names and Paul added pleasantly that he was one of Jack's teachers, so they wouldn't assume he was his father. Gilly asked which school and when he told her she said oh yes, she'd heard it was very good. 'We're fee payers, for our sins,' she added.

It was rather like being at a dinner party. I was thinking

361

that just because we ate tomato and mozzarella sandwiches from the posh deli and talked about schools, Gilly and Andrew automatically assumed we were on the same side, whereas Audrey with her fierce solitude and her cats and garden full of rotting cardboard never would be. My sympathy was with her.

'Well,' Gilly concluded, 'we'd better get a move on, we're going out to lunch. Let us know if we can do anything to help, won't you?'

As they were getting into their car they stopped to talk briefly to a man who was trimming his hedge and I saw Andrew nodding in our direction. The news of our sit-in would travel fast around Turnmill Street.

The afternoon trickled by in a daze of heat.

It was surprisingly pleasant, idling in the semi-shade, doing nothing in Paul's company. A couple of the cats slithered over the wall and picked their way around our feet. Paul rubbed the head of the slightly less feral-looking one while the other leaped on to the windowsill and stared into the gloom within. I heard the sound of some fracas in the distance, yet again announced by the blare of converging police or ambulance sirens, but nothing disturbed the drowsiness of Turnmill Street. I dozed for a while and woke up with a start, remembering the first evening when Jack didn't come home. It was comforting to be sitting only a few feet from him, even though I couldn't see what he was doing. I wondered if he might, just possibly, be finding my presence a comfort too. Either way, I reasoned, sooner or later he or Audrey – or both of them – would have to emerge.

I walked round the corner to find a pub that was open and as I strolled back I saw a small movement behind the tattered curtains at an upstairs window. Jack was checking up on my whereabouts.

Paul was talking to the two young men I had met the other day. They were both in Spandex cycle shorts and tight vests, and their bikes were resting against the party wall. He introduced them as Tim and Gavin.

'I was just saying to your friend, we do worry about the old lady,' the slightly less muscular one confided to me.

'We offered to do some tidying up out here in the garden for her, didn't we, Gav? But she wouldn't let us. She's very protective of her privacy. I'm surprised she's letting you sit around on her property, as a matter of fact.'

'We'll have to see what happens,' I said neutrally.

'Well, you want your boy to come home, don't you? Is there anything we can bring you, by the way, while you're out here?' Gavin asked.

'A cup of tea would be very welcome, thank you,' Paul said.

They brought out a tray, with a big white teapot with 'Earl Grey' lettered round the lid. It was, too. With lemon. Tim and Gavin sat on the wall and while we were all drinking our tea Gilly and Andrew came back.

'It's a street party!' Gilly cried. 'I've always said we should do one for the Jubilee or something but Andrew wouldn't hear of it, would you, darling?' She had clearly enjoyed a few Pimmses, and her husband's face was a dark reddish colour that was at odds with his polo shirt.

'I'm going to come and join you,' she said suddenly and tripped across the geological strata of cardboard in her sandals. 'Bring out a bottle of nice white vino, Andrew, and a few glasses.'

Five minutes later our numbers were increased by the man who had been trimming his hedge. He didn't know Tim and Gavin, so Gilly introduced them as well as Paul and me. His name was Mike and he had a loud voice and a highly confident manner.

'How's the siege progressing?' Mike boomed, accepting a glass of Andrew's Sauvignon and lounging against Audrey's gatepost in his Gap shorts.

'Um, it's not a siege, exactly,' I mumbled. 'We're just sort of keeping him company. He'll come out when he's ready.'

Mike was one of those people who don't listen to the answers to his own questions. 'Have you heard the news?' he was already demanding.

'No, what?' Andrew asked.

'It was on the local bulletin. There's been a street fight over on the Ullswater estate. A pack of skinheads set on some Muslim kids, or vice versa. Stone-throwing, knives, several casualties, police in riot gear. It's still simmering over there.'

In this crowded inner-city borough, the toughest areas and the most expensive often lay next to each other. The Ullswater was barely half a mile from the far end of Turnmill Street. Paul and I exchanged looks. Now that it was actually erupting, it had seemed inevitable all along that violence would boil out of the city's overheated cauldron. We all listened, but the street was eerily quiet with purple shadows lying under the dust-coated trees.

'I think they should all be sent right back where they came from,' Andrew said, surprising no one.

Two blond children emerged from Mike's gate, one of them riding an expensive bike. They came across the road to us.

'Hello, Ollie, hello, Jamie,' Gilly carolled. 'Having a lovely summer? Freddie and Mills are at adventure camp in the French Alps. They adore it.'

'We're going to Greece next week,' one of the boys said. 'Are those your bikes?' he asked Tim and Gavin.

The four of them clustered round to exchange technical information. The garden was getting quite crowded. In my bag, my mobile rang.

'Mum,' Jack hissed. 'Who are those prats with the bike? What are all those people doing in Audrey's garden?'

This was the first contact of the day and Jack had voluntarily initiated it. Even if it was only to make a protest. Clever Paul Rainbird, I thought.

I said airily, 'Just hanging out. Why don't you come down and join us?'

'Don't be stupid. Audrey's going mad.'

'Maybe tomorrow, then.'

'Mum, for God's sake. And what's Mr Rainbird doing here?'

'Keeping me company. Is that okay?'

'Shit,' Jack said despairingly. But he didn't say it wasn't.

After another bottle of Andrew's good wine and a trial for each of the boys on each of the bikes, Tim and Gavin said they had to get ready to go out. Gilly had suddenly gone quiet, and Andrew and Mike were talking at each other about how to prevent the arrival of illegal immigrants from across the Channel. Fifteen minutes later Paul and I were alone in the garden again. The light was fading to the colour of dust.

'I think we should call it a day,' he said.

I went to the front door and called through the letter box into the listening space of the house, 'Audrey, I hope you don't mind too much that we were here today. You've got some good neighbours. 'Night, Jack. I love you. Call me any time you want. I'll see you tomorrow.'

Paul and I drove home. The streets near the Ullswater estate were uneasily deserted, except for white police buses with fluorescent-jacketed occupants parked on almost every corner. A pair of police horses paced slowly by with their riders in riot helmets and with heavy sticks swinging. The peace sat uneasily and there was the smell of burning in the air.

'Where are you?' Mel demanded when I answered my mobile.

It was the next evening and Paul and I had resumed our comfortable vigil in Turnmill Street. People were stopping to chat as they passed by.

I told her and she laughed. 'We'll be along in half an hour.'
'Mel . . .'
But she had already rung off.

She was true to her word. Jasper's car nosed to a halt under the trees and Mel leaped out. Jasper followed her with a cool box in one hand and two more folding chairs in the other. Mel's presence, as always, made the light seem brighter. She called joking greetings to Jack through the letter box and introduced herself to Gavin as he arrived home from work. Mike's wife Andrea came across because, she said, Mike had told her all about what was going on and she didn't want to miss anything. Within minutes Mel and she discovered that they had worked at different times for the same company.

'Whose idea was this?' Jasper asked me. He was wearing an immaculate white linen shirt and his height and breadth made Paul look shorter than he usually did and severely crumpled. Even so I reflected that I wouldn't have accepted an exchange.

'Paul's,' I said proudly.

'There's Jack now,' Jasper said. I swung round and saw my son's face at the downstairs window with the other Jack, Audrey's alpha cat, like a furry sack alongside him. My Jack was watching us all with surprise and, I thought, a degree of satisfaction. All this was happening because of him.

'Hello, Jack,' I called.

Mel caught sight of him, and broke off her conversation with Andrea and Gavin to blow him a kiss. Jack responded with a quick, embarrassed smile.

A big part of his life had come to the doorstep of Turnmill Street to meet him. All he had to do was walk back into it. When he disappeared from the window, I was convinced that was what he was about to do.

But when the front door did open, it was Audrey who

stood there. 'What are you doing in my garden?' There was something commanding about her and we fell silent, even Mel.

I took one step forward. 'Audrey, let me try to explain. We're not trying to invade you. I just want Jack to know that he's also got a life to live out here with us. It doesn't mean he can't spend time with you, of course. It doesn't have to be exclusive, an either-or. I want him to come home, that's all.'

Audrey half turned and behind her we saw Jack, standing in the gloom at the foot of the stairs. He was small and serious and determined.

'Jack?' Audrey said.

Before he could answer quick footsteps came along the pavement and bounced in at the gate. 'Mum? Jack?' Lola asked. 'What's happening now?'

Mel and the others stood aside to let her through. 'Hello, bruv,' she said. 'I brought you some sweets and magazines and stuff. And I wrote you a letter. I was going to put it through the letter box.' She held the package out to him and there was a moment's silence.

Then Jack came out on to the step and took it. 'Thanks, Lo.'

He hovered, poised between us, his family and friends and the regular world, and Audrey's fastness. I felt his indecision and also the tug of his loyalties. It would be easy for him now to step outside, and much more difficult to cleave to Audrey and the lonely house.

There was a whisper in my head, *go on Jack*. But I wasn't willing him to step my way.

Jack would be all right, I knew that much now. He wasn't helpless or full of fear, as I had been. He was loyal to Audrey and he wouldn't be seen to climb down. For the time being, he had made the right choice. I wasn't regretting having forced it on him, either.

It was Audrey I felt sorry for.

He stood up straight. 'Thanks, Lo,' he repeated. 'And you, Mum. But I'm staying here, you know?'

I saw the flash in Audrey's eyes and then she had her hand on the doorknob. 'You are on private property,' she warned us. The door closed with a firm click, shutting us out.

The neighbours murmured goodnight and tactfully dispersed. The exchange they had just witnessed didn't quite fit with the party atmosphere. Mel and Jasper and Paul and Lola and I were left in the garden.

I took Lola's hand. 'Jack will be fine.'

'I know that.'

We were subdued by the taste of Audrey's loneliness and her need to hold on to Jack, and by Jack's solidarity.

'I don't think we can do any more tonight,' Mel murmured.

Jasper wanted us all to have dinner, but I shook my head. It didn't seem right to go off and sit in a restaurant now. In the end Mel and Jasper said goodnight too. They hugged me in turn.

'It isn't easy, is it?' Jasper said. I guessed that he was talking about Clare as much as Jack.

After they had gone Lola said, 'Hi, Mr Rainbird.'

He smiled at her. 'Hi, Lola. You can call me Paul, now you're out in the real world.'

Her smile in return was sad. 'Actually, I'm not sure I'm that crazy about the real world.'

'If anyone's up to dealing with it, Lola, that person is you.'

She brightened up. 'Really? Well. Thanks. Look, Mum, I've got to go. I promised I'd meet Kate.' As ever, Lola had her own priorities.

'Go on, then. It was good that you came over tonight. What did you put in your letter?'

'Oh. Just that he's my favourite brother and I miss him being around. That sort of stuff, you know?'

'I know,' I said.

Lola hoisted her bag, ready to depart. She looked straight at Paul. 'I'm glad you're taking care of my mum.'

'I will do my best,' he said gravely.

When we were on our own again Paul said, 'Do you want to go now?'

I shook my head. 'I'll just sit here for a little bit longer.'

He understood immediately that I wanted to do it on my own. He kissed me on the forehead and said he would see me tomorrow.

I sat down on one of the folding chairs and thought about Jack.

It was nearly the end of August and the evenings were shortening. At half past eight the light had faded out of the sky, but there was still no respite from the breathless heat. A police car sped down Turnmill Street, silent but with the blue light splashing a warning in the twilight. Another followed a minute later.

There was no sound or light leaking from Audrey's house. I pictured the two of them ensconced in the back room, watching television and spooning food for the animals and themselves out of a frying pan. Without warning, two running figures pounded out of the darkness. They flashed past the gate, hooded tops pulled over their heads, and I was reminded of the evening when Paul had walked me down the hidden street. I sat forward on the chair, aware of the thick shadows under the trees and hedges. A helicopter thudded overhead and turned in a tight circle, a shaft of harsh light spreading from its nose. The noise it made sawed over the rising cacophony of sirens. I had become used to these signals, they were the summer's refrain, but there was a fresh urgency to the clamour now.

I sat for a few more minutes, listening and wondering.

Then the snap of the letter box made me jump.

'Mum? You've got to go home,' Jack's disembodied voice piped through the darkness.

'What's happening?'

'You can't sit there. We've heard it on the news. There's riots, gangs fighting and breaking windows. They're setting fire to cars on the Ullswater.'

I could smell it now, acrid smoke on the thick air. Just at the limits of my hearing there was the crunch of smashing glass and metal.

'It's *dangerous*, Mum. Go home,' Jack begged.

I stood up, methodically folding the chair. 'All right.' I knew better than to ask him to come with me. Instead, I went to the door and crouched on the step. I could just see his eyes through the slot.

'I'm proud of you,' I said. Then I stood up again and pushed my fingertips past the flap. Jack's touched them at once. We told each other goodnight.

'I'll be back tomorrow after work,' I said.

I drove home in a thick stew of diverted traffic, past roadblocks and vanloads of policemen. The helicopters endlessly circled overhead as I waited for Lola. When she came in we sat down together and looked out at the sliced sky.

'It's like a war zone out there,' she breathed.

SEVENTEEN

Another hot day crept by at the Works. We didn't have much paid work on, but that wasn't unusual for August. Leo and Andy were both on holiday, so at least Penny and I didn't have to cast around to find employment for them.

I sent out a pile of invoices, then tidied some shelves and catalogued our supplies of paper and calf while Penny worked on a set of leather display boxes for a local jeweller. We listened to the radio news and learned that last night's rioters had been surrounded and overpowered by large numbers of police. Several arrests had been made. During the unrest extensive damage had been done to shops and homes and cars on and near the Ullswater estate. There was still a heavy police presence in the area and for the time being the streets were quiet. Thunderstorms were forecast, although when Penny and I sat outside in our lunch break the sky's dirty blue-grey haze was unbroken by cloud.

Throughout the heatwave Evelyn had been putting Cassie to bed for the hottest part of the afternoon and letting her stay up later in the evenings. Today she slept until past four o'clock, and Penny and I heard her irritably wailing when Evelyn finally brought her downstairs again. When the end of the day came I went across the yard to look in at the house and found her in her wet red starfish-patterned swimsuit, standing up on a chair to sail toy boats in the sink full of water. 'See, ships,' she

371

shouted to me. Waves slopped over the draining board and ran into the puddles already covering the floor.

Evelyn was sitting at the kitchen table, her hair knotted away from her pale, glistening face. She looked tired and peevish. 'Hasn't Penny finished yet?' she asked me.

I knew Penny wanted to glue the leather on the last of the boxes so it could dry overnight. 'Shouldn't be long.'

'Sadie, d'you mind just keeping your eye on Cassie for a minute? I want to make a phone call and have a fag in peace. She's been a nightmare all afternoon.'

I had promised to meet Paul at Turnmill Street straight after work, but it wouldn't matter if I was a few minutes late. 'Sure.' I stood at the sink beside Cassie.

Her corkscrew curls were damp and her fat little arms and hands shone with water droplets. She plunged a plastic mug in among the boats and another wave splashed over us both. My sandals squelched in the puddles. 'This your ship,' she told me, handing me a wooden yacht with a sodden triangle of sail.

'Thank you. It's a beauty.'

We sent the boats gliding across the tiny lake. She was leaning so far forward that I hooked my fingers under the slippery straps of her swimsuit in case she toppled head first into the water. The skin between the tiny wings of her shoulder blades was warm and furred with the faintest trace of downy hair.

After about fifteen minutes Evelyn wandered back again. She was still holding the telephone handset and a pack of cigarettes.

'Eve, I've really got to go,' I said.

'What? Oh, right. Is Penny still not here?'

'Shouldn't be long,' I repeated. I kissed the top of Cassie's head. 'See you tomorrow, Cass.'

I dried my hands on a tea towel. Evelyn was sitting at the table again. She didn't look round when I said goodnight, just sighed a response.

I could see Paul, as I walked under the trees up Turnmill Street. He was standing beside Audrey's gateposts talking to three boys. Two of them were hulking creatures with baggy cut-off pants and billowing T-shirts. Their close-shaven heads looked too small in proportion to their bodies. The third was small and skinny, more like Jack, except that he was wearing red and white football strip. I slowed down to give them a chance to move on, then realised that they were settling in. The largest one sloped into the garden and peered in through the downstairs window. I heard him calling in a friendly way, 'Oi, Jack? Wha's gwa'n, man?'

'Come out of there, Jason,' Paul ordered. He saw me and beamed. 'Here are three boys from Jack's year. Come back here on the pavement, please, all of you. That means you too, Wes.'

They didn't look quite so huge at close quarters. I could see they were really only twelve or so.

'This is Jack's mum,' Paul said.

They shuffled into an awkward, eyes-averted line. 'Yeah. 'Lo.'

'Is Jack going to stay in there, like, for good?' the one in the football strip asked.

'Of course not. How do you know about this?'

I was startled by the thought that Paul might have told them, but the middle one jerked his head towards the other end of the street. 'Jase's posh cousins, right, live up there? They heard something about the mad old cat biddy . . .'

'That's enough,' Paul said sharply.

'. . . and this kid who was in there with her and wouldn't come out, right? And the law coming round and all that. Some other mega-posh tossers they know in the street, they told them.' Jamie and Ollie, I thought. News travels. 'So we're on the way up the park 'cos half the roads are shut round the estate, and we see sir, so we ask him if it's true about it being a kid from our school.'

'I told you. Yes, it's Jack, and there's nothing else to tell or to see. The three of you may continue on your way to the park. Only a few days' holiday left, remember, so you might as well make the best of them.'

'Oh yeah, sir, d'you think we'd forget?'

'Can we just shout summat to him?'

Paul glanced at me. 'Yes, if it's quick and polite.'

They darted up to the door and clustered round.

'Oi, mate? It's Wes, right? Come up the park if you want, when you get out.'

'If you do.' The small one sniggered.

They heard a sound from within and stepped back so hastily they almost fell over each other. A second later they were back on the right side of the gateposts.

'It's well creepy in there,' Wes said.

I understood that somehow, according to their impenetrable value system, Jack was judged to be doing something quite cool.

'See ya, sir. Bye, Mrs, er.'

They scuffled away up the street, pushing and trying to trip each other up.

'Well,' I said, watching them go. 'Those are the leaders of the pack, aren't they?'

'They're all right. Not as hard as they pretend to be. They're pretty good kids, in fact. Wes Gordon in particular is very bright.' Paul looked down at me. 'Why are we talking about schoolchildren? I thought you weren't coming.'

He wouldn't kiss me under the eyes of Audrey's house and probably the rest of Turnmill Street, but I knew he wanted to.

'Here I am.' I smiled.

We went into the garden and I called a greeting through the letter box to Jack.

As I peered in through the slit he emerged in the usual way

from the back room and came to stand on the other side of the door. 'Are you all right, Mum?'

'Of course. Are you?'

He nodded and rubbed with the toe of his shoe at some piece of debris on the floor. I waited while he struggled with himself. I guessed that he probably wanted to come out now, but he would have to work out the right way to do it. 'Wes and Jason and Darren were here,' he volunteered.

'I know. Paul and I were talking to them. They said you should go up to the park, when you can.'

'They probably didn't mean it.'

'How will you find out, if you don't go and see?'

He pondered this, then shrugged, with a touch of regret. 'Anyway, Mum. Be careful. It's dangerous out there, I've been watching the news.' Anxiously monitoring one of the worlds from which he had chosen to withdraw, while mourning the loss of his involvement with the other.

I wanted very much to hold him close to me, but I only said, 'I will. Don't worry about me.'

'We do just worry about each other, don't we, Mum?' He sighed as he made his way back down the hallway to Audrey and the cats.

Paul and I sat in the folding chairs. After we had exchanged the news of our separate uneventful days, we divided the *Evening Standard* between us and read the reports of the clashes. There had been an attempted robbery at a Bangladeshi-run curry house. A fight between rival gangs had broken out in the street outside the restaurant and the violence had then spread across the estate. A couple of cars had been overturned and torched, and some shops had been looted. Smouldering embers of aggression had finally been fanned into flames by the heat.

There was an acrid mass of frustration and an indefinable anxiety balled within my own chest. It was so stifling and airless tonight. The air tasted as if it had been breathed too many times. I had to work to keep inflating my lungs with the oxygen-depleted residue.

I was listlessly folding the newspaper when my mobile rang.

Penny's voice was so jagged with panic that I sat up sharply and sent the contents of my bag spilling over the ground. 'Cassie's disappeared.'

'What? When?' My heart lurched and started hammering in my chest. Paul froze in the act of retrieving my belongings and stared up into my eyes.

'After you left. Evelyn thought she'd come across to be with me in the bindery, but I hadn't seen her since before her sleep. She's gone.'

She had been there, in the kitchen. Wet in her red swimsuit. Evelyn listless and sulky with the phone and her pack of cigarettes.

'How long?'

'An hour. We're searching. The police are coming. Did you see anyone? Anything at all, before you left?'

I made the pictures, a little innocent loop of film, play over in my head. The boats in the sink, the empty yard and the bindery doors open, dusty light, Evelyn sitting at the table. Nothing I could identify as unusual. 'No. I'm on my way,' I gabbled. I took my bag out of Paul's hands, almost falling over the chair in my haste.

'I'll drive you,' he said at once, not yet knowing where or why.

I called a rapid goodbye to Jack and then we were in the car. Paul trod on the accelerator and we shot forward. 'Cassie,' I said. I saw his knuckles go white as his hands gripped the wheel.

There was a police car outside Penny's house. When I ran into the kitchen I found an officer with a notebook trying to talk to Evelyn who was weeping hysterically with clenched fists pressed against her mouth. 'A red swimsuit.' She choked. 'With a pattern of starfish. Blue canvas shoes.'

The boats were still in the sink but the puddles on the floor had almost evaporated. A little knot of neighbours was gathered in the yard, and Penny was directing them to take a street each and knock on every door. Her eyes were staring and her face was a terrible dead white.

'Jerry? Could Jerry have taken her?' I shouted. It was only on Friday that I had seen him singing at the gig. It felt like five years ago.

'No. Jerry's coming. He hasn't got her.'

Two more policemen came round the side of the house, moving with massive calm. The neighbours fanned past them. I ran, hearing Paul in my wake, out of the yard and down the alley to the canal towpath.

There was no one there. The water was an unrippled sheet of khaki under a layer of dust. The grass at the land side had recently been cut and it was baked to a light toast-brown and scattered with empty cans, polystyrene food trays and dog mess.

I stared wildly up and down the path, then knelt down at the water's edge, trying to see into the depths. All I could actually see were Cassie's limbs flailing and her mouth, open to scream, filling with water as she sank out of sight.

'Oh, please, God,' I whispered.

Paul's hand touched my shoulder. 'You go that way, I'll go the other.'

I scrambled up and made off towards the lock. The gasometers loomed against the whitish sky. The band of shade beneath the bridge dropped across my face and I touched the crumbling brickwork. There was nothing on the no man's land under the opposite pier except broken glass and half-bricks torn up from the playground next to the bridge. I ran on and came round the corner before the lock. A fisherman was sitting there, his beefy bare arms and chest livid from the sun. 'Have you seen . . .?' I began but he cut me short.

'That kiddie not found yet?' I shook my head. Penny had been here before me, of course. The man quickly reeled in his line and put his rod in its cradle. 'I'll walk on up this way for you,' he said.

'Thank you,' I panted. The sight of him stirred something in my mind. Whatever it was glimmered like a fish in deep water and I pressed my fists against my temples in a vain attempt to hook it.

I ran back in the other direction. Paul was shouting the question to a narrowboat full of startled people and the boatman cut the engine in order to hear him. In the quiet, the prow of the boat swung gently towards the near bank.

'Anyone seen her?' the boatman called to his passengers. They shook their heads, smiles fading on their faces.

'Nothing,' Paul said to me. The engine started up again and the boat chugged on, cutting a swath of green water. The shoulders and arms and legs of the people were all bare and sunburned, like the fisherman's. Then the submerged memory flickered again and I jerked my head in pursuit.

This time I had it.

Only two hours ago. I was driving away from Penny's. My attention was focused on getting to Turnmill Street but out of the corner of my eye, on the opposite side of the road, I caught a glimpse of a man wearing a beige knitted cardigan. It was too hot even to think of wool, let alone wear it. Everyone else in the city was half naked. So I let the brief image, and its associations, fade away before they even printed themselves in my consciousness. But it had been Colin, near his usual bus stop. I was sure of that.

I snatched at Paul's wrist. I was already running and he pounded in my wake. 'I've thought of something.'

In the house, Evelyn was still crying hysterically. Her

mouth was square and wet, and her eyes were squeezed shut. A policewoman was trying to make her drink a cup of tea. Penny was sitting on her chair beside the computer monitor, answering police questions. She had aged twenty years in as many minutes; she looked like a frail old woman.

Names and addresses of our customers were all computerised, but I kept an old-fashioned notebook for my own use in my drawer in the bindery. I dashed across the yard again and took it out, fumbling with the pages. There was an address for Colin, but no telephone number.

It was a long shot. 'Quick. We can check this ourselves,' I called to Paul.

He thumbed the pages of the *A-Z* as I drove. 'Here it is. Left at the end, straight on, under the railway bridge. Left here. No, wait, it's one way. Take the next.'

The traffic was thin, for once. The heat and maybe the smell of violence, kept people penned within their own boundaries like Audrey's animals. It took us only five or six minutes to reach the address in my book.

It was a cheerless, featureless block of flats, concrete-faced with ugly blue-painted slabs beneath the metal windows. The gardens of the gound-floor flats were weed-filled and littered, reminding me of Audrey's. But Audrey's was an eyesore in the groomed expanse of Turnmill Street, whereas every one of these looked as if they never had and never would have the opportunity to be anything but squalid and neglected, and barren of all hope.

We dashed past a group of pallid teenage girls and up a flight of stone steps to a first-floor landing. Colin's door was one of a pair, but his had a metal grille over it. I pressed the bell and then rattled the grille.

From the other side of the flimsy door his loud, blurry voice demanded, 'Who's this?'

'Colin, it's Sadie. From the bookbinders.'

There was a silence. Another voice, a woman's, called something I couldn't catch from further inside the flat and Colin answered, 'It's all right, Mum. I'm getting it.'

There was another silence. I put my thumb to the bell and leaned on it.

'All right. All right, hold your horses,' Colin muttered. There was the sound of bolts being slid back, then the door opened on a chain. His spectacles and thick nose appeared in the gap.

'It's me, Colin. Let me in.'

'I can see it's you. You can't be too careful, you know.'

He took the chain off and unlocked the grille. I edged into the tiny hallway, with Paul right behind me. It was very hot in there and thick with Colin's body odour. There was a framed picture of the young Queen, in tiara and garter sash, on the wall.

'Who are you?' Colin demanded.

'My name's Paul. I'm Sadie's friend.'

I sidestepped very slowly and carefully towards an open inner doorway. I could hear the plink-plink of a child's musical box. The sweat on my back had turned icy.

The cramped room was almost entirely filled with a sofa and a huge television.

On the sofa Cassie was sitting, wide-eyed, gripping the musical box. Beside her was a little old woman, her teeth bared in a smile that was almost a grimace. Her gums were bright pink and shiny, revealing them to be old-fashioned dentures.

'Sadie-lady,' Cassie said. She let the musical box drop and slid off the sofa. Her plump legs made a squeak against the sofa's plastic covering. The old woman caught the discarded toy and set it carefully on the sofa arm. I saw that there were framed photographs on the walls, the windowsill and on top of the television, all of them of a little girl.

I held out my hand to Cassie, smiling at her as calmly as I could. With the other hand I extracted my mobile phone from my pocket and gave it to Paul. He stepped smoothly back into the hallway. I held Cassie's warm, sticky hand in mine for a second, then I stooped down to her level. 'Hello,' I whispered. I couldn't see any fear or pain reflected in her wide brown eyes. She looked surprised and mildly curious.

There was no sign of the red swimsuit. She was dressed up like a living doll in a lemon-yellow smocked-front dress with a matching hand-knit cardigan, tiny white ankle socks and white leather bar shoes. Her hair had been combed flat and centre-parted, and fixed with hairgrips and bows of lemon-yellow ribbon.

Colin's mother smiled. 'She wasn't properly dressed, you know. But she looks a picture now, doesn't she? These are some of my Susan's things. Lucky that I'd kept them all this time, isn't it?'

I lifted Cassie into my arms and held her tight. She settled herself astride my hip as she had so often done before. I could just hear Paul, outside the flat, talking rapidly. He had found Penny's number, stored in my phone. *Yes, yes. She's fine. Safe, yes. No. Nothing at all.*

I was hot again now, and trembling with relief. I didn't want Cassie to feel me shaking in case it frightened her. From all around the room the huge eyes of the other child gazed down at us. She looked nothing like Cassie – she had a thin little face and pale straight hair. The only point of similarity was the clothes and hair ribbons. On an otherwise empty shelf I saw the bright-red case we had made for Colin's recipe collection, with his name tooled on the spine.

I turned slowly to face him. 'Why did you take her away? Didn't you know how worried everyone would be?'

His cheeks turned a dull red and his lower lip protruded. His mother wound up the musical box and set it tinkling again.

'I was coming to see you and Penny about my new book and the kiddie was there in the yard. She said she wanted to play. She's a nice little thing, even though she is a half-caste. It was hot so I walked her down to the canal. I don't usually go down there because you get all sorts hanging around, you know. Druggies and blacks and whatnot. But it was nice seeing the boats. And you easily can walk from there to here. Although generally I prefer to take the bus because it's safer. Especially with all this fighting and that going on.'

His voice was the same as usual, prim but sounding as if his tongue were too big for his mouth, and he told his story without hesitation. I replayed the route in my mind's eye. The canal route was direct. By road it was twice the distance.

'I used to have a little sister, you see,' Colin confided. The whole apartment testified to that. 'But she died.'

His mother heaved herself to her feet. She was tiny and as frail as a bird. Colin towered beside her. She said, 'Don't talk about that now, love, or it'll get us all upset. Let me put the kettle on. We'll have a nice cup of tea and maybe a bit of cake.'

'All right,' Colin mumbled and she patted his hand. 'I brought her home to say hello to my mum, you know.'

The words fell unemphatically in the thick, sour-smelling air but the sadness in them weighed down on me. I tried to imagine what life must be like for the two of them, walled up in this tiny flat. I also thought of Jack and Audrey at Turnmill Street and then, finally closing the circle, about Jack and me. I understood that whatever might and whatever would happen from now on, I must stand back and give him room to flourish. Children who don't have enough light and space around them grow up spindly and lopsided, just like plants deprived of sunlight.

Paul came back and stood beside me. 'Great relief,' he murmured in my ear. 'We should take her straight back home now. Someone will call in later to see Colin.'

I held on tight to Cassie, who was beginning to squirm with impatience. 'We'll have to be off,' I said brightly.

'Wouldn't you like a cup of tea?' Colin's mother asked, politely but vaguely. Her grip on reality seemed fragile. She didn't understand who we were and she didn't want us here, strangers invading her cramped sanctuary.

'We can't, this time.'

'Wait a minute, then.'

She eased past Colin and left the room. He stood at the window, gazing blankly out at the sky as if matters had all got too complicated for him. His mother came back a minute later and handed me a Boots plastic bag, and when I opened it to look inside I saw the red swimsuit and Cassie's little canvas shoes. 'You can keep the things she's wearing. As a present from Colin and me. Doesn't she look a picture in them?' Then she lowered her voice. 'I'm afraid she can't keep the music box, though. That was one of my Susan's favourite things.'

'Thank you,' I said. From her vantage point on my hip, Cassie gave her wrist-angled wave.

I strapped Cassie into her car seat and once we were all inside, even though it was as hot as a furnace, I checked that the windows were closed and pressed the central locking button. I took some deep breaths and Paul touched my hand.

'Let's get her home.'

Penny and Evelyn were waiting on the pavement outside the house. The car hadn't even stopped before they opened the rear door to reach Cassie.

Paul and I sat in our seats, staring at the buses pulling away from Colin's stop and the cars lining up at the petrol station nearby. A few cellophane-sleeved bunches of pink and yellow carnations wilted in their bucket next to the newspaper stand. The *Evening Standard* headline was the same one that I had read with Paul, in Audrey's garden, not much more than an hour ago. Time seemed to stretch and assume strange dimensions, distorted by heat and the aftermath of fear. There was a pain like a migraine behind my eyes and I told myself that it was just shock; there was nothing to worry about; Cassie was safe with the people who loved her.

Evelyn was still crying. Her racking sobs were interspersed with jagged gasps for breath. Together she and Penny were holding Cassie and the three of them made a tangle of arms and wrists and hair. Jerry loomed directly behind, frowning, his hands hanging loose at his sides. He looked as if he were ready to start blaming and accusing as soon as the opportunity presented itself.

The small search party was breaking up. As they turned away Penny touched people on the shoulder or briefly shook their hands in mute thanks, but she couldn't speak or let go her hold of Cassie. An air of profound relief hung over the group, but there were no smiles or jokes. This outcome had been a good one, yet an unidentifiable threat still seemed close at hand, waiting in the wings of the sultry evening. It must be the promise of thunder. The lead-grey, swollen sky loomed too close to the rooftops.

'Let's go inside,' Penny murmured. A police panda car waited in front of the house and now an officer was coming towards us.

Evelyn said to Cassie, 'Let's take that pretty yellow frock off, shall we? You don't want it to get all dirty, do you?'

The policeman wanted me to make a statement. He took off his cap and I sat down facing him at the kitchen table. In the background Penny mechanically switched on the kettle, clinked ice cubes into glasses, trying to occupy herself.

I told him what had happened at Colin's and he wrote it down. I didn't say anything about the photographs, the lost daughter and sister.

'I see. You glimpsed the man at the bus stop and he is a customer of yours. He knows the child.'

'A little. Hardly at all.'

'Anything else?'

I shook my head and the policeman closed his notebook. We were advised that Cassie's doctor should take a look at her as soon as possible, although it seemed very unlikely that there had been any physical interference. A social worker would call to see Evelyn and the community officer and another social worker would visit Colin and his mother. Unless there were any unexpected findings or concerns, that would probably be all.

The radio clipped to his shirt pocket issued a constant stream of voices and commands. There were plenty more urgent matters to attend to, tonight and every night. The policeman picked up his cap and straightened it on his head. 'Keep a closer eye on her in future, please.'

'My feelin's pre-cisely,' Jerry growled.

After the policeman had gone and before Evelyn and Cassie came back, Penny squared up to Jerry. Her back was rigid; the top of her head came level with his shoulder. In a small, even voice she said to him, 'Listen to me, Jerry. Are you listening?'

Unwillingly, Jerry nodded his handsome head.

'Evelyn and I look after Cassie. What happened today was terrifying for us all, but it's over and thank God Cassie came to no harm. Evelyn doesn't always know what she wants, but she's learning to trust her instincts. She loves Cassie and so do I. I love Evelyn too, but I care for Cassie more than I have ever cared for anything, or anyone, in my whole life. I will not let anyone harm a hair on her head, or Evelyn's. Not now, or in the future.' Her voice dropped even lower, but the intensity in it made me shiver. 'And that includes you.'

Jerry shifted on his feet. I saw his eyes slide in my direction, then settle on Paul. He struggled with himself for a moment and then evidently decided that he didn't want any further discussion of this in front of the trumpeter from his pub soul band. He lifted his hands and laughed, making an exaggerated backing-off movement. Penny stood quite still, stiff-backed, regarding him. 'Hey. Whatever you say, my lady.'

'I do say.'

'You just take proper care of my women from now on, right?'

To Jerry they *were* his women. That would always be the way. Penny didn't even deign to blink. Jerry hesitated, then turned away to clap Paul on the shoulder. He held out his hand. Drily Paul shook it.

Jerry grinned. 'Thank you, my man, for what you did tonight. And I'll be seein' you at the gig Friday night, is that right?'

Paul said yes, he would be there, then I said we ought to go. We left Jerry, and Penny followed me outside.

'Sadie? Wait, Sadie.' Her mouth was quivering now. She took both my hands in hers. 'Thank you, thank you for finding her,' she whispered, and she lifted my hands and pressed her lips to each set of knuckles in turn.

The gesture touched me deeply. 'What did I do? Nothing. Say goodnight to Cassie for me.'

'I will,' Penny said. 'Thank you, both of you.'

Paul drove me home, but at the door he said, 'I think I'll leave you to yourself this evening.'

He was perceptive. I did want to be on my own for a while. I nodded, then I leaned across and kissed him on the mouth. I thought how natural and logical a kiss seemed. 'Good night. I'll see you tomorrow.'

I wandered through the quiet house. Occasional flickers of lightning whitened the sky and the bass mumble of thunder answered the drone of a circling helicopter. I turned on the television news and clicked it off again. There was a small sheaf of post waiting for me on the kitchen table – Lola must have put it there. I opened the first envelope and saw that the estate agents who were handling the sale of Ted's house were confirming an offer at the asking price. The purchasers were in a hurry and wanted an early completion. I would have to sell the last few pieces of his furniture as soon as possible and dispose of the remainder of his belongings.

Ted's volumes of notes stood in their place on the bookshelf, and I took one down and turned the pages. Lavender, verbena, bergamot, sandalwood. The perfume formulae kept their secrets from me, locked within Ted's scribbled lines, as complicated and remote now as the long-ago seductions they had been designed to promote. I didn't care. I had my own memories of him and of past times. Good times and bad times, sometimes so closely intertwined that I couldn't separate them. The flavour of Madame Lesert's bread and the scent of jasmine. Vinegary winkles, salt sea air, Viv's Vivienne scent and Ted's cologne. Objects, things, even houses and places didn't matter. They changed past the point of recognition, or they broke, or else they were scattered and sold. For me it was smells and tastes that endured, tiny droplets of life's essence containing and supporting the whole labyrinth of memory.

In this, I was my father's daughter.

I closed the book and gently replaced it beside its companions. 'Goodnight,' I said, aloud. It was Ted I was speaking to and I felt the closeness of our connection, for once without wishing for anything to be different or better.

The phone's sudden ringing makes me jump. I can almost feel the sound waves stirring the humid air. 'Hello?'

'Sadie? Is that you?'

'Who else would it be?'

'I dunno,' Mel says.

'Your voice is a bit strange.'

'I'm fine.'

And I truly am, I realise.

'I've got some news. I want you to be the first to hear.' Mel's voice is so tight with happiness it's like the skin of a ripe peach, ready to split and spill its juice.

'What is it?' I ask, although I already know.

'Jasper has asked me to marry him.'

'Mel, that's wonderful.' I'm smiling; there are creases at the corners of my eyes and bracketing my mouth, sticky because my skin is slicked with sweat. I sit down, cradling the phone, letting my head fall back against the sofa cushions. This news transforms the feeling of the night. It's friendly now and the heat envelops me like a bear-hug. 'Did you say yes?' I wonder.

'Not yet.'

'What?'

'Oh, Sade. I wanted to think about it, hold the idea to myself, taste it before I swallowed it. I was too happy to answer properly. Does that sound crazy?'

'No.' It sounds like Mel.

'I am going to tell him tomorrow night. Tell him that I want to marry him so much, I'll die if I can't.'

Some of the night's new benevolence fades. A finger of threat touches me, leaving a tiny cold print. I remember that I sensed it earlier, trapped like the promise of thunder in the heavy air. 'Don't say that.'

'It's the truth, Sadie. Wish me luck?'

'I wish you much more than luck. I wish the two of you happiness and more happiness, and contentment together for ever. It's what you deserve.'

In my mind I can see the wide curve of Mel's red mouth and I think again of luscious ripe fruit.

'Thank you, my dear friend,' she murmurs and then blurts out, 'I want you to be happy too.'

As you do, when your own world is so full of joy that you long for it to be reflected onwards from face to face and heart to heart, all the way down the hall of mirrors and into eternity.

'I am,' I tell her gently.

EIGHTEEN

At first, from under the skin of sleep, I thought it was the thunder that had woken me.

Then I was properly awake, coming to with the cold certainty that something terrible was about to happen. Cassie was safe but there was more to come, there was an even bigger threat trapped in the brooding air. I could smell it and taste it. There was a heartsick moment while I lay in the darkness and then the phone began to ring.

I hardly recognised Jasper's voice. He was hoarse and his words were disjointed, and when I did begin to piece together what he was saying it was worse than my fears.

It's Mel. Oh Sadie. What if she dies. I'm sorry, I know it's . . . I can't. She looks so . . .

'Tell me.' My own voice had taken on the edge of panic.

'She was coming to see me. Oh God, I shouldn't have. I should have gone to her. Instead of letting . . .'

'Jasper. What's happened?'

'She was knifed.'

Knifed. Knives, blood.

I tried to work out how these words could relate to Mel, of all people, and how to frame the next unthinkable questions. 'Where?'

'In her chest. The blade punctured her lung. She lost so much blood. She . . . they . . . she might not live. Sadie, I . . .'

He was crying. The hoarse sound of his voice came from trying to suppress his sobs.

I had meant, where was she? Where had Mel been, to put herself in the way of a flashing knife blade?

'How?'

'She . . . went to buy. Went to . . . to an off-licence. Champagne, for . . .'

I knew what for. She had been going to tell Jasper that she would marry him. 'When?'

'Ten. This evening. Yesterday, now. I'm sorry, I'm not . . .'

'Jasper, I'm coming.'

'It was a robbery, you know? Nothing to do with Mel at all, she was just . . . just standing there. They ran in, tried to grab money. Booze off the shelves. It went wrong. They, the police, told me. One of them had a knife, a very sharp knife with a long thin blade. They think he might be a butcher.'

A real butcher. A slaughter man.

I had a vision of Mel lying on the off-licence floor with her hair fanned about her head and bright blood spilling. Feet milling around her body and her lipstick another slash of red in her death-white face.

'I'm coming.'

As I drove to the hospital, oily raindrops spattered the car's windscreen. I remembered driving up the motorway to Ted's deathbed and how I had prayed and bargained for him not to go before I could reach him. I didn't try to pray this time. I just drove through the dead-of-night streets that still managed to be thoughtlessly busy. Yellow and red lights reflected queasily off the tarmac, now slick with rain.

Jasper was sitting in a grey-walled side room that smelled of anguish. He stood up as soon as he saw me and we held tight to each other. He seemed boneless in my arms, an inert weight with all his sunny certainty drained away.

'Come on,' I whispered at last. 'Sit down again and tell me as much as you know.'

I had to lead him to the row of chairs. They were bolted together in a straight line against the wall.

They were operating on Mel. The long thin blade had missed her heart, but her left lung had been punctured and then collapsed. She had lost a huge amount of blood. Jasper had called her mother just after he spoke to me. Lois Archer was on her way.

'Did the police get them?' I asked.

'Get who?' Jasper was dazed. His eyes followed the minute hand of the clock on the wall and I knew he couldn't properly concentrate on anything but Mel on the operating table and how long it might be before we could hear any news.

'The people who did it to her.'

'Not yet.'

Thieves had burst into the shop and one of them threatened the assistant with the knife while the others raided the till and the shelves. They were sweeping bottles and cigarette cartons into a holdall, shouting over the noise of breaking glass.

Mel and another customer were trying to back away as two more people ran into the shop. The thieves panicked and turned to escape but found Mel blocking their route to the door. The blade had gone straight between her ribs. This much Jasper had learned from the police.

I tried to swallow but my throat was dry. 'It will be on the security cameras. They'll catch them.'

'I suppose so,' Jasper said. It didn't matter much to either of us at that moment, only Mel mattered, but it was something to say.

Silence seeped between us as we waited.

Outside there were flashes of lightning followed almost instantly by long rolls of thunder. Rain smashed against the room's windows like handfuls of gravel flung at the glass.

I thought about how arbitrary this act of violence was, and how massive and inescapable it had now become. It wasn't a dream or an illusion, however much I wanted it to be. The waiting room was real, with its seats and chipped paint and overbreathed air, and so was the hospital that contained it. Somewhere down these corridors, under bright lights, Mel's life was hanging in the balance. I remembered sitting in the car park of that other hospital, on the day my father died, knowing that the births and dying and the pain happening inside it were part of the natural order, and believing that all of us belonged within the order. Tonight felt like the opposite of that. Mel had been singled out, for no reason, and the order had gone all awry. None of us, no one I knew even, had ever been touched by such a thing before. It belonged in half-heard news bulletins and glimpsed newspaper headlines, not in the ordinary fabric of our ordinary lives.

As I sat with my head hanging, staring at the toes of my shoes against the dull red floor, I thought of the knife thrust as another lightning bolt, discharging the static threat that had built up all this hot summer under the canal bridges and between crawling cars and at the dark end of fetid alleyways. Cassie's disappearance had presaged it and the relief that followed her discovery now flipped back into fear that was the more intense for having been temporarily allayed.

And this had happened to Mel, the most vital person any of us knew. It made me afraid of our place all over again and I shifted my weight on my hard chair, trying to square up to it, refusing to fear the city where I had spent my life. We belong here. Mel, Jack, Lola, Audrey. Paul and me, Jasper and Caz and Graham. I ran through the names, drawing the love and affection around us like a good spell.

'I don't know what I'll do if she dies,' Jasper said suddenly. It was a simple statement of the truth. He didn't know and nor did I.

I took his hand again and massaged it between mine. 'She isn't going to die.' I spoke firmly, refusing to admit anything else even though the opposite possibility hammered in all the chambers of my mind.

Jasper stood up and walked down the corridor. I could hear him asking a question of someone out of sight and the brief monosyllables of a reply. When he came back he shook his head and my heart almost stopped. 'No news yet.'

I breathed again.

A young Indian couple came in. They nodded patiently at us and took the two seats furthest away. The young woman was beautiful, with delicate features, but there were tears running down her face. Her husband put his arm round her shoulders while she cried, silently, so as not to draw attention to herself. Like us, they were waiting for news. I wondered if it was of a parent or a child.

After a few more minutes I looked up to see Lois Archer. She was wearing a silky two-piece with a cashmere wrap and a little beaded handbag over her arm. Her huge frightened eyes with mascaraed lashes took in the four of us and the bleak room. 'Sadie? What's going to happen now? I was playing bridge. Playing bridge with the girls, you know. I couldn't get a taxi . . .'

I had met Lois a handful of times, Jasper just once. We both stood up and now it was Jasper's turn to guide her to a chair. 'You're here now, that's all that matters. There's nothing new to report. And all we can do is wait,' I told her.

In a low voice Jasper repeated what he knew. Lois was trembling but she held her head up. The brown-spotted backs of her hands were gnarled with veins. The huge diamond on her wedding finger reflected the overhead neon strips in chips of rainbow light. I noticed small details: there was a dark scuff on the heel of her pale suede shoe and a tiny catch in the ankle of her sheer stocking. She had been in an unaccustomed hurry.

To bring all my concentration to bear on this helped to keep the other thoughts at bay.

'How can it have happened?' she whispered. I knew she had been asking herself this all the way here.

Jasper said, 'We don't know. The police will find out. I'm going to fetch you a cup of coffee, Lois. It's only from a machine but it will make you feel better.'

With Lois to take care of, with someone who needed his support, Jasper was more himself again. He seemed to have grown back to his normal size. Lois would look to him for protection, of course, because she was used to being looked after by Steven and then by her children. But it was just as much help to Jasper to be able to offer it as it was to her to receive it. I thought how we are all made who we are by our needs as much as by our strengths.

'He seems a good man,' Lois murmured when he'd gone.

'He is.'

'If only Steven were here.'

Steven was Mel's legendarily charismatic father. The only man Mel had ever loved, she told me. Up until now.

I bit the inside of my cheek to stop the tremors. 'Yes.'

'Stewart's in Melbourne, you know. And David's away in Greece.'

These were two of Mel's perfectly matched pairs of younger and older brothers. There had been so much good fortune in the Archer family. Steven's triumphant career and the children's looks and talent and ambition had been nurtured by the deceptively fragile matriarch who now sat beside me with her old hands clasped on her beaded handbag. It was hard not to think of the family's progress like an express train, forever gathering momentum and confidence, and travelling faster on its parallel lines, until it plunged without warning into the black tunnel of tonight.

Stop it. Don't think like that.

'Don't worry, they're only a few hours away,' I soothed Lois.

A young doctor who reminded me of Dr Raj Srinivasar appeared. He murmured to the young couple and they stood up at once, clutching at each other. Meekly, they followed him out of the room. Lois didn't speak and neither did I. Their child and Lois's child, both fighting their battle somewhere out of our sight. I thought about my own children, Jack behind the locked door at Audrey's, and about Audrey with no child of her own. And then Ted was there.

I felt his presence as strongly as Lois's beside me, smelt his cologne and heard his entirely familiar voice that I would now never hear again except in my memories. 'Well, my girl,' he said. 'This is a shaky old do, isn't it?'

I tilt my head, listening and gazing at the images in my mind's eye.

We are in the kitchen of our old house, the one that Tony and I shared, and into which Stanley erupted with the mission to build kitchen cupboards. Neither of them is here now, though. Tony has already moved out and Stanley is absent during this family colloquy, neatly presaging what's to come. It is always Stanley's way to take the easiest route and that is to absent himself from responsibility. He's probably in the pub. It's Ted I'm looking at and at Jack standing on my father's lap. He is about three, not much older than Cassie now, with fat babyish legs emerging from a pair of green shorts.

Ted has never been physically demonstrative with my children, any more than he was with me. He likes to keep his clothes uncreased and his hands clean. But today Jack has demanded a connection and Ted has yielded. Jack is rocking up and down, feet planted on Ted's thighs, pretending to ride a horse. Ted looks uncomfortable; he is smiling but there is an evasiveness in his eyes that I know of old. But at least he's here, I think. My marriage is ending and Ted has come to visit us in order for me to be able to talk to him about it. He has rallied round in a crisis, as he would put it.

Lola is in the room too, somewhere on the margins. A smouldering, currently mute, perpetually angry adolescent presence. Clothes, hairstyle, language all unsuitable for her age, designed to provoke.

I put a drink at my father's elbow. 'Yes,' I agree, choosing my words with care. 'I know it's a big decision. I didn't make it lightly, please believe that . . .'

In fact, I am shell-shocked by my act of desertion, by my wilful destruction of our nuclear family when it had been my strongest intention to preserve its security for Lola and Jack. And yet – I am convinced that I am doing the right thing, because I am so helplessly and passionately in love, as I have never been before.

I am turning to my father, looking to him as a fellow-traveller. Ted will comprehend what I feel, surely, with his history? I need his understanding, his wisdom, his sympathy, and most of all to know that he doesn't condemn me for what I have done. He takes a sip from the gin and tonic that I have prepared for him, replaces the glass on the table. From behind Jack's energetically bouncing body I hear him say, 'Think of your children, Sadie. Is this what they want?'

There is a clatter behind me. Lola slamming down a knife or the kitchen scissors. I dread her scathing response. I take a breath, count five long seconds, then tell the truth: 'It's what *I* want.'

It's like uttering a blasphemy. I don't think I have ever deliberately made such a choice before, let alone articulated it. In this instant I feel free and powerful and – in spite of all the pain I cause and feel – I am happy.

My father shakes his head. 'That's not the point. You're a mother. Your responsibility is to these two and then to your husband.'

The hypocrisy makes me gasp. I stand with my hands hanging loose at my sides, staring at him.

He does disapprove and he makes no attempt to hide it, even though he has always dismissively referred to Tony as 'your whatsit . . . accountant' and on the other hand considers Stanley a man's man, a proper chap. He is going to condemn me for daring to please myself even though, as it seems to me at this moment, he has consulted his own inclinations all his life.

But *you* do what you want and always have, I want to shout at him. Isn't anyone else allowed to do the same? Yet I don't shout, or even speak.

In the silence that follows, the last drops of my longing for his approval turn to chips of ice.

In the end it is Ted who breaks it. He says sorrowfully to Jack, 'Come on, then, old son. That's enough of that. Let's you and me go out in the garden and look at the birds.'

He probably didn't say exactly those words. But I know he took Jack outside, and Lola shot me a look that was pure bewilderment veiled with belligerence before she slammed out of the room as well.

I'm sure neither of the children remembers that day and it's quite likely that Ted didn't either. But after that I was always angry with him. We were cordial to each other, there was almost nothing that was different, not on the surface, but I cut him off. I became implacable.

I finally knew that I was on my own, instead of wishing and longing to be otherwise and all the time coming up against the brick wall of disappointment. The understanding helped me to survive the loss of Stanley. In the end, when enough time had passed, I even felt a kind of gratitude for my independence. I was strong because I reckoned I was invulnerable – as long as I had Lola and Jack, and the company of friends.

I wanted to tell Ted all about this when I drove up to his bedside, but I never found the words. I should have explained that I was wrong to be angry, because we all do things wrong and we are all flawed. Even my glamorous father, the perfumer and con artist, whom I wished to be perfect. I wanted to tell him that I regretted my selfishness. But it was too late.

It has taken me until now to understand this sequence properly, as I sit in a hospital side room waiting for news of Lois Archer's child and my best friend.

I'm sorry, I tell him. I am truly sorry. And I did – do – love you.

Jasper came back with three polystyrene beakers clutched like a sloppy bouquet in front of him. Carefully he handed one each to Lois and me, then sat down again. I sipped the weak liquid and blinked at the clock. It was two twenty-seven in the morning. Time seemed to be playing tricks. It was only five minutes since I had last looked, when Jasper offered to fetch the coffee, but it could easily have been two hours. I licked my dry lips and resumed my study of the floor and the toes of my shoes. The minutes creaked by and painfully turned into an hour. Outside, the thunderstorm had passed. It was still raining, I could see the drops bursting like tiny ripe fruits against the window, but the air was fresher and there was a welcome breeze stirring.

At last a nurse looked in. She asked if we were still waiting for news of Melissa Archer and when Jasper said yes she asked us to follow her. We marched in a silent line, none of us able to speak or even look at each other. Unvoiced, unworded bargains did form themselves in my head now.

If only she's all right. Let her be Mel again.

The doctor was at a busy nursing station looking through a sheaf of notes. Even though it was the deadest hour of the night there were bright lights here and people moving briskly.

When we identified ourselves he motioned us into an office cubicle. He spoke drily, unemphatically, but the words flared in my head.

Repaired. Transfusion. Optimistic. Recovery, he said.

Mel was going to live, I understood. The bags under the man's eyes, the way the overhead lights showed the pores in his skin and the creases in his neck, the smell of anaesthesia, all became hyper-real, vividly illuminated by our collective relief. Lois groped for my hand and I put my arm out to support her. I realised how tiny and light she was, and that she was quivering like a bird.

Jasper rubbed his hand over his face. I could feel the wash of relief in him, a big, heavy tide, with no undertow of happiness yet. That would come later. 'Can we see her?' he asked.

'Are you all relatives?'

Lois lifted her chin. 'I am her mother.'

'I am her fiancé,' Jasper said in a low voice. I felt rather than heard Lois's indrawn breath. This was the first she had heard.

I realised I was smiling, a stiff smile that almost hurt my lips and cheeks. Everything was going to be all right. 'I'm a friend,' I murmured.

'Only two of you,' he apologised. 'And then only a couple of minutes. She's very tired.'

Of course she was tired. But only people who are alive feel weary.

'Go on,' I said to Lois and Jasper. 'Give her a kiss from me.'

I drove back to my house through the thin drizzle. Coming home had never seemed so pleasant, or the security that my home offered felt so welcome. I went slowly up the stairs and lay down on my bed, intending to get up in a minute and undress properly. The room was blessedly cool after the stifling weeks that had just passed. I pulled the covers round my shoulders and let my eyes close. My last thought before I fell asleep was of Cassie. Sleeping too, in her safe bedroom, with the curtains closed on the night.

When I woke up again I was aware first that it was broad daylight, then that there was someone snugly fitting like a spoon against my back. I thought in sleepy confusion that it must be Paul, but when I stirred he stirred too and I knew it was Jack.

'Mum.'

I turned over and looked into my son's wide eyes. 'You're home.'

And as if through his ears I could hear the shuffling and the throaty calls of pigeons on the roof.

'We heard the early news on the radio. Audrey always listens to it. I came straight away because I thought you'd want me to be here.'

'I do.'

'Do you know how Mel is?'

'I went to the hospital. Jasper called me. She's going to be all right.' I stroked his hair. His clothes smelled of Audrey's house.

'It would be against the laws of nature for someone like Mel to die, wouldn't it?'

This was what I had tried to tell Jasper last night. 'I'm not sure that there are any laws, Jack. It's frightening.' I was speaking to him like an adult. We had passed a milestone.

'There are in nature,' he said calmly.

We lay still for a few minutes, lapped in quiet. The traffic in the street, even the pigeon noises seemed a long way off. It was only hours since I had watched Cassie playing with her boats in the sink. An afternoon, an evening, a night and half a lifetime seemed to have intervened.

'It's quite cool outside. It smells of autumn,' Jack remarked. After another pause he went on, 'It's cool to be home as well. I've had enough of Audrey's. I want to go up the park before school starts. I might see Wes and the others.'

'Okay,' I ventured. 'Good. Do you want some breakfast now?'

'Haven't you got to go to work?'

'I think Penny'll understand if I don't make it this morning.'

'Yeah. All right, then. I'd like a bacon sandwich. White bread and red sauce.'

One of his favourites. I sat up. 'We'll both have one.'

Jack watched me rummage around for clean clothes. I was half out of the door on the way to the bathroom before he asked, 'Will they catch the people who attacked Mel?'

He was still young enough to look for my reassurance that wrongs would be put right. He wasn't quite grown up yet after all. 'I should think so.'

He nodded and lay back against my pillows. The threads of life were tight. They might have unravelled or been torn into shreds, but this morning they were still intact and they knitted us all together in love and friendship.

I went on into the bathroom, and in my gratitude and happiness I didn't even blink at the mess of smeared make-up and crumpled tissues that my Lola left in her wake.

NINETEEN

There were so many chairs crammed in round my table that they had to stand at slight angles to each other, like crooked teeth in an overcrowded jaw. People leaned on their elbows among the dishes and pressed their knees together between the table legs, shouting to make themselves heard above the rising noise. Caz and I passed more plates over their heads and room was made, somehow, to put them down.

Mel sat at the head of the table with Jasper opposite her at the foot. We were celebrating their engagement. It was five weeks since the night in the off-licence and she had been home from hospital for almost three. 'I would have died if I'd had to stay in there any longer,' she said.

She was much thinner and there were grey streaks among the tight coils of black hair, but most noticeably of all she had stopped wearing lipstick. Her mouth was its own colour now so that you noticed the curve of the top lip and the fullness of the lower one, rather than just seeing the bright crimson. When I mentioned it she considered and then shrugged, with a hesitancy that was new too. In the past, Mel had always been so sure of everything. 'It's not important, is it?'

'No,' I agreed. After what Mel had been through, after looking death straight in the face, it would be surprising if the hierarchy of what was and was not important were not completely overturned.

I thought she was more beautiful than ever, especially now in repose, as she sat listening and watching the faces around her. Once, she would have been talking louder and faster than anyone, without waiting for answers.

Then when her eyes reached Jasper it was like shutters opening to the inside of her skull. The look was so naked that I had to glance away, as if I had been caught spying.

Jasper sat with Lois on his right and on Lois's other side was Mr Rainbird. She rested her leaf-dry hand first on Paul's arm, then turned the other way to murmur to Jasper. She seemed even tinier and more fragile than on the night at the hospital, as if the force of one of Graham's hoots of laughter might blow her away. But she could still turn on the considerable wattage of her charm, especially near personable men.

Caz was beckoning me into the kitchen, so I went to join her.

We were ready to serve our pudding.

When we planned the celebration dinner, we knew that Chocolate Nemesis had to be on the menu. Of all the chocolate puddings Mel had flirted with in her time, it remained her true love and this one was the best I had ever made. The rich dark square was firm on the outside, but only just. It had taken all our combined dexterity to coax it out of the tin and on to the cake board in one piece. On the top I had piped two big interlinked sugar-pink hearts of icing and a cupid's arrow. There were other puddings, but these were incidental. Nemesis was everyone's nemesis.

Graham was opening more bottles of champagne and filling glasses. Caz and I lifted the cake board and I balanced it flat-palmed at shoulder height. Caz clapped her hands for attention. Everyone's eyes turned.

I rotated my wrist and lowered the cake in front of Mel. She sprang half out of her chair to admire it, forgetting the great sickle-shaped wound that ran from her spine to her breastbone. Emergency surgery had meant the opening up of her whole chest cavity. The pain showed before she managed a smile.

'Be careful, darling,' Lois called.

'I am just greedy,' she murmured. Then she looked up at me. 'Sadie, thank you. It's beautiful.'

I stood next to her, facing the table, my fingers just resting on her shoulder. I could feel the protuberance of bone at the top of her arm.

Lola and Sam were at one corner, heads together, their two chairs wedged in a space only strictly big enough for one. They had left the festivities of the first week of university term specially for the party. Paul Rainbird sat with his elbow hooked over his chair back, smiling when his eyes met mine. I had begun, I realised, to look for him to be there.

Jack had asked if he could sit next to Jasper. 'He seems all right,' he said, which coming from him was the highest praise. Jack hadn't talked much during the meal, but he looked composed, even with the embarrassment of Mr Rainbird sitting right across the table.

'Does he *have* to be there?' he had asked when I warned him. But it was a routine complaint rather than a real objection.

'Yes, I think he does. I'd like him to be, unless you particularly object,' I said. Jack only sighed.

Graham made sure that everyone had a full glass. There was a waiting pause while I suddenly wondered if I was going to be able to speak at all because my throat was tight. Mel's head was bowed and I could see the silver hair radiating from the crown of it, and her left hand with the ring that Jasper had lately given her resting in her lap.

Caz nodded encouragement at me, her face lit with warmth, so I began, regardless. I said, 'We might so easily not have been here tonight. But we *are* here and that's mostly because Mel has been so brave. Jack said to me on the day after it happened, people like Mel don't just go and die. It's against the laws of nature.'

Jasper was looking at her as if there were no one else in the room, or anywhere in the rest of the world for that matter. As if they were the only two people on the planet. I glanced sideways, just for a second. Next to Lola was Clare, Jasper's daughter. She was dark-haired, small-featured, with narrow shoulders and long pale hands. She looked straight ahead of her, her lips closed but not compressed.

'And I told him I wasn't so sure that there are laws out there any more, not after a summer like this one.' The long hot weeks did have a lurid, unreal quality now, like scenes remembered from a film. 'But Mel's her own law, as we all know, and she came back to us. Most of all, she came back for Jasper.'

Mel lifted her head and laughed out loud, momentarily her old brash self again. 'Was I ever going to let him go, once I'd found him? Not for any old knife wound, believe me.'

Everyone else laughed too, including Lois. 'And I really had given up hope. Never to be mother of the bride, that would be very hard, wouldn't it?'

'I'm not surprised you didn't want to let him go,' Caz called. Clare turned her head towards her father, her pale cheeks colouring, proud of him and wary and possessive all at the same time. Yes, I thought, that's how it is.

'Let's drink a toast to them,' I said. 'To Jasper and Mel. May you always be as happy together as you look tonight.'

Everyone stood up, pushing back their chairs and lifting their glasses. The tears in my eyes didn't just spring from the champagne's sharp prickle on my tongue and against the roof of my mouth.

Jasper and Mel. Clare smiled gamely too as she called their names.

Mel picked up the knife I had laid beside her plate and sliced deep into the heart of the Chocolate Nemesis.

Amidst the cheering and clapping I was thinking that evenings like this were the best reward. They made sense of all the work that had to be done in an ordinary day and for life's routine that occasionally seemed too tedious to endure.

And then there came tonight, when everything shimmered with happiness and a sense of rightness.

The faces went all blurred and I blinked.

Ted was here again, standing close beside me, not in his Spencer Tracy youthful glory but shrunk and hunched over as he had been in old age, with his hands blotched and veined like Lois Archer's. He would have loved this party. 'Well, Princess.' He chuckled. 'Not so bad, is it?'

I was reminded of the afternoon of Ted's funeral when his neighbours and the cousins from Manchester had also spontaneously clapped and cheered, out of affection for his memory. The circle was closing. Ragged ends met and began to knit together again.

An arm slid round me. The touch made me jump and then I saw that in the noisy aftermath of the toast Paul had left his seat. His breath warmed my neck.

Jasper was standing up now. He cleared his throat and looked solemn, and then couldn't maintain the solemnity. He was too happy to be serious.

'Get on with it,' Graham called. 'I want my cake.'

Jasper thanked Caz and me for the dinner. Then he turned to Mel. A glance passed between them and at the same time a little arrowhead of anxiety pressed in my throat. 'I want to propose another toast. To the woman I am more proud of than anything else in my life.'

Oh, be careful, I thought. The dart's pressure was actually painful now. The room seemed to have stopped its collective breathing.

'To my daughter, Clare.'

Relief made me almost gasp. We clapped again and echoed

her name, and Clare's flush darkened. She scrambled out of her chair, hesitated as if she didn't know which way to go, then crossed to Mel and briefly laid her cheek against Mel's hair. She was doing the right thing because this was what was expected of her and she expected it of herself too, but there was reluctance as well as compliance showing in the stiff angles of her head and limbs. Mel tried to draw her closer, even though the movement was physically painful, but Clare evaded her and circled round to her father instead. He sheltered her in the crook of his arm, as if she were Cassie's age, and she nestled triumphantly up against him.

It wasn't all a fairy tale. Even for Jasper and Mel there was some rough water ahead.

Mel banged on the table. 'Now it's my turn,' she called out. She looked tired, with dark patches under her eyes, and she didn't try to stand up. The evening was beginning to tell on her. 'I have another toast. To family and friends,' she said.

'To family. And friends.' We drank to that.

The talk broke up while we ate our chocolate pudding. Mel managed only a couple of mouthfuls of her helping before her spoon drooped, and Caz took her plate away before anyone noticed. Lola poked her head round Sam's shoulder and called to me, 'How amazing is this, Mum? Clare knows Chloe and Seb.'

'That is amazing,' I agreed. In fact, it wasn't surprising at all. Wherever she went Lola seemed to encounter someone she knew or who knew someone else she knew. She moved blithely and unquestioningly through a huge, loose web of friends and friends of friends from school, and boys she had been to discos with when she was thirteen, and their brothers and their networks of mates and girlfriends, who connected in their turn and intersected one another's social groups in an endlessly complicated Venn diagram. I often thought that to Lola and her friends the city must seem like a vast disorganised club that was constantly yielding new connections to further consolidate their membership.

This notion was pleasing. It went against the current of threat that had swollen through the long hot summer and had finally broken out in random violence and a knife blade.

The four youths who had robbed the off-licence were arrested the day after the stabbing. Their hoodie tops were pulled down over their faces so that the cameras couldn't distinguish their identities, but one of the eyewitnesses had recognised them anyway. One of them had indeed been an apprentice butcher.

There had been a couple of days of newspaper headlines, after the arrest and while Mel's life was still in danger, but then events in the Middle East had commanded the news again and the story had faded. It was as if the waters had closed over the rocks, temporarily at least until the trial, and the waves subsided into ripples that were only felt by those of us who loved Mel.

Now the cool windy weather stripped drought-browned leaves from the trees and piled them in autumnal heaps in gutters and doorways. Relief at the return of normality fluttered under the prematurely bare branches.

Sam and Lola and Caz's Dan took Clare off upstairs to Lola's room.

Caz and I were piling up plates and making coffee when Jack left the table and sidled up behind me. He stood close, frowning and fidgeting, and then said, 'Mum, you know, you should have asked Audrey to come tonight.'

I straightened up from loading the dishwasher. 'Should I? She doesn't know Mel.'

Jack shrugged. 'Well. You know.'

I did know that Jack was still a regular visitor to Turnmill Street. Sometimes he went there after school and stayed until supper time, or else he called in on weekend afternoons and fed the animals for Audrey and then sat with Jack the cat on his lap to watch television. I found tell-tale tufts of the creature's fur on his trousers and sweatshirts. He answered truthfully when I asked where he had been, but he didn't volunteer information. And in my turn I didn't press him, or demand that he came home in time to do his homework. He was going to school every day and not complaining too much about it either. The brief interest in him shown by Wes and Jason and the other cool ones hadn't led to a friendship, of course, but on the other hand my son didn't any longer seem quite such an isolated figure. He reported that there was a boy in his new class who wanted to be a naturalist.

Paul and I hadn't spent the night together since Jack came home from Turnmill Street. I wished he would stay tonight, so that we could have one more drink among the remaining dirty glasses and coffee cups, and do a post-mortem on the evening before going upstairs to bed.

Jack splayed the fingers of one hand on the breadboard and with the other picked up the knife that Mel had used to slice the cake. Still frowning, he began gouging the point of the knife into the sliver of wood showing between his knuckles. Slowly, at first, then faster.

'Jack. Stop that. You'll chop your finger off.'

The knife's serrated tip stuck in the board and he let go, leaving it standing upright. He removed his hand just in time before it toppled sideways, blade down. I retrieved the knife and put it aside.

'She doesn't get invited out very much. Not at all, in fact.'

I sighed, recalling my own pleasure in this evening. 'I know. You're right. I'll go and see her soon, and ask her to come and have dinner with us.'

Jack was leaning up against the counter now, blocking off the sink and the kitchen bin. He always picked the most inconvenient moments for his obliquely telling questions.

I edged him sideways so that Caz could reach the sink but without losing eye contact with him. 'Mum?'

'Yes.'

'You know you've sold Grandad's house?'

The sale had been completed in the previous week and the money was in my bank. 'Mm.'

'And some of the money's supposed to be mine?'

'That's right. A quarter of it.' I planned to put it in a special account for when he went to university, or wanted to travel to somewhere remote to look at particularly desirable birds.

'Well, the thing is, I don't really want it. I don't need it, do I? So I want to give my share to Audrey.'

Caz rattled beans into the coffee grinder and called the routine 'Sorry, everyone' before the din began. I waited through the seconds and when I could hear myself speak again said, 'That's very generous of you. But Audrey owns a house, quite a valuable one I should think, in that street. Does she need your money?'

Jack frowned even harder, so that his tufty eyebrows pulled close together. 'There's a reason. A pretty good reason, actually.'

I waited. 'Are you going to tell me what it is?'

'No. I think she should tell you herself.'

Jasper towered beside me, saying that Mel wanted camomile tea instead of coffee and Lois was wondering if we had any Earl Grey. This last made me think of Audrey's neighbours Tim and Gavin and their big white teapot and the siege of Turnmill Street. It seemed a long time ago. 'Coming up,' I told Jasper. Then I said seriously to Jack, 'All right. I'll go and see Audrey this weekend and she can tell me whatever it is.'

'Okay,' Jack said and shrugged. He drifted over to switch on the television, quelling its sudden blare of noise by aiming the remote. He yawned and stretched out in an armchair.

The evening was winding down. Caz had done most of the washing up and now she and Graham were making a move to go home. Lois was deep in conversation with Paul. Mel's face was waxy with exhaustion and Jasper nodded when I raised my eyebrows at him.

'Have we got to go? Just let me finish my tea,' Mel insisted. In the old days she was always among the last to leave the party: she would feel the need to stay at this one that was being given in her honour.

'Mel,' Jasper warned her and she blinked at him.

'So is this how it's going to be? For ever?'

'Yeah. Home by ten thirty, or else.'

'Maybe I'm making a terrible mistake.'

'Don't say that, darling.' Lois looked shocked. Mel always did say that her mother had trouble with irony.

It took time to find Lois's cashmere wrap and then she kept remembering something else she wanted to tell Paul about her early days with Steven. By the time she was ready to go Mel looked as if she could rest her head on the table and go straight to sleep.

'Where's Clare gone?' Jasper was asking. More or less on cue, Lola and the others languidly reappeared.

'Mum, we thought we'd go on to a club. That's okay, isn't it?' Lola murmured.

Sam was welded to her side, as usual, and the other two were hovering just behind them. Clare was all slender tapered ovals – face and long feet and fingernails, and big blond Dan looked huge and square-cut next to her. They were very obviously not looking at each other and every movement they made betrayed their interest. Dan was sheepishly grinning and eager, and Clare was feline and supple with her head tilted away but her hips angled towards him.

'How'll you get home from this place? Where is it?' Jasper asked.

'I'll see her home,' Dan offered, to no one's surprise.

'Lo, you're always going out. You're always at some stupid

club.' Jack was frowzily trapped in his armchair, irritable with jealousy.

'Chill, bruv.'

Then with amazing rapidity the four of them were gone.

Mel and I laughed together on the doorstep as I put my arms round her to say goodnight. Strong perfume, as ever. Lilies of the valley, *muguet*.

'Did you see that with Clare and Dan?' I said. 'It looks rather promising.'

'Doesn't it make you feel *old*? It does me.'

I wasn't drunk enough to consider the question seriously. 'Hey. Maybe we *are* old and haven't noticed. Are we ready to crumble to dust when the light touches us?'

She wasn't laughing now. She was frail, standing on my front step with the door open and the night's darkness at her back. Her eyes were on Jasper who was bringing Lois down the hall with her bag and her wrap and her small, slow steps. The wine had made Lois unsteady and she held tight to Jasper's arm.

Mel whispered, 'It's not much of an exchange, is it? His lovely daughter's fled with a giant into the night, and he's left with my old mother and me.'

This was invalid's talk, not Mel's voice. She was weaker and sadder than I had realised, but I also knew for certain that the old Mel would re-emerge in time. Jack was right. She was too vivid just to fade away.

'Go home to sleep.'

'Oh yes, to sleep. I will.' There was as much longing in her voice as there used to be for wine, or fun, or chocolate.

I kissed her on both cheeks. 'Goodnight. I love you.'

'And me. Thanks, Sade, and for this evening. Tell Penny I said hello, will you?'

Penny and Evelyn weren't going out much at the moment. They wouldn't leave Cassie with a sitter and even Evelyn didn't seem to want to bring her to parties any more. Mostly they stayed at home in Penny's house, looking after the baby and each other, and they didn't seem particularly unhappy with that.

'I will,' I promised.

I stood in the doorway until they were safely in Jasper's car, then I stayed watching the red tail lights until they turned out of sight.

Downstairs again the house smelled of congealed food and smoke and lilies of the valley, but it was too cold outside to open the garden doors. Jack was staring sightlessly at the television in defensive posture, his knees drawn up against his chest and his arms wound round them. Paul was the last remaining guest. He was making tea, with small tidy movements. He handed me a mug. Silence was silted up in the corners of the room; I knew they hadn't spoken to each other while I was upstairs. Or maybe, most probably, Paul had tried to talk and Jack had rebuffed him.

'It's very late,' I said. 'Jack?'

He ignored me and went on gazing at the screen. In fact, it was only just after eleven thirty. In a minute Paul would leave and Jack and I would retreat to our bedrooms. I was waiting for Paul to say that he must go home, but he only leaned back against the sink with his fingers laced round his mug of tea. The atmosphere reminded me of the day, the terrible day, with the thunderstorm all the time waiting to break.

Paul tilted his head, semaphoring a question.

He was wearing the same blue shirt as that first time when I went to school to see him about Jack's truancy. His face had lately become blurred with familiarity but the sudden awkwardness of the moment made me look at him afresh. Neat but unremarkable features, it was true, with eyelids that sloped downwards at the corners. Kind eyes, though. Lines of resignation as well as laughter at the corners of his mouth. A good, mobile mouth; I remembered how it felt against my skin.

My own mouth was stiff.

He watched and waited as my eyes turned to Jack. I didn't know what to say. For some reason I thought of Auntie Viv and then the hated Maxine. So I said nothing at all.

I disappointed Paul. I knew it, because he put his mug down very carefully and turned away from me. The television babbled between the three of us, an insane commentary.

'Jack, could you turn that off, please?' His voice was crisp. Startled, Jack pointed the remote and we descended into silence. Paul went and sat down on the chair nearest to him. He said, 'I'd like to stay here tonight with Sadie. How would you feel about that?'

Jack's back went rigid. But he managed a small shrug, affecting indifference.

'You don't mind?'

Jack said coldly, 'You're not my dad, are you?'

'No, I'm not.'

Jack nodded as if he had scored a point but Paul went on, 'Only your dad can be your dad. But do you think that no one except him should ever be able stay here with your mum?'

'Yes.'

'Not just now, that is. How about in six years, say, when you've gone to college like Lola?'

The shrug. 'Dunno. Well, I'll be gone then, won't I?'

Out of sight, out of mind.

'Hm. It's just that it's quite a long time for her to wait until then.'

'*Is* she waiting?'

I broke in. 'Just a minute. I'm not some . . . some cow in a pen, you know, to be discussed between the two of you.'

Paul's mouth twitched.

Jack glared at him and then at me. 'What do you want?' he demanded. And that was the question.

I said slowly, 'I would like him to stay, Jack, you know. If you don't feel too bad about it. I'm sort of realising that I've been a bit lonely, sometimes, even though I've got you and Lo.'

Jack said tragically, 'Mum, *everyone*'s lonely. Not just you.'

I would willingly be crippled with loneliness every hour of my life in order for Jack never to feel such a thing.

Paul was less stricken. 'Everyone feels lonely some of the time, yes. But nearly all of us feel the opposite as well, quite often. I've seen you at school, lately. You like Max McLaren, don't you?'

'He's okay.'

'And what about tonight? You've got this wonderful family and there were all those friends sitting around the table eating chocolate pudding. It wasn't lonely for any of us, was it?'

I would have treated this as a rhetorical question but Paul waited teacher-like for a reply.

'No,' Jack admitted. And then, logically enough, 'So therefore my mum's all right as well, isn't she? She doesn't need you.'

'She doesn't *need* me, no. That's one of the things I value in her. But there's a difference between needing and enjoying. There are times when it might be nice for her to have a partner. I think you'd concede that, wouldn't you?'

Grudgingly he said, 'I suppose.'

'I like your mother very much. I wouldn't do anything to hurt her, you know. If that's what you are worrying about.'

'You mean, if you were her boyfriend?'

'If I were or not. Either way, I wouldn't hurt her. Or you.'

Jack considered this. 'Do you think she'd be less sad?'

'I hope so. Yes, I think so.'

I was surprised to learn that my son thought I was sad.

Jack turned back to me. 'What would Grandad say about him staying here?'

So Ted was in Jack's mind too. A grandfather to my son, as well as the perfumer and con artist for me, with his battered film star looks and his repertoire of aunties. If only he were still here, to tell us himself what he thought.

I turned the question around in my mind. 'I think he'd probably say good luck.' *And he'd probably add something like, let's face it, Sade, you're not getting any younger, are you?*

Jack suddenly tired of this. He launched himself out of the armchair. 'Whatever,' he pronounced, that most infuriating of adolescent non-acquiescences that still put an effective stop to all further discussion.

I loved him so much, in his slovenly T-shirt and untied trainers, and the jeans that were noticeably too short in the leg. He was growing fast. At the same instant I *knew*, as certainly as if I had photographed it, that he looked straight at Paul and the glance was collusive and disparaging, and it said something like *women*, or *mothers*. Jack was crossing the boundary into manhood.

'Night, then,' he muttered. He drifted up the stairs, one shoulder dragging against the wall. Soon it would become almost too much effort for him to walk or even move – like Lola at the same age – except in the pursuit of personal gratification. And in that he would be able to travel faster than light.

Paul and I were left alone in the kitchen.

'I'm sorry,' I said. I was disappointed in myself. I wanted to avoid hurting anyone and all I had managed was a failure to show loyalty in either direction.

'It's all right.'

'You did the right thing.'

'He's more resilient than you think and you should take credit for that.'

'Maybe.' I didn't want to talk about Jack any more. 'I'm glad you're here, anyway.'

Paul Rainbird's face split into a smile. He came to me and put his hands on either side of my face, smoothing my cheeks with his thumbs. I blinked, feeling that the light was cruelly bright and briefly wishing for candles and music and less debris around us.

'I'm glad I'm here, too, and Jack will get used to it. Do you want to finish the washing up, or shall we go to bed?'

'Bed.'

I didn't care about the unflattering light after all. It was like Mel not needing or wanting the red lipstick any longer. With Paul, I am who I am. I don't feel old, or young, or swamped with passion, or tacky with relief at finally having a man. What I do feel is *right*.

The next day was a Saturday.

Jack came down to breakfast and was no more or less uncommunicative with Paul eating toast at the kitchen table than he would have been if he and I were alone. When I asked him if he was going to Audrey's later he countered sharply by asking if he did whether Paul and I would be coming to stake out the front garden.

Paul held up his hands. 'Not me, thanks. I've got marking to do today.'

Jack looked as if he didn't quite know whether he was supposed to scowl or to smile. It was quite hard to tell, with Paul's deadpan style. 'Anyway, I thought *you* were going to see her.'

'Was I? I'm not sure I meant today, necessarily.'

'Mum. You said, last night.'

Paul gathered up his jacket and his shabby black bag. 'I've got to go. See you, Jack. Sadie, I'll call you later. It was a great evening, by the way. I'll let myself out.'

We were left on our own. There was something sticky either on the floor or on the sole of his shoe, I could hear the tiny crepitation in the sudden quiet. He was looking hard at me now, as if he expected or feared that I might be somehow different and I waited through his scrutiny.

'Did you mind about Paul being here last night?' I asked at length.

'Well. It does feel kind of odd.'

'I know. It must do.'

'You won't, you know . . .?' His voice trailed away.

He hoped that I wouldn't embarrass him more than was bearable, that I wouldn't withdraw from him or favour Paul Rainbird over him and Lola, and that I wouldn't allow myself to be hurt. In other words, that life would go on for him as usual. Or maybe even improve slightly.

'I won't,' I promised.

'Good,' Jack said in a tone that indicated that was more than enough discussion of the subject.

'I'll go and see Audrey this afternoon,' I added.

Turnmill Street was full of cars, some of them double-parked. I finally found a space in the next street, closer to the Ullswater estate, and I walked back to Audrey's past privet hedges dripping from an earlier shower and honeysuckles and wisteria trailing flags of yellow leaves.

I knocked at the familiar door and waited.

'You again,' Audrey said when it eventually opened.

'May I come in?'

'It'll make a change from sitting in my garden in your bloody deckchair.'

She stalked back down the hallway, indicating that I could follow her if I chose. The tide of rubbish seemed to be rising. There were busted cardboard boxes, piled two and three deep, spilling old clothes and magazines.

'I'm having a bit of a sort-out. You'll have to take me as you find me.'

'It looks fine,' I said weakly, stepping around a rusty oil heater and a pile of dismembered telephone directories. A junior cat was sitting in the remains of a green satin-covered eiderdown with feathers floating around it like a figure in a child's snow dome.

In the back room I edged around the furniture and glanced into the garden. The cages stood along the walls, and the no man's land in between was still littered with vegetable peelings and greasy enamel bowls. Tim and Gavin had either abandoned their clear-up campaign or got nowhere with it. I turned back abruptly and caught Audrey unawares, standing in a shaft of stained October sunlight. She had aged. There were food marks on her cardigan and her grey plaid skirt was matted with cat fur. Her pink scalp showed through the strands of colourless hair. Even her mouth looked thinner and the zipper lines that fanned from the top margin were more deeply indented.

'What are you gawping at?'

Caught out, I mumbled, 'I'm sorry. I didn't mean to.'

She stepped out of the path of the sunshine and moved softly around her lair. 'What are you here for anyway?'

She was as combative as ever. I felt the same antipathy to her as I had done from the beginning. There had been a natural discord long before our tussle over Jack and that issue was in any case becoming irrelevant now. Jack had changed, even in the short time since last term. He would grow up and away in the end, just as Lola had done.

'Jack asked me to call and see you. He said you had something to tell me.'

'Did he? Do I?'

'Audrey, may I sit down?'

Every chair was heaped with bulging polythene bags and cats.

'All right, if you're staying.'

I removed most of the stuff from the nearest chair and sat. Audrey now loomed above me.

'I think you know that Jack is going to inherit some money

419

from Ted. It's one quarter of the proceeds from the sale of Ted's house. The rest goes half to me, a quarter to Lola.'

I felt it necessary to explain this in detail, because Audrey had once asked me about Ted's will. 'Now Jack tells me that he wants to give his share to you. I asked him why but he said that you should tell me yourself.'

Audrey smiled and her face briefly lost its pinched lines. 'You've got an interesting child there.'

Her affection for him was plain to see. The sadness that was coupled with it acknowledged what I had known all along, that she had no one of her own to care about and was lonely.

While I waited, a cat unfurled itself on the rug. Its claws emerged, sharp hooks the colour of brittle old celluloid, and were sheathed again.

Audrey seemed to come to a decision. She went over to the drawer in the gate-legged table and took out a sheaf of creased and stained documents. She leafed through them and slipped one out of the pile, smoothed it flat on the table and studied it. Then she held it out to me.

'What is it?' I asked.

A pucker of anxiety inside my chest made me lean forward. I knew that I didn't want to learn any more about this, whatever it might be, but the document quivered only inches from my hand and I had to take it from her. I studied it for a long moment. Faded buff-pink squares, names handwritten in ink in an even, official hand: Edwin Lawrence Thompson, Bachelor. Audrey Ann Nesbit, Spinster.

It was a marriage certificate.

I checked the date: 1956.

'No,' I said, out loud. But it was a vain contradiction.

My parents married in late 1949 and I was born in 1950. My mother died suddenly ten years later. And in the middle of that time, according to this paper, Ted married Audrey Nesbit.

As well as a perfumer and con artist, my father was a bigamist. A grand master of deception. I felt a dull reverberation of shock, but no particular surprise.

I let the certificate drop. My fingers were thick and blunt, like sausages. 'Did you know?'

'When I married him? No, of course not.'

I had read similar stories. There were men who maintained whole families, sometimes only a few miles apart, living duplicated and duplicitous lives of perfect domesticity shared out between two wives, two sets of children . . .

My head jerked up. I recalled as clearly as if she had just uttered it Audrey's claim to the two police officers who had come to investigate our stupid siege on that hot summer's day.

I am his grandmother.

What if it were true? I had feared it once and chopped down the fear. Now my eyes met hers, searching for evidence. I could see nothing, but relatives never can detect their physical similarities. She gazed straight back at me.

I asked, 'Did you have children with him?'

'No. I had an abortion. He made me do it.'

The words fell out of her mouth like stones. There was such desolation in them that my suspicions and confusion melted, and I felt nothing but sympathy for her. 'Audrey. Please tell me about it. Just tell me everything that happened. It's not too late.'

'Isn't it?' Her eyes were dry but they looked sore, as if it were painful to move them in their sockets. At last, she tipped cats off one of the chairs. She sat turned away from the light from the window. 'Well, then. I fell in love with a man who made music, but it was music more subtle and elusive than the kind you play with instruments. He told me he could create a perfume for me.'

'My father.'

My father's routine.

'I worked for a company called Phebus Fragrances. Just a couple of weeks of temporary telephone and secretarial work. I was eighteen years old.'

'I remember Phebus.'

'Ted was important there. Very enthusiastic indeed, very good at what he did, but he was irreverent too. He laughed at everything and he made me laugh with him. I thought he was very gentlemanly.'

I knew what that meant. Pigskin gloves and cravats. A car, usually. A confident manner with barmaids and waiters, and an unshakeable belief in the illusion of himself.

'He never suggested anything while I was working there, but when I moved on to the next job he got in touch. Took me for a drink at a pub by the river.'

On one of those evenings when Faye put me to bed, read me a story with half an eye and half an ear cocked to the street outside, and then sat downstairs on her own. An evening when Ted was working late. There had been many, many of them. Times when he was away on business, meeting contacts. Enough opportunity, I now saw, to fit in another wife, another entire home life.

'He told me he was lodging with a family in Hendon because he'd had some money problems. It wasn't very nice, he said, but he was paying off his debts and he'd soon have a place of his own. I had a room in a house belonging to my married cousin. I grew up near Macclesfield and I couldn't wait to get away from there to London.'

The picture she painted was clear enough, in its grainy monochrome mid-Fifties way. Audrey, buxom and fresh-faced, Ted cupping her cheeks between his hands and murmuring, *I could create such a perfume for you.*

'It's not what you imagine,' Audrey snapped. And, indeed, I was imagining.

'We made plans. Business plans, for a shop, a perfumery

and cosmetics line. We went to Paris together. My first time abroad. We were going places, Ted and me. I loved him. And he was in love with me.'

Audrey lifted her chin and I saw beneath her skin into the face of the young woman she had been. An excited traveller, in her checked costume, with clouds of dark hair waving round her face. Or sitting on a wall, windblown, in the photograph Ted had kept and I had found so many years later. She was telling the truth. He had been in love with her; it was that simple.

'I was a decent girl, I'll have you know.'

The kind of girl who insisted on a ring on her finger. Ted loved her, they were a team and he looked into the future with her the way he never did with Faye. Hungry for Audrey, seeing no other way to get her for himself, he married her and overlooked the detail of an already existing wife.

For the first time in my life I properly understood my mother's pallor, her not-quite-there quality. The impression she gave, even at this distance and in the shallow recesses of a child's memory, of being an onlooker in her own life. She must have known. Poor Faye. She was the hollow, the empty space at the centre of this sad story, not Ted or even Audrey.

'Why didn't you become his proper wife, after my mum died?' I tried, but I couldn't quite keep the harshness out of my voice.

Audrey was still looking away. She was sharply silhouetted against the light and I could see the line of coarse hairs at the corner of her mouth. She would tell her story at her own pace.

'We rented a little flat. Not so very far from here. Just two rooms, on the first floor, but there were tall windows overlooking a square. I went on working as a shorthand typist, kept house for him, sat and waited for him to come back when he was away.' Audrey gave a little cough of laughter. 'I was a proper fool, wasn't I? But you can make yourself believe what you want to believe. My grandma died and left me a legacy, and I made the money straight over to him. He wanted to get out of Phebus and start up on his own. It was going to be our big chance. Then I got pregnant. I thought he'd be pleased, but he was angry. He told me he didn't want children, never did and never would, and I couldn't tie him down that way. *Tie him down*, those were the actual words. I thought married people didn't think things like that about each other. He gave me the money to get myself sorted out. Some of my own money back, it must have been. Really, I paid for my own abortion that I didn't want to have anyway.' She was talking as if she had forgotten I was listening, talking out loud to herself as truly lonely people do. 'Afterwards, he was good to me. Flowers, presents, promises and stories about all the successes we were going to have. But it didn't work. It was as if my silly innocence had been skewered out of me along with the baby. I started putting two and two together. Anyway, I ended up going through his things one night while he was asleep. Found an address in Hendon and when I went up there, what did I see?'

I said nothing, but I could guess.

'I saw Faye coming home with her shopping bags, and you in hairslides and white socks skipping along beside her.'

She laughed again, a sound that made the nearest cat stir and turn its yellow eyes to her. 'Ha. Do you remember the perfume? *Innominata*. Nameless, faceless. A wife all right, but one to keep hidden.'

At least there had been a perfume, which there hadn't been for Faye or for me. And had my poor mother spotted her rival, spying on us from the opposite side of Dorset Avenue? I left my chair and stooped down in front of Audrey so that our eyes were level. I tried to take her hands in mine and after a moment she let me. 'What did you do?'

'I told him I'd found him out. He begged me to forgive him,

told me he couldn't bear to be without me. He could be very eloquent, you know. Very hard to resist, Ted was.' As if I didn't know. 'He thought we'd go on in the same way, once I'd got used to the idea. But I wasn't having that. Anyway, I didn't feel the same way about him.'

'And so?'

'I shut him out. Changed the locks, all of that. There was a big to-do, of course, but I stuck to my guns. What else could I do? I wasn't going to go to the police, was I?'

'You might have done.'

Audrey glared at me. A lesser woman might have done, I understood her to mean.

'Then, about ten months after, your mother died.'

The wording on her death certificate might read brain haemorrhage, but I was sure that Faye had simply given up. She had faded out of her own life, and Ted's, and mine. I looked straight into Audrey's eyes. 'Then, if my father loved you . . .?'

'Oh, he came back to get me, we tried it out. We even went away together, a week or something, down to Devon. It was no good for me and we both knew it. I loved him but I couldn't have lived as his wife if he was the last man in the universe. I would have felt contaminated.' Audrey withdrew her hands from mine and folded them inside her sleeves.

That was the worst time for me, too. When Ted came back home at last he had been dejected for reasons that were way beyond my childish understanding. He relit the pilot light in the cold house and we ate fish and chips.

'There was a problem we couldn't get round. You.'

'But . . .'

Audrey interrupted. 'You were always there, getting between us. He had you and I didn't have the baby we should have had together. I used to think you were like a splinter under his skin. He couldn't charm you, could he? You were the only one it didn't work on. Sometimes he didn't want you because you got in his way, but he loved you all right because you held out on him.'

I tried the words out. *If my father loved me.* They didn't seem to make much difference now. And I could work out the rest of the story for myself. Audrey was the wife he wanted and had taken for himself, but the contract had turned itself inside out. Faye died, Audrey rejected him, and he was left with a beady-eyed and unpliant child. There had been the serial aunties as compensation, and Scentsation followed by a spell in prison, and the uneasiness that lay heavy between the two of us for the rest of his life.

His charm *had* worked on me, but after he left me I was cunning enough to hide the effects of it from him. Power to the powerless. Ted may have traded in dreams, but he had lived with lost love and the finality of death. He wasn't wicked, or really even a bad man. He was just what he was. I thought I knew him but when I tried to catch the scent of his cologne, or a glimpse of him within the glittering box of Scentsation, there was nothing there. Only the stink of cats and Audrey's peeling wallpaper.

'I think I understand,' I said, meaning the effects of history that had marked us all.

'Maybe. Or maybe not.'

I stood up because my thighs and back were aching. 'Shall I make us a cup of tea?' I asked.

'That would be nice,' Audrey said.

I washed the teapot thoroughly, found teabags that were still in their hygienic sachets, located two cups. While I waited for the kettle to boil I cleared some of the potato peelings and expired teabags and eggshells out of the sink, and tied them up in a plastic bag. I swabbed the sink with a cloth and wiped the crusted taps. There must be a very fine line, I thought, between choosing and having to live like this. Audrey had probably started on the right side of it, but I wasn't sure about now.

I poured the tea and gave a cup to Audrey. She puckered her mouth and blew on it, then sipped and sighed appreciatively.

'What about the money?' I ventured.

'I never saw it again. You might say, more fool me.' She put her cup down and retrieved the marriage certificate from where I had left it. She folded it neatly and stowed it in her pocket. 'I never asked him to pay it back.' That was a matter of pride, I could tell.

'Did you see each other?'

Audrey smiled, for the first time a genuine smile that made her look much younger. 'Once in a while.'

I said, 'We'd like to pay you back. Out of the house sale. I can't speak for Lola, but Jack and I will make it up to you, with the proper interest.'

She looked up to where the laths showed in one corner of the ceiling behind a broken lip of plaster, and at the back door listing in its frame and plugged against draughts with twists of newspaper. 'Better late than never, I suppose.'

Optimistic plans were tumbling in my head. I could help Audrey to fix up her house, maybe even advise her to sell it. She could live in a more manageable flat, not too far away. Jack's real grandmother had died so long ago, Tony's parents lived in Canada. Audrey's wild claim might prefigure a real, valuable relationship.

'You and Jack get on well . . .' I began.

I was going to extend an invitation into the Thompson family. In my fired-up imagination I saw snapshots of Sunday lunches, birthday celebrations, Christmases. A grandmotherly rehabilitated Audrey figured in a rosy group picture of Lola and Jack and, in time, their spouses and children as well.

'That's between Jack and me,' she snapped.

The pictures dimmed, but even as I bit my tongue I knew she was right. She was Jack's ally in the first place, not mine. You can't direct other people's friendships for them, even your children's. If there was going to be a connection between Audrey and me, it would come later, and it would have to grow of its own accord. 'You're right. I'm sorry,' I said humbly.

Audrey seemed mollified. 'You mean well, Sadie,' she conceded.

And that would have to stand as our first, teetering step towards friendship.

My cup was empty and so was hers. 'Shall I pour you another?'

'No, thank you. I'm having a sort-out. I've got to get on with it.'

That was my cue and I took it. I put my arm, very briefly, round Audrey's shoulders and withdrew before she could nudge me away. 'I'll be getting back home. Maybe Jack'll pop over later, or tomorrow. If you want a hand with anything.' The words sounded so ordinary, after the exchange of such momentous information. Involuntarily my eyes slid to the pocket where she had stowed her marriage certificate.

She covered it up with her hand. 'I don't know how all the rubbish piles up,' she said.

'Thank you for telling me the truth,' I added, but she didn't reply.

She walked down the hallway behind me and let me out of the front door. It closed firmly.

I walked back up the street, past Tim's and Gavin's front door, towards the grim concrete ramparts of the Ullswater.

Lola and Sam had got up, finally, and gone straight out to the pub. Jack was still in the kitchen, waiting for me. He seemed to have grown even in the last three hours. I noticed the pale knobs at his wrists and his Adam's apple like a small bird's egg protruding from his childish throat. His voice would start to crack soon and in no time he would tower over me, like Caz's boys.

'Did you talk to her?' He was eyeing me anxiously, trying to gauge whether I had done it right and if so whether I was upset by what I must have discovered.

'Yes, I did. Jack, what was it like, all that time you were staying with her?'

He chewed the corner of his mouth but he didn't give even the ghost of a shrug. I realised with a sudden beat of happiness that we were going to have a proper conversation, one where we listened to each other and made responses based on what we had learned. 'We talked quite a lot. She told me things.'

As I belatedly understood, Audrey didn't treat Jack like a child. To lonely people, to Colin even, the distinction between one condition and the other isn't so clear. I imagined Jack sitting in the back room at Turnmill Street with the debris and the peeling wallpaper, listening to Audrey while she talked and talked. Telling her husband's grandchild all the truths that she kept to herself for so long.

'They weren't always things I wanted to hear, as a matter of fact. Like about Grandad and her, and the way they got married when he was already married and had you.' He glanced at me, checking my reaction.

'I know.'

'But some of it was really interesting. About what it was like in England in the war and stuff. Children got sent away from London, with labels on their coats, to live with people in the country to be safe from the bombs. Did you know that? Audrey and her mother had two sisters who came to stay with them and they'd never seen cows before.'

'Evacuees, they were called.'

'Were you one?'

'*Jack*. I wasn't *born* until 1950.' Then I saw that he was joking. 'Very funny.'

'Did she tell you about how she gave Grandad money?'

'Yes, that too.'

'That's why I thought of giving her my share from his house. She hasn't got very much to buy food or anything, you know.'

'That's a good and very generous thought, Jack. But it might be better to keep your money for when you want to go travelling, or to help you through college. I'm going to pay Audrey back out of my share.'

'That's not fair, though.'

I smiled at him. 'Yes, it is, actually.' His face remained clouded for a second, but then an answering smile broke through. It was the same smile that had been his from babyhood, but now the changing planes showed me a glimpse of the grown man too. There he was, just briefly: Jack fully formed.

It was a moment of great delight, and also an instant of bereavement. As always, I wanted to wrap him in my arms, make him a baby again, but I held still.

'By the way,' he said. 'The postman came. There's a package for you.'

A brown padded envelope lay on the counter. I picked it up and saw French stamps, half-familiar handwriting, crossed sevens. I put it aside until later.

I made Jack a late lunch and we sat down to eat together. Then he mowed the lawn for me, for probably the last time before the winter, while I raked up leaves and cut back waterlogged summer growth. It was good being out in the thin sunlight. The garden smelled of wet earth and benign decay. Afterwards Jack said he was going on the tube to see his new friend Max, and I agreed that he could make the complicated journey on his own if he called me when he got there. Then Paul rang to ask if I wanted to go to the cinema later or have dinner with him. I was replacing the receiver and thinking that I would make a cup of tea when I saw the brown envelope still lying where I had left it.

I used the bread knife to slit the parcel tape that sealed it. The envelope had been used before and a new white label had been thriftily stuck in place to cover the first address. Inside, wrapped in a protective collar of corrugated card, there was a plain glass bottle of perfume with a round gold-coloured screw cap. I slid my fingers inside the envelope once more and found a letter with another sheet of paper folded inside it.

As I had already guessed, the letter was from Philippe. 'Your visit', he wrote, 'prompted me to look through some old boxes of my mother's things. And I found this.'

Carefully, I unfolded the second sheet. This handwriting was familiar too. It was Ted's and I recognised a complex perfume formula. I stared at the heading, and my heart thumped in my chest. I glanced down the list of essences, noticing some of the names that chimed from my childhood: lavender, bergamot, vanillin. But my eyes were drawn to the foot of the page where my father had added a note: *My dear friend Marie-Ange. I think this is a fine fragrance, maybe even one of my best. If you can use it, please take it as part payment of my debt to you.* The date was October 1965, just after the end of my Grasse summer. I looked back at the page heading again. It read, 'Orphan. For Sadie.' Well, I thought, with a lump in my throat. The name isn't going to do much for it.

I took the liberty, Philippe continued, *of making the fragrance up for you.*

Very carefully, I unscrewed the gilt stopper and lowered my nose to the neck of the tiny bottle. The scent flowed into the chambers of my head. It was fresh and flowery, innocent with a marked sweetness, like an afternoon's sunshine in a bright garden. A young girl's scent from almost forty years ago.

'It is a pretty fragrance, I think, but not a record breaker. I think my mother must have shared my opinion, because she put it to one side. But I am sure that you will like to have it, just the same.' He signed himself, 'Your old friend PL.' Philippe was quite right. I did like to have it.

I looked searchingly around my kitchen, as if I might catch my father there, but there was no trace of him. On a shelf stood the photograph of Lola and Jack and me on holiday in Devon. Next to it was the one I thought of as Ted's film star picture, and tucked into the frame was a snapshot of him with Lola and Jack. They were posed in front of a Christmas tree and they all had red-eye, but they were laughing. Beside it was the one of Faye and me in the garden at Dorset Avenue. I longed to look into my mother's eyes and read her thoughts, but she was still looking away, out of the frame, while my frowning gaze locked with the camera lens. Faye was the mystery. She would remain so, now.

My fingers closed round the smooth contours of the scent bottle. 'Thank you for this,' I said aloud to Ted. I couldn't hear his voice or smell his cheating citrus cologne. It was so like him to use my perfume to try to settle a debt. It was so like him that I found myself laughing as if I had just heard the best joke in the world.

'Mum?' Jack called from the stairs. 'Is that you?'

I thought he had already gone out. 'Yes. I was just thinking about Grandad.'

'Oh. Right.'

Bravo, I was saying in my mind to Ted although he couldn't and wouldn't ever hear me. You did what you wanted, just as far as you could. Bravo for that.

TWENTY

A whole year has gone by and it's October again.

Mel chose autumn colours and they work well. There are big urns all around the room, filled with thick-petalled bronze chrysanthemums, coppery leaves and sprays of golden ivy. The effect is gorgeously theatrical rather than bridal. Mel herself is wearing a plain pale-gold sheath dress, with her hair wound up in a loose knot and threaded with flowers. She has never regained the weight she lost after she was stabbed and the dress fits tightly round her reduced curves. But she did dye her hair to blot out the grey and the red lipstick is triumphantly back. Altogether she looks as beautiful as any woman could look on her wedding day.

As her (very) senior bridesmaid, I am sitting at the top table. My partner is one of the Archer brothers who is currently between wives, but he is busy talking to Clare who is seated on his other side. Paul is at another table and I can't even see him from here. There are well over a hundred of us and the circular tables stretch right down the room. I am glad to have this interval of quiet to look around me. It has been a long, lovely day and there is still the dancing to come.

It started nearly twelve hours ago with Mel and me drinking champagne for breakfast, and then giggling so much at the absurdity of dressing up in wedding finery and going through wedding rituals at this late stage in our lives that we finally had to be bullied into line by the make-up woman who came to paint our faces.

The ceremony made me cry. In front of their families and friends Jasper lifted Mel's hand and kissed the wedding ring before he kissed her on the lips. My tears washed pale runnels in the unaccustomed layers of foundation, even though they failed to dissolve the sob-proof mascara that even now makes my eyelashes feel as if I am peering at the world through spiders' legs. At the signing of the register I leaned down to take Lois's hand and the vast feather plumes in her hat tickled my nose and set off a sneezing fit, so the tears flowed even harder. Clare looked embarrassed for me but the other two bridesmaids, tiny nieces from a brother's second marriage, roared with unashamed laughter. I stooped down to their level and gave them the handkerchief that I was supposed to hold in readiness for discreet clean-up operations on their round, penny-bright faces. They were enchanted with this role reversal, and their stiff gold paper-taffeta skirts crackled as they rubbed at my cheeks and nose.

'Hold still,' the younger ordered me with bossy delight.

'I am holding.'

'Sadie never worries about a thing, does she?' Lois said and, just as I was silently mentally contradicting her, I realised that today it is the truth.

Today there is nothing to worry about. These marriage rituals represent enough happiness and good luck to face down every possible threat from any corner.

Today is inviolate.

Not all days are like today and history's cruelly shifting perspectives may even come to alter this one in time, but I am certain that the here and now couldn't be bettered. I won't forget it. I will keep it safe in my memory and refer to it like a text.

Jasper and Mel linked hands. The two tiny girls fell in behind them, and Clare and I paired up in their wake. Lois and Jasper's best man, and a couple of brothers made up the procession. The organ music swelled and broke like waves around us as we made our way back down the aisle through the avenue of beaming faces, and the drifts of simple scent from the towers of autumn blooms and the complicated symphony of women's perfumes. All those bottled dreams.

I felt, and feel, a lightness that is beginning to be familiar, as if a weight I have been carrying for a long time slips into a new position and then drops away altogether. It makes me want to smile and look up at the sky.

On the broad steps of the church the photographer's assistant lined us up for the lens and posterity. It was a perfect autumn day, with the blue sky softened by a thin veil of mist and the leaves of the massive plane trees all ochre and crisp and ready for the gales. We could look down at passing cars as they hooted good wishes and the pale faces peering from the top decks of buses were level with our eyes.

Paul slipped out from the crowds of guests. It was the first time we had seen each other today because I stayed the night at Mel's. 'I hardly recognised you,' he murmured.

'Good or bad?'

As well as the make-up I am fastened into an unfamiliarly tight arrangment of tiny metallic bronze pleats fastened with dozens of spherical buttons that remind me of aniseed balls. The skirt fans out behind in broader pleats like a mermaid's tail and the assistant was crouching at my knees busily arranging these on the stone step behind me.

'Good. But I certainly wouldn't dare to touch you.'

'I do dare you.'

'Well. I like a challenge.'

'Could the senior bridesmaid come in closer behind the little ones, please?' the photographer ordered.

'See you later, then.' I smiled at Paul.

It's time for the speeches. Mel's eldest brother offers some winsome memories of the bride as a little girl and Lois obediently dabs the corners of her eyes. Next he introduces Jasper's best man who does a good funny one, not too long or too rude, and proposes a toast to the bride and groom. I love this about weddings, the rhythm of them and the way that however different and original they try to be they are always the same, with the principals happily reduced from themselves to Bride and Groom figurines from the top of the cake. As we stand to drink to their long life and happiness I see Mel smiling at me across the table, as if she can read my thoughts. She wanted a proper big wedding and this is it.

Jasper's is the last speech. He doesn't look quite sure of himself, as if even now he can't quite believe his luck, but his is the easiest job and he does it well. He thanks Lois and the Archer brothers, and proposes the toast to Mel's beautiful bridesmaids. I keep my head ducked for this one and so my eyes rest on the single-fold menu, thick cream paper with a thin thread of gold ribbon, placed next to my champagne glass. I didn't need to read the menu when the food was being served, because I know it off by heart. I set the type by hand and printed off the sheets on our old press. Leo and Andy did the folding, and Penny tied the ribbons. We hand-set the wedding invitations too, and as part of the wedding present we made big photograph albums with pale-gold calfskin covers, ready for the pictures. Now I am idly reading my own handiwork, and approving of the faint but elegant unevenness that almost no one in the room except Penny and me will recognise for what it is. But then I notice something, and I gulp and almost swallow my own tongue.

The pudding we have just eaten was iced berries, red and black currants, with white chocolate sauce. Very well chosen and very good, too.

Except I now see that I have spelled it *currents*.

I proof-read the list and checked it three times, and I still didn't notice the mistake. After all the years that Mel and I have joked about and collected menu misspellings, I have made a classic error on her wedding one.

I look up in horror, but Jasper has already taken her hand. According to plan, and exactly on time, they will sail down a grand sweeping staircase to the colonnaded ballroom and lead off the dancing. They process between the tables and a tide of applause sweeps with them. I want to kick myself and I want to laugh at the same time, and the person I have shared these tiny comedies with has been Mel for so long that I miss her already.

Then a hand touches my shoulder.

I look up into Paul's eyes.

'AC or DC?' he murmurs and now I am laughing, full-throated head-back laughter that makes Mel's brothers turn to stare at me. Mel will laugh too, when the photographs and the menu and the guests' signatures are all pasted into the albums, and we sit down to share the memories.

Among the dancers I can see Lola. She has recently split up with Sam and tonight she is thinner in the face, winged with melancholy, and attracting a good deal of attention. She is cloaked in Ted's perfume, Orphan.

When I gave it to her she was wide-eyed. 'Is it really your own? I mean, Grandad made it for you and no one else can smell of it?'

'The only bottle in the whole world is in your hand.'

She fingered the gilt stopper knob. 'Don't you . . . want to keep it for yourself?'

'I never wear scent, Lo. I'm not going to change now. It's yours.'

'I'm not an orphan, though. And it makes me sad to think of you being one. You were sad, weren't you?'

'Let's change the name, then. I know. We'll call it Lola.'

'Noooo. *Can* we?' I could see the flash of delight in her eyes.

'Yes, we can.'

'I'll never wear it. I'll be worried about using it up.'

'I'm sure Philippe will make some more when you need it.'

'Really? I can wear it for ever, my own signature scent?'

'That's the idea. That's what Grandad did. Bottled dreams.'

'I love it.' Lola sighed. I wished Ted could have seen her satisfaction.

I am dancing with Graham, who is doing his elbows-out knees-in twist and shuffle. There are dancers pressed all round us and the music is not unlike Jerry's band but more polished and these musicians are wearing wedding-gig matching band jackets. Of course Jerry isn't here, but Cassie skims across my field of vision. She's in a blue dress with a long sash, and she is especially pleased with her little white socks with lace cuffs. There are plenty of other children. The two tiny bridesmaids spin with her, both of them plainly at the edge of exhaustion.

I can see Jack, too. He is occupying a table next to the wall with his inseparable friend Max, and something in their louche postures tells me that they have had a lot of champagne. There will probably be a few problems later on, but whenever were there not, after a wedding?

It's half past ten. Mel and Jasper are due to leave, and suddenly we are all surging out and crowding at the foot of the sweep of stairs.

Mel has changed into a red dress and her leather jacket. She has let her hair loose and it corkscrews round her face and her eyes are brilliant. I see that Penny and Evelyn are right next to me. Penny is holding tight to Cassie's hand and Evelyn is cradling the baby. Mel and Jasper have been laughing and calling out from their vantage point on the stairs but now Mel holds her bouquet up like Liberty's torch. Jasper gently turns her so that her back is to the room.

Evelyn nudges me and lifts the baby from her shoulder. He is five weeks old, the final product of Jerry's grudging communion with a jam jar. I circle his minute ribcage with my hands and his frowning, crunched-up tiny dark features twitch slightly. His head lolls on me and I know that he is hungry because his mouth moves like a tentative kiss against my neck. When I cup his velvety skull, the skin rides over the soft plates of bone.

Mel's bouquet makes a full loop as it sails upwards and falls. A forest of arms stretches but Evelyn leaps like a basketball player. She catches it securely and then jumps up and down so that the Pre-Raphaelite hair streams out. 'I got it, I got it.'

Penny grins. She doesn't know what this means; no one does, with Evelyn.

The crowd separates just enough to let Mel and Jasper pass through. Outside, at the foot of some more steps, a car is waiting. There are ribbons and lipstick scrawls all over it and tin cans tied to the back.

'Oh, no.' Mel laughs. Her wide red mouth blows a kiss and they run down the steps together. The weather has changed and a thin drizzle sets haloes round the street lights. We close round the car, thumping on the roof and shouting good wishes. Slowly it moves forward and we fall back, watching it go. The red tail lights go into formation in the thin traffic, blurring in the distance, and we turn away with the rain in our faces. I can still see Mel's smile vividly in my mind's eye, Cheshire cat-like, as the surrounding features fade.

Inside again, we are all blinking in the lights. The band is still playing – there will be some slow numbers now, Mel promised.

I can see Paul standing in the doorway. I thread my way

towards him and reach out my hand. He takes it in his familiar grasp.

'Hello, Mr Rainbird.'

'Hello, Mrs Rainbird. Shall we dance?'

I *am* Mrs Rainbird.

Paul and I were married in the summer, on the anniversary of the first day of the siege of Turnmill Street.

Neither of us wanted a big set-piece wedding like this one. Paul's father was his witness and Audrey was mine, with Mel's blessing. Jack and Lola were there too, and no one else at all.

But I was happy then as I am now and I long for everyone around me to feel the same joy. I recognised this yearning months ago in Mel and now I know the force of it.

Today comes close to satisfying the wish.

We start dancing together, turning in circles to the slow number.